BLACK FOREST

LARAMIE DEAN

Published by Inkshares, Inc., Oakland, California
www.inkshares.com

Edited by Sarah Nivala and Pamela McElroy
Cover design by Tim Barber of Dissect Designs
Formatted by Kevin G. Summers

ISBN: 9781950301454
e-IBN: 9781950301461
LCCN: 2022938637

First edition

Printed in the United States of America

For Ryan

I

THE SÉANCE

"Lie close," Laura said,
Pricking up her golden head:
"We must not look at goblin men.
We must not buy their fruits;
Who knows upon what soil they fed
Their hungry thirsty roots?"

Christina Rossetti, "Goblin Market"

1

THE MAN HAD found him finally and stood on his lawn now, just below his bedroom window; he'd followed Nathan home from school, which was maddening, because Nathan had been so certain that he'd lost him along the way, ditched him by cleverly ducking across dangerous Sprague Avenue and fading into the shadows of the trees cast by the weak, late-winter sun. Yet there he waited, this persistent man, tall, gaunt, nearly graceful, swaying like an aspen or willow stirred into a dance. When he caught Nathan gazing down at him, he grinned wildly and trotted back and forth across the winter-weathered grass, which gleamed silver and black in the moonlight. Back and forth he trotted, back and forth, like a horse that found it could stand on its hind-legs. His grin grew wider, and wider still; naturally, he's grinning, Nathan thought, his head throbbing and his stomach roiling. Naturally. Grinning was all the man could do. His face was only a skull.

"Go away," Nathan murmured, wiping ice-sweat from his forehead and rubbing it unconsciously against his bare leg. *Go away*, he thought as ferociously as he could, but the man outside just grinned and grinned and trotted back and forth.

The man had followed him all the way home, and they had never done that before; what could be next, Nathan wondered, what fresh hell? *They wouldn't come into the house*, he thought, shivering; *they wouldn't come into my* bedroom.

The man trotted outside, the physical embodiment of Nathan's fear; the man looked up with eyeless sockets; the man grinned his yellow grin.

Nathan wasn't born with a caul over his face, or possessed of an extra finger, or with a pair of clever little horns protruding from his forehead. Nevertheless, he was considered quite strange by his peers, as he saw what they did not see and heard what they never could, though he learned, eventually, not to talk about these things.

Or about *them*.

The deaders, he called them.

Sometimes, when he woke in the early, evil hours of the morning and stared into the blackness of his bedroom, he thought, *I've been dreaming, only dreams*: drums in a dark forest, lilting songs, and fires, and the moon. *Someone is waiting for me there*, he would think, still half-asleep, allowing delicate electricity to rill up and down the length of his body, alternating waves of desire and terror.

Sometimes he knew that nothing was a dream, and everything was real.

We make our own realities, he would remind himself; *we knit them all up around ourselves every moment.*

Because there was someone waiting for him; he knew it, there *must* be: at the beginning of a path that would lead, finally, satisfyingly, through trees and darkness, and if Nathan could just brave the deaders and the monsters, he could find the path's end. He could take the steps to reach it.

His Tarot cards, just before the skull-faced man appeared on the lawn, predicted changes coming. Nathan imagined a great wind, cold, like it swept down fresh from the Montana mountains that surrounded Garden City and its valley, ready to rearrange the comfortable pattern of their lives into something cleaner, maybe sweeter. But then again, the cards, as Nathan's best friend Logan enjoyed pointing out, always predicted changes. "We're graduating," Nathan knew Logan would say with his easy grin, "moving out into the world. We're going to tear the damn place apart and you know it. You're seeing changes everywhere because everything is about to change, chumly." And he would laugh, but good-naturedly. Nathan and Logan had, for the last three and a half years, attended Royal High School, which Nathan couldn't wait to shed like the carapace of some soon-to-be powerful insect.

But Nathan also knew that Logan was undoubtedly right. They'd been best friends—fast friends—since kindergarten, but now Nathan feared an uneasy kind of drifting. He already felt isolated from his older brother, Terry, and his mostly absent father, while his mother was currently fighting a battle with depression she seemed destined to lose. He couldn't remember the last time he'd spoken to his father; Terry never emerged from his bedroom, which he had transformed into a dark cave that stank of unwashed adolescent boy and cigarettes; his mother always worked late now, until she finally slunk home near midnight, trembling ceaselessly on the verge of crying. On occasion, smoking and tapping her ashes into a tray made of thick, clear glass that Nathan secretly believed to be composed of all the frozen tears fallen from her eyes over the years, she would stare at him wordlessly, and he wondered if she found him wanting, or if she wanted him too much, if she wished it could be just the two of them, or if she wished it could be just her, all alone.

You imagine all these things, he would tell himself sternly; but he wondered often if he shouldn't fear his imagination most of all.

I'm not imagining this weirdness with Logan. Because the weirdness was real, he was certain; of all the terrible things that happened to him now, the return of the deaders and the dissolution of the little world he'd constructed for himself over the last eighteen years, the chasm he sensed between him and his best friend growing wider every goddamn day was the *most* real.

And he didn't think he could stand Logan drifting away, too. Possibly forever.

Nathan had always loved Logan more than anyone, ever since kindergarten's first disastrous day. At recess, Nathan, sitting alone on the playground, had cradled gently a green-faced witch-doll he'd insisted on bringing to school despite his mother's protestations; a little witch, he'd said, to keep him company in case no one else did. He'd looked up, inexplicably afraid, a gazelle scenting danger on the vast Serengeti, to find a towheaded boy with startling green eyes looming over him and smiling. The boy possessed the improbable name of Seb Candleberry, and Nathan, with six grand years of unbroken naiveté behind him, thought Seb's monster's smile kind.

"H'lo," Nathan said, unsure how to react; his experience with children—with *anyone*—was limited, and words eluded him, always jumping away like tiny fish. He'd felt a rush of heat and his eyes blinked rapidly, uncontrollably. "Dolls," Seb had proclaimed, and only then did Nathan perceive the cruelty in the other boy's curling smile, "*dolls* are for *girls*."

"She's not a doll," Nathan said, but Seb had only laughed, seized the witch, and with one swift, brutal jerking motion, tore off her head.

"Dolls are for girls," Seb sneered, "you girl." He threw the little witch's torn body and stepped on her head and left Nathan to stare after him, his eyes brimming, swearing ferociously, *I won't I won't I will not cry*. But the tears came regardless, as he might have expected they would. Suddenly, Logan was there: a tall boy with a perfectly square and symmetrical head that was, perhaps, just a little too big for his body. Logan said, brightly and kindly, an unstoppable flow of words: "You okay, kid? Jeez, that dude's a jerk, huh? You can have some of my Mountain Dew if you want, but you can't tell anyone that I even have it 'cause my dad's a dentist and he says it'll make my teeth fall out, but they're falling out anyway, see? I lost one last night and the tooth fairy brought me a dollar and some floss. I don't care about the floss, and I couldn't catch the darn tooth fairy, but I tried, see. Jeez, I'm sorry about your toy. Let's see if we can get her head back on. If you wanna play with my LEGOs, we can build a fighter jet and shoot bombs at Seb Candleberry."

Logan was kind; Logan was perfect; ten years later, Nathan's under-celebrated and unsurprising coming-out announcement followed on the heels of Logan's, which had proven, per usual, far more successful.

Nathan counted on Logan, though he knew he couldn't forever, because, no matter what Logan thought or didn't think about Nathan's Tarot, big changes were coming, the icy wind Nathan heard at night hooting in the eaves outside his bedroom. *But he's my best friend*, Nathan would think. *We can't lose each other. I tell him everything; I always have!*

Which was why, even now, Nathan found it so surprising that Logan didn't believe him about the deaders.

The man no longer stood on the lawn, which remained flawless and unmarked, despite his trotting, his crushing the frost-silvered grass with the jagged bare bones of his feet.

Nathan turned away from the window and padded back to his bed. The wind moaned softly; he whispered back to it, "Can't get in, won't get in, can't, can't, won't." He caught the pale flash of his reflection in the oval mirror that bedecked the dresser his mother had purchased for him at the antique mall downtown. *Before it turned bad*, he told himself, though he didn't like to think about it, his first experience with a deader. He stopped, held by his own eyes, and gazed at himself. His face was thinner than it probably should have been, cheekbones higher and startlingly sharp; hadn't Logan just complimented his cheekbones the other day, earning Nathan a pointed look from Logan's ordinarily chipper little boyfriend, Derek?

Nathan had lost significant weight over the last month or so; who knew that being stalked by the walking dead would make for such a great diet? Probably he shouldn't feel proud of himself, but he did, a little.

I'm almost handsome now, he told himself, *or I could be*. His hair, dark, had grown wavy as of late; it fell in near-ringlets over his forehead, which had recently cleared of the acne that had plagued him so fiendishly through the first half of high school. He leaned in farther, gazing harder at himself, and thought, *Narcissus, Narcissus*; a movement behind him caught his eye and he felt a flash of guilt (*caught, caught; freak; fag; checking yourself out in the mirror; freak*) and he spun, already knowing, sick, what he would see.

"Where's your camera?" Logan had asked him the day before, handsome in his letterman jacket and aviator sunglasses and a red ball-cap perched far back on his head, the slogan in bright rainbow block letters, proclaiming "SOUNDS GAY . . . I'M IN!" Nathan had given him the cap for his birthday the previous spring and Logan wore it faithfully every day. "Don't you need a few more shots for your show? The last ones were awesome, and I'm not just saying that because most of them featured me. Hey, Amy didn't back out, did she?" Amy Wilson, the owner of You've Been Framed, a combination frame shop, art supplier, and gallery for artists from the Pacific Northwest, had promised Nathan an entire wall for his photographs after he started working for her last summer. He'd been developing like crazy. Until the photos had . . . changed.

If Nathan closed his eyes, he could see them still, all his pictures laid out on his bed, straight and neat: Logan outside the school, leaning against his car and gazing serenely up into the vast bowl of sky that made Montana famous; a hallway at Royal High, deserted and forlorn; the twists and knots of the trees that composed a small forest growing forcefully on the Waxman University campus, where the trails lacing the woods had sprawled empty. Empty, dammit; Nathan would swear it. But, nevertheless, in every photo, he saw—and he couldn't think of another word to describe them—figures.

Extra figures.

No one else had been present when he took the pictures. Only Logan. The halls of the high school under his eye had lain devoid of life; the mouth of the woods on the Waxman campus stood barren and empty.

But *they* were there in the photos: reflected in the passenger window of Logan's car was a slim white form, swimming black holes where the eyes should be, hard to see but there if you knew where to look. And in another, an impossibly tall, gangly man waited at the end of the hallway, nearly hidden by the shadows, taller than anyone Nathan had ever seen, head bowed, arms dangling, enormous hands ending in long white fingers far, far below his knees. And in *another*, an old, hunched woman scuttling between the trees, barely visible, her face a raddled hag's mask as she hissed into the eye of the camera, seeing Nathan, despising him . . .

They've taken even this from me, Nathan thought as he'd gone through the photos, flipping through them again and again. There was a face in that one, and there, a white waving hand; and another, and another, and another. On the verge of hateful, burning tears, he thought, *They've taken the thing I love and made it theirs, goddamn them all to hell.*

And there was so little left that he felt safe loving.

"Go away," Nathan said flatly, but the face in the window only continued to stare in at him, preening, its teeth yellow and chipped, its skeletal face not completely denuded after all; not a bare skull, as Nathan had first assumed, but covered in a withered layer of skin that shone blue before him, blue as an electric flash, blue as a river locked with winter ice.

His stomach turned over, but he couldn't look away from it.

How did it get up here? How in the hell—

Patches of bone peeked through the blue skin of the forehead and cheeks; the empty eye sockets flickered with an azure glow, way down deep. A deader. It saw him, as it had before, down on the lawn, and waved its thin, blue hand ecstatically.

"Go," Nathan moaned; but wasn't there something fascinating, just a little, about being so close to the thing? About the blue luminescence that sparkled and danced in its eyeholes? He didn't necessarily have to look away, did he; he could open the window for the thing, couldn't he; he could take it into his bed and press his face against its withered, sunken chest and whisper songs into its ears, which had dried and curled up like desiccated apricots against that sky-blue skin; he could open the window and do these things.

It isn't as if my life is so perfect, he thought dreamily. *It isn't as if I'm so loved, or that anyone would miss me if I just disappeared.*

He lifted his hand, brushed his fingertips against the glass, and the thing lifted its own thin blue hand and pressed its bony fingers to his, separated by that tiniest, most delicate barrier. Together, they sighed in time.

Nathan hated Royal High, though he didn't want to; his contemporaries had identified him long ago as different, whatever that meant, when they first met him and realized that, in myriad innumerable ways, he stood out from the herd. Could be the gay thing, though Logan's popularity only surged after he came out. Maybe it was how, in the beginning, he'd talked to anyone who would listen about the ghosts and witches and vampires who populated the horror movies and novels he'd loved since he first learned to read, until Logan told him, kindly yet firmly, that maybe he shouldn't mention those things so much. "Or at least," Logan said, "maybe not as conversation starters."

Didn't matter; Nathan's classmates sensed his otherness, whether he talked or didn't talk or simply entered a room, or sat, or blinked, or breathed. Friendship with Logan eased some of the awkwardness, a bit of the bullying, but not all. By early senior year, Nathan had already begun fantasizing about his last day of high school, the day he could start again, all shiny and new.

College—Waxman—beckoned him, a sparkle at the end of the moronic tunnel of high school. A place for remaking. He knew, absolutely and with conviction, that someone waited for him there; it only stood to reason that there'd be other people like him, and, searching among them, Nathan would find *him*. A hand to take. Belonging, delicious and well-earned. *At the end of the journey*, he would sing to himself, *at the end of the day—the long and terrible day . . .*

He can keep me safe, he told himself at night. *Whoever he is, or will be, he will keep* them *at bay*.

Blue hand, thin blue fingers, so near to his own.

Blue fire. Empty sockets.

A fatal glamour.

Nathan drew back from the window, pulled back his hand, and hissed, "Stop it," even though he knew it wouldn't stop. It nearly had him just then; he had nearly opened the window, almost invited it inside . . .

The thing—the deader—nodded happily. Scratched, frantic, at the glass.

"Go away," Nathan said louder. "Son of a bitch. Bastard. Disgusting thing. You are disgusting, you are vile—*go away!*"

The deader uttered a squealing sound, horribly porcine, but full of joy. It began to bang its head against the glass of his window again, and again, and again.

And the glass cracked, and the cracks widened, spreading out like the magical web of an unseen spider, preparing to allow the thing entrance to his bedroom, to his *bed*—

But it didn't; the glass of the window held.

For now.

The next morning, the blue-faced horror gone, evaporated like mist, Nathan looked at his window, where the cracks from the thing remained, between him and his reflection. They danced laughingly across his face, his shadowed eyes; his reflection might as well have been a skull, too.

Somehow, he'd fallen into a thin, dissatisfying sleep after the blue-faced deader had ceased its assault on his window; bathed in painful gray, early March sunlight, he looked at his windowpane despairingly and thought, *How am I going to explain these cracks to Mom and Dad?*

And, worse: *What if it comes again? What if it gets inside next time? What then?*

"It won't," he whispered uneasily to himself. "I won't let it get in. I won't let it get in my *head*. Not again."

Liar.

Because they'd never shown up in his pictures before and they'd never tried to come inside his house, nor inside his mind; they'd never invaded him so *personally.*

My pictures; my brain.

What am I going to do? he wondered, tracing one of the cracks with a finger. *What am I going to do?*

The answer came in Logan's voice, though not a suggestion Logan would ever make:

Easy-peasy, chumly. Have another séance. One that actually works this time.

Because he'd tried a séance before. Unsuccessfully.

Now he thought to himself, *Maybe I can make it so I never see them again; a nice big push; I can be loud and exceptionally brave, and they'll go and never come back again. Then I'll have a palace of my own, a great estate that stretches throughout the woods. My home. And a prince will come riding to me, or soaring on wings that cover the whole sky. His eyes will be jewels; his hands will be strong; he'll ride or he'll soar, but he'll come for* me, *flashing in the light of the sun or the glow of the moon, and together, yes,* together, *we'll have a place to belong and we'll never feel lonely again.*

But first he had to confront those things that had once been people, dead, broken, and starving, and a séance, Nathan decided, was obviously the only logical course of action.

2

ON A RANDOM, rainy Saturday afternoon when he was nine years old, Nathan was inexplicably invited, along with his grimacing older brother, to accompany their mother on an antiquing expedition into downtown Garden City, to the last three secret streets, where most of the city's antique, junk, and pawn shops abided. Nathan's mother held a private passion for antiquing that she shared with few people; on Saturdays in mid-autumn like this one, with the sky leaden and brooding and pregnant with rain, it was her habit to slip away by herself without a word. But on this particular day, unaccountably, she decided to whisk the boys with her to her most beloved place: a five-story antique mall, a building of century-old red brick shaded by sycamores and willow trees, presiding at the termination of a dead-end street.

Garden City began its life in the late 1880s as a close-knit village that expanded and strengthened itself around the seed of a paper mill, and soon enough, taller buildings sprang forward as if from the ground; before this one evolved into an antique mall, it had performed as a hotel for the wealthier elements of the city. The floors were (mostly) firm, but the entire building tilted shockingly whenever a strong gust of wind rushed over its frame. It smelled old, wide-eyed Nathan thought as he crossed the threshold for the first time, but not *bad* old. It was, he decided, the smell of promise, of possibility and adventure; he had very little experience with adventure, which alternately saddened and comforted him. Something could happen to me here, he thought; something could begin.

He saw rows of glass cases and cabinets, little wooden tables crammed full of knickknacks, what his mother called "tchotchkes," and his father called "crap." A silver polar bear the size of a kitten posed humorously beside a menacing wax pumpkin carved to display its jostling Halloween grin; a box of comic books blared color and the excited, sweating faces of men with bulging muscles; a delicately carved wooden mask hung beside a framed portrait of Shirley Temple, her faded child's face bisected by a crack that shivered across the glass.

Nathan was in love, enchanted; Nathan, amid the hundreds of vessels of history, touched by who knew how many hands, thought, *This is home.*

Adventure, yes. *Maybe I'll just run*, he thought dreamily. *I'll run until I find the dragon and the dragon's gold, until I meet a knight and we go together out into the whole wide world. Something will really really happen to me at last.*

Terry looked bored; he'd wanted to play video games with the boy in the house next to theirs today. But Nathan was as itchy to go, he found, as his mother.

Before him, the first of three staircases beckoned him up to the next floor.

Up there, yes. That's where it'll be, whatever it is, waiting for me.

Nathan mounted the staircase.

The boards squealed somewhat alarmingly beneath his sneakers, and he reached out with quick fingers to grasp the railing.

He climbed. The stairs creaked but they held him, and he relaxed a bit, inch by inch. The walls were lined with old photos, brown and sepia tinted, and several paintings depicting people Nathan supposed were intended to be Native Americans. Some were cartoonish maidens with large, incongruously blue eyes, or men with craggy faces, scowling, always scowling, with feathers in their hair and dressed in buckskin.

"All of that is bullshit," Nathan's friend Roger Charbonneau had told him just a few weeks ago, and Nathan had grinned at the epithet, which Roger was supremely fond of, among others. "All those Indians, painted like that. That's not real. Bunch of white nonsense. People think we live in teepees and wear big ol' headdresses. Shit," and he had spit, disgusted.

Nathan had grown quite fond of Roger, ever since Roger thumped the hell out of Seb Candleberry, the roughest boy in their class, and who always, *always*, came to school in ratty clothes that smelled like fish and mildew. Seb was known for saying especially horrible things to the girls; he had called Amelia Lane a whore at Christmas, and no one really knew what that meant, including Amelia, except everyone could tell that it was *bad*, and using it marked Seb as *bad*, too. He called Roger "Chief" and "Tonto" and asked him once, with an evil little glint sparkling in his eyes, how many scalps he had in his teepee; Roger, who was Blackfoot on his mother's side and Salish on his father's, immediately proceeded to thump Seb quite soundly. The thumping itself was literal: Roger's fist connected with the crown of Seb's head until he'd collapsed, semi-conscious, onto the concrete of the playground. "He doesn't mean too much harm," Roger told Nathan and Logan later. Together they had watched the thumping, wide-eyed and frozen; Nathan felt only delight, though they both agreed that Seb deserved it. Roger had grinned and said, "But I *do* think he needs a little thump from time to time." He'd winked. "Keep him in line."

Once, last year, Seb spent an entire afternoon calling Nathan "Natalie" and asking him if he preferred panties to Fruit of the Loom; when Seb seized the belt-loops of Nathan's jeans, Nathan, horrified, realized Seb intended to pull them all the way *down*. He kept demanding to know if Nathan was really a girl underneath his clothes, pulling, pulling, until Logan, a furious thundercloud, materialized behind him and ran him off.

But Nathan didn't want to think about Seb right now; he just wanted to explore.

If only the people in the paintings and the photos rising steadily up the wall at his side weren't so *creepy*. Men in buckskin and business suits; women in long dresses, wearing enormous hats prickled with feathers, all glaring, their eyes seeing nothing and everything.

They looked dead, Nathan thought with a shudder, but also horribly aware.

And yet, the photos were interesting. Nathan held a deeply rooted fascination with photography that his mother had nourished since he first picked up the old Polaroid camera that had once been hers; the way the photos developed inside the black plastic shell and then just appeared, as if from nowhere, was magic, he decided, had to be. One of his earliest, most vivid memories was of the joy he'd felt capturing the image of an owl, great and shaggy and gray, like something out of his favorite book of fairy tales. It had declared the tree outside Nathan's bedroom window its home, and all he wanted to do since first making its acquaintance was to pet it, to gently sink his fingers into the ruff of feathers surrounding its mammoth head. He knew how they would feel, how thick and how soft; since he couldn't do that, he'd settled for a photo. Nathan remembered the weight of the camera in his tiny hands, holding it steady, *steady*, and squinting through the viewfinder, much to his mother's quiet, unspoken amusement, until he found the owl puffed up on the branch of the tree, golden eyes glaring. He'd pressed the button, startled by the angry whir of mysterious gears deep within the magic box, then squealed with excitement as the flat, blank square ejected itself and fell solidly into his hand. Within moments, his mother beaming over his shoulder, it developed before his astonished eyes: the owl, framed perfectly, its yellow talons gripping the branch, haughty, golden-eyed, captured forever. And he'd wanted to be a photographer ever since.

He reached the top of the stairs and stood there, slightly out of breath. He wouldn't allow himself to run—that was what babies did, babies couldn't control themselves—but he walked quickly, his hands clenching and unclenching into fists of excitement. His thoughts raced. Would his mother let him buy one of the photos on the wall? Were there even more upstairs in cool old frames? What if there was an antique camera he could have? Excitement sparked and flared inside him. He thought he belonged there, in a place stuffed to the guts with the olden days.

He stopped first at a bookcase stacked high with empty glass perfume bottles, then picked one up to hold in his hand, glancing around as he did to make sure he remained unobserved. A big woman tucked like a sausage into a straining purple coat lingered nearby, carefully picking through a wooden carton of ancient Christmas decorations that jumped and jostled with color and light. He looked away from her and back to the perfume bottle, which was not smooth but contained hundreds of faces, the way a diamond must. Peering closely at it, he saw himself, reflected over and over: all tiny Nathans with dark, wondering eyes and an invisible line of a mouth. He smiled; the hundreds of Nathans smiled back. The bottle was sealed with a delicate stopper shaped like a teardrop, which he lifted, but carefully, then closed his eyes and held the open bottle to his nose. He inhaled. At first there was nothing, and he felt a pang of disappointment. But he tried again, and this time managed to catch the last vestiges of the bottle's essence: the barest whiff of ancient ladies' perfume, heady even now, sweet, but with an undertone of bitterness.

He imagined, eyes still closed, the woman who had belonged to it. She lived in a big house, Nathan decided, not at all like the tiny, cramped house he shared with his brother and their parents, but a big house all alone in the deep dark wood. Her bedroom was the size of an entire floor of the antique mall, and she owned an immense bed with a white canopy (Nathan dutifully watched his mother's beloved black-and-white movies with her during especially useless Saturdays, and since the Old South was a prominently featured setting in many of them, he recognized a canopy when he saw one), and she owned a thousand bottles of perfume, but this, *this* was her most precious. She would dab it on each wrist and behind each ear and then recline on that giant bed and close her eyes, the white satin nightgown she wore spreading out around her like the feathers of a delicate bird. She would close her eyes and wait for her lover, holding the perfume bottle loosely in one hand until the sound of his footstep met her ear, climbing the stairs outside her bedroom or tapping gently on the glass of the French doors outside her boudoir . . .

Nathan tittered a little bit, nervously, and opened his eyes. This happened sometimes when he wasn't careful. The woman's lover in his imagination would become a monster if he let it: a demon outside her window, an incubus, a creature with glowing eyes and inky black wings, or a pale-faced ghost from the grave, hungry, with reaching hands. He had learned long ago not to discuss these fancies with the kids at school. "They already think you're kinda weird," Logan told him apologetically a year or so ago. "Not me, *I* don't; I'm just telling you what I hear." Nathan had felt bewilderment and a hot, unpleasant feeling in his gut; later he would recognize it as shame, useless and painful. He cared what people thought about him, though he didn't want to. While Logan listened to him talk about his dark and dreamy stories without judgment, he knew Logan was right, that the other kids sensed the difference between themselves and him. And they weren't afraid to let him know exactly what they thought about it.

Nathan was grateful for Logan, who had only tried to warn him instead of beating him up or, worse, icing him out. Nothing terrified Nathan more than being alone or left out; the thought of Logan moving away or changing schools or, worst of all, turning into one of *them*, the mean kids, the bullies, scared him most of all. Nathan didn't know where he'd be without Logan, where he'd go.

Seb Candleberry was usually the worst of all his tormentors, as he had been since that first day of kindergarten. But there was no Seb there now, nor any of the other kids in his class who stared at him or laughed at him or called him a freak or a weirdo or a fag, and so he could think of the dark things, the strange things, the creepy things that caused him a delight he had a difficult time articulating; what kind of person *really* likes to be scared? Logan would ask him. No one else in their grade, it seemed, liked creepy things. Except for Nathan.

But now he allowed himself a delicious shiver. He enjoyed scaring himself with the most unnerving of the fairy tales he knew, or with the novels he was exploring, comic books, movies, and, ever-burgeoning, his own fantasies.

The big woman in purple had moved away and left Nathan alone. The temperature on this floor felt warm; so, he thought, did *her* room, the imaginary boudoir of the woman he'd just invented, the original owner, he was certain, of the perfume bottle he still held.

Waiting for her demon lover.

The past, the long ago—he loved it, and he wished for it; he would surround himself forever in those things if he could.

Without thinking, he slid the bottle into the pocket of his jeans. It created a noticeable bulge, nestled there. *I'm not doing this*, he assured himself, *this is never something I would do*. He told himself that he wasn't taking it because he didn't need it. The bottle belonged on its shelf, so of course he wasn't taking it; it was some other kid, some terrible stranger.

He whistled a snatch of a song he didn't recognize and wandered away from the shelf of perfume bottles. Next, he found a box of stuffed animals that looked peculiarly hand-sewn; some were riddled with holes that leaked their guts out into the bottom of the box, yellow fluff, or, from one unfortunate little creature intended to resemble a dachshund, disturbing red. He shuffled around with his fingers inside the box until they brushed against the husk of what had once been a spider, desiccated, empty, but still horrible somehow, and *spiny*. Nathan recoiled with a sound that was half grunt, half gag. He scrambled to his feet and whirled around.

A boy stood behind him.

Nathan froze, his heart slamming in his chest. The boy was as tall as he was, just as tall, and his eyes were as blue as Nathan's, but solemn and bruised looking. His hair, darker than Nathan's own, swept across his forehead in an odd series of spikes, like clawed fingers.

"Hello," Nathan said, cramming his hands into his pockets. His heart trip-hammered in his chest until he could hear the sound reverberating deeply inside his ears.

The boy remained silent. His eyes drifted down to the box of animals. "You play with those?" he said at last.

Blood flooded Nathan's cheeks; he tried to laugh, but the sound emerged as a cough, a mouse's squeak. "No. They're not mine. They're for sale."

"Oh," the boy said. "I thought you might, is all." He knelt down, bumping Nathan out of the way. Nathan took a mincing half-step to avoid stumbling. He frowned. Rude, he thought.

The boy pawed eagerly through the box, shuffling the animals around. Nathan considered mentioning the giant dead spider inside but thought better of it, and so, smugly, kept his mouth closed. He watched the boy instead. He wore dark clothes, a ratty old sweater, and his hair, though dry, seemed thickly wet somehow, as if he hadn't washed it in a long time. He looked all over unwashed, and suddenly Nathan could smell him, too: wet, sickly sweet, like fruit gone bad in a forgotten basement room; like feet, after enduring hours of dampness, shockingly removed from wool socks and exposed to a warm room. Still shuffling through the box, the boy turned in time to catch the wrinkle of Nathan's nose and the frown creasing his forehead. He beamed up at Nathan and said, "They're real nice, some of them."

"I'm sure," Nathan said stiffly.

The boy laughed and turned back to the box. "This place has so many things. Have you been on all the floors?"

"No," Nathan said. His bladder contracted unexpectedly, and he bit his lip. The urge to pee was strong, not all-consuming (not yet), but strong. Then it passed as swiftly as it had come. There's something about this kid, Nathan thought. He was horrible, and yet . . .

Come with me.

Nathan shivered. He'd heard the words clearly, but the boy's lips hadn't moved.

"So many things," the boy repeated. He closed his eyes and tipped back his head.

Come with me. There's a place we can go.

No one is saying that, Nathan thought ferociously. *There are no voices. No one wants you. No one wants you anywhere.*

Adventure. Sudden. Unexpected.

"They're neat," the boy said. "I come here a lot."

Nathan didn't know what to say. He didn't especially like this boy, but that wasn't so unusual; Nathan often found it difficult to communicate with strangers—adults or children or *any*one. He couldn't always find the words he wanted, or the words wouldn't come together, and so it was often safer to stick to monosyllables: "yup" or "sure." He would pray that his face wasn't burning in a noticeable way or that his clothes didn't look stupid or that no one would notice the sweat that sprang out heatedly onto his brow.

I just want to belong, that's all. What's so wrong about that?

The boy giggled softly to himself. He held up the stuffed dachshund with its guts trailing out of the hole in its stomach. They were wet now, too, probably, Nathan thought with another shudder, from the boy's hands, which he saw were white and fishy-looking, the way Nathan's own became if he lingered too long in the bathtub. The boy was trying his best to stuff the guts back into the hole, but there were too many of them; he started to pull them back out and then stuffed them back in, out and then in, and those trilling little giggles came in a constant stream from his mouth.

Nathan had to pee again.

"Don't be so goddamn nervous," the boy said, glaring up into Nathan's face. "It's just a toy."

"You're ruining it."

"I am not." The boy's face wrinkled with indignation. "Besides, they're just old things," he said before putting his teeth onto the place where the dog's throat would be if it were a real dog; with a sudden jerking motion, he tore the little animal's head off. Nathan took a step backward but made no sound. The boy was laughing, and Nathan could see those red guts (*fabric*, he thought, *it's just cotton or something, not real, not like real guts*) in shreds protruding from the sizable cracks between the boy's crooked teeth.

"Why'd you do that?" Nathan said. Like Seb, Nathan thought mournfully, just like Seb and the poor lost little green-faced witch. The urge to pee was painful now. He dug his fingernails into the soft meat of his palms, and it helped, but only a little. "Why'd you have to go and do that?"

"Because it's not a real dog, dummy. I wanted to show you that."

"Your teeth," Nathan said weakly, and the boy sprayed more of that diseased laughter.

"No one can see us up here," the boy said. His eyes flashed, and Nathan saw they were silver, that they glowed. But they didn't; they were ordinary and brown. No, they were blue. Weren't they blue? Nathan was so sure they'd been blue before. He shook his head as if to clear it. "We're all by ourselves. So don't worry. We won't get caught or nothin'. Not up *here*."

"You shouldn't have done that."

"Why not?" The boy cocked his head in a strangely animalistic fashion, like a curious dog trying to understand. "Why not? Why not? Why not why not why not not not?"

Nathan looked down at his own hands and saw dark arterial threads and bits of crimson fluff clinging insistently to his fingers and their nails. "Because," he said, wiping his hands on his jeans, "it was old."

"So?" the boy said, shrugging. He held something cupped in his hand, but Nathan couldn't see what it was. "All this stuff is old. Old doesn't make it *good*, does it?"

"Yes?"

More tinkling laughter. "You don't sound so sure. You wanna play? We can play. That old bitch downstairs ain't coming up here. She won't stop us."

"My mother—"

The boy waved a dismissive hand. "She's miles away." He took a step closer, and Nathan realized with a rush of sensation and that overwhelming urge to urinate that he'd been backed against a wall. There was nowhere to go.

Oh my god, Nathan thought, sweet horror filling his mouth, *is he going to touch me with those white, wrinkled fingers?*

The boy seemed taller than before, and his eyes were silver and amused. "It's just us."

Come come with me. You can belong; I could love you; we all all could love you all we. I promise.

"So we can tear the heads off more dogs?" Nathan tried to laugh, but it was a whispery sound, scratchy and weak. "No, thanks."

The boy opened his fist, and there he held the desiccated husk of the spider. He shoved it under Nathan's nose. Nathan, disgusted, cried out and turned away.

"Yeah," the boy said with a cursory glance at the horror in his palm, "it's pretty awful, huh."

"I *hate* them," Nathan whispered.

"I do, too. That's why I'm glad it's dead."

"Get rid of it."

"But it's kinda neat, don't you think?" He ran the tip of one finger over the thing's bristling back. "Like an artifact. You're the one who likes old shit so much."

"It's awful."

"Relax. It can't hurt you. It's dead."

"I don't care."

"Maybe," the boy said, as if considering, "*maybe* it don't have to *stay* dead."

Come come come along with me.

"Stop it!" Nathan cried.

The boy's face showed a trace of sympathy finally, and he lowered his fist. "You really hate it that much?"

It twitched.

His eyes widened.

Its leg, moving, just a bit, pawing at the air; another leg . . .

Nathan, afraid that it was some further trick, nodded slowly. *It's alive,* he thought, afraid to breathe. It couldn't be, but it was. *It's alive—*

"Yeah, I guess," the boy said, and with a quick flick of his wrist, he flung the spider's corpse far away from them both.

Nathan relaxed a bit. He told himself that he'd imagined it. It hadn't been real. Impossible. But the boy remained awfully close to him. Awfully, dreadfully close.

"I have friends," the boy said quietly. "So many friends. So could you."

"You should be good."

"Why?"

"You should go where kids are."

"You're here." The boy came closer now. His smell washed over Nathan, sickly sweet. "I'm not good."

"Sure you are."

"I'm not," the boy grinned, a shred of purple-red stuffing still caught between his front teeth, "and neither are you."

"You don't know me."

"I know enough. I watched you." He laughed. "I watched you take that bottle." His hands flew out and were *on* Nathan. Nathan cried out, a strangled rabbit sound. The boy's fingers squirmed around inside his pockets like thin, hot snakes, until, triumphant, he pulled the little perfume bottle out and held it aloft. It caught the overhead lights and sparkled magnificently. "See? You're not so good."

Nathan could only pant; he couldn't move because the boy was still there, his chest against Nathan's, flattening Nathan against the wall with tears pricking his eyes. "I was going to put it back."

A grin; a flash of those teeth. "Sure," the boy sneered. "Oh, I bet you were."

"You don't know."

"Cry. Baby. Cry, then."

Nathan's hand curled into a fist. He pushed it roughly against his right eye, and then the left. He snuffled; he couldn't help himself. "I'm not."

"You are. That's what you are. I see it now. Crybaby. Goddamn crybaby."

"I'm *not*."

As Nathan lifted a hand (to force away the tears? To claw at his own eyes?), he froze.

The boy cast no shadow on the floor.

The boy smiled his wicked little smile.

But Nathan had felt him, felt his touch, could smell him still; he thought of the spider; *it moved, it did*.

"Aren't you tired of being alone?" the boy said, teasingly.

Nathan's shadow lay all by itself on the slightly warped planks of the floor at their feet.

The boy threw his head back and howled wild laughter, then, with the same swift movement he used to invade Nathan's pockets, he hurled the perfume bottle to the wooden floor. It shattered, a bomb of glass. It *exploded*. Nathan cried out as shards of glass, some of it rendered useless powder, went *everywhere*.

Nathan closed his eyes and waited, his heart trying to shatter his chest; he waited for the inevitable slamming of footsteps on the staircase, for the woman at the cash register, for his mother, for the police, for men with angry eyes and reaching hands to come and find them both and grab them *hard*—

Nathan moaned and opened his eyes.

The boy was gone.

The shards of the bottle still lay like a sparkling carpet, but the boy, probably grinning, probably laughing, had run off, leaving Nathan alone to deal with the inevitable angry eyes and writhing, furious mouths.

The urge to urinate was now a cramp, and he clutched at his genitals, still moaning.

But no one came.

He snuffled once, trying to drag all that foul snot back into his nasal passage where it belonged. The boy was gone, and no angry footsteps stomped up the stairs, and somehow, blessedly, no one had seen what had happened. All he had to do now was move, get away, abandon the scene of the crime and everything would be okay.

I made it up. He had a shadow; of course he did. And he ran away while my eyes were closed. He was just . . . quiet.

I am good, Nathan told himself ferociously; *that boy was wrong. I am good, I am.*

He came around the corner and thought he saw the boy, that he'd come back. But it wasn't the boy, and it wasn't his mother or his brother or the lady in the purple coat. Another woman stood before him, someone he'd never seen before. She faced away from him, her shoulders slumped, her head bent, and he thought that she must be looking through the books on the shelf before her. She wore a red dress, simple, plain, but bright, exquisite and hot, like a flame. Her movements were quick and jerky, and her head cocked, first to the right, then to the left, and he heard the sounds she was making: little frenzied noises, tiny squeals, like a pig, amusing almost. He smiled, unable to help himself.

She froze, and he wondered if she had heard him approaching somehow, or if she sensed his smile, the muscles in his cheeks creaking perhaps, his teeth grinding together. She lifted her head from the awkward position where she held it, dog-like, and turned to face him.

All the air went out of his lungs; his eyes bulged; his hands clenched and loosened and then clenched again. He felt his bladder let go, finally, as it released a stream of burning urine to run down his leg.

"*Oough?*" the woman before him said through the hole in her face that should've, in a saner world, been her mouth. Her face was grated, brown and orange and black and red all over; in some places it flashed whitely, and Nathan knew that he was seeing bone, that those white patches were places where her skull showed through. The flesh hung in strings; she had no eyes or holes where her eyes should be, only more shredded strips of dried skin. They hung in flaps over the gaping hole where jagged white shards gnashed and ground together. "*Ouugh,*" the woman said again, not a question this time, and held out her hands, groping, reaching. Dimly, Nathan wondered if she could see him or only sense him somehow. And then, as the boy's had only moments before, her smell washed over him: high and sweet, but fishy, ruination, decay, old shit, thick and clotted, flooding his nostrils and filling his mouth. Her hands were close; they fluttered beside him like furious owls, descending on him.

What is she? he wondered. *Christ Jesus god Christ, what is she?* But it didn't matter then, because one of her hands touched his face. The flesh of her fingers was white and withered, like a mummy's, and from each digit he saw a tiny tip of bone. Three of these brushed against his skin; he recoiled, screaming, his shrieks deafening and echoing around the high ceiling of the room. *This isn't happening,* he thought, *isn't happening, can't be happening, can't can't can't.*

He broke away from the horror-woman-thing still groping blindly for him, making her piggy squeals of excitement or anger, the miasma stink of her hanging over him like foul perfume, and he ran for the stairs, struck the wall, glanced over his shoulder. She was coming for him, still coming, those bone-shards in her face gnashing wildly, and he reached for the railing and missed and thought, his arms pinwheeling helplessly, *I'm going to fall all the way down, I'm going to fall and I'm going to die*; and the woman's porcine squeals, emerging from that awful ruined face, continued to echo in his ears.

She was the first of the deaders. More followed. For *years*. Until, after one summer afternoon just before sophomore year began, they didn't anymore.

3

NATHAN LEFT HIS bedroom window and its wicked new cracks, and showered and dressed and styled his hair as much as it would allow itself to be styled; passed silent, staring Terry in the hall, who, unsurprisingly, yet painfully nevertheless, did nothing to acknowledge him—not a nod, not a smile, not a slug on the shoulder—and finally left the house and made his way outside, where Logan waited at the curb as he always did. It was an ordinary Friday morning in March, except that it wouldn't be ordinary at all, Nathan knew. Not if the cards were right. Not if they had the séance, as he currently schemed, feeling only the tiniest bit absurd. *Logan will think it's absurd. Stupid. Pointless.* But all Nathan had to do was conjure up last night's blue-faced horror and its amazing hypno-eyes, and any lingering feelings of absurdity curdled, dwindled, and disappeared.

Yes, Logan would think a séance absurd. But he could be convinced. Nathan already had a plan.

Nathan paused to look at him fondly, his Logan, beautiful and waiting.

He won't be here much longer, said a familiar feminine voice in Nathan's head. *The end is drawing, drawing, drawing nearer and nearer, darling; just admit it, dearest.*

Sometimes Nathan heard voices, though he had decided long ago that they meant nothing, couldn't possibly be a sign of mental illness; creativity, perhaps, or hitherto undiagnosed brilliance, but not *mental illness*, nothing so frightening as *schizophrenia*, for Christ's sakes; he'd know, wouldn't he, if he were *schizophrenic?*

Voices. This one belonged to a woman he imagined as eminently lovely, icily blonde, and swathed in a dress of emerald-green that would sparkle beneath any light that dared shine upon her.

But she loved to taunt him, whether she was real or . . . or *not*.

Change, she purred. *Coming, coming, coming. Today will be unusual; tonight will be terrible. You don't have to wait and see; might as well just come back to us, darling boy.* And she laughed wildly.

Shut up, he snarled at the voice, and it retreated.

Logan hunched over the wheel of the car with his chin resting on his extended elbows, yes, just as he did every morning. Nathan could see from the stoop where he paused that Logan was, as always, mouthing with big enthusiasm the words of a song he loved; Nathan could just hear its steady, siren's beat from where he stood, and he felt that familiar, susurrating pulse of love for the other boy.

He trotted across the lawn, wincing as he slid almost gracefully across a patch of icy grass, long dead, yet somehow able to retain its summer hue; but he righted himself in time, and besides, Logan hadn't seen. Shouldn't matter if he had, but it did. It always did, when Logan didn't notice him.

The passenger door was locked against him, and Nathan bounced backward and barked, "Hellfire," as he did so. The curb was icy, too, and he nearly fell again. He thought that if he did, he would disappear forever beneath the car and into the heat and dark and fumes of gasoline and oil and no one would ever see him again.

I'd become one of them. *Is that what they want?*

His mother thought he was depressed, that he was suffering from the same kind of depression she had battled since she was his age. "I'm not depressed," he would say brightly. "I don't need Prozac or Xanax," or whatever other prescriptions she suggested. He wondered now. Was she more than just depressed? And even if that was all (*ha*, he thought without humor, *all*), even if that was *all*, couldn't depression be something that you passed down to your kids? It wasn't the first time the thought had occurred to him. *Maybe I'm just scared,* he thought. The end was coming, changes were coming; who *wasn't* scared? *Séance it up*, he thought with that same dark humor. *Make all of this go away. Magic versus medication.*

Nathan tapped on the window, suppressing thoughts of the blue face and its bony fingers, and Logan looked up, startled, his eyes wide. Nathan saw him mouth the word, "Oh!" then wince, embarrassed. Logan embarrassed was interesting because it was so unusual. Nothing embarrassed Logan, which had to be, Nathan was certain, the key to his success at school and everything else; Logan knew how to do everything and it seemed he had always known. He was never a jerk about it, or an ass, and he never hung it over anyone's head. His teammates voted him captain of the basketball team that year for the first time because they knew—*he* knew—that he could do it, just as he had played the perfect quarterback the year before. This year, he claimed, football held no interest for him, and it didn't matter that he had never played basketball, not seriously, until then. When Logan thought he could do something, he just did it.

"Going my way?" Nathan purred, mock-seductively. Logan, grinning, pushed the button on his key that unlocked the doors. Logan's mother was a lawyer and his father a dentist and they were, by Garden City standards, fairly comfortable, which explained the new car Logan had received, solemnly, as a gift on their first day of senior year.

Nathan opened the door, releasing a rush of warm air, still sweet with the scent of new car, leathery, lemony; he tossed his raggedy brown messenger bag into the backseat and slid inside, then buckled his seatbelt, grumbling as he did so. "Don't grumble," Logan said amiably. "I didn't lock you out on purpose, you know."

"I know, but it's freezing out there," Nathan said. He looked down at his hands, which were red and chapped. "And I forgot my gloves again. Damn. My hands are gonna swell up like Mickey Mouse." He waggled his fingers before Logan's face. "See? Fat white sausage fingers. Boogedy boogedy."

"No worries." Logan cranked the heat up three notches; dragon breath flooded Nathan's face and he drank it in. "You'll thaw by the time we get to school. Then we can shrink your fingers back down to size. Donald Duck maybe, instead of Mickey."

"Does Donald Duck wear gloves?"

"Maybe his feathers are too thin. Not enough coverage. If he doesn't, he should."

"He totally should. Only the classiest ducks and rodents wear gloves."

Logan laughed; then they laughed together like they always did. Maybe the day wouldn't be so unusual, so *strange*, after all. Logan pulled away from the curb, and their laughter faded until it disappeared completely. They drove for a time in silence; frightened, Nathan realized how frequently these weird little pockets occurred, lags between conversations, more every day. Change, the wind whispered outside, change coming fast.

The day at Royal High started when the first bell rang at 7:45; Logan always picked Nathan up at 7:00 sharp, even when he used to drive the old beater car he'd selected himself sophomore year and paid for with money he'd earned by working summers on his uncle's farm outside the city. And while working with Amy at the frame shop was amazing—she encouraged Nathan to design the window displays that frequently won local awards, especially around the holidays—Nathan found that he still couldn't save enough money to afford a car of his own. (But he swore he would; he just hadn't yet.) So Logan did the driving, and Nathan would settle back against the comfortable cushioning of his best friend's car and let him. Logan was always punctual, and they rode together every day this way in the bland late winter darkness that wouldn't clear until well after 8:00.

Except Logan wasn't punctual today, Nathan realized with a glance at the clock on the dash. 7:15. *Change, oh, change,* that woman's voice jeered, and a cold finger stroked his heart. Two years ago, after he'd given her form and shape, he'd attended a party she'd thrown in his honor.

No. You didn't. That wasn't real, chumly.

Such a kind imitation of Logan's voice.

He blinked, cold; try not to think about her, about *them*, he hissed at himself in his own voice. *The party wasn't real, stupid;* even if she was beautiful in a green dress that made her look like a mermaid,

flared like Beyoncé's in *Dreamgirls*, even if there were a million people in his mansion—

You don't have a mansion.

There was no party.

Maybe I'm just crazy, he thought, and sighed.

Logan glanced over at him, squinting his concern.

There are still the photos.

Right. Photographic evidence that the deaders existed.

Except that he'd destroyed them, every one. And the negatives.
On the off chance that it might destroy the deaders themselves. It
amused him now: witchcraft against the dead, voodoo dolls, pins.

"The cards," Nathan said suddenly, and Logan looked over at
him again while maintaining perfect speed. "Last night, the cards
were weird."

After a careful moment, Logan said, "I thought you put the
cards away."

"I know what I'm doing," Nathan said stiffly. "I've worked really
hard to understand them." He was enveloped with heat now, and the
walls of the car were starting to press in. He laid his forehead against
the window, seeking coolness, some relief.

Logan, knowing, clicked the temperature dial down three
notches. He smiled kindly while he did it. Nathan felt the rancor draining away, while the familiar and irritating gnaw of guilt
returned to replace it. "I just think they're, you know," Logan said,
"kid stuff. Junior high."

"They don't work for just anyone, you know. You have to pay
attention. You have to *listen.*"

"I don't want to hurt your feelings."

Nathan said nothing, merely gazed out the window.

"Shit. I did. Hey, I'm sorry, chumly."

Nathan grinned despite himself. "I told you not to call me that."

"Clarabell?"

"Not that either."

"Dude? Bro? Man? Dude-bro-man?"

"Sounds like a superhero," Nathan said gravely. "The Toxic
Masculine Avenger."

"Is that a movie? Sometimes I don't get the references you're—"

"I know, I know," Nathan said hastily. He didn't like to be reminded of Logan's admonition since they were children: *Don't talk about that stuff so much.*

"Okay, so I don't mean *kid* stuff. Could just be," and Logan heaved a dramatic sigh, "that I'm over-thinking these last few months of school."

"Me too," Nathan said quietly.

"I'm fixated on shit that seems so . . . juvenile. Because we've got to grow up and be adults, right? And your cards . . ." He trailed off, thinking. Nathan watched him carefully, lovingly. No more rancor, he swore, no more vast waves of irritation. "They're *creepy*," Logan said. "That's it. They creep me the hell out."

"Yeah?" He felt genuine surprise. Logan never really talked about things that creeped him out; he'd long ago decried a belief in ghosties or ghoulies or long-leggedy beasties, which was one of the reasons Nathan had stopped trying to convince him about *them*.

"A little. Like, to know that something silly, these little playing cards, can look through us and into us, and forward, and find out." He blinked. "Things." Shivered. "I don't like it. I don't want to think that everything is predictable and all laid out. Like a funeral suit or something."

Nathan snickered. "A funeral suit?"

"You know," Logan insisted. "It's like being too prepared for something. The zodiac, the Tarot, all those things. What about free will?"

"We have plenty of free will. And this isn't your intro to psych class."

"I'm taking intro to ethics."

"Whatever. This isn't that. I just . . ." He toyed with his bangs, a habit he had developed in elementary school; occasionally, when he wasn't tugging on his bangs, he would pull at his eyebrows, thinking, *These are long, these are too long,* and out they would come. They always proved to be great black curling hairs, like severed spider legs on the tip of his finger, and he would throw them away from himself with a mixture of grim pleasure and disgust. "I'm not talking about ethics," Nathan, tugging, said helplessly. "I need them."

"I can see why."

"Oh?" Nathan stopped tugging his hair and raised a single eyebrow.

"Don't sass me," Logan said, amused. "Yeah, I can see it. Because they're right sometimes. Maybe even a lot. What did they say about today?"

Nathan shifted uneasily in his seat. "That it would be weird."

"Just weird?"

"That big changes are coming."

"Don't you think that there are always big changes coming?"

"Not always." Too defensive; he could hear it in his voice. He smoothed his hands along the leather seat. "Sometimes things stay the same. People get into ruts."

"Maybe you're just reading into them. Maybe it's all coincidence."

"Maybe," Nathan said. He ground his teeth despite himself. *Just breathe*, he thought; *one, two, breathe, three, breathe—*

But some demon, Poe's Imp, Nathan thought cynically, forced him to add, "Screw the cards. I want to have a séance."

Logan turned his head to stare at Nathan, opened his mouth, and then closed it again. "A *séance*?" he said. "Oh man. Oh Nathan. Not really."

"Really." His mouth grew firm; his hands clutched each other tightly; he stared out at the mountains, which resembled the slow, exhausted ghosts of elephants covered in white shrouds.

"That's even worse than the cards."

Nathan's eyes flickered. *My last chance*, he thought obscurely. "I don't think so." Teeth pressed together, hands knotted. "I want this."

"But a séance? Why?"

"Because I'm interested. I want to see, you know, what could happen." *Tell him, tell him the truth, try again; now's the time, do it, do it—*

"Listen, chumly, people already think—"

"I don't care what people think."

"Maybe," Logan said quietly, "it's about time you did."

"God," Nathan said, his irritation really rancor now, spilling out over his tongue and teeth and into the warm enveloping air holding them inside Logan's fancy car. "Why do you have to shit on the things I love? Why can't it be enough that I *like* something, that I'm *interested*?" His nostrils flared; horrified, he found that his eyes burned with tears.

Logan didn't say anything for a long time. They sat at a stoplight, and the white fluffy clouds of exhaust from Logan's car and the car in the lane beside his obscured the fading winter world so that all Nathan could see was his own reflection in the window, milky, his eyes wide dark holes, his mouth a small empty circle. "I don't mean to shit on anything," Logan said at last, carefully. "I love you. You ass. I *love* you. You're my best friend."

"Yeah," Nathan said miserably.

"You know it."

He did.

"I don't want to tear into the stuff you like. If you care about it, I care about it, to a point. But I want you to be safe, too, and we've got just a little bit of this race to run before someone hands us our diplomas and pronounces us grad-u-muh-cated, and until then I don't want you to get hurt."

"I don't talk about this stuff with everyone, you know. Just with you."

Logan looked at him piercingly. "Nathan," he said. "Séances?"

Nathan stared back at him in his most challenging way, but eventually he lost, as he always lost, and dropped his eyes.

"They used to call you 'the Succubus,'" Logan said quietly. "Emphasis on 'suck.' And 'Dracula's Daughter.'"

Nathan tried to smile. "Sounds like the jag-offs at school are getting more creative. Good for them. Or maybe they're watching those movies, too. I'm doing the Lord's work."

"They don't talk about it, if they do."

"Like me, you mean."

"Like you."

"And I shouldn't. I shouldn't talk about sexy boy vampires in those Anne Rice movies, or how the books are better. I shouldn't talk about gender roles and queering narratives, or how the movie *The Talented Mr. Ripley* is better than the book and how rare that is, or how the special effects in *The Birds* are really super awesome and everyone today is an idiot. I shouldn't—"

"I stamp it out. When they call you names. I do that. Me."
Logan remained stern.

"Thank you *ever* so much."

Logan took a deep breath and glared at the steering wheel.

"What?" Nathan said jeeringly. "You getting tired of being my manly defender? Listen up, Sir Galahad. No one asked you."

"You don't have to ask—"

"Maybe I don't want your help."

"I just want to—"

"And maybe," Nathan said, biting down savagely on each word, "maybe I don't actually like it. Maybe I want to stand up for myself for a change."

"Maybe you should, then," Logan said angrily.

"Maybe I get just the teensiest bit tired of *you* doing everything for *you*, pretending it's for *me*, so *you* can feel better about yourself." Logan's mouth gaped.

Nathan, horrified at himself, knew this wasn't true, but he was unable to stop.

But isn't it, that sibilant woman's voice whispered. *Isn't it just a little bit true?*

He's my best friend, Nathan thought.

But he only cares about himself, tittered the evil little voice.

Which was why Nathan was unable to hold back the thundering climax of his little diatribe: "If you cared more about me than you do about yourself—"

"Look," Logan exploded. Nathan startled, cringing back against his side of the car, the seatbelt cutting into his windpipe. "I don't help you because I want to hold it over your head, so I can make myself feel better. Is that what you think? Really? That I'm like that?"

Shame rose like bile up inside Nathan's chest and esophagus, where it burned hatefully.

It's because he's just so good, that wicked woman's voice insisted. *He's so good, and he's so good at* everything. *Darling, little lamb, doesn't it make you crazy? Doesn't it drive you absolutely mad? It will, you know, if you let it; darling, come with us, you'll see—*

Go, goddammit it, he hissed at the voice, and it receded again.

None of those things were true. Right? They couldn't be. *Couldn't.* And since they couldn't possibly be true, the shame burned hotter, corrosive and hateful and exactly what he deserved. Soon his teeth would dissolve, his hateful tongue.

And since he needed his teeth and his hateful tongue, and since he didn't enjoy feeling the bitter burn of shame—he told himself he didn't—there was really only one solution, wasn't there?

He needed to get the fuck out of Royal High.

"No," Nathan said quietly. "No, I don't think you're like that."

"I hope not," Logan said, calmer now. His hands on the wheel were clenched so tightly that his knuckles glowed white. "We've been friends for how long, Nathan?"

Nathan said nothing.

"Too long to fight over goddamn Tarot cards," Logan said, then spat, "Séances."

The drive was almost over. School waited a mile away, an old brick building constructed in 1913, when Garden City first rose like a bright and worthy sun, a jeweled star in Montana's firmament, offering civilization in what had mostly been, according to the spreading white population, and in spite of the hearty presence of the Salish and the Blackfeet tribes, a wilderness. Royal was the first of Garden City's high schools, and only a decade or so younger than Waxman University, which sprawled four blocks away, with its oaks and aspens and its series of green grassy knolls that surrounded solemnly all the buildings comprising the campus, and where Nathan would be headed in six short months.

Logan had dated a Waxman theatre major when they were sophomores, a boy only three years older than they were, but he was a *college* boy nevertheless, and Logan and Nathan both thought it was like something out of a movie.

"He was the worst kisser in the world," Logan had admitted with a mixture of melancholy and longing and a wicked sort of amusement after it was all over. "Wet and sloppy. His tongue was too long. All the acting classes in the world won't make his tongue any shorter." Then, amused, he added, "Frog tongue. Slimy frog tongue." Then he waggled his own tongue around and around until they were both laughing so hard that tears ran out of their eyes; they each threw back another glass of the wine Logan had spirited from his father's vast collection in the cellar and then laughed some more.

"I'm sorry," Nathan said. He held his hands together and they fought each other, fingers pressing against fingers, forcing them down. "I shouldn't have said those things. Any of those things."

Logan stared at the wheel.

"I love you."

Logan sighed.

"I mean it."

"Yeah," Logan said after another of those scary little pauses.

"I'm an asshole." He heard the desperation in his voice and was helpless to prevent it.

Please don't leave me alone, a little voice inside him whispered, a remarkable imitation of nine-year-old Nathan. *I only said those things because sometimes I lose control, and I won't, not ever again.* But the child's voice continued to whimper inside him, *I don't like it here, I'm afraid . . .*

"You *are* an asshole," Logan agreed, then grinned. His grin was contagious and beautiful. Nathan felt a pang when he saw it. Foolishly, wantonly, Nathan had accepted long ago that he loved Logan more than as just a simple friend; once, he might even have allowed himself to think about all the ways they could be together, which were clearly impossible. Sometimes he even dared to wonder if Logan thought about him in that way, too; neither of them ever spoke the words out loud. He feared that if Logan felt that way even a little (and Nathan had to admit that, no, he probably didn't), then he'd already accepted that their friendship was the way things were, friends forever. Just friends.

And who wasn't attracted to Logan? He was fucking gorgeous: smile sparkling with straight teeth, square jaw, hair so blond it was nearly white, and a head-size he'd finally grown into back in junior high. No one hated Logan, not even the worst of the assholes at school. He was friends with the jocks and their girlfriends; he could spar with those same jocks while complimenting (sincerely) their girlfriends' hair and shoes and fingernail polish. He possessed a passable singing voice, nothing glorious, but serviceable. He was *nice*: he held the door, not just for Nathan, but for everyone; he brought coffee on days when Nathan hadn't slept and felt irritable and logy, because Logan just *knew*; and he always predicted what Nathan secretly wanted for his birthday and then got it for him, that book, that movie, that beautiful sweater he'd ogled at the mall. Logan was, overall, friendly and chatty and confident. And pretty. Well-muscled. Broad-shouldered, broad chest.

Nathan jealously wished to hoard their friendship, to tuck it away like a mouse does crumbs. He told himself that Logan was nice to everyone because that's the way he was. But Logan didn't belong to anyone else.

"Yes, you are an asshole. But you're *my* asshole," Logan said. His grin widened and he shook his head with mock sadness. "Oh man. I wish I hadn't said that."

"You only need the one," Nathan said laconically.

"Hell. Don't let me do this to you."

"Do what?"

"Lay all my shit on you. You wanna do Tarot readings at lunch in the caf dressed like a swami, go right ahead."

"That's very magnanimous of you."

"Isn't it?" Logan grinned again, but just a hint, the sun peeking above the mountain. "I mean it though. We've got, what, three months left? What are those dickwads gonna do to you that they haven't already done?"

"College, then." Nathan sighed luxuriously, then quickly added, "Just Waxman. I'm *excited*."

"I can tell."

"I'm ready for adventure."

"At Waxman?"

"Adventure. A journey. I want to go right this very now."

Logan laughed. "You should come with me to Washington."

"Scared to go by yourself?" he teased.

"Absolutely," Logan said with a straight face. "Wouldn't you be?"

"It'll be same old, same old for this kid. Except everything will be different."

Would they *follow you if you went?* Can *you go, Nathan? Can you really?*

"You hope."

"I," Nathan said grandly, silencing that wicked voice in his head, "will make it different."

They laughed together and the sound fluttered around the car like a small bird that escaped as soon as it could. Logan pulled into the school parking lot. Most of the spaces were occupied since they arrived later than usual, and Logan hunted for a spot, his brow only slightly furrowed.

But it was out now. The conversation that they had only tiptoed around for the last five months, since college applications and letters of recommendation and decision-making became such a huge part of their lives, splitting them, slowly but surely separating the membrane that had connected and sustained them all these years, inevitably and certainly, but slowly enough that it wasn't as painful as it might have been. That was the fiction, anyway, that had grown so comfortable between them: that there was no pain, would be no pain.

But there must be, Nathan thought, because the world was a god-damn hateful machine and it turned anyway, no matter what, despite connective tissue and membranes and plans; both boys were only just now, they realized without articulating their new, mutual knowledge, beginning to understand this.

Logan pulled his car into the last available spot, then pushed the button to turn off the engine. The exhalation of warmth was caught mid-breath, one last puff of comfortable air.

"This is it," he said inadequately.

"Yeah," Nathan agreed, feeling equally inadequate.

They inhaled at the same time.

Nathan thought about all the things they never talked about. He wanted to ask Logan about Derek, find out how many times they'd fucked, *really*, not just blowjobs in the back of the car. He wanted to ask if he was any good, how big his dick was, all that stupid shit; what would happen to them at the end of summer, when college started and Logan left Garden City and Derek stayed? What, then? Nathan felt sudden insight and what felt passably like wisdom:

Change will come, fast or slow. Let it start now, then, by god, let it blow these idiot times away.

I can have a life.

I can be normal. Do normal things like have a job and go to college and have a real boyfriend at last.

He imagined, with relief, coming clean to Logan, what he would say:

I see dead people. Like the kid in that movie, I guess, the one we watched at your house last summer even though you didn't want to, and I kind of didn't either, but then I felt like, oh my god, this is me, I'm seeing myself. It sounds stupid, but I do see them. I call them "deaders." I always have. I tried to tell you once and you thought I was joking. You said you didn't believe me; you said I have a vivid imagination; you said you loved me but I watch too many movies, so I stopped. I see the deaders and I'm trying I'm trying I'm trying so hard to make them go away. Crystals and séances and Tarot cards; I went a long time without seeing one, and now—bam—they're back. It's like they're swarming everywhere, and I can't figure out how to make them stop. I wish you could help me. You're my best friend. We could do it together, Logan. Banish them together. Just you and me. Forever, you and me.

The words danced on his tongue, against his teeth.

"And . . . the séance?" he said instead.

But Logan, opening his door, hadn't heard, or ignored him, which didn't seem likely but was possible. Nathan closed his mouth and opened his door and sucked in a bitter pull of late winter air that burned his throat raw. He tried to call out, but the wind took whatever words waited on his lips, tore and tattered them, sent them into nothingness, and so, helplessly, Nathan could only follow.

4

THE HEAT OF the school was the jungle's heat, a tangled snarl of invisible currents, thick air, hormones, pheromones. As he did every morning, Nathan reeled back momentarily, overwhelmed by the rush as he followed Logan through the door. Logan didn't notice; Logan never noticed. He was looking for his boyfriend. Nathan watched him glance around the long hallways lined with their schoolmates, a blur of washed-out, blank faces.

Nathan thought about how pissed Logan would be if he knew that he'd already broached the idea of a séance with Derek, Logan's little boyfriend since last Christmas or so. Derek was a cheerleader now and bound to be a cheerleader for the rest of his life; he was also a theatre geek and a choir geek and Logan had, starting a month or so ago, been very into him, "Even though," he'd admitted once when he and Nathan cruised around aimlessly in Logan's car, "he's, um, real emotional." Logan had blushed—Nathan could see it, even in the dimness of Logan's car—and stammered a bit in a distinctly un-Logan-like fashion. "I mean, he, um . . . he *cries* sometimes. Out of the blue. For no reason. It just kinda . . . happens. He says it's because he loves me so much. That's nice, right? Cute. I mean, I think it's cute."

Then, almost pleading, with a sideways glance: "Don't you think it's cute?"

"It's cute," Nathan had replied obediently, and then, looking pensively out the window, he wondered if he'd be in control of his emotions if he were dating Logan, if Logan loved him like that.

How did people control their emotions when they were in love? How did they stay *sane*? The darkness of Garden City outside Logan's car had thickened, laughing at the very idea of sanity.

"I think I love him," Logan had said shyly, and Nathan had closed his eyes.

He's waiting for me out there, at the end of a path, Nathan thought as he followed Logan through the halls, *or in a lost garden, or deep in the still and secret heart of a magical wood. A forest living under an enchantment. That's the word, the perfect word: enchantment. I'll come riding on a white stallion, and I will find him and love him and break the enchantment; only I can break the spell, of course. And he will be so grateful to me, whoever he is, that he'll marry me on the spot. I will love and be loved.*

Pretty words; magic words. But now here was Derek, jolting Nathan out of his reverie. He bounced toward them through the crowd, bugling to Logan: "I wanted to tell you first, so that you wouldn't say no, because I *really* want to do this, so we have to." Then he saw Nathan and brightened even more, if possible. "Hi, Nathan!"

Looking at Derek, Nathan wondered again at the nature of his relationship with Logan, and what he thought their future held. He knew there had been blowjobs for sure, but anything more than that? Derek had once waxed romantic while they all ate lunch together and sighed about "making love." Nathan grimaced thinking of them together like that, "making *love*," as if fairies sprinkled magic dust over their supine bodies and fireflies spelled out their names in great glowing explosions of pink and purple light.

Nathan had to admit to himself, though, that he was curious to know what it would be like with Logan.

"When you lose your virginity," Logan had said once, smiling kindly and touching Nathan's hand, "we can compare gay sex notes."

And Nathan had smiled secretly to himself. Because Logan didn't know everything there was to know, did he.

Deals, deals, deals with the devil.

"Hi," was all Nathan said, and Derek's eyes flickered away like twin butterflies and settled on Logan's face.

One very particular devil.

"They asked me because I'm in drama," Derek said. He took both of Logan's hands in his and squeezed them. "I said yes, because it's going to be cool, but it's *tonight*, and so I had to say yes right away, otherwise it would be too late."

"Is this about that ghost thing again?" Logan asked.

"You know Mikyla Simmons," Derek said, "and her friend Essie? Essie is that girl who always looks like someone dug her up in the graveyard after a hundred years. She's all mascara in clumps and I don't think she's ever washed her hair, probably." Logan made a face. "Anyway, they have this club, and *I've* never heard of it." His eyes flickered back to Nathan. "Have you, Nathan, heard of this club?"

"Ghosts," Nathan said.

"You *do* know! For hunts. Like those guys on TV. They bring cameras and make recordings and I think they have a special fan page. It's all kids from Royal High; I think they worship the devil. But Mikyla is friends with Heather Addams; Heather's cheer captain, Nathan. Jeez, don't look at me like that; I wasn't sure if you *knew*, that's all; you don't have to *growl*. So, Mikyla is friends with Heather, and Mikyla told Heather and Heather told me because she thought it sounded fun."

"What," Logan said, his smile less defined now, "sounded fun?"

"They're going to do a hunt tonight."

"Here?" Logan said, scoffing. "In the school?"

Derek nodded eagerly, his little head bobbing up and down.

"Isn't Mikyla dating Seb Candleberry?" Nathan asked.

"Yes," Derek said. He turned and clutched Logan's hands again and said, "Come on, babe, it'll be fun. It'll be *wicked*."

"Why can't I just tell him it's your idea?" Derek had asked yesterday afternoon when Nathan caught him between classes, looking over his shoulders to scan the crowd for Logan. The blue-skull-thing had yet to appear, was still twelve hours in the future, waiting to follow Nathan home and trot across his lawn and beat its head against his window. He had already discovered, however, that the deaders had pranced and grimaced and snarled their merry ways through his photos; Nathan figured it best to be proactive.

"Because it'll sound better coming from you," Nathan had said, trying to maintain a pleasant smile and his patience at the same time. "He's tired of hearing me talk about stuff like this."

"You're *way* more into it than even me, and *I'm* pretty into it."

"I know," Nathan had said, feeling exhausted; talking with Derek always left him feeling at least slightly exhausted. "Just trust me. I'm going to bring it up to him, too, but he'll probably say no. But if it's your idea—if *you* suggest it—he'll do it. I'll back you up. Just don't let him know that we had this little conversation."

Derek's big brown eyes had grown bigger and, somehow, browner. "You want me to lie to him?" he'd whispered.

"No, no, no," Nathan said swiftly, his hands cutting the air. "Of course not. We're not going to lie. We're going to *protect* him."

Derek frowned. "Protect him?"

"From himself."

Derek's frown deepened. "How?"

"Because," Nathan had said, smiling, a used car salesman, "Logan doesn't get how cool this could be. How awesome." Derek was, Nathan knew, inordinately fond of the word *awesome*. "So it's up to us—or you, really—to convince him. To bring us all *together*."

"Up to me," Derek said, scrunching up his face like a little rabbit. Then he brightened. "Yeah," he said brightly. "Yeah! I want him to like all the stuff that I like. I want us to be even closer than we are now. I love him, Nathan."

"I know you do."

"More than anything or anyone." Derek had grown solemn, all Disney princess eyes and trembling rosebud mouth. "I will love him forever and ever."

"Sounds like a long time. So . . . will you do it?"

"So . . . will you do it?" A high-pitched, lisping voice pierced Nathan's ears, loud, sharp with cruelty. He stiffened; Derek glared. Three boys who looked vaguely familiar—juniors, maybe even sophomores—jocks in ball-caps, as the assholes always seemed to be jocks in ball-caps, mocking them. *Or me*, Nathan thought darkly, *it's usually all about me.* The jocks minced about, flapping their wrists like birds with broken necks. "Faggots," the biggest one, Rory-something, sneered. "*Suck*-ubus."

"Fuck," Nathan said, "you."

"*Fuck you*," the other boy mimicked in a soaring soprano. His friends laughed their simian laughter, their faces ape-like and ruddy. "Good comeback, Bride of Fagenstein."

"Bride of Fagenstein!" Nathan called after them as they strolled, shoulders rolling, blithely down the hall. "It's a classic! But why not Boris Queer-loff? Or Bela Luh-gay-see? Try harder, you jags!"

"They're gone, Nathan," Derek had said quietly.

"Yeah, yeah." He pulled at his bangs and then his eyebrows but forced himself to stop. "And people are staring. You sound like Logan. He's always worried about people staring. So. Will you ask him?"

Derek had placed one finger against his lower lip and attempted to look thoughtful.

"So, will you do it?" Derek pleaded now, his excitement unyielding.

"There are janitors," Logan said reasonably. "And teachers."

"We're going to *hide*," Derek chirped. "We're going to stay here after school—"

"That'll take hours."

"We'll hide in the auditorium, because that's where the *most* ghosts live—"

"Ghosts," Logan said, "are not alive."

"—and Essie has her dad's camera and we'll have our phones, just in case, to catch something. But I don't care, I just want to *see* one."

"The auditorium is supposed to be haunted," Nathan told Logan. "Some girl said on the first day of school."

"*Ghosts*, Logan," Derek said, his voice now plaintive.

"What if ghosts don't show up on camera?" Logan said.

Derek's eyes shone brighter, if possible. "But they do! There's books. I read one in Barnes and Noble. Ghosts," he said to Nathan, conspiratorially, "show up in pictures all the time."

"It sounds like bullshit to me, babe," Logan said.

"Don't say that." Derek traced circles with his fingertip on the inside of Logan's arm. "Essie said she and Mikyla brought a Ouija board in here last week and the little plastic indicator thingie totally moved."

"It's called a planchette," Nathan said.

"Planchette, yeah, sure," Derek said. "It *moved*."

"Because she moved it." Logan's patient façade was crumbling.

Derek's bottom lip quivered. "Why shouldn't there be ghosts? People must have died here. You can't have a building where no one ever *died*, right?"

Nathan thought of what he'd seen in the antique mall nine years before. Had she died there, that ghastly woman? Did she wander through those aisles loaded with meaningless mementos? Did she giggle mindlessly to herself, caressing lightly the staring faces of dolls and moth-eaten dresses and tables with scarred surfaces from a hundred-thousand meals; did she know where she was, or *what*?

Logan looked at Nathan. "What do you think?"

Nathan thought Logan would bring up the Tarot cards, but he didn't. He only watched. Derek's eyes danced back and forth between them.

Nathan pretended to consider. "I think they'd show for you," he said, ruffling Logan's hair.

"Yeah?" Logan said. He grinned. "Yeah. Sure, they would."

"But it has to be a séance," Nathan said, more loudly than he intended. "Not just a hunt."

Logan's grin faded.

Derek frowned. "Séance?"

"We sit in a circle," Nathan said, smiling sweetly at Logan. "We put out a call. And we see who—or *what*—answers."

They can finally tell me then, the bastards, what the hell they actually want.

"Awesome!" Derek trilled. "I'll figure out the how of it all. I'm research boy!"

Logan shook his head in exasperation. Eventually, though, his radiant grin resurfaced, and Nathan felt a spear of hope. "Okay," he said, "you got me. I'll add 'ghostbusting' to my résumé." He pressed his lips to Derek's.

"Who else will be there?" Nathan said casually, looking away.

"Me and Logan and you," Derek said, counting on his fingers, "and Heather and Essie and Mikyla and Seb, of course."

"Of course," Nathan said, and felt demure.

"He won't be a dick," Derek promised.

Logan said, "But he's always kind of a dick, isn't he?"

"He is," Nathan said.

"Is that a game-changer, do you suppose?" Logan frowned at Nathan. "An unexpected guest appearance by Mr. Sebastian Candleberry?"

"I don't think so. There'll be enough of us that it won't make any difference. Besides, it's like you said: How much time do we have left here? I mean, really?"

"Enough that he could make your life fairly shitty," Logan said grimly. "If he wanted to. Every day for three months."

"I've got a thick skin," Nathan said, waving a hand.

"I'll tell Mikyla to make him behave," Derek said.

"No," Nathan said instantly, and they both looked at him, Logan with his eyebrows raised. "I mean," Nathan added weakly, "I don't want to make a big deal out of it. We don't like each other very much, that's all. It isn't like nuclear war. We won't fight."

"You'll have to resist the urge to hit him with something," Logan said.

"I'll use your car if I have to."

Logan laid a hand on Nathan's shoulder and squeezed. It burned pleasantly as Nathan looked at it. Then he looked up into Logan's smiling eyes.

"That's the first bell," Derek said happily. "School."

5

"DO YOU BELIEVE in ghosts?" Nathan had asked his boss, Amy Wilson, as they were closing up the shop on Monday night, after the deaders first started to return, and he began turning the idea of a séance over in his mind.

"Oh, hell yeah," she'd said immediately, grinning at him. "Of course I do! I watch that *Ghost Hunters* show on Bravo all the time."

"Bravo," he'd said weakly. "Have you ever seen a ghost?"

"No," she admitted. "Not really. Which sucks. I've always wanted to, and I have this feeling like I could, or like I'm about to. I could turn a corner in my house and—boom!—there one would be. But it never happens. You ever feel that way?"

He didn't trust himself to answer, so he only nodded.

"Why are you wondering about ghosts now?" she'd asked, her eyes sparkling a little. Amy's eyes, Nathan had noticed immediately upon his hire, were always sparkling or preparing to sparkle. She was an artist herself, went to Waxman before deciding that Garden City could use a frame shop that doubled as an art gallery. She'd looked at Nathan's work and saw potential, encouraged him to practice more, and then, she'd said, he should go public with his photographs. She'd recommended a specific teacher at Royal High, a woman whose class Amy had taken herself once upon a time. "She taught me a lot about perspective," Amy had told him, "and shadow and how to use darkness. There's a lot you can learn about how darkness functions. How to make it work for you. She'll teach you that." So he'd enrolled in the class and found that Amy was right.

"Halloween isn't for another eight months or so," she continued. "Prepping to get your spook on all over the window display? That'd be okay, actually," she smiled, "if you won me another award from the Garden City Downtown Association."

"Get your spook on. Heh. You make it sound dirty when you say it like that." Nathan smiled a little. "I was just wondering . . . how you might get rid of them."

"Like . . . Ghostbusters?" Her forehead creased.

"I was thinking something a little less out of the movies. Maybe a bit more, um, ritual-y."

"You mean ritualistic."

"Sure. That."

She closed her eyes. "Well," she said at last, "when I went through my Goth Wicca feisty feminist phase in college—you will, too, just you wait—a friend of mine totally swiped this book from the Waxman bookstore that was supposed to be full of real spells. Hocus-cadabra, all that."

"Abra-capocus. Did you try anything?"

"Sure did."

"And?"

She waved her hands through the air, miming mystic passes, then turned them palm-side up and shrugged. "Nothing," she said. "Absolutely nothing. In retrospect, we probably should've smoked more weed beforehand."

"Peyote," Nathan said, and they laughed together.

"Are you okay?" she said as their laughter faded. "Seriously, Nathan. Dark shadows under the eyes, unsuitable pallor . . ."

"Maybe I already started my Goth Wicca feisty feminist phase."

"You can tell me if something is wrong. I'm a cool boss. I mean, come on: look at my eyeshadow! Who wears electric blue eyeshadow these days?"

"You are a totally cool boss."

She jabbed her chin out like a sword. "Damn straight."

"And I'd tell you if something was wrong."

"You just need . . . what? An emergency exorcism?"

"I saw that movie," he said, shuddering, "and it did not end well. Priests throwing themselves out windows all willy-nilly. No, thank you."

"Ghosts, Nathan?" The amusement was gone from her voice now, and she sounded, he thought, genuinely concerned. "Really? This isn't some kind of pre-graduation freak-out?"

"Let's call them bad dreams."

"Okay," she said, clearly unconvinced. "Something to get rid of bad dreams." She considered. "I think Eleanor's witch book said that crystals were the way to go."

"Crystals."

"Yuh-huh. Good for channeling energy."

"So if I was trying to get rid of something bad," Nathan said thoughtfully, "I could, whadda ya call it, channel it . . . somewhere else."

"You just have to concentrate, I guess. I'm not sure; I was never a very good witch. Probably why I decided to stick with art instead. That's a kind of magic I understand." She beamed at him and brushed his bangs out of his eyes. "I'm sorry you're having bad dreams, sweetie. I wish I could help."

"Nothing I can't handle," he said as the door opened behind them and two older women entered, swathed in scarves and bangles that clinked and chimed as they moved. Amy saw them, recognizing the Sunderson sisters—twin painters, and ancient—known throughout the state for their meticulous depictions of cows and barns and the more bucolic elements of the valley where Garden City nestled. She made a face for Nathan when the Sunderson sisters' backs were turned, then she flowed toward them with her arms spread, calling, "Myra! Bedelia! It's been so long! What can I do for you girls today?"

Nathan chuckled to himself. The Sundersons were harmless, though they would undoubtedly occupy Amy for the next hour or so, which was perfect. He could look up crystals and channeling on his phone in the break room while she discussed hay bales and barley prices.

As it turned out, candles *and* crystals were recommended when attempting to summon spirits, so Nathan procured them both, silently thanking Amy as he purchased them at the same new age shop where Logan had taken him once to buy his Tarot cards.

"Spirits," Nathan had intoned on Monday night, sitting cross-legged on the floor before his bed, the flame of a black candle trembling at his breath. In his right hand he held a crystal, though he wished he possessed something witchier, like a black hooded cloak or the skull of a ram or some chicken feet. Where did people even go to get chicken feet? Did they chop them off the chicken themselves?

"Spirits," he said again, before reconsidering and adding, "anyone who has appeared to me. Any*thing*." He concentrated on the flame, squinting until his head ached. *I should feel something inside*, he thought, squinting harder. He searched within himself for an answering flame, or a shiver of cold, or a golden tide opening, something, anything, to let him know that he was doing it right. But he felt nothing.

Perhaps, he might have felt a chill, but it could've been the branch of the ancient oak outside his window that scratched at the glass like a hag's hand, urged by the wind, whispering, *Winter, not over, not yet*.

He stared into the reflection of the candle's flame trapped within the crystal he held. He realized then that all he could see was his own face, and it was trapped there as well.

So, he'd failed his first séance. Later, when he'd looked out his window and saw the man trotting across the lawn, he felt absolutely unsurprised.

"I don't want you there," Seb Candleberry said to him immediately, after they'd all sat down for lunch and Nathan had explained to him, using as few words as possible, about the séance and Seb's planned part in it.

Logan and Derek, holding hands beside the Coke machine, chattered brightly. Seb's girlfriend, Mikyla Simmons, was dolled, painted, and tucked neatly into a black spaghetti-strap top that revealed the white half-moon of her belly with jeans so tight that Nathan could see her panty-lines. She giggled endlessly with her friend Essie, who sported a black camisole, black beanie, clumps of black eyeliner, and black-and-white striped tights. She looked like the Wicked Witch of the East, Nathan thought absently; his eyes, meanwhile, were drawn back to the ghost of Mikyla's underwear, which, he assumed, interested Seb more than anyone else.

But Seb wasn't paying attention to either of the girls. Nathan realized that no one was looking at them, that no one could hear them, and that they could say whatever they wanted.

"Maybe that's shitty," said Seb. "But it's true. I don't want you there tonight."

"I don't want you there, either," Nathan said brightly. "Guess we'll have to rock-paper-scissors 'til we die. Maybe even after that. Maybe that's what the afterlife *really* is: eternal games of rock-paper-scissors."

Seb made a sound of irritation, then bit his lower lip and ran a hand through his thick mane of hair. He glanced for a second at Mikyla. "Goddamn," he growled under his breath.

"We won't have a chance to even say anything," Nathan said. "We don't want to scare away the ghosts." He snickered.

"Succubitch. Countess Dracula."

"That's Dracula's *Daughter* to you, jag. Why don't you want me there?"

"Fuck." Seb grimaced. "I want a smoke."

"Principal's patrolling now, harder than ever."

"I'll go to an alley, then."

"Still."

"Fuuuuuuck." Seb closed his eyes, then opened one and regarded Nathan lazily. "Come with me."

"I gave it up."

"The hell you did."

"I like my lungs crystal clean, thanks. Thought you didn't want me around."

"I didn't say that. I just don't want you there *tonight*."

Nathan fluttered his eyelashes. "Worried for my safety? How gallant."

"You can be pretty goddamn girly, you know."

"So? I thought you liked girls." Nathan looked over at Logan and Derek. Derek said something into the shell of Logan's ear until Logan threw his head back and guffawed. Nathan looked away quickly. "Do you think something's going to happen tonight? Really?"

"Really?" Seb tousled his own hair again. It grew thick and darkly golden and fell down just below his earlobes. "Yeah, I guess."

Nathan raised an eyebrow. "You do?"

"*You* do." He half-smiled. "Ghosts got as much right to exist as the rest of us."

"Have you really believed me? All this time?"

Seb shrugged. "Hell. Maybe I do, maybe I don't. Maybe I don't know what I believe in."

"But you said you did."

"Maybe I'm a liar. Or I'm just a really good actor. It's why I'm always cast in school plays."

"You could be. You just never try. You always—"

"Fuck you."

"I mean it."

"And fuck you, I said."

Stung, Nathan shoved his hands in his pockets. "You and Mikyla are going to the prom," he said at last, surprised at the words, though they'd been bobbing around his brain for the past few days or so.

"Yeah." Seb sighed. "We are."

"She got a dress?"

"She does."

"Did she make you go with her to get it?"

"She tried." That same lopsided smile again.

"She look good?"

"She will."

"And . . . after?"

Seb looked at him, right in the eyes, for the first time. "Why do you want to know?"

"Are you gonna . . ." Nathan swallowed. "Did you get a hotel?"

"Maybe." Hint of teeth.

"You can't afford a hotel."

"Show's what you know, bitch. I hawked some of my mom's jewelry. Turns out not all of it is crummy costume shit."

Chilled, Nathan crammed his hands further into his pockets, as far as they would go. He wished he had claws; he wished his hands would tear through his jeans.

If I were an animal, he thought, *I could sprint away, blow apart the wall, and just run. I'd scream and howl and laugh as I did it.*

"I'm going," Nathan said suddenly.

Seb stared at him blankly. "Why?"

"It's senior prom. I'm a senior."

"But you're going alone."

He hesitated. "Yeah."

"Shit. You shouldn't do that. That's fuckin' stupid."

"It's not," Nathan said, stung again.

"It is. Go with someone, anyone. Just . . . don't go alone."

He wanted to ask why he cared, but he knew what Seb would say, or the kind of thing, remembering, as he did from time to time, his poor decapitated witch-doll on the first day of kindergarten.

"It won't be so bad," he said instead.

Seb shrugged, knelt down, and retrieved the green army coat he wore every day, rain or shine, didn't matter, and slid his arms inside it. "I gotta get out of here," he said curtly, then, to Mikyla, "Hey, babe! I gotta get out of here!"

Mikyla looked up, mid-conversation with Essie. She waved him away impatiently.

"Fuck," Seb said under his breath, then started to walk away, head lowered, hands curled into fists.

Mikyla called after him: "And no ciggies!"

Seb glanced over his shoulder, glaring at her. Then he turned to Nathan. "Don't let the ghosts get you, bitch," he said, winking, before he thudded away.

Nathan thought about ghosts and séances and about the past week or so and how everything was about to change.

Logan extricated himself from Derek and stood beside him. "Don't worry about that guy," he said, laying a hand on Nathan's shoulder. "I'll be there if you need me."

Like always.

"I know," Nathan said.

"Listen." His lips, close to Nathan's ear, vibrated the sensitive skin of the lobe, down the back of his neck. "We don't have to do this if you don't want to. Or *you* don't. I can make excuses for you if you—"

"No," he said, smiling. "I want to go. I want to be there."

"Maybe the ghosts will get *him*," Logan said, inspired.

Seb, nearing the end of the corridor, lunged forward without a backward glance and disappeared out into the courtyard and the wide world beyond it.

"Maybe," Nathan said softly. "Maybe they will."

6

LAST SATURDAY, ALMOST a week before that final day—the day when everything unraveled—they lay together in Seb's bed, not for the first time or the hundredth, Nathan astride Seb, Seb pressed tight inside Nathan, staring at each other, unblinking. Seb allowed Nathan's sweat to drip down onto him so it mingled with his own, and then to run in a salty river over his forehead, off his cheek, and onto the flattened pillow that barely supported Seb's head.

Nathan wasn't thinking of deaders, as no deaders had shown themselves for almost two years, long enough for him to seriously consider that they'd been, what, childish fantasies? Dreams? Just his imagination, as Logan had always insisted? Didn't matter; the deaders had disappeared long ago, and now he had this thing with Seb.

There had been no talking, which was usual, only the frantic sounds of their thrusts, well-timed by now, and their moans, until Nathan finally erupted with a gasp of relief, and Seb finished after him seconds later. Then there was only the sound of the empty house breathing and the roaring of the trains outside, less than a block away, the wrathful, endless clanking and crashing and rushing sounds of their machinery, and Seb's breathing, which sounded like the house; not for the first time, not for the second time nor the hundredth.

Pressed tightly together in Seb's single bed, stripped of sheets—"They're in the washer," he'd said with his customary defensiveness when Nathan showed up on his doorstep after receiving Seb's summons—the mattress cold and lumpy. It was usually Seb who performed the summoning, Seb who demanded, commanded. Seb had stared up at him furiously during the moment of release, but now, Nathan observed, his eyes were closed. *He doesn't look angelic*, Nathan thought. He always assumed he would, but he never did. He didn't look peaceful, or at rest; but he *was* beautiful in his own way, and Nathan wondered idly if Seb ever thought about him like that. Very probably not, he concluded. He felt a shiver and a pang simultaneously.

This is a game; this is animal for him, it must be; any hole's a goal, that's what those jock assholes at school say; it's just a game.

Unless—

Nathan drew a breath.

It's not really *impossible. He could watch you while you sleep and trace circles on your forehead; he could.*

It was possible.

Don't do this thing.

But it was rising inside him, he could feel it, and he was helpless to prevent it.

Nathan had first told Seb about the deaders during the summer after their freshman year; he first touched Seb's cock at a party Logan threw the following autumn.

They'd shared a single class in their initial year at Royal High: P.E., the most awkward of all the classes they might have endured together; and Nathan, having nurtured since they were children a dislike for Seb mixed keenly with a very particular yet indefinable kind of lust or desire or *something* else equally stupid, especially since Seb was so-very-fond of referring to Nathan as a girl, or a homo, or queerbait, or whatever other vile epithets went stomping about his brain, was alternately elated and frustrated to spend fifty minutes every day watching Seb run and jump and spin and then take off his clothes in the locker room and put them on again. He never allowed himself to strip down completely, he was never *naked*, but Nathan faithfully observed how he always wore blue jockey shorts, and how, Nathan saw, Seb filled them out quite nicely; Nathan always enjoyed these secret observations immensely.

Seb hadn't been popular with most other kids as far as Nathan could tell; he was pretty enough, certainly, in his own way, mostly, with that mane of thick, tough-looking hair. But the jocks didn't care for him, and he generally irked the drama kids as well as the choir nerds. His voice, when Nathan heard his voice for the first time, was pleasant, if not always entirely on pitch. Seb chummed around with one or two friends freshman year, but Nathan tried his best to avoid them all whenever he could. Logan often said that Seb was a creature misunderstood by most people (even if he also muttered equally as often, "Dude is a serious *dick*,"), and that he should probably just be given a chance, even if Logan would later admit that he wasn't exactly certain what that chance might look like, or if he or Nathan or any of their friends should be the ones to offer it to him.

Mr. Rice, the choral director, held auditions for his advanced choir early in the spring, just as the last of the snow began to drop thoughtfully from the trees. Nathan was not possessed of a voice he wished to share with people, and Logan, whistling as they walked into the hallway from their final class of the day together, had stopped long enough to say, "I don't know if I want to be in choir, anyway. I'm just so stupid *busy*. Hey, I was thinking of trying out for the spring play. Whadda ya think the chances are I'd get a part?" which were, as it turned out, pretty good, since he ended up playing the lead in *The Crucible* a month later.

Thus, neither Nathan nor Logan stood in the line outside Mr. Rice's holy choir room for an hour and a half waiting to sing "America the Beautiful" in front of a room of two hundred other kids, who watched with faces grim or jaded or sourly amused. Mr. Rice was not a beloved teacher, but his choir class was revered—*highly* revered—and so it was something of an honor to be admitted into the Sacred Sixty, the best of the best. The rest were sent packing, most of them in tears, nearly all scarred by Mr. Rice's whip-quick tongue.

Nathan had waited inside the school that day for a ride from his mother; he knew she would be late, as she usually was on Wednesdays, and he found himself wishing madly for a car of his own. I'm going to get a job, he told himself, pacing through the now-deserted second floor of the school, watching the shadows outside as they crept closer to the building. He swore to himself that he'd save money and buy a car, even if it was a piece of crap, because it would be his and he would have earned it, and something would, at last, really belong to just him.

He clicked his heels absentmindedly along the tiles, amusing himself by pretending he was all alone in the school, that teachers weren't nearby grading papers so late in the afternoon, or custodians fervently vacuuming carpets and mopping up spilled cups of ranch dressing from lunch, or basketball players sweating out their energy as they ran endless laps in the upper gym.

He'd heard a sound halfway down the long hallway, blue shadowed with the darkness creeping in from outside, and he stopped. The back of his neck prickled. Someone crying softly, he realized, and trying to smother their sobs, sounding for all the world like a child. More gooseflesh rose on his arms. The sobbing went on and on. He decided that he didn't want to see it; he didn't even want to know why the deader was there, let alone what it wanted. He crept cautiously across the tiles, thinking of the woman in the antique store, then he shivered. *Why me?* he wondered, as he had wondered before.

Why don't I stop? Why don't I run?

But he didn't.

He came around the corner, peering, and there, instead of a deader, a child or otherwise, was Seb Candleberry, crammed up tightly inside a little alcove. Royal High often resembled a castle in its construction, full of strange little oddities in its architecture, tiny rooms that were especially useless, and crannies where kids would go to make out or smoke a joint between classes. It was Seb, Nathan understood, whom he'd heard crying, his head bowed, tucked up against his chest, his shoulders shaking with some volcanic grief. He looked up just then as Nathan approached. His face glared ugly and sweaty and wet and red; his eyes widened and then narrowed as he dropped his chin back against his chest.

"Leave me alone," he'd said.

Nathan, not knowing what to say, said nothing.

Seb hiccupped, then looked up, and his face grew even redder, if possible, and more furious. "Leave me the *fuck* alone," he said distinctly, then snuffled loudly and wiped snot on the back of his hand. It left a glistening snail trail in its wake.

Nathan shuffled his weight from one foot to the next.

"Goddammit," Seb snarled, launching himself out of his hiding place.

Nathan flinched but didn't move.

Seb froze then, a lion hovering impossibly above the back of a zebra, claws extended, his face a gaping maw. But he didn't complete the leap, and he didn't attack Nathan, didn't pummel him with his fists or slash at him or kick him. He simply stood there, glaring, his teeth bared.

Nathan, who, if asked even an hour before about his feelings for Sebastian Candleberry, might have described them as actually bordering on hate. You try being called a homo and a faggot for ten years, he might have said, and see how you like it. Now, miraculously, he found himself fascinated by the glint of pain he saw in Seb's eyes.

Seb relaxed.

"Fuck," he said at last. His eyes were puffy and as red as his cheeks; these expanded, twin blushing balloons, and then he released the collected air in a whoosh. Actually smiled a bit.

Nathan smiled, too, hesitantly. "You hungry?" he said. The words were unplanned, unexpected, just rolled, tiny boulders, off his tongue.

Seb stared. "Are you?" he said.

"I," Nathan said without consideration, "could eat."

They looked at each other, motionless. *I'm creating worlds,* Nathan had thought dimly. *I'm inventing them right now. Singing them sweetly into being. He hates me; I hate him; but in this world, perhaps, in this world, brave, new . . .*

"Sweet," Seb said grimly. "Let me grab my shit." He dug deeply back into the alcove, and, as Nathan watched, he pulled out a wrinkled green army coat at least one size too big for him and a canvas bag, flat, almost empty. He shouldered it nevertheless. "Come on," he commanded and charged toward the staircase, head down like a bull, shoulders hunched. Nathan followed him, not believing that he was actually doing it. Adventure, new worlds, magic around every corner; he found himself intrigued, and fear—though it was more like excitement than fear, he would think later—tingled in his guts like fireflies.

Seb said nothing as Nathan pawed through his locker until he pulled out the black peacoat he insisted his mother purchase for him at Christmas, necessary with the day's afternoon chill, even with the snow dropping tentatively from the trees as winter receded. He was letting his hair grow—too long, probably, and it curled all around his head in tiny waves—and so he shoved the jade knit cap his mother had made for him when the weather turned cold down as far as it would go.

"Your ears are showing," Seb said, looking at him.

"Yeah," Nathan said.

"Looks stupid."

"Yeah," Nathan said again, sheepishly.

"Christ," Seb hissed, yanking the hat down over Nathan's ears. He stood back, admiring, and said, "Tons better. You almost can't see your face."

"Fuck you," Nathan said, surprising himself. He felt a happy grin start to spread.

"Yeah, yeah." The air smote them as they left the school, tasting of cold iron, and Seb said, "See? Ain'tcha glad? Your ears should be thanking me if nothing else."

"Where are we going?"

"Gas station? I got a few bucks. Or pizza? DeFazzio's gots pizza."

"Pizza," Nathan said immediately.

"You buy your own fuckin pizza," Seb said, grinning back. "This ain't a *date*."

Nathan's face burned, and he stared at the broken sidewalk beneath their feet as they walked.

"I hate this town," Seb said; DeFazzio's, which made its humble living off Waxman University students and the kids from Royal High, was still a block and a half away. A car drove by them, blatting black smoke out its tailpipe, and a girl Nathan didn't recognize leaned out the window and cried something cheerful-sounding and derisive, but neither boy could understand her.

"See?" Seb had said with a sad shake of his head. "Bitches," he pronounced clearly. "Town's full of nothing but bitches."

"Yeah," Nathan said.

"They act like they listen to you, but they don't. Not really." He exhaled and shook his head mournfully. Then he darkened. "The old fucker won't even let me audition again."

A moment passed before Nathan realized who he was talking about. "Mr. Rice is kind of a jag."

"Oh," Seb snarled, "he's way worse than that. Fuckin' faggot."

"Don't say that."

"It's true."

"You still shouldn't say it." Seb was staring at him and he felt his face flush. "What happened in there?"

"Fuck," Seb said mournfully and glared down at the pitted sidewalk beneath their sneakers. "To start with, my voice cracked, which it don't usually do. Then after I embarrassed the hell out of myself in front of all those other son-of-a-bitching cock-sucking motherfucking—"

"Poetry," Nathan said, smiling a bit.

Seb's eyes narrowed, then he smiled back. "Heh. Right. That's me. I'm a poet and I don't know it."

"I could've said, 'You kiss your mama with that mouth?'"

The darkness was back, spilling across the other boy's face like sodden ink. "Shut the fuck up about my mom," he said quietly.

"Okay," Nathan said evenly. He felt a little giddy; Seb's darkness was exciting, causing sparks to dance and gibber inside him, evil revelers before a bonfire, in a way he'd never felt before. "So then what happened, poetry guy?"

"I said, 'Mr. Rice, can I try again? I really wanna be in this choir, it's the best choir, you're the best teacher,' waaaah, waaaah, whiney bull*shit*."

"He didn't go for it, huh?"

"Thank you, Captain Obvious." Then, imitating Mr. Rice's high-pitched, rather reedy voice, Seb said, "'You suck, Candleberry.

You suck worse than anyone I've ever heard in the whole history of suckage. I've seen a hundred trillion students in my career, Candleberry, and you are definitely the one who sucks the most.'"

"He didn't say that."

"He might as well have," Seb said, mournful again. "Didn't put me into his goddamn *honor* choir, but you know what? Who gives a fuck. I shouldn't have made such a big deal about it." He was proud, arrogant, wildness in his eyes and the toss of that thick mane of lion hair. "We're here," he said.

Nathan looked up, surprised; DeFazzio's, its sign announced in neon red letters that, Nathan supposed, were supposed to be vaguely art-deco-ish. The dining room lay empty.

They paid for their slices of pizza respectively and sat at a booth in the back, as far from the front door as possible. Seb devoured his quickly, messily, allowing crumbs to drop onto the table and into his lap and sauce to collect at the corner of his mouth. "Stare hard, retard," he said at one point, and then giggled.

"I don't cry very often, you know," Seb said, after he had finished his pizza and was slurping noisily from his can of Coke. "But Mr. Rice, man. Dude is a fuckin' prick."

"I've heard that."

"Nah, but he *is*. You can't talk to people like that, even if we are just kids or whatever. You *can't*," he said ferociously, crumpling up his napkin and throwing it onto the floor. He aimed a vicious kick at the wall next to their table. The dour-looking college girl at the counter glanced over at them blearily, then she looked away. "Fuck," he snarled. "I can sing. You believe me? Because I can."

"I believe you."

"You don't know, though, and I'm not going to show you or nothing. But I can. I know it, and that fat shitbag knows it, too. He just don't want me in his goddamn choir, that's all."

"Why not?"

Seb smiled humorlessly. "Because I live on the Northside," he said. "Because I'm total trash. I like to break windows out of broken-down houses with chunks of brick. I stole a book on the last day of school in third grade and Mrs. McFadden was too afraid of me to call me on it. Fuck, I don't know, do I. I can't read minds. But he don't like me, and I know he don't, and *he* knows that I know. So. I'm fucked. See how that is?"

"I never auditioned for anything before," Nathan said.

"It sucks. You shouldn't."

"You could try again."

Seb glowered. "Why would you say that? Fuck, that ain't the point, jeez, aren't you *listening* to me anymore? It. Don't. *Matter*. It wouldn't matter how many times I tried or didn't try or how much I offered to pay him or blow him or whatever. Christ. He *won't have me*."

Seb's eyes were glistening again with tears he struggled to restrain. He bared his teeth and slammed his fist against the table, and Nathan, thrilled, couldn't recoil, could only watch, fascinated.

I would like him to bite me with those teeth; I would like him to hold me down and put those teeth in me. Am I sick? Is that a normal thing to think?

Something dark lurked within Sebastian Candleberry; Nathan had sensed it, heard it. A song, some familiar melody. He thought about the long-ago bottle of perfume and how satisfying it was to shatter it against the uneven wooden planks of that floor in the antique mall; he considered fire, how there might be fascination in watching everything around him burn. *But it's not me*, he thought with sudden alarm; *it couldn't possibly be me*. It was Seb, just him.

Logan, Nathan knew, would tell him he was fucked in the head; Sebastian Candleberry, of all the boys in their school, wasn't gay, not even a little. "He'll be the first one to tell you that," Logan would say, "just before he calls you a faggot for the trillionth time."

"And he can fuck himself anyway," Seb said, dropping his eyes. "I don't want to be in his goddamn fucking choir. I'll wait. This will be over before too long."

"What will?"

"*This*," Seb said, gesturing. "High school and this place and you and me and everything. So why does it matter?"

"Maybe it doesn't," Nathan said. "Or maybe you just have to wait."

"Could be." Seb was watching him closely, and Nathan couldn't look away. *Mongooses*, he thought, *cobras*. "Maybe I really do bust out windows. Maybe I look for bricks, big honkin' chunks of rock. Maybe I go hunting for houses to break all the windows in. What do you think of that?"

"I think it sounds . . ." Nathan closed his eyes, considering. He could see Logan, tall and broad-shouldered and handsome; he could see his own house, two stories, a light shade of blue, barely room enough for all four of his family members. He saw the town of Garden City spread out before him, clean, neat, well-ordered.

But it's haunted, Nathan thought, and he opened his eyes; *there are things nobody sees beneath its pretty postcard veneer, but they're dark and they're there.*

There are the dead. The terrible, hungry dead.

". . . freeing," Nathan concluded. "You aren't pretending."

"No," Seb said, and he sounded surprised. "I guess I'm not."

"Better than being locked up in a cage. Better than being a monkey in the zoo or something."

"Monkeys got it real easy."

"Until someone makes monkey-fur coats out of 'em."

Seb squinted at him. "That don't happen. Does it? It *can't*."

"Ladies *love* to wear monkey-fur," Nathan said, grinning. "All up and down the street you see nothing but ladies just *dripping* with monkey-fur."

"Dripping monkey-fur. Sounds hot." Seb shook his head, amused. "You're weird."

"So people keep telling me," Nathan said, cupping his chin in one hand.

"But you're funny."

"I don't feel funny."

"Funny," Seb had said. "Like a heart attack. Christ. Let's get out of here."

They did, and they walked together, laughing, down Sprague Avenue. "You tell anyone I cried and I'll beat the ever loving shit out of you," Seb said, and Nathan only rolled his eyes, and then they laughed some more, and stopped in front of one of the fancier-looking buildings in Garden City's bustling downtown.

"I do this sometimes," Nathan explained. "Just come down here by myself and walk around. Look in stores."

"But you don't go in?"

"I never know what to say when I do. The people who work there think I'm just some dumbass kid who's gonna bust stuff up."

"Aren't you?" Seb cocked his head.

"No. But they don't believe that." Nathan nodded in the direction of the door of the fancy building; a sign above them, in great florid letters painted electric blue, proclaimed the establishment THE RAVEN'S END GALLERY. "See that place?"

Seb squinted. "It's a gallery. So what?"

"I like to go in there. The only place I *do* go in. They've got this great photo exhibit now. Creepy-looking abandoned farms from all over Montana."

"You like creepy things?"

Nathan shrugged. "I like pictures. I like to take them myself."

"You got a camera?"

"Not yet," Nathan had admitted. "I have to get a job first, my mom says."

Seb lifted a hand and waggled it in Nathan's face. "Five-finger discount," he said.

Nathan laughed despite himself. *I couldn't ever do that*, he thought. *Could I? I couldn't.* Awe opened inside him like petals colored something surprising; a weird shade of coral, maybe, or a dark bottle green.

I didn't really *take that perfume bottle, did I. It wasn't me.*

A flash of movement across the street, where the Sprague Avenue Bridge ended and downtown began, caught his eye, but he didn't turn away from Seb. Just someone walking, he thought, another person out in the world, moving about, just like they were.

"What the fuck is a Raven's End?" Seb said. "Where the shit comes out?" and they both roared laughter.

"I could be a photographer," Nathan said after the laughter subsided. "That's what I want to be."

"*I* want to be a circus clown."

"Astronaut."

"President."

"Cowboy."

"President cowboy." Nathan laughed, then felt all the color drain out of his face. Seb, watching him, saw it happen, and stopped mid-chuckle. He glanced over his shoulder, then back at Nathan. "What?" he said, a mixture of concern and irritation coloring his voice.

Nathan couldn't find the words; he couldn't say, *Look, look at him, look at that man. He doesn't have any eyes, just holes. He doesn't have a shadow, and he doesn't have any eyes.*

His tongue became a dead worm in his mouth; a brick filled his throat.

It had been him, that purple-yellow-blue shambling horror man who caused the movement that caught Nathan's eye, shuffling and twitching across the sidewalk, hands out in the air, groping, his mouth gaping wide and a stream of black water pouring from it so that his chest, bruised purple and blue, was soaked. He was naked; his feet were bare; that foul water cascaded endlessly from his mouth and ran over his penis, small and shriveled amid the gray thatch of his pubic hair, which was patchy and missing in places. The missing patches gleamed, red and meaty. His eye sockets were empty and his hands sawed at the air blindly but insistently; he aimed himself directly at Nathan.

"What the hell?" Seb said again, but Nathan seized him by the arm and pulled him away so that they ran back the way they came, over the Sprague Avenue Bridge, away from the naked corpse. He was one of *them*; a deader; he had sensed Nathan somehow in the way that they always had, and so he'd come for him.

Finally they stopped, panting, on the other side of the Royal River. Seb's voice rang sharply with indignation: "What the fuck was that all about?"

"Sorry," Nathan had said in harsh, tearing gasps. "I saw . . . someone I didn't want to see."

"We ain't old enough for loan sharks," Seb said. "Ex-girlfriend?"

Nathan laughed despite himself. "Something," he managed through his gasps and semi-hysterical laughter, "something like that."

"Hell," Seb said happily. "Got my exercise for the day." He looked over his shoulder, down Blythe Street, which was lined with elm trees, denuded by the tender, cold caresses of Garden City's autumn and winter. His eyes narrowed, then he dropped his head. Nathan watched him curiously. Finally he lifted it again and smiled, the first genuine smile Nathan thought he'd seen from the other boy. "Come on," he'd said slowly. "I wanna show you something."

Curiouser and curiouser, Nathan thought, but he followed Seb as he led them down Blythe Street, first one block, then two, then three. The houses, so close to Sprague, were, at first, all two or three stories, stately, built around the turn of the last century when Garden City was puffing itself up and developing, realizing its potential, how beautiful it was, and how even more beautiful it would become. As they walked, however, Nathan noticed that the houses grew smaller and more dilapidated, the lawns less cared for, still overgrown despite summer's long ago promise, now faded. Grim, gray grass and weeds pockmarked almost every yard; windows were boarded up or covered with cardboard and duct tape. They walked, and though Nathan's fear of the dead man they'd seen downtown had faded, his unease grew.

They stopped abruptly before a burned-out edifice that was barely recognizably a house. The roof was absent and charred embers reached like deformed, clawed hands for the granite sky over their heads. It was nothing but a shell and badly scorched. Seb stared at it with something close to reverence. "That was my house when I was a kid," he said. "A *little* kid," he added, so softly Nathan almost didn't hear him.

"I remember this," Nathan said. "It burned down."

"Duh-doy," Seb said, a flash of humor that faded almost immediately. "When I was seven." He looked at Nathan, then down at the ground. "I did it. It was me." He looked up, then down, up, then down. Nathan watched him carefully. "*Me*," and he crammed both of his hands into the pocket of his hideous green jacket.

"Holy shit," Nathan said at last, because Seb had been waiting. What else could you say when someone told you something like that? It had never come up before.

"I didn't mean to." There was no rancor in his voice, no defensiveness. Nathan was surprised but also intrigued. *Oh yes, oh yes, that singing inside Seb, way down deep, like beautiful, lilting music, but so dark.*

The threat of something terrible.

Terrible . . . but intriguing.

Drums in the forest. Dancing; wilder dancing; wings, hooves, horns . . .

"How?" Nathan said.

"I was playing with this lighter I found outside. Probably belonged to my old man, the cheap prick. And he must'a lost it, like he loses everything. So I started playing with it. You played with fire before, right?"

Nathan said nothing. He and Logan had tried smoking the previous summer, but they'd used matches that Logan's dad brought back from a bar he'd visited in Denver. The cigarettes seared their lungs and they coughed and cried and then laughed at each other and neither of them had tried to smoke since.

Seb fumbled in his jacket, and finally revealed a crumpled pack of cigarettes in one hand and a little silver lighter in the other. "This is the one," he said solemnly. "It's old. You'd think that would make it so my dad wouldn't lose it, but he's a shithead, like I said. So I kept it."

He pressed a cigarette between his lips, clamped down with his teeth, then clicked the lighter one, two, three times until it sparked and flared up, igniting the tip of the cigarette. Nathan watched the flame dancing in Seb's eyes, fascinated.

"Here," he'd said, and thrust the pack to Nathan. He took one with no visible hesitation. Seb passed him the lighter, and Nathan imitated him, clamping down on the cigarette, flicking the lighter until the paper ignited. He drew a blazing draught into his lungs. He wanted to cough; his eyes burned, fairly bursting with water, but he held the smoke in, then released it in a stream. He didn't cough, and he didn't cry, though he was sure Seb knew exactly what he wanted to do.

Seb smirked. "First time, huh."

Nathan shook his head, smirking back around the thin white paper. "Nope," he said, then grinned. "Second."

Seb thumped him companionably on the back, exhaled a thin stream of gray smoke, looked back at the ruined hulk before them with more solemnity, and said, "I started the sleeve of my shirt on fire. You believe that shit? I freaked. Tried to put it out. Spread fire all over my bed instead." Seb laughed softly and, Nathan thought, with a decided lack of humor.

"Did anyone get hurt?"

Seb's eyes flickered over to him, narrowed; then he sighed and shook his head, took another ferocious drag on the cigarette. "No. We all got out in time. My folks don't know. I think they wonder sometimes. I remember the firemen and how they looked at all of us. Not just me. I didn't try to explain or nothing." He chuckled, a thin, papery sound. "They never asked me what happened. Faulty wiring is what they decided, whoever makes decisions like that. It was a crap shack, we were poor white trash, so who the fuck cared? It probably would'a burned down someday anyway."

"That's intense," Nathan said. His heart was a rabbit in his chest. He took another drag and closed his eyes. He enjoyed the sensation, the terrified animal running around inside him, kicking. "Do you ever feel guilty?"

"Sometimes. A little. And you ain't gonna tell anyone." It wasn't a question.

"No."

"I know," Seb said, grinning again. "That's why I told you. Shit, you think I just open up like this to anyone who finds me crying my poor widdle heart out?"

"I would hope not," Nathan said, clutching imaginary pearls.

"Yeah, me too. I just thought . . . you seem like you'd listen to me."

"I did."

"You did. You believe me when I say that I didn't mean to." He sneaked a look at Nathan. "And you're not afraid."

"What would I be afraid of?"

"Me."

Nathan smiled. "Normal people scare me. The people who say they're normal, I mean. Weirdos are usually more up front about their weirdness." He showed his teeth, and he felt like an animal baring its fangs. "Like me."

"You're kinda dark-sided, huh," Seb said.

People are drawn to evil, Nathan thought to himself, and took another drag on the cigarette. It burned less this time, and he held the smoke in his lungs for longer than he probably should have. *What is evil?* he thought. Destructive things. Things with goals that ran counter to the goals of humanity. Demons, darkness; all that was bullshit. Human beings were self-destructive enough all on their own. "Guess so," he said, exhaling.

They continued to look at each other, there in the dying embers of the afternoon, with the aspens and elms throwing soft blue shadows down all around them. Just looked. Finally, Seb dropped his cigarette and ground it beneath his heel, then moved away, back up the street, toward the school. Nathan crushed his own cigarette and rushed to catch up. They spoke of other things as they went, stupid, inconsequential things, and soon enough—too soon, Nathan thought—they stood before Royal High, where Nathan's mom had been waiting for him in her car in the parking lot. He waved goodbye to Seb, and Seb waved goodbye back and turned and walked away. Nathan watched him go and said nothing.

They hadn't spoken again, Nathan realized, with Seb sighing and sticky beneath him, hadn't seen each other at school or stopped or looked at each other or talked again for months, almost the whole summer after that. Then, one day, near the end of August, a week before they were scheduled to return to Royal High for sophomore year, Seb, crossing through, saw Nathan sitting in Rose Park, which was his favorite of Garden City's many parks, and he ran toward Nathan immediately, loping like a wolf; no, Nathan remembered, a *lion*. He'd lost weight by then and his face was relatively clear of acne, and he was smiling. Nathan had squinted at him through the haze of mid-August sunlight, thinking the other boy's smile might possibly be one of genuine warmth and excitement. But he also remembered kindergarten-Seb and his witch-destroying hands and how he'd worn that same smile then.

"You're all alone over here," Seb said, plopping himself down at Nathan's side. "Why?"

"Just sitting," Nathan, surprised, had replied, because, he scolded himself, *you have to say something,* and here was this big lumbering *idiot . . .*

"It's hot." Seb swiped at his face, grimaced, and wiped the sweat away on his shorts. He threw himself down on his back and supported his head with his hands, fingers laced behind it, and closed his eyes. Nathan, feeling helpless and hating the feeling of helplessness, only watched. "Christ," he said without opening his eyes. "I hate this town. I ever told you that?"

"Once," Nathan said stonily. *Am I mad now,* he wondered, *or just irritated that he disturbed me? I can't be mad, can I, genuinely angry; is that crazy? It is, isn't it?*

Maybe it was just the fear. He was afraid of being alone, because when he was alone— with increasing frequency, it seemed—inevitably one of *them* would find him.

The last one had stepped out of a crowd in the mall while Nathan was trying to shop for new sneakers. It had clutched a small bundle in its suppurated hands, holding it out to him plaintively. It had taken a moment for Nathan to realize that the little scraps of cloth and bones once belonged to a child, but still, separated and rotted and destroyed, they had moved and twitched in the arms of the corpse and aimed themselves inexorably at Nathan.

"Hey," Seb said, and opened one eye. "You're gay. I didn't know you were gay."

"Guilty," Nathan said, surprised.

"Everyone knows." Seb lazily scratched his tummy, browned by summer and glistening with golden hairs that matched the ones on his head. "Everyone knew but me."

"Now you do." *You called me those names,* Nathan thought furiously, *girl, faggot, all those times, but you never really . . .*

"You," Seb said, then, darkly, added, "and Logan. Everyone knows about *him.* You'd never think, looking at him, but everyone *knows.*"

"We don't care." *All those times—*

"I guess not. Live and let live, right? That's what they say." He opened one eye again and scanned Nathan, who was reminded of an enormous tiger he'd seen once at the San Diego Zoo, striped and fat, heavy, tucked up on a hillock across a false stream, lying asleep (it seemed) in the shadow of a tree. Its tail had lashed through the air urgently, then lazily, then urgently, and Nathan, face pressed against the glass of its enclosure, found with a shock that one of its eyes was open, but only one. It stared at him, glittering, golden, staring and seeing him, as if marking him forever. *Come with me, come lie between my paws*, the tiger seemed to say, preening; *I'm beautiful and you're beautiful and we can be beautiful together. Between my paws. In my jaws. Between my teeth. Pressed there, forever.* Then Nathan had looked away, his heart beating, fear and excitement mixed together thrumming in his fists and behind his eyes. "But," Seb said, "*I* didn't know."

"It's not very interesting."

"I think so. People still give you shit about it. They call you names."

"You knew about the names. *You* called me those names."

"Yeah," Seb grinned, "but I didn't know you admitted it."

"It's not something I'm ashamed of."

"You don't have to sound like a little bitch," Seb said placidly, eyes closed again, his grin melting into a slight smile. "I'm not gonna beat you up or something stupid like that."

That's big of you, Nathan thought sourly. "There's more of us than you'd think," he said. He felt stupid the second he said it. The words sounded threatening, like something from a horror movie about aliens or vampires, secret creatures blending in among humanity who only appeared when the time was right, when they were about to *strike*.

"Yeah? I don't know any. You and Logan."

"There are more."

"Okay." He sighed happy, contentedly. "It don't matter to me. I just do the things I want to do and everyone else can go to hell. Hey, can't you tell? I'm in a better mood than the last time we talked. Don't I look like it?"

He remembered. Lightning bugs flickered in Nathan's gut.

"We," Seb said, "should talk more." He ran his finger in whorls around the inside shell of his ear.

"School will start," Nathan said, avoiding his eyebrows and nervously tugging, instead, the grass growing dark and green around him. "You know how it goes."

"We'll be sophomores," Seb said idly. "Big fuckin' whoop."

"It is, though. A little."

"Nah. Remember what I told you? None of this shit matters. Not in the end. And there will be an end."

"I don't get you." Frustration tightened his vocal cords, buzzed in his voice.

"Of course you don't." Seb smirked charmingly. "Or, heh, maybe you do. You listened to me, remember? When I made big with the confession. I burned my house down, oooooh, scary. But you listened, and you never told anyone. And I know you didn't, 'cause something would'a happened. Look, everything ends, let's agree on that, but we don't gotta talk about it. That way lies shitty depression. Sun's gonna shine down on me, at least for a little while. So let's talk about just *that*. Deal?"

"Deal." Nathan watched him suspiciously.

Why can't I stop looking at him?

"I'm in a good place. I haven't even burned down another house, though I been *tempted* to, see."

Nathan lay down beside him. The sun was westering, and the shadows from the trees ringing the park were growing longer. *Logan was supposed to meet me,* Nathan thought, *but then he couldn't because of his new boyfriend from the university; fuck him, fuck them both.* Guilt at that sudden attack of vitriol struck him immediately. He knew he didn't mean it. He loved Logan; he just hated so much to be alone.

"You got your phone with you?" Seb said.

"Yeah," Nathan said, surprised.

"Put my number in it."

He squinted suspiciously. "Why?"

"Don't be stupid. So I can talk to you, dummy. You listened to me. Most people don't. You did."

"Only," Nathan said, "because you were telling me deep dark secrets. It isn't every day someone just comes right out and admits that they're a total pyro."

"Not a *total* pyro. I only burned down one house and it was kind of an accident and I haven't done it again, have I? So I don't know if you can call me a *pyro*, not really."

"But you want to call me."

"Yeah. To talk sometimes."

"About stuff."

"Stuff."

They looked at each other.

Nathan took Seb's phone and punched in his digits, and Seb nodded as if satisfied and stuffed the phone back in his pocket. They turned to watch the sun go down, and for a long time neither said a word.

"You owe me one, you know," Seb said quietly, staring down at the grass.

Nathan raised an eyebrow. "One what?"

Seb imitated him, raised one eyebrow, then the other, then waggled them both lasciviously. "Secrets, man. Trading secrets. It's only fair."

"I don't have any secrets," Nathan said uncomfortably.

"Oh, but you do. Oh, but you must. Everyone does, dude. Something deep down and freaky, probably. Freaky *deaky*. Even your best friend Logan the douchebag."

"I *don't*." He ignored the jab at Logan, but guiltily.

"You *do*." Seb poked him in the arm. "You got that dark side, like I said. You do," and again, in the chest, "you do you do you *do*," three pokes to the tummy, and Nathan, ticklish, laughed, couldn't help himself.

"Even if I did," he finally said, "you wouldn't believe me."

"Not with a sales pitch like that." Seb swung around on the grass, crossed his legs, then steepled his fingers so he could rest his chin there. "Go on. Tell me. We're, like, bound by secrets now. Nathan. *Tell me*."

Nathan closed his eyes. The world came rushing down around him; dimly, he heard the calling of a bird, giant and black, and the hiss of its wings as it lifted off the branch where it perched and rose now into the air. He thought, *Owls are magic; witches who turn into owls, or owls who turn into witches.* Fairy tale bullshit, but it wasn't. Now, in the lovely late summer twilight, he believed in it all.

Nathan opened his eyes and said, "I see things that . . . maybe aren't there. Or maybe they are." And in a rush, "Sometimes, I do. Think I do."

"Things," Seb said, frowning, "that aren't there."

"Like . . . people."

"Imaginary people?"

Nathan felt pricked all over by needles; his hands clutched convulsively at the grass, pulling it up in great handfuls. "No," he said, "they're there. I'm pretty sure."

Seb's frown deepened. "But no one else can see them?" He laughed. "What are they, then? Like, ghosts?"

Something cracked open inside him, spilling thick, sweet darkness. "It's not as good a secret as burning your house down. Or maybe for gay kids, queer kids, whatever word you want to use—"

"Fags," Seb said, nodding solemnly.

"Any word but *that*," Nathan said, and tried to sound stern. "Maybe for *us*, reality is different. We have to make our own realities because we live in so many of them. And it gets harder and harder to tell the difference, to figure out what is really real and what is only a little real or what we've just made up but we've forgotten and so we don't *really* know . . ." Nathan stopped, perplexed. Seb was staring, one eyebrow raised. Nathan sighed heavily; *what did I say, what was I saying?* "Or maybe I'm looney tunes," he said, and offered Seb a weak smile. "Maybe that's the secret."

"Or maybe you see ghosts," Seb said thoughtfully.

Nathan only watched him.

"Like, all the time? Like, *constantly?*"

Nathan shook his head slowly.

"But sometimes."

"Since I was little," Nathan whispered. He stared down at the grass. "Then for a long time, actually, nothing. Enough time passed that I thought I'd made it all up, or that I imagined them. But then school started, high school, and they came back. I call them deaders."

He lifted his head, afraid that Seb would see the tears pricking his eyes. But Seb's face was fixed, unmoving.

Nathan drew a breath. "Remember that day we went to pizza, the day you told me about your house?"

Seb nodded slowly; his eyes stared forward, unblinking.

"I saw one that day. Outside the Raven's End. I grabbed your arm—"

"And we ran," Seb said quietly. "Right. We ran back across the bridge. And I made some stupid joke about ex-girlfriends. What a dumbass I was."

"No, you weren't," Nathan said gently. "It was a man. He didn't have any eyes." He forced the words. "He was nuh-nuh-naked."

"Nathan. You don't gotta cry, for fuck's sake. So maybe you're crazy. Or maybe you see ghosts. There are worse things, don't you think?"

"Do you believe me?" Nathan whispered.

"Do *you* believe you?"

Nathan thought, then, carefully, he nodded.

"There you go," Seb said brightly. He looked around quickly, his eyes darting from side to side. "Do you see any now?" He twisted up his mouth so that the words, comically, came only from one side.

Relief washed over Nathan in waves, pulsing, beats timed to the rhythm of his heart. *He believes me*, Nathan thought. *He really does; someone knows.*

"No," he said, wiping his eyes with the back of his hand.

"Damn," Seb said. "I kinda wanna see one." He straightened his back. "Hey," he said, inspired. "Do you think you could, like, summon one?"

Horror washed over Nathan, replacing the relief, and it felt as if he'd been doused by icy water. "No!" he cried. "Jesus! Why would I?"

"Duh." Seb snickered. "To see if you can. That's never really occurred to you before? To test your powers?"

"I hate them," Nathan said fiercely. "You don't know. They're scary, not . . . not . . ."

"I think they sound cool," Seb said, folding his arms implacably. "You mutant. I'm gonna slap black Kevlar on you and send you out to fight crime. Go on. Give it a shot. Let's just see if you can. On command."

Nathan stared furiously down at the grass. The shadows grew ever longer; the sun vanished. He looked back up at Seb, who only watched him with that same implacable quality Nathan found simultaneously irritating and endearing.

Fine, he thought, *goddamn fine*. He closed his eyes, aggravated and afraid, unsure even of what he should *do*. Then, unexpectedly, he felt Seb's hand descend onto his leg. His eyes flew open to find Seb patting him just above his knee. His eyes locked on Nathan's own, his face a mask of sympathy and encouragement.

And he didn't remove his hand.

Nathan closed his eyes again. He felt his mind tugged as if a string were attached and someone had given it a hearty jerk. He felt himself go out; his mind escaped his body, soared outside the cage of his skull and rose above them. He could picture both he and Seb clearly, close to each other, down there below, with Seb's hand resting companionably on Nathan's knee. He soared high, up and up and *out*, until there was nothing but a starless expanse of dark, and he thought giddily, *Here I am, here I am at last.* Then, immediately, with a shock of horror, he realized he wasn't alone.

"It's okay," Seb whispered from somewhere far away. "It's all right. You're fine, *fine*. I promise, it's okay."

Not alone, Nathan thought. He heard a tinkling sound of laughter, like the sound of a wineglass being struck by the tip of a spoon; male, female, he couldn't tell, but there was someone there with him. In the next moment, he felt, rather than heard, a voice say two words.

Hello, Nathan.

He opened his eyes with a shock and scuttled backward, pulling away from Seb, who stared at him open-mouthed. Gasping for air, panic running in his head and his chest, Nathan cried, "What happened? Someone was here, someone was *there*; Seb, what *happened*?"

"I didn't see anything," Seb said. For the first time, he sounded legitimately scared. "Not really. Just for a second, though—"

He cut himself off, looking around in the dusk that swelled up around them; the shadows from the trees were long and purple, and might, Nathan realized miserably, conceal anything.

Anything at all.

"What?" he barked, angry despite himself.

Sly giggles. Someone's voice. Somewhere else.

Not his own.

Hello, Nathan.

"Just for a second," Seb said, his face very pale. "I thought . . . I th-thought I saw someone." He pointed. "Over there. By the statue."

Nathan turned and looked. Rose Park was also the Vietnam Veteran's Memorial, and someone had been charged, decades ago now, with the unenviable task of constructing a statue to commemorate the fallen soldiers in that long-ago war. What they'd come up with, Nathan had always privately believed, was just on this side of horrible: an angel statue, masculine, the face bearded and the eyes open and solemn and terribly, blankly white, with muscular arms wrapped around the chest of a soldier in his fatigues with his helmet slightly cocked. The soldier's face was open with surprise; as well he might be, Nathan would often think, as this winged celestial muscle daddy seized him and pulled him up to heaven. To fuck him? To eat him? Both? Nathan wasn't certain, but he never felt comfortable around the statue; the wings of the seraphim, he was always disturbed to see, melted into what seemed to be coils—or maybe even tentacles—that wrapped around the unfortunate soldier's fatigue-clad legs.

Now he looked in the direction of the statue, but he saw nothing. He looked back to Seb.

"It didn't work," he said flatly.

Seb was smiling a bit. Was there malice in it? Amusement? Love? "I think it did," he said. "I saw someone. Or the hint of someone. Just a hand. Little white hand. Just there in the shadows of that creepy fucking statue."

"No, you didn't."

"Maybe I didn't," Seb said placidly. "Or maybe I did."

"That could've been anyone. Or no one. Maybe you're making it up."

"Maybe," Seb said with a ghastly little smile quirking his lips, "I like to fuck with you."

"You're a bastard," Nathan snarled.

"Sometimes," Seb said, nodding as if he were very pleased with himself. "Sometimes I can be."

"So you didn't believe me at all," Nathan said, stung.

"No. I did."

"You did?" His eyes widened.

"I suppose I could come up with a few reasons for you to lie about something like that, but I don't think you would. And even if you did," and he laid his hand back on Nathan's knee again, and squeezed delicately, "I don't think you know you're lying."

They looked at each other again wordlessly, unblinking; carefully, delicately, Seb removed his hand from Nathan's knee.

"It's getting dark," Nathan said inadequately after a stupid amount of time had passed.

"Lots of shadows. Listen, I never seen a dead person, but maybe it wasn't as cool an idea as I thought it was." He mimed shivering, crossing his arms over his chest and clutching at his shoulders. "Could be anything in them shadows." He hauled himself to his feet and extended a hand. Nathan looked at him and thought, *Who are you, Sebastian Candleberry? Who are you really?*

But took his hand anyway.

"Good times," Seb said with exaggerated jocularity, then rocked back on his heels. "Good times with my friend Nathan. Hey. I gotta split."

"Sure," Nathan said. "Me too."

Seb began to walk away, hands in his pockets, whistling. Then he stopped. Glanced over his shoulder so that Nathan could see just a flash of one green eye, sparkling with good humor. "Could be," he said, drawling, "those dead assholes won't show up if I'm around. You ever think about that?"

Nathan swallowed.

"Maybe they're scared of me. Maybe I can keep 'em away. I'm a lot scarier, dude, than a bunch of moldy sheets. I promise."

"Okay," he said. His throat was too dry to say anything else.

"You need friends like me."

"I think so, too." His mouth shrank and twisted into a desert.

"I'll call," Seb said, patting his pocket where his phone rested, containing, as it did, Nathan's number. "Soon."

Then he was gone, leaving Nathan alone in the park, now grown into a solemn shadowland.

7

BUT SEB HADN'T called, not for the first month of school, or the second. Nathan couldn't admit that the bitterness he felt at this perceived exclusion squelched in his mouth like dirt, like gravel and old grapes and burnt tires whenever he thought of Seb or saw him in the hallway at school. Then Logan had decided he wanted to throw a party while his folks were out of town, and Seb was invited (somehow), probably because of Mikyla Simmons, who was in the fall play with Logan, cast, as Nathan anticipated he would be, in the lead.

The plan they constructed was for twenty or so kids to party in Logan's rambling house at the edge of town; by then it was nearly November, and Seb, without any warning, finally began calling Nathan the week before the party. His phone chirped warningly while Nathan and Logan hung out at Logan's house and watched TV on Logan's giant, comfy couch, leaning on each other, each savoring the other's warmth and comfortable, familiar smell.

No preamble: "Dude, I don't know what the hell I'm doing," Seb wailed into his ear, and Nathan stared coolly into the distance, Logan beside him, head on his shoulder, kung fu jittering and jiving its way across the TV screen. "I don't know how I'm even gonna *get* there," Seb continued, sounding abjectly, enjoyably miserable. Nathan rolled his eyes at Logan, who, considerately, rolled his eyes back. Then he was off the couch and up the stairs and into the little hallway that led to the kitchen where Logan's dad was busy boiling fettuccine for their dinner. "Listen," Seb whispered, "I'm not feeling good, okay, not so good, not so good at *all*."

"Logan's party," Nathan said, cool.

"That's what I'm trying to tell you. I'm freaking out here."

"Why?"

"Because I don't know why he even wants me there," Seb wailed, louder than before, and Nathan thought, *In some world there are Sebs and Nathans who have never met, who will never speak; in some there are Nathans who marry Sebs and run away to the end of the world, wherever the world ends, hesitating, dancing at the edge, but together, until they fall into air and mist and then into nothing. Other, other, other worlds than this.*

"Mikyla." Nathan opened his mouth and the word dropped out, and he felt amazed, but more followed. "Mikyla Simmons is going to be there. That's why."

"Mikyla Simmons?" Seb sounded blank, unintelligent, an ape.

"She probably likes you or whatever."

"Likes me." Testing the words.

"I don't know her very well. I'm just saying, you know, that it's possible."

"Sure," Seb said. He sounded calmer now. "Sure, sure."

"What's that popping sound?"

"Huh? Oh. Me. I snap my fingers when I'm nervous."

"Don't be nervous."

"It's weird, you know? Logan. I . . ." He hesitated, and silence ticked out in the emptiness between them. Far away Nathan could hear the water bubbling and boiling in the pot. Wickedly, he thought, *Fillet of fenny snake, baboon's blood; double, double, toil and trouble.* They were reading *Macbeth* in his honor's English class, and the other day he had, half-seriously, pondered aloud the potential efficacy of dabbling in witchcraft, which, he told an unbelieving Logan, might be a lark.

He heard the sounds of kung fu grow more turgid; somewhere far away Logan cleared his throat deliberately. "Hey," Nathan said, "listen, I gotta—"

"I never been to nothin' like this." Seb sounded furious, embarrassed, angry because of his embarrassment. Nathan could imagine the sullenness in his face, how his cheeks glowed red.

"Never?"

"Nothing," Seb said savagely. "Not like this."

"A party?"

"Don't laugh at me," he said darkly.

"I'm not."

"Look, I don't . . ." Another tortured pause. "I don't know how to talk to people. You know how to talk to people, so you—"

"*Me*?" And now Nathan *was* laughing. "The hell I do!"

"Better'n me. Maybe that's why I'm calling you."

"Yeah, about that."

"I'll know *you*, won't I." He shifted, sounded thoughtful, considering. "I'll know you when I'm there. I can talk to you."

No, Nathan wanted to say, *you won't catch me so easily.* "Of course you can."

"That's good."

"Seb."

"Yeah."

"I gotta go. I'm at Logan's right now. We're watching some stupid movie."

"What movie?"

Was he really interested? "Something with ninjas or kung fu. Logan likes movies like that."

"And you don't."

"I guess not."

"Then why don't you choose the movie?"

Because he's Logan, Nathan wanted to say helplessly, *because Logan always knows more than me and he understands the rules, I* never *understand the rules.* "It's his house," Nathan said foolishly.

"You should tell him that you don't want to."

"No worries. It's fine." His face was burning.

Another pause. "Okay," Seb said. "Well. You get back, then. To your movie."

"Okay." Smiling, unable to stop the smile. A nice smile.

"Mikyla Simmons, huh."

The smile flickered and died, just like that. "She's okay. Kinda weird."

"Mikyla Simmons."

"Seb."

"All right, all right. See you at school."

And Logan, looking at him with his forehead creased: "That took *forever*; who *was* that?"

The next night, studying, Nathan's phone blipped at him cheerfully, Seb's number, and once again, no preamble: "I been thinking."

"You shouldn't do that."

"Yeah, but I can't help it."

Mikyla Simmons, Nathan thought wisely, and steeled himself for the questions, the suppositions, the request or the demand for any knowledge Nathan himself might be withholding. He stared wistfully at his algebra book, spread wide before him, then closed it, resigned.

Instead, Seb said, "So you like . . . guys."

Blinking, Nathan could only say, "Yeah. Yes. I guess."

"You *guess*? Don't you *know*?"

"Of course I know. Yes. I do. Like guys."

"Dudes. Men."

"Dudes, sure." Nathan's eyes widened, and he glanced over his shoulder, but the door to his bedroom was closed, and his brother was out cruising in his ridiculous pickup truck, and his father was not back yet and his mother was in her room, smoking cigarettes and watching her soap operas, her stories, she called them, like it was the 1960s and she wasn't a woman who worked routinely sixty hours a week. His heart sped up, revving inside his chest; the room condensed and grew small, claustrophobic. "Guys. Dudes. Men."

"Yeah," Seb said, "but how do you know?"

Nathan opened his mouth and then closed it, thunderstruck. His face felt hot and flushed. At last he said, "How do you know if you like girls?"

"Dunno. I just do."

"So?"

"So?"

"So what the hell do you want, Seb?"

"I'm just," Seb said, grumbling, "you know, *wondering* is all."

"About guys?"

"No, no, no," Seb said quickly. "No. Fuck no. Just. Wondering."

"About what?"

"Hell, I don't know," Seb said. "I gotta go." Then there was nothing but emptiness against Nathan's ear. He sighed, and touched his algebra book, shuddering a bit.

But the phone trilled its merry laugh again the following night, and Seb, immediately: "But what do you do?"

"We have got to stop meeting like this," Nathan said dryly, but Seb seemed not to hear him.

"What? No, seriously. What do you *do*?"

"Well," Nathan drawled, and slammed shut with a dramatic flourish the complete works of Shakespeare that Mrs. McQuilkin required each of her sophomores to schlep back and forth from school on a nightly basis, "I like long walks on the beach and romantic movies, not the cheesy kind, but with *proposals*, and some kind of complicated chase, and roses, red, not—"

"Shut up," Seb said urgently. "Shut up and listen to me, would you? You're supposed to listen to me. You're supposed to be good at that."

Maybe I'm not, though, Nathan wanted to say. Instead he heaved a heavy sigh. "What do you mean, what do I do?"

"Well, maybe not you specifically, but guys."

"Guys."

"Guys. Together."

"Oh!" His face flooded with blood again, filling capillaries and burning in his cheeks, and he almost dropped the phone.

"I'm just wondering," Seb said swiftly. "Like I said, I'm curious."

"You are?"

"Guys can be curious," he said defensively. "*Any*one can be curious. I'm not the only one, you know."

"I suppose you're not."

"Don't laugh at me. I told you that."

"I'm not—" and the phone was dead again, leaving Nathan with Othello and Desdemona and Iago, all clamoring up at him from a heavy book with a closed cover.

He was prepared for Seb's phone call the following night, but it never came, and so, feeling discomfited and slightly bent, Nathan read all of *Othello* and half of *Macbeth* for the third time, fillet of fenny snake indeed, and fell asleep with his phone next to his ear, but it never rang.

When it finally did, Friday night, Logan's party right on schedule for Saturday, Nathan snatched it up and snarled, "Now listen, if you think that you can just—"

"I'm sorry," Seb said, small and contrite, "I just been thinking, and I'm not very good at it, or talking. So I just wanted to call you and tell you: I'm sorry."

"Oh," Nathan said, confounded. "Okay."

"I'm still scared."

"Of the party."

"That, too."

"What," and his throat was dry and his lips were dry, and he said, "else?"

Silence spooled out between them for what felt like endless hours, until Seb said at last, "I don't know how to do things either."

"I'm getting that."

"Shut up. I don't know how to do things, not boy things or girls things or . . . or *any*things."

"And you think that I do?"

"More than me. You belong in the world, don't you know that? I watch you, and you—"

"You *watch* me?"

"—you know things and how to do them, and you seem like you know *you*, no, shut up, you do, and *me*—" His voice was choked and trembling, and there came another great pause, and Nathan, wisely, thought that he shouldn't say anything, that it was definitely smarter to afford space to Seb Candleberry, who more and more reminded Nathan of the feral cats who lived delirious lives in the alley behind their house and who would approach, sniffing cautiously, mouths sneering, if anyone tried to entice them with, say, a piece of chicken or a little scrap of fish left over from dinner; they would flee given the first opportunity and then you'd never see them again. Nathan understood that it was better to allow Seb Candleberry to take all the time he needed and to wait until he spat out all the words on which he currently choked.

"And me," Seb said at last, "I just wonder all the time."

"What do you wonder about?" Nathan's voice was lower now; he couldn't help it.

"About how it feels. All of it. I don't know, see, and I don't know if I'll ever know."

"Like?"

"Like," and Seb was whispering now, "a dick."

"Oh wow." Whispered, whispered back.

"Hell." Seb's voice thickened. Nathan heard him swallow, heard him lick his lips. "Right? Like how another dick feels."

"Another guy's dick."

"And what it does. And what happens. Like, if you put it in your mouth. What it feels like. Tastes like. Would I choke on it? Would I gag?"

"I—"

"I can imagine," Seb said, singsong, "I can almost feel it. I'm feeling *me* right now, that's all I know, and I'm hard as a fucking icicle."

Nathan said nothing, he *couldn't*, and his room grew smaller. He swallowed; his eyes flicked involuntarily to his bedroom window, but there was nothing out there, certainly no face glaring in at him with empty, hollow eyes. *I haven't seen one in almost a month*, he realized, *maybe even longer than that. Maybe not even since the last time I met Seb.*

"I just want to know, that's all. Another guy."

"Another guy."

"How he feels. How he tastes. Does he feel like me? Taste like me? Is it like, you know, coming home? Coming?" He laughed.

"I don't really know," Nathan said apologetically.

Thunderstruck silence, and Nathan wondered if he hadn't made some terrible and irrevocable blunder. Finally, Seb, incredulous, said, "You don't."

"I don't."

"You and Logan?"

"Logan and I," Nathan said ruefully, "are friends. Just friends. *Only* friends. I mean it. That's all we've ever been." *And all we'll ever be.* But he didn't say that.

"So you never?"

"Never," Nathan said emphatically.

"Oh." More silence. *I've missed some great chance*, Nathan thought desperately, and then he realized he was unable to define what that chance might have been. He felt stupid and silly.

Then, wickedly: "Wouldn't you like to?"

Nathan's throat filled with wood, a great square chunk, like the kind his dad used to block the rear tires of the car when they'd had a flat the winter before last and Nathan could only watch, both unable and unwilling to help, feeling dull and angry and useless; yes, that same exact kind of wood. Nathan imagined it now, the way it sat in the darkness, crammed against the tire, digging into the snow, and it filled his craw, his throat, his mouth, with oily splinters.

"If you could," that insinuating, whispering little voice said in his ear, "wouldn't you? With someone? With *any*one?"

Nathan held his breath. It trembled; it burned.

"I spend a lot of time," Seb said hesitantly, "alone. Mom's not here. Hardly ever here. And, hell, my dad's not coming back. It don't feel good to think about it. It hurts to think about it, actually."

"I'm sorry," Nathan said, confused. "I guess."

"You *guess*. Shit. Listen, it don't mean nothin'. We're not gonna feel and learn and grow. I just want you to understand. I got no one to tell me things, you know?"

Me either, Nathan wanted to wail, wanted to scream and weep and laugh and go spinning out his bedroom door, down the hallway, out onto the front yard and into the street, spinning endlessly. Me either, he wanted to cry out his joy, I'm alone, too. Even Logan doesn't totally understand. How could he? He's *perfect*; but you . . . *you* . . .

"The party," Seb said at last, musingly. "I'll see you there." He paused; Nathan could hear him breathing still. And just as Nathan was about to whisper his name, Seb said, casual as hell, "You still seeing those, whadda ya call 'em . . . those deaders?"

"Oh!" Nathan said, startled. "No. Nothing. Not a one." Not a whisper, not a shadow, nary a shambling, decaying corpse; nothing, he was certain now, since that evening in the park.

"I been thinking. They're people, you say?"

"They were."

"But what if they *ain't*?"

Nathan blinked. "People?"

"Or not always. What if some of the things we think are ghosts aren't people? Maybe not now, or maybe they never was."

"I never thought about that before."

"Takes practice," Seb said dryly. "You gotta aspire to be a smart guy like me. You like that word, aspire? My counselor at school told me I gotta raise my sights a little higher. Gotta *aspire*." He chuckled. "Anyway, it's something to think about, yeah? I mean, if you want my opinion."

"I do."

"Good. Think about it. Maybe there are other things out there besides them deaders, and you're seeing *them,* too."

"Now you're freaking me out."

"Also good. Sometimes being freaked out ain't a bad thing. Keeps you on your toes. But maybe it don't matter anyway now. 'Cause you ain't seen any."

"No." Nathan licked his lips. "No, I haven't."

"I toldja," Seb said smugly. "It's all me, dude. You're welcome."

"I—" Nathan started, almost angrily, but only emptiness shouted bleakly in his ear again. Seb was gone. Nathan thought he would lie back and cry, but his eyes were as dry as the wind outside his bedroom window, the sly autumn gale that stripped the remaining leaves from the trees and rattled them, secretly, like little bones.

The party itself, the following night: the house smelled like fresh pine dripping sap from torn branches, because Logan's mother bought only the costliest candles from catalogues and websites that she spent hours combing; twenty-three kids from school had accumulated by eight o'clock. Nathan arrived first, of course, hours before the others; his mother, doe-eyed and grinning when he asked her that morning to take him to the mall so he could buy a new sweater, blue, so his eyes would pop, sang, "Is it a boy, sweetheart? You can tell me. Is it a *boy*?" and he had only smiled a little and stared out the window at the denuded trees and browning lawns they passed.

The sweater purchased and donned, his eyes glistening blue, Nathan gnawed at his fingernails until Logan, grinning, smacked them out of his mouth. The music blared and it was as bright and plastic as all the music everyone Nathan knew listened to with breathless devotion. Nathan continued to gnaw at his fingernails and Logan was too busy talking to Mikyla Simmons to smack them out of his mouth again.

"I don't care," Logan said. "He's an asshole."

"A college boy, though," Mikyla said, laughing. "My god, that's fuckin' ballsy."

Logan echoed her laughter. "Not as ballsy as you'd think. Like little acorns."

Nathan spun away from them, his heart trip-hammering in his chest. More people flooded the house with every minute that passed (it seemed that the door swung open and slammed shut again every fifteen seconds or so), but none of them were *right*. The house seethed with a sea of red Solo cups and the rich, yeasty smell of beer, which Nathan sipped; when someone handed him a joint he took a hit without even thinking. Immediately his head swelled like a balloon, and he smiled stupidly until paranoia came crashing down around him, pressing on him like the crush of heavy planks from above; even the stomping of feet from the floor over his head was heavy and driving.

Panic ran around and around on clutching little rodent toes behind the ridge of bone just above his eyes, and he coughed an explosive cloud of yellow-gray smoke that hung before him in tatters. Logan, holding a joint of his own and exhaling with expert efficiency, said gently, "You look like you're about to piss your pants. What's *wrong*?" and Nathan could only shake his head, unable to find the breath he needed, he had no *breath*, only the remaining shreds of the marijuana smoke; he was becoming, he was nothing *but* marijuana smoke; and then the door slammed open and it was Seb after all, alone, shrugging in his old green army coat, and smiling the way Nathan imagined his smile would be, perfect.

Seb, Seb after all.

"Shit," he said, "it's cold outside. Hey, this is a fuckload of people. Do you really know all these people?"

"No, of course not," Nathan said. "Here, come inside, give me your coat for the love of god."

And Seb, laughing, said, "Nah, I think I'll keep it on."

Then Mikyla descended on them like a harpy, shrieking, "Oh my god, you came, you came!" and Nathan felt brushed away as if by an immense wind. Seb, seeing her, narrowed his eyes, then beamed widely and opened his arms and she flew into them and Nathan felt as if he were about to vomit up a whole tide of darkness and blood and gray-yellow smoke like a genie materializing from inside himself. But he didn't run or cry or whimper; now his eyes were full of splinters instead of his throat, and if he were to weep, he knew he would weep perfect wooden chips.

How he ended up outside, he wasn't certain, but Logan's backyard was vast and shadowed and held him with its darkness so that he could stare unblinking into the empty night, arms folded over his new blue sweater that matched his empty wooden eyes.

I'm alone out here. There is no one here in all this great glaring darkness but me.

He looked down into the cup he held. It was nearly empty. He wondered blearily, and with a jab of hostility, if his parents knew, or even suspected, that he drank. Both his mother and father were recovering alcoholics, and had been since before Nathan even attended kindergarten, so he'd grown up under the monstrous, exaggerated shadow of booze. Oh, the horrors, the *horrors* of booze, life-ruiner, encourager of late-night fist fights, of throttlings, of driving too fast, too many near escapes, too much death, oh, it was all about death, wasn't it. Nathan poured the rest of the contents of his cup straight down his gullet. *You'd think they'd notice, they'd realize they have a sixteen-year-old son with friends (Logan, at least) who do all the terrible things everyone does (more or less). We party. This is what we do; this is how we do it.* His eyes burned with the threat of tears, and he thought, *Why don't they fucking* fucking *notice?*

Why don't they stop me?

He swayed, bit the tears back savagely. He didn't want to be alone. Not now.

Do you think you could just summon them?

His eyes widened. That was Seb, only two months or so ago; Seb in the park, suggesting that Nathan might have some control over his life after all; Seb, who thought Nathan could call the deaders up deliberately. Nathan rocked back and forth on his heels in the darkened shadowland of Logan's backyard, staring, staring, staring into the darkness.

He began to smile.

Maybe he's right. Maybe I can do things. Maybe there's all kinds of magic, all kinds of control; maybe I don't have to be alone after all.

What if they aren't ghosts though? What if some of them are something else?

He felt wicked.

He felt powerful.

Maybe everyone will just have to do what I say for once.

He closed his eyes.

Took a breath.

I don't want to be alone; I won't be, never again. Somewhere to belong, that's all I've ever wanted, all I've ever—

And opened his eyes again.

"Oh, it's so good to *see* you, darling," said a woman in a mermaid-green dress that hugged her curves and then flared out below her as if she had her own fishtail, disguising her feet. She was exquisite, just as Nathan had imagined her. A face matched at last to the chiming laughter he'd heard that day with Seb in the park; laughter he'd thought was only in his head. Her mouth pursed as if she'd nibbled on lemons or as if she held a million kisses waiting to be unleashed; her hair was twisted into a chignon, Madeleine from *Vertigo*, because he and Logan were exploring Hitchcock's oeuvre together (*at my insistence*, Nathan thought dimly, *but Logan was such a sport, wasn't he*) and hadn't they just watched *Vertigo* instead of another kung fu movie?

"We never see you anymore," she chirped, "and of course we simply *leaped* at this opportunity. A party? But Nathan *never* has parties, I told dear Ernest that only this morning, so we *must* go. And here you are, poor dear, opening up the house at last after such a great sadness. But you mustn't be lonely, darling. No one, not one single person here, not one single person among the millions who love you and would do anything you ask, simply anything, not one of those millions of people who are all your nearest and dearest friends wants you to be *alone*. Your tuxedo is beautiful, your hair is flawless; and here you are, here you are at last." She touched his face lightly with the tips of her fingers; they were warm; they were real.

The party thronged around him, and there they were, golden and glowing in his mansion, his friends and family and vast multitudes of lovers. Finally he stood at the top of an immense marble staircase and raised a silver goblet and said, "Dear friends," and they all turned to look at him, eyes avid and adoring, because of course *Nathan* was speaking, and when Nathan spoke *everyone* listened and caught their breath so as not to miss a single syllable, "I must thank you all for coming. It's been a dreadful year, and I know I've been a hermit here in this lonely old manse. You've all been so wonderful and forgiving, but we're all together and so tonight this party, *this* party is just for you, because the darkness has flown, the journey over, the tests all passed, and now . . ."

His eyes widened; his tongue froze mid-word; his breath puffed out before him in a delicate frosty cloud, like lace.

They stared up at him adoringly, the throng below him, with glaring molten eyes, red as lava. Some wore the heads of animals: dogs with long wet snouts, ferocious jungle cats colored nighted-black, here a vulture with a simpering beak, there a gorilla with enormous jabbing teeth, and what must be a jackal, Anubis, Nathan thought, nauseated and staring and unable to move. Some were things that had never been human, bulging eyes and stalks or jointed legs emerging from their faces, and these moved and jittered and danced on the air, beckoning.

"I—" he tried to say, but he choked on the word, and the jackal threw back its head and emitted a single, shrill scream, which the panther-headed creature took up, wrapped lovingly in its blue sarong; then the dogs, howling, the loneliest sound Nathan had ever heard, their canine heads tilted back from the collars of their tuxedos, their human hands locked together tightly. The sound was deafening and grew louder, and somewhere the woman in the mermaid dress was laughing, laughing—

He realized that he was sobbing and shaking his head. *No, no, god no*; and he was alone with his special, monstrous party that collapsed spectacularly all around him like sodden ashes, his hands pressed to his ears, there by himself in the darkness of Logan's backyard. The wind hooted through the trees and raised gooseflesh on his arms beneath the pretty blue sweater. He could hear the crash and crush of the party behind him; *the* real *party*, he thought desolately, *Logan's party, not* mine *at all, even though it felt real, like I was there, could it have been?* And those people, those *people*. He had to force his hands down to prevent them from covering his face again—through the glass of the sliding doors that had opened and admitted him out into the darkness of the backyard in the first place, and he thought, *I have to go back to the real world. Because what happened just now, whatever I saw, wasn't real. People see ghosts; it's conceivable that* I *can see ghosts or whatever the deaders are; I can accept* that.

But a roomful of animal-monster-werepeople and those other *things . . . that just isn't possible. No way.*

And even if it is, I will never, never *be lonely enough to go back there again.*

He tried to shake away the last gasps of his high from the pot they'd offered him and the two (or three) cups of beer he'd consumed, then lifted his chin and moved determinedly toward the house, where Logan waited—surely *Logan* had missed him—toward the house and the *real* party where no one was a monster and he could find a place to fit in if he just tried hard enough, said the right words, stopped saying the wrong words.

But, as he moved purposefully through the October shadows that held him still, a tiny voice inside him whispered with tinny glee: *You did it; it was real; you were there. See what you can do?*

And then Seb's voice again: *What if they ain't always people? What if some of them ain't people . . . and maybe they never were?*

The air inside the house stifled him, a damp wool blanket descending after the blessed coolness of the outside nighttime, and Logan was nowhere to be found. Mikyla Simmons he picked out almost instantly, in the kitchen with Essie, waving a potato chip in the air to illustrate some astute, well-considered point, surely, before she crammed the chip into her mouth and chewed it into yellow wet crumbs. Seb, Nathan thought, Seb? But I don't care, he thought viciously; I don't; which was, of course, when Seb caught his arm and pulled until he followed, helplessly (he told himself), or willingly, maybe he was just willing, or maybe *he* did the pulling, Nathan himself, down hallways Logan had expressly forbidden people to travel, and up a staircase to a back bedroom, the existence of which Seb Candleberry had no business knowing.

"Nobody saw us, so don't worry," Seb said.

"I don't give a fuck," Nathan replied, more loudly than perhaps he should have, but he found, with some relief, that he really didn't.

Seb stared at him with wide eyes, perhaps a bit hurt, then hooded them and glared instead. His chin was blond with stubble, unshaven, no thought put into it, unprepared, and not the way Nathan believed one should prepare for a party.

He is foul. He is indescribably terrible, with that ridiculous army coat. He is despicable. He is vile.

"*I* give a fuck," Seb said. "I'm not like you."

"I don't know what that means."

"Shit," Seb said, grinning and throwing back his head. "Me neither."

They stood there, simply looking at each other, in that little back room with the bed Nathan only then, belatedly, noticed. Or had he been headed there all along? He knew Logan's house as well as his own; had he, and not Seb, brought them there?

The heat didn't touch them. In fact, Seb rubbed his hands together, said, "Cold," apologetically, and blew warm breath into his cupped palms.

"I don't understand anything," Nathan finally said. He tried to summon up more appropriate words—*vile*, he thought, concentrating, or tried, *vile*, but it wouldn't come—and he certainly couldn't ask a question like, "Do you want me?" or, worse, "Do you love me? Could you?"

Could I love you?

Seb raised his eyebrows, comically surprised, and said pleasantly, "You understand more than me." He closed the door softly, casting the room into absolute darkness. Fumbling, cursing, Nathan found a lamp beside the bed (oh, the bed) and snapped it on. It offered soft, warm light that did little to illuminate. Shadows sprang to life, and their shadows, Seb's cast beside Nathan's own on the wall, were largest of all. "Better," Seb said.

"I really don't."

"Don't say that." Seb's eyes gleamed in the half-light of the room.

"It's true though. I never really feel . . ." He gestured helplessly, aware of how long his fingers seemed, how thinly and exquisitely feminine. He clutched them, hid them. "I feel like a watcher," Nathan said at last. "Like, I just *watch* things. They're here and they're real and I'm not. Or maybe they're not real either, and I'm somewhere else." He shook his head wearily. "Or some*one*."

"But you are. You're real." Wickedly, "Aren't you?"

"Beats the hell out of me."

"That's why you see them," Seb said, inspired. "Those *things*."

"Things," Nathan said weakly.

"Yeah, yeah." He snapped his fingers in a rapid pattern, the firing of little guns. "Because you *watch*. Because you *listen*. You got this light, and it shines out of you."

"Poetic."

"That's me," Seb said, beaming. "If it makes you feel any better," he said, and sank backward onto the bed, "I often feel that way myself. That maybe I ain't real."

"You are." He laughed drunkenly. "It's all all *all* real."

Seb said nothing in return, but instead patted the bed beside him. Nathan didn't move, only watched, one eyebrow raised. "Oh Christ," Seb moaned, and threw his head back. "Oh hell. Don't look at me like that. I hate when you give me that look." He patted the bed again.

"I don't have a look."

"Oh, but you do."

"I don't want to be in here anymore, Seb. I want to get back to the party."

"Party'll be there when we're done."

The words froze on Nathan's lips: *With what?*

Irritation gave way to exasperation, and Nathan made a sound to indicate his displeasure, watching Seb lounge there on the bed before him, supporting himself with one elbow, his eyes wide and absolutely full of guile; Seb Candleberry was a creature possessed of *much* in the way of guile.

"You," Nathan said, "are a confusing creature."

"I'm a creature now?" Amused, he jumped up from the bed and stood, only inches away from Nathan.

"You have always been a creature," Nathan said, pronouncing each word clearly. "You brought us here, creature."

"I guess I did, didn't I."

"I don't understand why."

"We talk, you and me. Yeah? Don't we?"

"We do."

"And you get me."

"I do?"

"You do. And stop that shit."

"What shit?"

"*That* shit. Throwing my words back at me like questions. I don't want to hear any more stupid goddamn questions. Listen," and he was calmer now, "you and me, we got this understanding. We got something between us." He locked the door, then stood there, his face complicated and twitching with shadows and some emotion that Nathan couldn't quite understand; beast, Nathan thought, creature.

"Seb—"

But he knew.

In that moment, he knew exactly what he wanted.

Why am I fighting this? Stupid to fight. Idiotic; obscene.

"Hell," Seb said savagely, cramming his hands into the pockets of his jeans, faded, torn at the knees, then pulled them right back out again.

"No more talk," Nathan said, his voice thick in his own ears. Seb watched him, wide-eyed, unblinking. "I don't want to talk anymore. I just want this."

His hands were trembling, Nathan saw, wide-eyed, as they fumbled with Seb's belt and then his buttonfly, which didn't want to come open until finally it did, and, with an overwhelming feeling of triumph, he released the other boy's cock. It stood out stiffly before him, furiously red and trembling like Nathan's own hands. He looked up at Seb's face: a portrait, frozen and unmoving. His mouth gaped and his breath came hard.

Now what am I supposed to do? Nathan thought stupidly, but he knew, of course he did, he'd known all along; he reached out firmly and decisively and put the other boy's erection into his hand and held it, but gently. Seb made a sound.

"Down," he growled. His voice was thick, an animal's. "You have to get *down*."

Yes, that comes next, Nathan thought. His hand was sticky already with the liquid that seemed to bubble endlessly from the tip.

Seb's eyes were ferocious, and Nathan didn't think any longer. He held his breath instead and sank down onto his knees and opened his mouth as wide as it would go.

And so, for the last two years, they had their sex, as they'd had it with more or less regularity ever since the night of Logan's party, and nobody, not even Logan, knew about it; they were bonded together by their sweat and by their semen, mingled now irrevocably. Nathan had felt warmth open and spread inside him just before coldness rose up, and the trembling that came with what he'd known he was about to do, this new and marvelous thing, this terrible, disastrous thing; what he knew he was helpless to prevent himself from doing.

They spent time together, driving about town, passing back and forth bottle after bottle of sweet red wine, and over the course of those years, Seb told Nathan about how he wanted to join the

Marines because his dad, whom he rarely mentioned, had been a Marine, but he didn't think they'd take him because of his peanut allergy; he had considered becoming a nurse, or a lawyer; talked loudly and at some length about the card tricks he'd taught himself because, when he was twelve, he'd decided that he was destined to be a magician. Once, drunkenly, near tears, Nathan had finally confessed, "I just want a place, you know, a *place*, and I don't care," and he had nearly started to sob. "I just want *somewhere*," but Seb only smiled sympathetically.

They met clandestinely for coffee downtown at The Spark, Nathan's favorite coffee dispensary in Garden City, or they returned to DeFazzio's, just they two, and they didn't tell anybody, and Seb was usually caustic and frequently critical, but Nathan had adjusted to the causticness. As if they were just friends. Secret friends, Nathan thought wryly on occasion, who you couldn't tell anyone about and who, once or twice a week, fucked you in the ass.

But Seb was proven correct: the deaders were gone. Or, if they *were* still hanging around, Nathan had thought, literally or idiomatically, he hadn't seen them. It was as if his thing with Seb, this secret, wicked, lovely thing, kept the deaders at bay.

It's like he's me, Nathan had told himself, attempting to analyze the situation when he was supposed to be working on his senior paper for English class. *He's a reflection of me*, he thought, sketching doodles of people with animal heads in the margins of his notebook. *Or my shadow, maybe. He said he could make the deaders go away and I believed him, and so they're gone. For nearly two years they've been gone. If they were ever really real to begin with.*

Then, suddenly, he recognized the doodles he was making. He narrowed his eyes and scratched the drawings out. He hadn't attempted anything like *that* again either, not since the night of Logan's party sophomore year. He told himself that he'd just been drunk and high, as he scratched away the doodles, scratch, scratch. There hadn't been a mermaid woman, no monsters in tuxedos and pretty dresses.

Maybe there are no dead people, and maybe there never have been.

The cat-eyes of the leopard-headed man he had sketched glared up at him, amused, lustful.

Scratch scratch.

Don't do this thing, he told himself now, Seb beneath him, three and a half years behind them, the blue-faced horror still a few days away, the séance more than that; no deaders, no magical parties, just the rest of senior year, and beyond that . . .

Seb opened his eyes and swallowed. "Christ, I want a drink of water," he croaked.

"Just water?"

"Gin," he said, grinning. "Vodka. Clear liquors."

"Your mom'll wonder."

"No, she won't. She never does anymore." He wiggled beneath Nathan until Nathan, sighing, rolled off him, releasing him to jump off the bed and scrounge on the filthy floor of his bedroom for his jockey shorts. The carpet now was brown, though maybe once it had been green or taupe or tan, and nubby in places, worn away almost completely in others. It held tightly to the dark and secret stains dotting it like distant galaxies.

"It's fuckin' freezing in here," Seb growled as he found his underwear and examined them critically (to make sure they're his? Nathan wondered), then slid into them.

"We could take a shower."

"Can't. Mom'll be back soon."

"She hasn't called the plumber yet, huh."

Seb's head flashed up and he glared over his shoulder. "What did I tell you? Fuck off."

"I'm just saying—"

"Well, don't. She'll call the plumber. Mind your own business."

Stung again, Nathan looked down at himself, his stomach still glistening with their combined fluids.

This isn't me; this is someone far, far away.

It could be real, darling, he thought in imitation of the trilling voice of the mermaid woman. *It could work out. Don't weep and gnash your teeth, it could.*

He scolded himself to be careful. It was too dangerous to think about. It wasn't real. He didn't want to go back there.

But he couldn't stop himself from thinking of the world in which there was a mansion that belonged to a man named Nathan, who had been alone for so long. The mansion was filled with his friends for a party that went on and on; in another world, there was a boy named Nathan who learned to drive and found a car and climbed into it and drove away until he discovered, at last, the very edge of the world, and it was so beautiful that it burned away everything he held inside him, and then it was easy, letting it all go away; and in still another, there were two boys, and no one knew them or cared about them; they had only each other and could do whatever they wanted.

He took a breath and blinked until he was back in Seb's room. Seb's terrible, disgusting bedroom.

He's been so prickly lately, Nathan thought, watching him uneasily. *Don't do this thing don't.*

"You should go," Seb said, now snug in his jeans and a ratty green hoodie covering the tiny perfect paunch Nathan loved to trace with the tip of one fingernail. "Before Mom gets back."

He sounded distant, cool. Nathan felt a spear of fright pierce him. Seb was just tired, he told himself. But he couldn't shake the unease—*don't don't don't do this*—that only continued to grow.

Nathan nodded anyway and stood up. He was shivering; Seb's house was eternally cold, small and tucked away in a forgotten neighborhood of Garden City's notorious Northside, by the railroad tracks at the northern tip of town, where a low, rolling hump of mountains, worn down by time until they were nearly just hills, formed a natural border.

"Regentrification" was a word tossed around a great deal by the Garden City hoi polloi, and it was applied, with near universality, to the Northside, where people were stabbed or raped or stabbed and raped more than in any other sector of the city. Nathan, grudgingly, admitted that, okay, sure, the Northside wasn't where *he* lived (or would ever choose to live, *probably*) but it wasn't like the inner city. Garden City claimed just under 60,000 citizens; the entire state of Montana boasted barely a million; *inner city indeed,* he thought, half-smiling. He wiped their mingled semen off his chest with one of Seb's tattered blankets that littered the floor; *this part of town isn't beautiful,* he thought, eying the terrible carpet of Seb's room with raised brows, *but it isn't the worst place in the world, not by a long shot.*

It had been a while, he realized, unease growing, since the mermaid woman crossed his mind, since he'd thought of the party even, that secret world he'd created within the real one. He thought that the danger was very real; by thinking about her, about *them,* he was always at least a little afraid that he would summon them back.

And maybe never be able to rid himself of them again.

That thought, that they were more than just fantasies or daydreams, that it might actually be a kind of mental illness (*what the fuck,* he thought, despairing, *do I know about mental fucking illness?*), scared him more than anything else, even more than being alone for eternity, and finally provoked him into leaving Seb's bed while the other boy poked eagerly at his phone.

He found his underpants with little difficulty, but his T-shirt had been kicked somehow beneath the bed, and the smell emanating from the darkness there caused his stomach to do endless airplane rolls. Nevertheless, he gritted his teeth and reached beneath, half-expecting small but sharpened teeth to sink into the back of his hand as he fumbled helplessly in the shadows beneath Seb Candleberry's lumpy twin mattress and shitty, splintered bed frame.

When they'd started their little whatever-it-was (and Nathan didn't even attempt to offer a definition), Seb hadn't owned a bed at all, just a mattress on the floor, thin and stained and shoved haphazardly into a corner of his bedroom. But his mother, Seb told Nathan with stony and practiced indifference, brought it home last Christmas, and he was happy to have it. People from her church donated it, he'd said. Seb didn't like to talk about his mother, or, especially, his mother's church. But he liked the bed.

Nathan wondered, pulling up his jeans and cinching his belt, what it would be like to live this life, in this place. Seb's room, Seb's house, Seb's life, and Nathan didn't understand it completely but remained fascinated, nevertheless.

Because he's my shadow.

He opened his mouth. He nearly said the words. He wanted to say the words.

Don't do this thing.

Then he realized that he was still sitting on the bed, that he hadn't moved. *He hadn't moved at all.* He hadn't pulled up his jeans or cinched his belt; he shivered and realized that, yes, he was still sitting on Seb's bed in just his underpants, staring stupidly at his hands.

Seb, noticing, growled, "What? You got this look on your face. And why ain't you dressed yet?"

Come with us, a tinkling, feminine voice said clearly.

Nathan told himself it was just his imagination. He didn't hear anything. Easy to convince himself. Years of habit.

Sometimes I do things and sometimes I only think *I do things, and that's scarier than anything else I'm about to try.*

"I just wonder what we really are," he said slowly, not sure what words were about to emerge from his mouth, even as he said them.

"*I'm* an astronaut," Seb grunted.

"A cowboy."

"Olympic figure skater. Opera star."

"Yes," Nathan said, smiling. "An opera star."

"Nah. Just a guy. Some stupid guy, goin' nowhere," he said, grinning, grinning. "That's me. And you're . . . whatever you are. Future photographer to the stars." He scowled. "But 'we'?" He shook his head. "I don't understand 'we.'"

Nathan didn't want to say Mikyla's name. Instead, "There's," he started, hesitated, and then, in a rush, because he'd been thinking it and it had bloomed that night when he was supposed to be writing his useless senior paper, he let the rest of the words fall out of his mouth one by one, and then it was far too late to stop them. "It's stupid, I think it's probably stupid; actually, I *know* it's stupid but . . . there's this dance."

"Uh-huh," Seb said. "Prom. It's, like, what everyone does, right? I mean, according to TV and movies and all that happy horseshit."

"Cowboy," Nathan said mildly, then, all in a rush again, "but we could go, is what I meant. *We* could. The . . . two of us."

Seb, moving slowly as if through water solidifying into ice, growled, "We? Could? Go?"

"It's a cliché," Nathan said. "A horrible high school cliché. It's crammed into our brains, and it's beautiful or it's horrible or it's beautiful *then* horrible, but this is almost over—"

"This?" He was fuming, being willfully ignorant.

"High school," Nathan snarled. "Come on, you *know*. It's almost done forever and then we, what, just *go*, and there's so little left except this part, and I guess I don't care that it's a cliché, I don't, because I want it."

"You want it."

"Stop repeating me back to me. Jesus, no wonder that makes you nuts when I do it. Yes, I want it."

Seb considered this, then, maddeningly, shrugged. "Okay," he said, "so go."

"Not," Nathan said, running his tongue over his teeth, "not me. I mean, not *just* me.

"You could go to the dance.

"*With* me.

"*We* could go. Things are better when it's 'we.'"

Seb's eyes were hard and they sparkled and Nathan thought them beautiful. Even when he was being deliberately obtuse, he was still beautiful; even his terrible, moldering room was part of his beauty. In a rush, Nathan wanted to hold him again, no sex, just holding. He'd take a kiss, just one, what he'd always wanted from Seb: for Seb to touch his face, for his eyes to go gentle, for Seb to say, "I'll go anywhere, do anything, just stay with me, please, don't go, don't go away," or "I want you, I do, only," or "Come with me, I love you, do you love me?" For Seb to want *him*. There wasn't a reason not to, so what did they have to lose?

I belong; we belong; this is my place, at last; here is my place after all.

Seb sat beside him on the bed.

Seb's eyes softened. He lifted a hand. He touched Nathan's hair. Then he grinned.

"Don't be a fuckin' idiot," he said, smacking Nathan lightly upside the head. "Why would I go with *you*?"

Nathan stared; Nathan swallowed; numbness washed over him and he sat very, very still. He wanted to touch his head where Seb's hand had landed, but he didn't dare; *doesn't hurt*, he chanted to himself, *doesn't hurt, doesn't*.

"Hell, we ain't *boyfriends*," Seb said, still grinning that hot and somehow feverish grin. But he didn't sound hateful; he didn't sound angry or mean or nasty; matter-of-fact, probably. "I ain't your *boyfriend*. You didn't think that, did you?"

Nathan opened his mouth, but he didn't know what to say.

"Hey," Seb said. "I don't mean to be cruel or nothin'. It's just . . . it's not like that for me. We're friends. This is a kind of friendship we got here."

"Right," Nathan said. His voice sounded bright, almost chipper, in his own ears. What was happening to him? He felt that his eyes should be leaking tears, should be overflowing, but they were like dried riverbeds that had known water once, long ago, and were full now of earth, cracked, crumbling, gray.

He pulled on his pants. He grabbed his belt. He really performed the actions this time, he knew he did; it was real, this was real, he did it.

"Sure," he said, and he knew he said it; he heard the word. Bright and false. He knew he said these words: "I mean, right. Sorry."

"We're friends." Seb waggled his eyebrows. "With benefits. Ain't that what they call it?"

"Right." Bright, bright, chipper. *I'm saying words*, Nathan thought. *He's making a joke out of it, he's trying to make a joke so that he'll feel better because he knows that I overstepped, that I gave away too much of myself, so he's trying to be funny.* "Fuck you," Nathan said, or thought he'd said, but Seb didn't react. He only smiled, so *that* must not have been real. It was getting so hard to tell.

"Let's be friends, then." He touched Nathan's hair again, but he didn't grin or pull it or smack him. He touched his hair, that was all, and gently.

"This is all your fault," the mermaid woman whispered at him. Everyone else at the party stared at him gravely: *you should've known*.

He glanced at his hand. For a quicksilver moment, it emerged from the cuff of a starched white shirt, which itself grew, telescopically, from a midnight-black tuxedo jacket.

He thought, *Flex*, and his fingers flexed. He felt a flash of heat. The party. The party was back; the party never ended.

He closed his eyes, took a breath, opened them, then looked down again. Just his hand this time; his bare arm, covered with goosebumps. He picked numbly at the Kelly-green sleeve of his T-shirt.

Seb's phone made a sound then. He grabbed it from the top of the plastic set of drawers that held all his clothing, glared at the screen, mouthed the word *Mikyla* at Nathan, then jerked his head in the direction of his bedroom door.

Nathan thought, *He could have sounded gentle; it's possible. He could've said those words pleasantly.*

"Get gone," Seb said.

Many worlds, Nathan thought numbly. He shrugged into his coat. *Many, many worlds, just waiting out there. Many worlds, farther away than this.*

"Deaders," Nathan said, but Seb didn't hear him.

And when he left Seb's house and closed Seb's door behind him and turned to face the street, still filthy with half-melted, dirt-stained clods of snow berms and ice, he was surprised, and then surprised at his surprise, to find that the yard was full, the *street* was full, and they were back after all.

The dead, the dead, the walking, staring, gesturing dead, some of them flickering like a light bulb about to die, some of them whole but washed of all color, men and women and a few children, one horrible headless little girl in a pinafore and shining patent leather shoes, *no head no head*, but her hands reached for him and her fingers, the nails painted a delicate, coral pink, flexed in his direction. They'd been there all the time, he now understood, fascinated despite himself, horror and a sick spark of delight mingling together, because he'd been right, and they were real after all. As he watched, more gathered, more coalesced. Their mouths opened if they possessed mouths to open; they lifted their hands and their fingers extended. They called for him silently, their mouths working, the air awash with the sickness of their smell. Nathan heard nothing, but he felt them nevertheless, their hunger for him.

You want us we love you we see you and we need, we are the place where you can belong, we. Suddenly it was too much, and he ran, and, when he glanced behind him, there they remained, fixed like statues in Seb's yard, staring, starving, staring at him still.

That was Saturday afternoon; Monday night, he tried his own little séance, with crystals, with candles. Thursday, and a dead blue skull smiled in at him and cracked his bedroom window; Friday, and he hated himself and tried not to, tried to hate Seb. What he wouldn't give to be out of that place; what he wouldn't give to have someone.

Drums in the forest, dancing before the fire, a blazing path that I can follow and it will lead me . . . where? He thought of his dreams.

Wings, drums, flash of scarlet, golden eyes, staring—

"Maybe the ghosts will get *him*," Logan had said, inspired, and—

8

IT WAS NEARLY seven o'clock, and Bert, the custodian in charge of keeping the Royal High auditorium in sterling repair, had just closed the doors with a resounding clapping sound that echoed throughout the vast space where plays and musical concerts and classes in dramatics played out day after day after year. They were hiding in the balcony, Nathan and Derek; Seb and Mikyla had disappeared immediately somewhere backstage, and Essie and Logan lingered outside in the hallway, "Keeping watch," Logan had said with an exaggerated sigh. Heather never showed, which, Derek said, madly rolling his eyes, was hardly surprising to anyone. Nathan wasn't certain how this arrangement had come to pass, or why he was stuck with Derek and why Logan was paired with Essie; but he reminded himself he truly, *truly* didn't care. He honestly did not care, he swore, that Seb and Mikyla were probably just now becoming pregnant together in the thick shadows on the stage below them.

Derek's feelings, Nathan knew, were hurt when Logan hadn't insisted on joining his boyfriend in the balcony with Nathan, hadn't even seemed bothered by the fact that they wouldn't be together while everyone waited for the clearing of the coast. Derek's little face had broken like a tiny plate, and Logan hadn't noticed. Nathan felt familiar slices of shame like a series of internal papercuts; he knew what it was like to suffer Logan's absence. Wasn't Logan's future, permanent disappearance from Nathan's life what he'd been trying not to think about all day? Wasn't that why he was focusing so hard on this séance?

"Of course they won't allow you to room by yourself," the mermaid woman said in his ear, but she had transformed, her voice and her clothes. Now she wore a sterling-gray starched suit, and not just the suit, but a pince-nez as well, and she was, what, an admissions officer? Someone on a board of directors? "You can't room alone, and your friends can't save you," she sniffed. "College is for adults, little man, contrary to the popular belief disseminated, I have no doubt, through the hallowed halls of your home institution by the unknowing vermin who always, *always* think they have a clue as to what exactly happens here. Like you. There are rules," she said, and the world gave a sickening hitch.

"And he didn't even notice," Derek was saying, his voice quavering, "and he *should've*, don't you think? Don't you—"

Hitch; and he stood in an office paneled with dark red wood that reflected back his white face and wide, terrified eyes. Plush furniture held up the walls and a massive mahogany desk spread itself vastly before him and supported the fish-cold woman leaning against it, arms folded, glaring at him. She had appeared several times like this over the last few days, ever since his final, disastrous coupling with Seb, in addition to the reappearance of the deaders.

The world hitched again, and he was crouched down next to Derek. "—just don't *get* it—"

Hitch, and he was staring at her and she stared back at him with cold eyes. A tiny, horrible smile lifted one corner of her mouth. "Rules," she said, "and those rules, as I have reminded you time and time again, include a roommate and a communal bathroom you will share with sixteen to twenty other young males roughly your own age."

"Do you know how we met?" Derek said, trembling, his eyes wet, and Nathan, disoriented, could only shake his head. "My sister has a class with him. Intro to Journalism. And he's out, and I've never been anything *but* out. I was never even *in*. And, of course, she figured Logan and I were the only two gay boys in all the world, so she decided to just hook us up. Bam." He smacked the flats of his palms together, then laughed, bitterly.

Nathan closed his eyes tightly, his stomach upset and his head throbbing.

I wish I wish I wish I could go back to when it was just me and just Logan. We could leave this terrible place together and just go; no Derek, no Seb, no deaders, no mermaid, no monster-headed beasts; me and Logan, Logan and me; I wish, he thought.

"I really don't think you should bother," the mermaid woman said airily, and tossed her head. "Frankly, I don't think you'll make it. Not *here*. You aren't prepared. There's no way you could be. Not *you.*"

But I have to go, he thought with some desperation. *I have to get out of this place. I'm going to be a photographer; I'm going to find the love of my life and we'll be together forever; I'm going far away from here. I don't care about living in a dorm or if I have to take a thousand classes; I need to get out of this terrible life of nothing but dead people* right this very second.

"There are more people out there like us, so it isn't like we *have* to be together," Derek said. "Do you ever think about that? That there have to be other people? And I love him," Derek said fiercely, bitterly, "like an idiot, I love him, but he doesn't love me back."

Hitch, and the party raged around them. The mermaid woman, back in her emerald-green dress, simpered at him. "This," she said, sipping from her martini glass, "is more like it. This is always better."

"Fuck it," Derek said, and wiped away the silver tear-streaks from his cheeks. "What do you care?"

"I . . . I do." *Do I?* Nathan wondered. *Does Derek matter? Derek knows he doesn't matter. Where are you, Logan?* Were the shadows creeping closer to them, pressing in around them? Nathan's eyes widened. *Don't leave me with him.*

"Whatever," Derek said, stirring. "It's gotta be dark by now."

And the mermaid woman sighed irritably, blackened, and faded away.

"I do," Nathan muttered, "believe in spooks." When he had first tried to tell Logan about the deaders, Logan had only nodded. Nathan was certain that Logan thought he'd been merely reciting back the plot of one of the horror movies he enjoyed that Logan didn't so much. His mother, after the incident at the antique mall, white-faced and with blue-purple shadows of exhaustion beneath her eyes that crouched there like small, biting animals for weeks after Nathan's tumble down the stairs, would merely say, "Don't start that again," whenever Nathan tried to broach the subject. "You know what people will say, my little love? Do you know what they'll *do*? Don't you want friends? Don't you want *Logan* to be your friend? Because he won't be. I promise you, he won't want to ever even be *seen* with you." So he never mentioned them to her again, not the voices he heard, not the plodding, staring, reaching hands and faces and *mouths*, and certainly not that he'd already tried to tell Logan.

And Logan hadn't listened.

Logan hadn't *believed* him.

But Seb did.

His stomach twisted into a knot.

"I hear them sometimes," Derek whispered.

Nathan turned to look at him sharply. "Who?"

"*Every*where. This school is stuffed with them. This whole town," Derek said dreamily, "this whole entire town. Ghosts. *Stuffed* with them."

Nathan looked back down to the seats below them, and the stage, and the shadows that gathered in its wings. "Is it," he said softly.

A séance. Yes, yes; a brilliant shining circle around the dead.

They stood there like that, Derek's back to him, Nathan watching, until at last Derek lifted his head and Nathan said, with as much gentleness as possible, "Come on. Let's go find your ghosts."

Logan and Essie were laughing as Nathan and Derek opened the auditorium doors and revealed them waiting outside, Logan's lips peeled back, showing his straight, white teeth, and Essie, nodding, giggled into her hand.

"Where's Seb?" Nathan said.

"Off with Mikyla," Logan replied, smiling and shaking his head, "totally making out. I'm kinda jealous. Sexy time sounds like a better idea than this." He touched Derek's hand, but the other boy pulled away. Logan frowned.

"Making out," Essie giggled.

"We should find them," Derek said quietly. "Mikyla's got the camera."

"Sex tapes," Essie said and giggled again.

"Oh my god, Essie," Logan said, but he was laughing, too.

"Scaring all the ghosts away," Essie cackled. She cupped her mouth with both hands and called, "Olly-olly-oxen-free!" and her voice echoed throughout the auditorium.

"Shut up, will you?" Derek snarled. "Seriously. The custodians aren't all gone, you know. There are still at least two on the third floor."

Nathan stared; he hadn't been aware that Derek was capable of anger, let alone snarling.

"So what?" Essie said. "Those doors are, like, iron. They can't hear us all the way up there."

"I don't want to take a chance." Derek's eyes flicked to Logan, then back to Essie. "Listen, I don't want to be kicked out of here before we see something. Can't you guys understand that?"

Nathan, placid, understood.

"I understand," Logan said soothingly. "We'll find you your ghosts, baby."

"What ghosts?" Mikyla said, appearing from the shadows that concealed the backstage. But she wasn't adjusting her skimpy black blouse or buttoning the skintight jeans she wore, Nathan noted, betrayed by his own relief. Seb materialized behind her, his face pale and sheep-like in the dimness of the auditorium, the darkness barely beaten back by the single ghost-light that glowed ineffectually upstage of them.

There is nothing inside me, Nathan chanted to himself. *Nothing but darkness, an entire world. An incantation to make it true. An entire world, and Seb Candleberry hasn't even ever* been *there*.

"None yet," Logan said pleasantly. "That's why we're here, yeah? Rattle some chains? Dig up some spooks? Metaphorically speaking," he said to Nathan, smiling his old friendly Logan smile. "Only metaphors. I didn't bring a shovel, see."

"They'll have to do all the work themselves," Nathan said. "I'm not lifting a finger, not *one* finger, to hold a shovel *or* to dig up a single—"

"You guys are assholes," Derek said tearfully, stalking out into the house and sitting, glaring, in one of the seats.

They stood there then, the five of them, and looked at each other with humor that quickly faded and was lost. The darkness felt palpable, and they all thought privately about the cold; the auditorium was never *really* warm, and if there was a haunted place in all of the school, it was there, in that vast, drafty room where invisible dreams were spun out, day after day, icy now, whispering with the growing chill, its ceiling a hundred feet high, maybe more.

Logan shrugged at the others before him, and, smiling apologetically, said, "Damage control. Don't worry. I'm the Derek whisperer. Be back in a sec." Moving slowly, gently, he sat beside Derek and laid his arm over Derek's shoulder, then placed his lips against the other boy's ear. Derek glowered.

"This is bullshit," Seb said at last, and Mikyla slugged him in the arm.

"Shut up," she said amiably. "It's gonna be fun. Derek's just being a little bitch. He'll get over it. Wait and see."

"I don't want to wait and see," Seb growled. His eyes flickered to Nathan. "What'd you guys do up there in the balcony all that time, huh?"

Nathan's eyes widened. Mikyla and Essie watched him curiously. Finally, his voice only a rattle, he managed, "We, uh, we played soccer. Several matches. And hockey. Derek won."

"Tonsil hockey," Seb sneered, then winked lasciviously. "Funny. Fuuuuuuunny. Like a heart attack."

"Don't be a dick," Essie said. "Derek's totally into Logan. Why would he fuck around with *him*?" She pointed at Nathan with one black-lacquered finger.

"Excuse me," Nathan said indignantly, "but I happen to be a *very* delectable piece of . . ." but no one was listening.

"Quiet," Mikyla said, eyes shining. "Do you hear that? Listen."

They all leaned in toward each other. It was a whirring, not mechanical, but alive somehow, like wings. Nathan envisioned, for one dreadful moment, an enormous owl rising up before them out of the dark, filling the entire auditorium, spreading its wings, razor beak agape, dull yellow eyes fixed on them; shrieking, tearing the darkness with those wings, tearing—

"Something's moving," Essie whispered. "Backstage."

"Bullshit," Seb said again. "See the ceiling up there? You know what's just above it? The third floor. Where the fuckin' janitors are. They're walking around and the floor is creaking. And the ceiling. Don't be stupid."

"I'm not," Essie said furiously, whirling away from him to face her best friend. "I told you about him talking to me like that. I told you."

But Nathan had already wandered away from them. The whirring hadn't stopped, and it wasn't the creaking of custodial feet on the third floor above them. It was heavy, dusty. The sound of wings. The auditorium was icy cold, as though somewhere nearby there lay an enormous body of dark midnight water sending up wave after sickening wave of frigid air that reached beneath his clothes, pinching and fondling.

The others were arguing still. Seb growled something; somewhere nearby someone smothered laughter. Nathan was sure of it; someone didn't want to be heard and covered their sniggering with the back of one hand.

The darkness grew as Nathan moved away from the group. He looked around but saw nothing clearly, and the ghost-light on the stage continued to dim. He stopped and marveled at his own shadow, cast, huge and ghastly, on the far wall. It moved, lifted a hand, cocked a head.

But I'm not lifting my hand. Shuddering, he whirled around, but there was no one behind him. He looked back to the shadow, which had grown in that bare millisecond and loomed over him, gesturing wildly. It was far too big, and bent at angles that were wrong and threatening.

"You'll get lost back here," Logan said behind him, flooding Nathan with warm relief. He spun and wrapped his arms around Logan and pressed against him tightly.

"Whoa." Logan smiled. "You look power freaked. You okay?"

"Did you see it?" Nathan whimpered. He dared to take a glance backward, but of course the shadow was gone.

"See it?"

Nathan hesitated. He saw Derek nearby, watching him carefully, not moving at all.

"Nothing," he said. "There was nothing." He took a step back and away, and Derek moved in and laid his head on Logan's shoulder. He stared at Nathan with those tiny slitted eyes.

"What should we do first?" Essie said.

"I got this," Mikyla said and revealed the tiny camera she held. "It's my dad's. Better than our phones for sure. I'll set it up, then we'll just talk to them and record what they say."

"Why should they talk to us?" Seb said.

"I'm with Seb," Logan said, and added, smiling, "for once. Why should anyone—or any*thing*—want to talk to us directly? Or at all?"

"We have to try," Derek said. "It can't hurt to try, not really."

"Unless we get all possessed," Seb said, waggling his fingers.

"Don't be an idiot," Derek said unexpectedly. "Nobody gets possessed outside of stupid movies. Ask Nathan. You don't even know what you're afraid of."

"Sure I do," Seb said. "I seen those movies, too."

With me, Nathan thought, piqued. They'd watched them together, just the two of them.

"I don't want my head to spin around backwards or to puke up gallons of neon green goo." Seb clutched his throat and opened his mouth: "*Raaaaaaccchhhh,*" he said.

"I'd love you even if you puked red, white, and blue," Mikyla said and kissed him noisily on the lips.

Nathan didn't blink. *Feel nothing*, he thought to himself, *feel nothing*.

He heard that sound again, whirring, the rising of enormous wings in the darkness, but no one else, he understood, could hear it. A strange dark delight rose up from the midnight pools inside him.

Nobody heard it but me.

"Gross out," Essie said.

"Come on," Derek said. "We're gonna start the séance."

"Oh, you have got to be fuckin' kidding me." Seb threw his head back and groaned. "Really? Bitch, you been watching too much TV."

"Honey," Mikyla said softly, stroking his hair. Seb subsided.

"Let's sit on the stage," Derek said, inspired. "Then we can all put our hands out so that our fingers touch. The fingers have to touch," he said to Nathan conspiratorially, "or it's just no good at all. I spent all day on my phone figuring out how to do it. Mr. Rice almost caught me but I was sneaky."

As they joined the others, Nathan, dismayed, found himself spaced equally between Logan on his left and Seb on his right. Logan's eyes met his, and he smiled warmly and shrugged. *See what you've gotten us into?* that smile read. Nathan relaxed. He'd imagined the whirring sound, that was all.

"Spread out your hands," Derek said. Any trace of the melancholy and doubt Nathan saw in the balcony had been wiped away. "The tips of your fingers should touch the tips of the fingers of the people on each side of you."

"Faggot," Seb snarled. Mikyla elbowed him and Essie giggled, they giggled together, both girls, and Nathan found that Seb was staring at him, directly into his eyes.

"Wait," Nathan said. "Mikyla, leave the camera on the stage, but turn it on. In case we hear anything. In case we make contact."

"Contact," Seb sighed heavily.

Derek smiled at him gratefully, and Mikyla, nodding, set the camera off to her right and pushed record. The little red light blinked, blinked, blinked, then caught and glared with crimson intensity.

There will be proof, right there on camera.

"Now," Derek said, pleased, "let your fingers touch."

9

MONTHS LATER, WHEN summer showed her emerald and gold face and the winds that blew gently through the valley where Garden City nestled were once more soft and caressingly warm and graduation was somehow two months in the past, Nathan saw the dead woman from the antique mall again, the first deader he'd seen since that final night in the Royal High auditorium.

"I can't meet you," Logan told him over the phone that day, and Nathan thought darkly about how all their conversations recently seemed to take place over the phone. "I'm really sorry, chumly—"

"Don't call me that," Nathan said distantly, trying to smile.

"Sorry, Clarabell, but I got packing to do." He heaved a tired sigh. "Aaaaaand I'm meeting Derek after lunch. He knows what's coming and so do I, but it doesn't make it any—"

"Oh," Nathan breathed. "Oh shit."

"Yeah. Oh-oh shit." Logan sounded gloomy.

They let the silence hang there between them.

"I'm sorry," Nathan said at last.

"Ain't no thing." Logan, trying to sound light, failed, so the heaviness between them only increased. "It was inevitable, right? He'll be at Royal for another year, and I won't. I won't even be in this *state*, and after that . . ." His voice trailed off. "Things haven't been the same anyway since . . . you know."

Logan didn't need to qualify; Nathan knew exactly what he meant, and which night, and under which set of circumstances.

"Is he okay?" Nathan was surprised to find that he cared, at least a little. *Poor Derek*, he thought wistfully, *poor tiny Derek, the eternal cheerleader.*

"I guess. Or no. Probably not. I'm his one great love, you know." Logan's voice sharpened with cynicism, and Nathan, shocked, was a trifle scandalized. He hadn't known Logan possessed a single cynical bone in his body.

"He's just a kid."

"Shut up. So are we."

"Haven't you heard? We matriculated. Got our diplomas and tucked 'em under our arms, so we're grown-ups now. All official-like."

They laughed together, and even separated by distance, it felt nice. Then the laughter rustled and faded and died away and only the distance remained. "Doesn't feel like it," Logan said at last. "Unless this is what grown-ups do."

"I'm pretty sure it is." He tried to think of Seb but then wouldn't allow himself. They hadn't talked since that night. No more calls, no more Nathan listening, no more lying together with their fluids combined. That part, it seemed, was over. Nathan refused, when he thought of Seb, to let his eyes burn or his chest hitch, though his eyes and his chest wanted those things every time.

At least he wasn't seeing the deaders anymore. A few times, once or twice, he suspected that he'd spied one out of the corner of his eye, standing outside his house, down the block, in Rose Park. But when he looked, really looked, there was no one, nobody watching him with unblinking, marble eyes or empty holes; no one struck his window after midnight until it threatened to shatter.

And he'd stopped taking photos. That part seemed over, too. Amy had asked him curiously about them, if he was planning his show; there was, she told him, an opening. But he hadn't, and he couldn't think of any viable excuse. *I don't take pictures anymore*, he'd tried to say, but the words crawled behind his lips like ants and then retreated dutifully down his throat and into the darkness beyond it.

Also, no more party. Also also, no more mermaid woman.

He wasn't sure how he felt. Relieved? Probably. But it felt, ominously, as if everything were holding its breath—metaphorically, of course—and waiting.

For what?

"It sucks," Logan said. "I don't wish it on you. Not ever."

"It happens to everyone, doesn't it? I mean, it's a thing everyone goes through."

"I'm tempted—this is shitty—but I'm so freaking tempted to text him and just, oh balls, take the easy way out, you know?"

"Yeah," Nathan said, thinking of his last conversation with Seb. "Sure." He paused. "So why don't you?"

"Because I think he deserves better than that. We were together for almost a year. It's a crummy thing to do to anyone; I'd hate like hell for someone to do it to me."

Nathan, thinking of the absurdity of anyone ever breaking up with Logan, could only smile.

"So that's the reason I can't hang out," Logan said. "He's just one more chore for today. Four o'clock: pack. Four-thirty: break up with the boyfriend. Six o'clock: meet parents for dinner. Easy-peasy."

"Lemon squeasy," Nathan said absently. *Rituals, rules, rhymes, and regulations.* "Don't even trip. I was just going downtown for a while. Maybe get some coffee."

"I wish I could go. But Mom'll kill me if I don't get the last of my shit boxed up. I tell you what: we'll hang out the last Saturday before I leave town, just you and me. We'll stay up all night and drink wine spritzers because you like wine spritzers, which are absolutely disgusting, by the way, but I'll cut you a break because I love you. Then we'll go out or stay in or stay in and then go out and then stay in, and we'll watch the sun come up and sleep all day Sunday and then get up on Monday and start our lives. Our shiny brand-new grown-up lives. What do you say? One last night to be kids before adult-onset adulthood sets in."

"I'm in," Nathan said. He knew it would never happen; they both knew it. He felt something start to tear inside him, somewhere between his guts and the cavity inside his chest, and he suppressed it, wouldn't allow it. No tearing, he thought ferociously, no breaking.

"College," Logan said, marveling. "You think we'd ever get there?"

"I'm the Succubus of Suck," Nathan said humorlessly. "I'm Dracula's Daughter. I'm gonna live forever, haunting the halls of Royal High and sucking the blood of the freshmen."

"Sucking the *something* of the freshmen," Logan said. They laughed again, and for the flash of a second, flaring up hot and golden, it felt real, the way things had always been. When the laughter died away again, there was nothing Nathan could do to resuscitate it. He knew that now.

"Hey," Logan said, and Nathan, panicking, knew what words were to come. "I gotta go, man. Seriously. Mom will gut me if I don't get these last few boxes loaded. Who knew I had so much shit, anyway?"

That awful, oily wooden block was back in his throat, but Nathan spoke around it anyway. "I'll call you. Or you call me. Or we'll call each other at the same time and leave frustratingly cryptic voicemails."

"Sounds like a plan."

"Okay."

"Okay."

The silence, the goddamn spool of silence, hanging there.

"Well," Logan said, "bye."

Then the inevitable nothing at all, an absence of sound. No crackling, no voices whispering, *Nathan, Nathan.*

He closed his eyes, then opened his eyes, then went downstairs and out the door and stood on the porch and felt the boards, warping now with time and moisture and heat and cold, beneath his bare feet. He was supposed to paint them, or Terry was, but their father the enforcer had been absent most of the summer and their mother was working more shifts, later each night.

"Dad'll be back in time to move you up to the school," she had told him the other night. "So don't worry, honey. No one's abandoning you just yet. It isn't like you're even moving out of town. God, we'll probably never see you, even." She laughed to show she was joking, but her eyes had been dark and trapped and hurt-looking. He hated her to look like that, but there was nothing he could do. She had looked wounded all her life.

He supposed he could paint the damned porch right then, he thought. He looked at the boards between his toes. He laughed. *It isn't my house*, he reminded himself, *not anymore.*

The next time he crossed that threshold, the next time he tread across those boards, warped and newly painted or not at all, they would not be his boards or his chosen color or his threshold or his home. When he returned to that place, if it continued to exist across the span of years and decades, it would be as a visitor only; *if I haunt a house, it surely won't be this one.*

Terry was at work and his mother was at work and Logan was working toward a new, Derek-free life and Amy had given Nathan the week off—"To pack, to plan, to run around, footloose and fancy free," she sang to him over the phone. "Also, I can't believe you've never seen *Footloose*. So you should probably watch that instead of another horror movie you've seen a bajillion times. See your friends. Hang out with your folks. Keep ignoring your brother because he's a tool. Do the things that make you happy. Maybe get your camera out. When was the last time you even took a picture?"—so he slipped on shoes and hopped on his bike and rode it downtown. The sky was flawless and painted that deep and somehow creamy blue that made Montana famous; here, however, the mountains surrounding Garden City broke up the sky, but even they were green and gentle and not forbidding in the slightest. The temperature soared in the high eighties, so by the time he crossed the Sprague Avenue Bridge and zipped past the first of the shops and restaurants that composed Garden City's great and glimmering downtown, he had already developed a line of sweat at his hairline that dried in the breeze created by the swiftness of his passage. As he slowed, he was struck by the heat, nearly solid feeling with the encroaching humidity, which meant that the calm and placid nature of the sky belied a peace that would undoubtedly be shattered later by a thunderstorm. Tomorrow there would be news of forest fires out beyond town, in the hills and mountains outside the valley; now, however, the only shade lay beneath the awnings of the businesses that lined Sprague Avenue.

Nathan walked his bike slowly for a few blocks, then parked it before The Spark. He went inside and purchased a peach-flavored Italian soda loaded, he requested shyly, with extra half-and-half, then re-emerged into the day, which enfolded him in its hot, wet arms. He decided to leave his bike parked at the coffee shop and just walk around, sucking on his straw and moving it around with the tip of his tongue.

He wasn't even thinking about that day years ago in the antique mall when he realized suddenly that he stood in its shadow. He stared at it, sucking away the little bit of water from the ice melting at the bottom of his cup, and felt afraid. The air remained still with no hint of breeze. He had come to the very end of Garden City's downtown, two blocks off Sprague, just across from the railroad tracks. He stared up at the giant building as if hypnotized. He felt himself ease into the memory of that last night when they were all together for the final time, and what had happened in the Royal High auditorium; he remembered, too, the slow, lazy terror he felt that long-ago day when the woman with the ruined face turned and squealed and reached for him and he wet himself like a goddamn baby and then fell for a bit, just a bit, down the first set of stairs, and how his mom finally found him, screaming, and she didn't see the dead lady. Even though the dead lady still gibbered and squealed and fumbled for him with her fingers that ended in bones, Nathan's mother hadn't acknowledged her existence. Which was, of course, worst of all.

Don't talk about those things, honey. You know what's real and what's not real, don't you, honey? Don't you? Don't you?

She *had* sensed that something was wrong; he remembered her face, how her nostrils twitched, like a deer. Or maybe she had smelled something . . . *bad.* And she'd looked around. She'd looked over the shoulder where the dead woman stood and made a face. Like she could feel her . . . or *smell* her.

She sensed her, that terrible rotted dead creature, and she ignored her.

He removed the straw slowly. His chest was closing in on itself.

She ignored me.

Of course she did, he told himself angrily. *What did you expect her to do?*

He thought about something she'd mentioned once, obscurely, when he was a child: *Sometime I'll tell you, my little love, about a thing I saw one time. It wasn't real, though. It . . . couldn't've been real. But I saw it. Or thought I did. And I've never forgotten it. Only in Garden City would I see something like that, that's what I've always thought. Something like* that. *Someday, when you're older . . .*

But she'd never told him. Whatever strange thing this town offered up for his mother, she never told him what it was.

He wondered then if Garden City was weird for anyone else. It couldn't just be him, could it? Was he the only one who saw these things, who *felt* them?

He knew only a little about the town's history. The Native tribes, the Salish, Blackfoot, Pend d'Oreille, could have lived in the valley before white settlers invaded, but Roger Charbonneau told him once a few years ago, maybe sixth grade, maybe seventh, that they hadn't.

"My Gramma said they called it the Valley of Ghosts," he'd told Nathan somberly. "The people of her tribe." Then he broke into a great big grin. "Sounds dumb as shit, right? Oooooh, spooky. But I believe it."

"You do?" Nathan had said.

"Hell yeah. My Gramma told me that. She's full Blackfoot and, like, a billion years old. She said that her great-gramma told *her* that this valley was a place where *things* lived. No people. Just things." Any trace of the wicked, usually ribald sense of humor that emerged habitually from Roger had faded completely. He was absolutely serious. His eyes, looking far away, grew dreamy.

After an awkward amount of time, Nathan said, "Like . . . what?"

"Huh?" Roger jerked as if stung. "Oh. Spirits. Animals that aren't animals; people that aren't people. You could chase them if you wanted, and they'd almost let you catch them. Then they'd disappear. Or something worse."

"What kind of worse?"

Roger smiled humorlessly. "They'd turn around and they'd be . . . something else."

Nathan considered this.

"She said there's something bad about this place. Everyone can feel it. Even you white assholes."

"Sounds like a movie."

"Racist pieces of shit," Roger said cheerfully. "Fuck you, Stanley Kubrick. Fuck you, *Poltergeist*. Why does everything that's bad have to be about ancient Indian burial grounds? Fuck, I don't have any obligation to educate my goddamn oppressors." He'd sighed. "But this valley wasn't a burial ground. It wasn't *anything*. No one lived here. Not 'til you white assholes showed up."

Nathan, sipping his milk, had said, as casually as he could, "Have you ever seen a ghost?"

"Once," Roger had said, and all the humor evaporated from his voice. He stared, suddenly brooding, at the remains of his hamburger. He picked at it, scattering little crumbs of meat about his tray.

Finally, after another interminable stretch of time, Nathan said, "And?"

"And nothing," Roger said, glaring. "I'm not going to tell you about it." He chewed his lower lip. "Besides. Maybe it wasn't even a ghost."

Nathan watched him carefully. "What was it?"

Roger said nothing for a long time. Nathan remembered how the light outside the cafeteria windows looked that day, winter light, cold and gray, leaching all the color from the dead grass that peeped through the crust of snow and from the oak tree that guarded the school's gate. It looked gray, too, branches denuded, gnarled and reaching; everything out there looked dead.

The Valley of Ghosts.

"Tell me," he whispered.

"It wasn't a ghost," Roger said furiously. "Okay? It was me."

"You?" That was unexpected, Nathan thought, starting.

"Yeah. Me." He looked around, eyes darting, then lowered his voice. "Older than I am now. I saw him—me, *it*—downtown. Outside the bus station last year. I was with my folks. They didn't see him. But I did. And he saw me back. His hair was longer and he was probably twenty, at *least*, but his eyes were the same as my eyes and he had a scar right here." Roger touched a long pink indentation about two inches long that zagged above his right eyebrow. "And I just knew that he was me. He looked sad and tired and washed out and angry. He was just so *angry*. I could feel it coming off him in waves, you know? Like a cold wind. He stood up off the bench where he'd been sitting like a fucking snake coming out of a basket. Mom and Dad didn't see. I tried to tell them, but they didn't listen. They're goddamn *college professors*." His nostrils flared. "He started walking toward us. He tried to talk."

Roger's eyes were wide and far away and full of distant horror, and for Nathan the horror was contagious, and he shuddered. "But nothing came out except this high-pitched whine. It got louder and louder. No one heard it but me. Then he . . . h-he . . ." Roger glared, and he turned the full force of this glare onto Nathan. "If you laugh at me, Nathan, I swear to fucking god that I'll—"

"Do I look like I'm laughing?" Nathan said quietly.

"No." Roger relaxed. "I guess you're not. Thanks." He took a breath. "Anyway, he kept making that sound. I wanted to scream just so I didn't have to hear it anymore. Then he lifted his arms and flew away."

"He flew away."

"Yes." Roger's forehead screwed up. "No. Not exactly. He just wasn't there anymore. He was gone. And my head hurt. It *really* hurt. You ever get migraines? I get migraines. It was like that, bad like that. Spots in front of my eyes, just dancing. When I got home, I puked. But he was outside my window later, after it got dark. He was looking in at me. And he was still angry. I felt like he was mad at me, and I know why."

"Why?"

"Because he knew *I* knew. That he wasn't me." Thunderclouds, dark, pressing, grew above his eyes.

"It pretended to be you."

"Maybe. I tried to tell my parents. They didn't listen. They didn't believe me."

"Yeah," Nathan said, and sighed. "I bet they didn't."

"Fucking *professors*. But my Gramma did. She hugged me and told me that I was lucky. That there are other *things* out there, worse than ghosts. Things that look like people or that look like ghosts but they're not. She called them *skinwalkers*."

"Skinwalker." Nathan tested the word.

"Grams said that there were some things that were never people, and they could turn into whatever they wanted. They could fool you. She said what I saw was probably a skinwalker pretending to be me. I don't really know what that means, because she wouldn't talk any more about them. She said that talking about them attracts them. She said sometimes things like that, they can appear to you, they try to lure you places, and then they . . . take you."

"Take you where?" Nathan's eyes were wide.

"Who knows? Somewhere else. And no one ever sees you again. Spirits, demons, werewolves, what the fuck. Shit that ain't *human*. Gramma said I was lucky that it didn't come inside the house. She said it was good that I didn't invite it. What the fuck? Why would I let a thing like that inside my house? But I saw it. I *did*. And I think Garden City is an attractive place for things like that. I think there's something here in this valley that calls out to them."

"I think you're right," Nathan whispered.

Roger looked at him closely. "You know, don't you?" he said.

"Maybe."

He considered. His eyes softened. "Be careful, okay? It's not like movies. I think they like to hurt. That all they want is to hurt."

They'd looked at each other somberly.

They'd never talked about it again.

Nathan stood outside the antique mall, thinking about Roger. Was that around the time he'd started seeing less of the other boy? Or had he started to see less of Nathan?

Another casualty of . . . whatever it is that's wrong with me, or about me, or around me. The thing that people can sense, that pushes them away.

Garden City is an attractive place for things like that. He remembered Roger's words.

A cloud passed over the sun, or something huge passed over the sun, and he turned to look behind him but he already knew what he would see, and he was right: there she was, the deader woman. The cup of ice and the foaming remains of the whipped cream that topped it fell from his nerveless fingers and spilled onto the concrete at his feet.

She wasn't standing, and she wasn't squealing this time; she lay at the side of the railroad tracks. Her body was in two pieces, bisected, but not neatly. Staring, Nathan could see that whatever had separated her top half from her bottom had done it just below her stomach. She was naked; her guts gleamed beneath the glare of the sun, and her eyes, open, held no life or avidity but merely stared, glazed and stupid and empty, up at the sky. Flies lighted on them; Nathan turned away, stomach roiling. He hadn't seen her actual face that last time, Nathan marveled through his nausea; last time her face had been nothing but orange and red and brown shreds.

A man came out of the Dalva Bar beside the antique mall, a grizzled man with a white curly beard and a battered old cowboy hat made of damp-looking felt perched on his head. He regarded Nathan with no surprise. "Hot today," the man said.

"You don't see her," Nathan said dully, and didn't know why he bothered to speak at all. He knew the man wouldn't believe him, no matter how much he pleaded and begged for him to see her, to see the flies, to even *hear* the flies. Maybe the Dalva was his real home. Maybe he passed outside its doors once or twice a day, going right back to the darkness inside. Maybe it comforted him. Maybe it would comfort Nathan someday, too.

The man's eyes squinted and his mouth became a thin line. "There ain't no one here. No one but you and me, boy."

Nathan nodded despairingly and cast a glance back over his shoulder. But there she was, lying beside the tracks neat as you please, and blood had started pooling out of both halves of her, shiny and black and fresh, as if whatever terrible accident or act of violence that separated her without consideration for life or neatness had just that moment occurred.

"I suppose you're right," Nathan said dimly.

"You're a little young for the DTs," the man said.

"What are the DTs?"

"Delirium tremens," the man said proudly. "Confusion." He grinned, revealing a passel of missing teeth. Those that did remain were yellow and stumpy. But it was a pleasant and sunny smile, and so Nathan took a step nearer to him, casting another glance as he did at the dead woman bleeding out beside the tracks. Maybe she'd gotten bored with the antiques, he thought. Gallows humor, but he couldn't stop himself.

"Comes from the generous imbibing of alcohol," the man sang. "Oh, too much alcohol, don'tcha know. You probably shouldn't play down here," the man said.

Nathan raised an eyebrow. *Play? Of course, yes; I came down here to play. The last day for playing, and then we're grown up. Just like what Logan and I talked about: one last day and then we get to be adults. We are allowed. They gave us paper certificates and everything; we wore hats.*

"Even in the middle of the day," the man said, "it ain't safe. Garden City ain't the way it used to be. I grew up here, you know, and it's just not the same. No one's *safe* anymore."

"I suppose not," Nathan said.

"Makes me sad sometimes. I don't know what you think of me and I guess I don't care. But I'm telling you, boy, once upon a time Garden City was fresh, it was *nice*, and the people were nice, too. They *cared*. They gave a damn!" He shook his head sadly.

Valley of Ghosts, Nathan thought. *Murders, cannibalism. The drinking of human blood.*

"Now we're getting bigger all the time, just growing and growing. Progress, they call it. Sad bullshit, I call it."

Sacrifice.

"That's what happens, though," Nathan said. "You can't stop it."

"No." The man sighed. "You certainly can't. Or I can't. That's why I like it in there." He jerked a thumb in the direction of the Dalva. "I'm actually part of the problem. Came out here to take a piss, you believe that happy crappy?" He grinned, and Nathan grinned back; he felt that he could do little else. "Just because the john was occupado. I'm not a patient man. So I came out here to take a leak and found you. You wouldn't think it, would you, but not many people come down this street anymore."

"I was thinking about going into the antique mall."

"Good luck," the man said, squinting at him. "Can't you read, kid? That place closed up shop a long damn time ago."

"Oh." He felt a strange kind of dismay. *Don't be stupid*, he hissed at himself. The past was the past, and time marched on. *Blah blah bullshit platitudes blah.* Just because he'd never bothered to go back doesn't mean it would stay open just for him. It was dead, just as dead as that sad woman behind him.

He dared a look and there she was; more flies had gathered on her corpse. Both of her wounds throbbed with them, and the somnolent buzz as the flies did their work grew louder.

"It's too bad," the man said. "Antique mall used to be real nice. 'Course, they'd never let someone like me in there, not for long. All those little knickknacks and such, and me, hell, I'm like a goddamn bull in a china shop half the time. But I suppose they thought I'd steal something. I wouldn't. I'm pretty sure I wouldn't, but you never know." The man shook his head sagely, then reached into his pocket and pulled out a can of Copenhagen and deposited a fat wad into his lower lip. "Shit," he said reflectively. "Whole damn town's gone to hell."

"And you really don't see her," Nathan said tentatively, then, inspired, "Or hear them? Those flies?"

"'Course I hear the flies," the man said. "I'm drunk, not deaf, kid."

Horror and relief washed over him simultaneously. He looked again and saw a dog had appeared at the woman's side, a small gray mongrel with ribs like slats protruding from his thinning hide, and the dog was sniffing about the woman's face.

"Oh Jesus," Nathan said through numb lips.

"You crazy, son?" the man said, cocking his head. "I'm not trying to be an asshole, but maybe that's why you come down here?"

"I'm not sure," Nathan whispered. "I've never been sure, to be honest."

He couldn't tear his eyes away from the spectacle before him. The dog, growling, lunged forward and sank its fangs into the place just below the dead woman's staring eyes, covering her face with its mouth. It shook its head in an angry frenzy.

"Ghosts," the man said sagely. "Haunts. You read something about Railway Mary, came down to see if it was all true."

"Railway Mary," Nathan said, as if tasting the words. That rang some bells, didn't it? He closed his eyes, but he could still hear the dog at its savage work. It hadn't scared away the flies; they continued to buzz and clack and chew, even when it snapped at them with bloody jaws. Vomit rose into the recesses of his mouth, peach flavored and bilious. "Tell me about her," he said.

"That sad woman. We didn't really know her name, or what to call her, because we only seen her just the once. She came into the Dalva one night—hell, this was twenty years ago or some such—but she came waltzing inside one hot night, just like this one, with her fancy red dress and her fancy red shoes and her hair all did up, but you could tell she was a lonely thing, and she just drank and danced and drank and danced. I didn't pay too much attention to her, but I did dance with her. Just once. Didn't exchange no words. But one minute she was there and the next she was gone, and we didn't see her again until Mike O'Shea, a real sweet feller who used to own this place, came out to close up and found her there." The old man pointed at the place where the dog continued its ferocious repast and the flies sang in their hellish chorus. "Lying there beside the train tracks. Well," he said unhappily, "she'd been cut in two, but they never figured out how or why and they never caught nobody and never even learned her name. So we called her Railway Mary, and sometimes people say they seen her walking beside the tracks or standing in the shadows of the alley. Horseshit. What's a sad little bitch like that got to do with haunting a bar, I'd like to know?"

"Maybe she doesn't know any better," Nathan said. The dog was gone, but the woman remained. Her face was a mess of yellow and red and black and white. But her arms twitched and shivered; her fingers reached and clawed at the dirt, pulling her torso, and he understood then what she wanted.

"I don't believe in ghosts," the man said stoutly. "And I should! I know enough dead folks. Like dear old Mike O'Shea. Christ, what a man. Ran this place for nearly fifty years. Never had a cruel word for no one. Let me sleep in the back nights when it was too cold to walk home, or when the snow was too deep. What a man."

The woman's scrabbling hands succeeded in dragging her torso, still bedecked with its shroud of flies, through the dirt, until it met her sternum and legs, then *pressed* until they came together with a thick, wet, slapping sound. Her hands beat at the ground in a mad tattoo, and her entire body trembled and thrashed; her head lashed from side to side with no face and no eyes to see, but her mouth gaped open and revealed those terrible shards of bone Nathan remembered so vividly from their previous encounter. A sound came out of her then: that familiar, dreadful squeal of triumph.

"I have to go," Nathan said. The sweat dripping down his forehead and his back and the crack of his ass was deadly cold. His hands clenched and unclenched, and he thought about Seb, about how he'd kept them away, just like he said he would. Except there at the end he fell down on the job.

It was up to Nathan now. He thought of Seb mournfully. *I wish I wish, oh Seb oh.*

"I'm sorry, really, very sorry, but I have to go," he said to the man, smiling idiotically.

The man blinked at him. "I didn't mean to upset you, kid. It's just a story."

"No," Nathan said, "it's not that. It's just—"

He turned and uttered a small, hysterical jag of laughter, because the woman was standing, tall and ghastly purple-green, her face a ruined wound and the flies covering her nakedness in a writhing black gown. Though she swayed slightly, her head turned until it found him. She squealed again with delight.

The man's eyes widened. "Do you hear something?" he said, his voice a whisper made harsh with fear.

"Nope," Nathan said. Only the buzz of the flies and the dead woman's cries, he wanted to say, and he giggled again. That sad dead woman who's got no eyes.

"I do," the man whispered. His face was white as cheese. "I smell something, too."

Got no eyes, dog ate her eyes.

"Nope, nope, you're wrong," Nathan sang. "Railway Mary is just for me, just for me," and there she was, inches away and reaching for him again with her fingers nothing but the tips of bones. He screamed laughter into her ruined face, and he touched her and his hands burned icy cold when they met her flesh, because she was real, she wasn't ectoplasm or a simple ha'ant, as the old man would have said, and anyway, there went the old man now, backing away from Nathan slowly, as if Nathan were dangerous. And he supposed he was. But as he backed away, just before his back met the door of the Dalva, Nathan was sure he *did* see something, more than just a crazy teenage boy dancing with empty air and screaming loony laughter into the afternoon heat. A hint of something, a flash, Nathan was sure, that was all the old man saw, but it was enough, because he screamed then, high and womanish, the shriek of a panther in the deep dark woods, and the front of his dirty old chinos darkened with piss. He threw open the door of the Dalva and vanished within, leaving Nathan alone with *her*. Good ol' Railway Mary, darling of the Garden City jet set, drunks, railroad men, and anonymous bisectors of women.

They regarded each other, Nathan and the dead woman, who did as well as she could with her missing face and lack of eyes or even sockets to support them.

"You," Nathan said at last. The air shivered before them; wide-eyed. Nathan watched ice crystals appear despite the crush of heat, embryos of snow, dancing dizzily, spinning in little vortexes, until they vanished. The woman swayed a bit, as if she might fall at any time. "You're here," he said shyly, "you're actually here."

Did she nod? Did she shake her head just a bit? Nathan thought she had.

"I was afraid that I imagined you. Or that I'm crazy. It's been so long, see."

Somewhere gears were grinding noisily inside cars; somewhere someone shouted a word Nathan couldn't understand; somewhere snow wasn't manifesting under the August sun and the lives of the people of Garden City ran on and on, whether, Nathan realized, they were there or not: *the machine of time and earth just goes.*

She reached for him with unforeseen speed, and he flinched away from her. Her hand paused then, and she held it in mid-air; her head cocked like a dog's, as if she watched him, confused. He saw the denuded flesh of her hand, purple and frayed, at the places where the yellowed tips of bone emerged.

"Who were you?" he said into the face of such ruination, but she didn't move. "I—"

That terrible squealing sound began again, rattling phlegmatically deep within her chest and exploding out of the hole where her mouth once existed, gaining force and volume as it went until it became a siren. Somewhere, a dog howled. Nathan, shocked and horrified, clapped his hands against his ears and backed away from her, but she came at him relentlessly, still making that dreadful squealing sound, the tearing of metal, the end of the world.

"I can't help you!" he screamed into her not-face. "Don't you get it? I don't know what you want and I don't care because there's nothing I can do for you. *Nothing!*"

Her mouth gaped; the shattered remains of her teeth jutted forward and out, lengthening as Nathan watched, becoming the tusks of some hellish, oversized boar.

"No!" he screamed; somewhere a door slammed and an angry, slurred voice yelled, "Shut the fuck up, asshole, some of us are trying to sleep!"

"I can't help you," Nathan forced himself to say through chattering teeth. "I don't know if that's what you even want, but if it is, you are fucked, lady. I can see you and that's all. Look, I tried to ask you. We held that séance. I held my own séance," he said furiously, "and none of you came. None of you bothered to speak at all. And I gave you a chance! I did! So go away! Leave me the fuck alone!"

She sighed then, or he thought she did. Some kind of sound emerged from the hole in her face; perhaps only a gust of errant stomach gas. He wanted to laugh again; he wanted to shriek.

"Go away," he whispered, and lowered his head. "That's all I want. Please leave me alone. I'm begging you. I'm begging. Just go."

He dared to look up at her, then recoiled, gagging, rocking backward, buffeted as if by a ferocious, foul-smelling wind; his mind, as he went stumbling, pinwheeling his arms, was flooded with images of that night in the auditorium last spring. He could hear his friends as if they were beside him now, reciting their lines: "The fingers must touch," Derek had said. "Do it," Seb had slobbered in his ear. "Fuck, *do it.*"

Nathan screamed miserably, remembering. At that same moment, the woman lifted her head to the sky and *she* screamed, and screaming still and rising, she was gone.

Nathan stopped. He blinked; one second she was there, the next not at all. She hadn't faded away like smoke or dematerialized like a ghost on a television show. It was as if the sky were rent behind her and she, swallowed by the rent, vanished, and then the rent was healed and he was left alone.

He remembered what Roger had told him, what he had seen.

He licked his lips. The flies were still there, though, clacking and buzzing and rubbing their clever little hands together. The smell of her remained, too, thick and meaty.

"*Quelle dramatique,*" a silken voice purred in his ear. "Thank the good lord above or the bad one below we're not all such drama queens."

He shuddered uncontrollably as if an electric current ran from the top of his head down through his spine. He was standing outside the Dalva, hearing the buzzing of Railway Mary's cadre of flies, and then—

Hitch.

"It's really very simple," said the mermaid woman; the party clashed and roared as it opened its jaws and swallowed him whole again. He stood before her, swaying, giddy at the transformation into this new reality that had knitted itself up around him. Her eyes held the green of her dress, flashing and wicked, and she said, "You wanted to know. You told her. You asked. But all she could do was scream, poor, stupid, confused, crazy old thing. That's all *she* could do. Let me clue you in. They need you, baby boy. The dead, the dead, the hungry dead."

"The hungry dead," Nathan whispered. The martini glass in his hand sweated tiny crystal diamonds.

"Oh yes. Your . . . what do you call them? Deaders? Your deaders are people that died hungry."

A dreadful suspicion rose in his mind like a bubble, and then became a certainty.

"But you aren't like them, are you."

She smiled and lowered her eyes and swirled her drink.

"You're not a deader."

"No," she said, amusement puckering her lips. "I'm really not."

"You're like what Roger said. You're some kind of monster."

"Now that's a little uncouth, don't you think?" She was only miming anger; beneath her words a terrible mockery underscored everything.

She thinks this is funny, he thought angrily.

"Do I look like a monster?"

"You had animal heads before," he said, coldly. "And other things. Not . . . human."

"Your friend Roger was closer to the truth than he realized. And so was your little boyfriend. Sebastian, yes? We aren't human. We never were. But sweetie, darling . . ." Her pointed fingernails, sharp, danced across one of his shoulders.

I'm not wearing a tuxedo this time, he thought with a dim kind of amazement. *I'm not one of them, then. So what am I?*

"Don't you know? You don't need to *ask*. You *are* one of us."

"No," he said, appalled. "I'm not."

"Of course you are. We're outside. Outsiders. Yes, Outsiders, proper noun status accorded. Oh, I *like* that." Her eyes threw emerald sparks. "We are Outsiders, that's what we are, and so are you."

Nathan closed his eyes. "Let me go back."

"Not yet." She said this pleasantly, with no hint of menace. "I think it's time, darling boy, that we lay out all our cards." He opened his eyes. She offered him a charming smile. "Tarot, that is."

Nathan realized he was shaking, trembling all over.

A man with slick and shining hair parted perfectly down the center of his skull walked toward them. "Charlie!" the mermaid woman called out, lifting her glass to him. Nathan saw how the amber liquid inside splashed and foamed; perfect little details, he thought, wide-eyed, such attention to the detail of the fabric that composes this world. But who had built it? "Charlie, sweetheart, you simply *must* try this. I invented it myself. It's div*oon*."

"Divoon," Nathan whispered. His head throbbed. "I don't believe in any of this," he said savagely.

The mermaid woman sniffed. "Stop fighting us. I'm not one of your idiot deaders." She gestured about the room. "None of us are. But we see your light, as they do. You know that you have a light inside, don't you?"

"Yes," he whispered. Seb had told him so.

"There you have it! So many of us, and so few like you. And because there's so few of you, we fight sometimes, you see. We *feud*. There's a hierarchy."

Now *that* was interesting. "A hierarchy," he said, testing the word. "Made up of . . . ?"

She ignored him. "We exist outside, my friends and I; we don't often get the chance to feel things, or to hear them, or to see or to touch." Her smile became beatific, but nasty somehow, too.

What would a thing like her touch, Nathan wondered, and *how*?

"We float in and out of consciousness. For us, it is eternal blackness." Her voice grew sad and bitter at the same time. "Eternal nothingness." Then she brightened and lifted her glass. "But then there's you, and with your light . . ."

"I don't want it," Nathan declared. "I'll give it to you. You can have it. I just want to be normal."

"That's a stupid thing to say. What does that even mean? I spit on that word!"

"I wish someone would just take it from me," he said darkly.

"That's fair. But impossible. It's inside you, and it will always be inside you. And we, we beautiful monsters, whom you've made so beautiful, we love you because you make us real, you give us shape and form, and we do *so* enjoy a feel, a taste."

She raised her glass again at a passing couple, beautiful, as she'd said, a man and a woman, and they nodded at Nathan, and the woman tittered behind her hand as they passed.

"We enjoy shape and form, and we want you to stay with us forever and forever. Better us than *them*. Your deaders are stupid, as I've told you. They'll eat you."

"What?" he cried, horrified.

"Chomp chomp," said the woman, leaning in and putting her mouth close to Nathan's, then inches away his throat, "smack smack," and her mouth stretched and her tongue came out and licked all around her face before retreating. She smiled at him with perfect pursed lips that bore crimson lipstick, only slightly smudged.

"They can't," Nathan said, horror flooding his throat. He could still feel the heat of the outside world, where the Dalva cast its shadow grimly against the pavement, so hot with August's glare that it was nearly steaming. But he also saw the snow striking the endlessly tall windows of the mansion—*his mansion?* It didn't seem possible; but what, and he wanted to scream laughter, did a word like *possible* even mean anymore, especially in a place like this?—enormous fat flakes buffeted by the December wind that was merely, eternally, a clock-tick away from becoming January.

The mermaid woman leaned in. "You know that we're here," she said in a voice that was hard and cutting and thin as a knife blade. "You know that we are always watching.

"And you know that we'll come for you." She sipped mildly at her drink. "One of us will get you," she said pleasantly, "sooner or later. We'll convince you that it's our way or no way. We've been working at it." She placed her lips centimeters away from his earlobe. "Because ours is the *only* way. We'll get you, oh yes, oh *yes*. Then you'll stay with us and the party will go on and on."

"I won't let you," he said through gritted teeth.

Her eyes searched his. "You are such a lovely darling boy," she whispered, and for a moment, here and then gone, so fast that he wondered if he hadn't imagined it, he saw a glimpse of howling cold, icy wind, a hatred for him and for all humankind in the eyes of this creature, glaring at him; *filthy*, she was thinking. He could feel her thoughts, her hatred; *filthy beast*, she thought, *abominable creatures*.

Then she was lovely again, just as he'd imagined her to be. He'd given her that face, that hair, her drink, the *house*; it was him. *I did it all*, he realized.

"But you must come willingly," she said. "That's the rub. You must join us of your own free will. Why, you're asking yourself, should I tell you such a thing?" Smirk. Spark of emerald. "Because I'm confident that you will. Do you think that you're strong enough to live the life you think you want? You want to belong, out there, with *them*?" She threw her head back and barked cruel laughter.

Nathan stared at her helplessly, clenching and unclenching one fist.

"They don't want you. They won't even want to bother with you. Oh, you can be sweet, sure, and loyal, ask your friend Logan. But you can't ask Logan," she said nastily. "Can you? When was the last time you saw him? Spent any time with him? Does he always answer the phone? Does he always return your texts? Or sweet, chaotic Seb? You can't. Because they left you. They'll always leave you. Just like that." She snapped the fingers of her free hand so unexpectedly, so near to his face, that Nathan uttered a small cry and looked away from her miserably. Still she droned on and on. "All of them will leave you. It will be so much easier if you just stay. Here. With us."

He looked down at himself, following her gaze, which sizzled with emerald lightning: he was sheathed after all, he saw, in an immaculate tuxedo; golden cuff links sparkled against his wrists; his shoes reflected back his face, which was, somehow, adult and handsome in its confidence. His hair was controlled, for once, and styled neatly, shining with pomade.

"You will fail," she whispered, her lips brushing against his earlobe and sending razors of sensation dancing up and down the length of his body. "If you go out there. You aren't prepared for the real world. And you know it."

"I . . . can . . . do it," Nathan said through gritted teeth, but it was an effort. Maybe she was right, he thought, overcome with a wave of dizziness. He sipped unthinkingly at the glass he held. Gin, he thought, licking his lips; gin with a splash of tonic. Cold. Delicious. He closed his eyes and savored it. It burned in the back of his throat, but pleasantly.

She tapped her crimson upper lip with the tip of one finger. "But there's still *him* to worry about," she said, frowning. "He could ruin everything, and we need you so, Nathan darling. We've stayed at this party just for you; everyone has come together for you, darling. Oh, poo!" she cried, and stamped her heel. "It would be terribly unfortunate if he ruined it all for us, ducky, just rotten."

Confused, he said, "Who are you talking about?"

"Don't be dense," she said dangerously. "*Him*, of course."

"But who is *he*? Seb?"

She stared at him with flat eyes and a mouth grown terrible with displeasure.

Everyone was watching him. He blazed with embarrassment from the weight of all their stares. *Seb is gone, Seb will never come back; oh god, god.*

"Darling," she said, an admonition, and he understood then that she didn't mean Seb at all. "*He's* coming, but he'll need an invitation. We can all be so silly with our rules and regulations."

The party was gone and Nathan found himself sitting on an unmade bed, one of a pair of twins that had been pushed together, in a small room with scuffed floors and a low ceiling, and the single window looked out into the eye of the same blizzard that continued to roar and shriek, only now the mermaid woman wore that beautiful dove-gray suit again and her tiny pince-nez. She grinned and was severe and cold as she gripped his shoulder with one hard hand. He cried out with the pain and iciness of it, even as she spoke in a voice of swirling winter.

"He will appear to be exactly what you think you want. He'll seem to be the answer to everything. But he's worse than us. Far, *far* worse. Trust me on this. There is," she said again, and maddeningly, "a hierarchy. And you must never forget it."

"Who are you talking about?" Nathan screamed. The walls of the little room pressed in against him; the wind howled; his teeth chattered against the force of that demonic cold.

"Don't call for him and all will be well," she chanted. "Trust us, we Outsiders. We know you and we love you and you know us because you always have. You've heard my voice for an eternity. We are familiar."

"Is he like you? Who is he? What is he? Tell me who he is!" he screamed into her face.

"You don't need him," was all she said, implacable and deadly. "So don't call out for him, Nathan, whatever you do. Don't call out for him, do not, do not, *do NOT!*"

Sudden heat smote him; he staggered and nearly went down onto his knees. A sickening spike of pain stabbed at him in the center of his forehead, and he moaned. These transformations, shifts of time and place and world, were proving effective. He gritted his teeth and thought, *I will stop them; I will not be their victim, Outsiders or the hungry dead. I will not submit to them. I will NOT.*

He opened his eyes, and, as he knew he would, found that he stood outside the Dalva Bar. There was the abandoned antique mall; the dog that had chewed so disparagingly at the rotten flesh of Railway Mary watched him balefully from the safety of an alley across the street.

"Ghost dog," he whispered, and it turned and trotted away into the deeper darkness.

He knew now that he saw them, yes, Outsiders and deaders alike, but they weren't wise; they weren't knowledgeable spirits, good ghosts or even friendly, Casper, ha. They were broken, damaged by their hunger, and they thought that he could . . . make them whole again? Or had that dreadful woman been right, and he was just some kind of tasty treat?

Anger flooded him, more than the despair, and it lifted a veil that had fallen over him the moment Railway Mary reappeared, what felt like hours ago.

They want to eat me up, he thought distinctly. *Until there's nothing. Until I break apart and dissolve and there isn't any Nathan. Until there's nothing left.*

"Fuck," he pronounced clearly, *"that,"* into the shimmering afternoon heat.

A hierarchy, she'd said. Deaders, Outsiders, and . . . ?

He thought of Roger, of Roger's beloved grandmother, and what she believed.

Don't call for him and all will be well.

Deaders, Outsiders . . . and . . . *and* . . . ?

"No," he said firmly. "I don't even wanna know. I am done with this shit."

He walked with his head held higher than before back up Sprague to The Spark, where he'd left his bike. As he went, and despite himself, he thought of that final night, the last time things were really okay, when he'd let Seb go, finally, or had tried to. Time shifted then, too, he recalled, frowning as he pushed through what felt like hot, wet, invisible sheets; time came unbound and he saw things all out of order. *Seb,* he wanted to whisper, *I'm sorry. Please come back. I didn't mean it. I'll do anything.*

But that wasn't true either.

Let him go, he thought, *finally and for true. You have to let him be gone.*

He thought about that last night and closed his eyes against the sick throbbing in his temples, when they all sat together on the stage in the auditorium and reached out their hands because Derek said the fingers must touch, the fingers *must—*

10

THE AIR PRESSED down around them, and now it was clammy as well as cold. Nathan forced himself not to shiver. He wanted to see something, even though a part of him cried and wept and covered his face, and he felt absurdly like the Cowardly Lion, clutching his tail.

I do believe in spooks. I do believe in spooks. I do, I do, I do.

"Is anyone out there?" Essie quavered in her exaggerated, little-girl voice, and Mikyla giggled helplessly; they giggled together until Seb growled, "Shut the fuck up," and they did.

"Listen," Essie said, her eyes flashing and wet in the dimness around them, "you don't have to be so—"

"No," Derek said serenely. "He's right. Shut the fuck up, both of you."

But Essie only giggled again. The sound held no amusement, however, and her voice was horribly shrill, the scraping of a bow by untrained hands against innocent violin strings, and she only stopped when Seb cried, "Oh my god, would you please, *please*, shut up, you fat old *fat* bloated cow?"

Essie's giggling was cut off as if by knife and all the color fell from her face.

"Yeah, I got your number," Seb said, grinning at her furiously. "What, are you afraid that someone leaked your very worst secret? Are you afraid that *someone* told *someone* who is me and now everyone's gonna know that you run off to the goddamn potty to yak up your lunch every single day? Why do you want to hide it so bad, babe? What," he snickered, "isn't bulimia cool anymore?" And he mimed gagging himself with his finger and, again, made that terrible vomiting sound: "*Raaaaaaach.*"

There was sudden, shocking silence. Then Essie began to sob, a braying, wet wailing sound.

Logan leaped up. "Not cool, asshole," he snarled, raising his fists. It was almost ludicrous, that pose, except that Nathan knew Logan could beat the shit out of Seb if he wanted to, and Seb knew it, too. He merely sneered up at Logan, though, sitting in his place in the circle, showing his teeth.

"I thought you all wanted to see dead people," Seb said. "Thought you wanted to *make contact.*" He hummed three jagged chords, all off-key. "So let's get to playin'. No more fucking around."

"You didn't have to do that," Mikyla said solemnly, but she didn't move to help her friend, who remained where she had fallen, sobbing.

"Ah, hell," Nathan said under his breath. He heaved himself up off the stage and trotted over to the place where Essie lay in a heap.

"Get him back," Derek snarled to Logan, who ignored his boyfriend and took a step instead toward Seb.

"Come on," Logan said, fists still lifted. "You wanna hit someone? That it? It's always been that way, hasn't it? You just push and push and *push.* Fuck it. I'm done with you and your shit. So hit *me*, motherfucker. Hit me if you can."

"Stop it," Mikyla whispered. Her eyes were very round in the dimness. "You'll scare them away."

"No, we won't," Seb said, grinning. "They like it. Deaders want to feel alive, yeah?"

Nathan flinched at Seb's casual use of that word, *his* word. The betrayal was hot, sharp.

"Because they can't really feel anything on their own," Seb said. "I mean, it just makes sense. No bodies, no feeling. So they get off on shit like this. They must. They wanna feel what we feel. They're probably hunkering down beside us right now, soaking it all up, watching, and laughing."

"He's right," Derek said again. His eyes were closed. He held out his hands. "We have to make the circle again. Please."

Logan hesitated; Nathan, trying his best to comfort Essie, but feeling idiotic and slow and clumsy nevertheless, whispered, "Come on, get up. It's okay. Let's just get this over with."

She nodded, hair lank before her face, puffy and smeared with mascara, and allowed Nathan to help move her back to her place in the circle where she sat, sniffling and glaring.

He returned swiftly to his place in the circle, thinking, not about Essie, but about *them*; he didn't think he could handle seeing one of them now, with everyone here. *They've never hurt me before*, he thought, *but what if they try? What if they succeed?*

There was a part of him, though—maybe only a small part, but it was there nevertheless—that was . . . what? Flattered? That felt, god help him, *special*? Did he not feel some sort of deadly charm or attraction to it all? Even though *they* were horrifying, even if *they* meant him harm, there was something cool about the fact that he could see them. He wondered, in a daze, how that had never occurred to him before. He'd always been too terrified of them to really consider that no one else saw them like he did; sensed them, maybe, but they never saw them.

I'm not crazy, I'm not.

And this will prove it.

Let them come through, then. Let them do whatever they want.

He took a breath and opened his eyes, but only Seb was looking at him, with his eyes like slits and an unreadable cat smile dancing at the corners of his mouth.

"We seek a spirit," Derek said; his voice carried throughout the auditorium with effortless clarity. "We seek a spirit who watches and who will come to us. Are you there, spirit? Are you watching? Do you know what lies beyond this world we inhabit?"

Seb smiled his cat smile; Essie's and Mikyla's were closed, and both their faces glowed with fervency. Beside him, Logan squeezed his hand. Nathan squeezed it back.

"Spirits of the dead, those who have passed, those who walk in a world we cannot yet inhabit: give us a sign that you hear!"

Seb sighed delicately and dramatically.

I hate him, Nathan thought. *I despise him. How dare he use me, how dare he refuse me, how dare he make me feel this way for him.*

Goddamn him to hell.

Didn't matter; if a spirit came, it would be for Nathan; Nathan's body would be their vessel; perhaps that's what they'd wanted all along. *I'm special; I'm the one; I am.* Seb didn't matter, and now Nathan only loathed him more.

"Spirits," Derek continued.

"Ouch, dude, my hand," Logan said.

"Shut up!" Mikyla hissed.

"Spirits," Derek cried, his voice rising into a tenor and beyond. "Spirits, ghosts, ancestors, those that were and are no longer! Be known to us! Appear if you can! Appear! Appear! Appear!"

They sat, clutching each other tightly, and even Seb's smile had faded. The air pressed down against them, colder and colder still, and they all realized that their breath had taken form, emerging from their mouths in small white clouds like little clumps of moths that hung, suspended and fluttering, before them.

"I'm not seeing this," Logan said.

"Shit," Essie whispered.

It will be me, Nathan thought dreamily. *It will only be me.*

Seb's eyes closed; his lashes, so blond they were nearly white, lay softly against his cheekbones. His face seemed placid and thoughtful.

"APPEAR!" Derek commanded, thundering and immense.

Me, Nathan thought clearly. *Me.*

Seb's eyes flew open.

"Idiot child," Seb said, but it wasn't his voice, or even a clear approximation. It was deep, ferocious, and grated like the door of a tomb, long unused. His eyes glared darkly at Derek, who seemed frozen amid his exultation. No one moved, no one spoke. "Words, nothing but stupid words. *Mori*; *mortuum*; *vivere*; *vixitque*. You don't know *anything*." It laughed, that voice, but Seb's eyes stared forward, utterly without feeling.

"Tell us your name," Derek said, an approximation of bravado.

"I have no name," came the curling voice from Seb's mouth. "Nor do you. Will anyone remember you? I think not. Will anyone know you? I think not. I am nothing and you are nothing, too."

"I have commanded you," Derek said angrily, "and you must obey me!"

Dazedly, Nathan wondered what kind of research Derek had done for his role in this little melodrama.

Seb isn't faking.

Dear Christ, it's one of them. They're inside him now; it's one of them.

Seb showed his teeth, which seemed, in the uncertain light, longer than they'd been before. They gleamed and sparkled enticingly.

But what if it's not? What if it's something . . . different?

"*Mouri*," the voice said smugly, "*halott, shinda, mrtvi, martwy, mort, wafu, marw*." It laughed, a scraping sound. "'These being dead, then dead must I be.' Unless," and it winked in Nathan's direction, "I'm something . . . *different*."

"Did you die here?" Essie whispered hesitantly.

Seb's eyes flicked to her; they glowed, golden and luminous, and split down the center like a cat's.

Nathan thought dimly that he recognized those eyes, that he'd seen them before. Or did it mean that he *would* see them? Someday, in a future far away?

"Car accident," the voice said clearly, with precise diction, fixing Essie and holding her. "When you are just forty-one. It will be painful. The engine of your car will be pressed by necessary force into your lap two seconds after the collision occurs. You'll live long enough to feel it, I promise you. The pain will seem to go on and on, forever, before you finally give up and die." The voice grew deeper as it spoke, the crushing of vast plates deep within the earth.

"Sonofabitch," Logan said, "leave her alone, I *told* you." But he didn't move, and he didn't break the circle, and all their breath continued to hang like tattered cloth in the air.

"You love him," the voice from golden-eyed Seb said to Logan, jerking his head in Nathan's direction. "Isn't that a joke? You do. You always have."

"Fake," Logan growled.

"But not enough."

"*Faker*. Of course I love him. He's my best friend."

"You've thought about him before," the voice buzzed, "when you were jerking off. Whacking, smacking, jacking. At that moment of jack jack ejaculation. You've thought about him. And," it added glee-fully, "with revulsion. Repulsion! You are repelled!" It cackled. "Vile, despicable, foolish, vain! Repelled! It poisons your love! It saps your strength!"

Logan looked at Nathan helplessly; helpless and frozen, Nathan could only look back.

"It doesn't matter," the voice from Seb's mouth continued relent-lessly. "Because they fuck. Without you." Seb's chest was straining. "They fuck and they fuck, just they two, they fuck and they fuck and they fuck. You doubt it, little girl?" Its golden eyes fixed on Mikyla, whose face glowed chalk-white. "You know. You've known longer than anyone else. That's how it is here: we see and we know, just like you said, little faggot, little poufter. We know."

"Who is he talking about?" Essie whispered.

"Shut up, Essie," Mikyla said colorlessly. She didn't take her eyes from Seb.

Seb rocked back and forth, back and forth, dragging Essie and Mikyla with him as he went, back and forth.

"It feels good, *sooooo* good." He trained his eyes on Nathan. "Don't worry, boy. He wants you as much as you want him. Isn't that what you want to hear?" It sighed happily. "Less than a year from now. Both of you. Less than a year. In the woods. In the dark. The Black Forest. You'll go. He'll come for this one, and then he'll come for you. You'll call for him. You can't help yourself, and neither can he. He is my kindred. They will tell you not to reach, but you mustn't listen. Call for him and he will come. Oh, my boy," and he cackled, "what wonders Waxman holds in store for you. Find him. You can do it. Go to the woods and holler holler hell for him. Eyes of gold, wings, ebon, strength, air, dark, crimson, fire, flash, blood. All over the snow, all *over* it. You'll see them first, those lost boys, then this one will come." It thumped Seb's chest with Seb's fist. "Then my kindred, and finally you'll both go. Oh, poor thing, poor, you'll never be anything but *his*. The forest is black, and when you go in you'll never come out again, never come out again." The voice was rising now, growing shrill, losing any trappings of humanity. "Never come out again," gibbering, furious, "*never come out again never come out again NEVER COME OUT AGAIN—*"

Logan leaped up, the circle broken; Logan seized Seb by his collar and hoisted him into the air, the muscles of Logan's arms bulging, his face purple and savage. He lifted Seb and then slammed him down.

But no, the circle wasn't broken. Nathan blinked, confused. Everyone remained where they'd been.

"Shut him up," Logan cried, still very much sitting at his place, hadn't moved, hadn't leaped up.

What the fuck, Nathan thought dimly. *I saw it*. But they all remained in their places and no one had moved, except Seb, who twitched and writhed.

Mikyla cried out in horror. "Help him," she screamed. "Oh god, please, help him!"

Seb pulled away from her and flopped onto the floor of the stage where he rolled and kicked in spasms. They encircled him and Mikyla was crying and Essie was crying and Derek's face was white and frozen with helplessness.

Then Seb was sitting up, laughing, as if nothing had happened; they all stared, frozen. "Oh fuck, you should'a seen your faces," he said. "Aw man, you big dopes, your *faces*," and he screamed his laughter and rolled and kicked like a child.

Nathan tried to breathe. *Time is skipping around,* he thought, *time is unstable.*

Something here made it unstable.

A presence.

"You asshole," Logan said furiously. His face glittered in the dim light around them and Nathan saw with a shock like icy water that there were tears there. *He loves me*, Nathan thought with some desolation. He remembered the talk they'd had only that morning; *he loves me, he does.*

But not enough. Not nearly enough.

"Oh my god," Seb said, kicking his feet. "Oh my *god*," helplessly with his laughter.

"I don't understand," Derek said slowly, like a sleepwalker; his face was white and his eyes round and shiny. "Didn't they come? Didn't one of them come?"

"Seb was fucking with us," Mikyla said quietly. There was something deadly in her voice, some awful inevitability. "Just fucking with us."

No. He wasn't.

"His voice," Derek said. "His eyes—"

"Nathan," Logan said and tried to touch him, and Nathan couldn't help that he flinched away. He told himself he couldn't help it.

But pain flashed across Logan's face nevertheless, quick, like lightning. Later, Nathan realized that that had been the end, the true end of everything. Of the world. That exact second.

"Get up," Mikyla said to her boyfriend, but Seb's laughter only intensified. He kicked and he rolled and his face was wet with tears.

"Your *faces*," he said.

"It wasn't a joke," Derek said. "I know it. And you know it, too. Didn't you hear him? Didn't you see his eyes?"

Mikyla's foot lashed out and connected with Seb's gut. But still he didn't stop; he roared his laughter, he shrieked it.

Essie said, "Hey, didn't the camera record it?"

"Oh, fuck," Mikyla said. "Where is it?" She moved about the stage in a fury, but the camera was not where she had placed it; no more blinking red light.

The camera was gone.

Nathan felt no surprise.

Beside them, Seb's laughter dissolved, fell apart, broke into little wheezes and snorts. His chest rose and fell.

Nathan watched him and thought: *I love him. I love him. I want to hurt him; I want him in pain.*

He wanted to hold him down, put his teeth in him. He wanted him to know what it felt like.

I loathe him, despise him. He is vile. The awful burning, the pain. *Let him feel it, by god.*

Who spoke just now? Whose voice?

He loved Seb, Nathan realized sadly, but he hated him, too.

I think I would kill him right now if I had the option.

"It was real," Derek said. "Real." His face trembled and then shattered and he ran up the aisle and out into the lobby, where the sounds of his hoarse sobs filtered back into the theatre and echoed off the walls.

"Nathan," Logan said again, but Nathan jerked his head in the direction Derek had just fled.

"Go," he said. "It's the thing you have to do. You're the Derek whisperer. Go on."

Logan hesitated, looking helplessly up the aisle. He took a breath, then, without another word, he charged down the steps and followed Derek into the lobby. Almost immediately Nathan could hear the sound of Logan's voice, soothing, and Derek's tortured sobs.

"Aw, fuck," Seb said happily from his place on the stage.

"We're getting out of here," Mikyla said. "I'm taking Essie home."

"Good," Seb said. "Cow."

"Is she okay?" Nathan said.

"You shouldn't have said that," Mikyla snapped at Seb, who grinned up at the ceiling like the Cheshire Cat. "Not any of it, but especially that crap about her weight." Her eyes darted around the auditorium, taking it all in, shadows and light. She shook her head, and some dim tremor, a tiny spasm of pain, trembled across her face. "Come on, doll baby," Mikyla purred, and Essie, nodding, crammed one fist into her mouth. Mikyla led her down the stairs and marched them both out into the lobby. Nathan heard her say something sharp to Logan, heard the dire, flat sound of Logan's voice; then the lobby doors opened and slammed shut, custodians be damned.

Now it was just they two.

"Freak, freak, freak," Seb said softly from where he lay.

"Sure," Nathan said. "That fits us both. Except I see monsters and you speak for 'em."

"You talk a lot of stupid shit," Seb said. He sat up, supporting himself on one elbow. "There ain't no monsters, dummy."

"So you lied to me before when you said you believed me." He felt nothing; no rage; no ice; nothing murderous. Just nothingness, like black wings opening within him and smothering all feeling and light.

"Maybe I did," Seb said. He swung his legs around and sat cross-legged, his chin in his hands. "The dead don't come back. They're gone. Dead is dead. Don't you know that by now?"

"Whatever you say."

"Stop that shit. Fucking little parrot faggot *freak*."

Nathan smiled thinly. "I know you are, but what am I?"

Seb's gaze narrowed, then he threw Nathan's smile back at him. "They got no word for what I am. You think you're so smart. Aren't you *lucky*, little gayboy faggot, knowing what you are—"

"I know who I love," Nathan whispered.

"Sure you do, sure." Seb stood, and his muscles were coiled and deadly looking. He trained his lion's eyes on Nathan. "You don't think I do?"

"No. I don't."

All the posturing faded, and in that moment Seb looked like what he really was: a miserable teenage boy who, Nathan finally and shiningly understood, hated himself more than anyone else ever could. All that chaos, Nathan thought sadly, just to distract himself from how much hatred he holds for himself. Rotting blackly inside him, a sickness.

You make up your own reality, too, don't you, Seb. It isn't just me; maybe we're more alike than I—

"Goddamn it," Seb said thickly. He put his face in his hands; his shoulders trembled and his chest heaved.

Leave him; he's an asshole, a monster; he doesn't deserve anything from you; there is a better world, remember, and Seb hasn't—

"Seb," Nathan said softly, reaching for him, which was when Seb, grinning, Nathan saw belatedly with a shock, locked his hand around Nathan's arm and dragged him deep into the backstage shadows.

"Hey!" Nathan cried, but one of Seb's hands pressed against his mouth; one of Seb's hands worked his own belt; one of Seb's hands worked *Nathan's* belt; one of Seb's hands—

Nathan was afraid again; someone, impossibly, held both of his hands.

There are too many hands; where did he get all those hands?

Icy fingers, burning, slid down the front of his jeans and folded around his flaccid penis and joggled it, attempting to move it into tumescence, but the fingers were too cold. Another probed at the crack of his ass; another cupped his balls.

This is what you wanted this is what you wanted this is what you wanted

Seb stood behind him, his lips on Nathan's earlobe. "Come with us," he whispered. "You want to, you want us, so come, come along now."

The heat of Seb's erection pressing against him, its strength, its steel.

"No," Nathan said clearly.

"Now," Seb panted in his ear, "isn't this what you wanted? I know, we know. We've always known. Isn't this what you wanted, Nathan, Nathan?" Seb groaned and Nathan tried to pull away, caught a glimpse of Seb, his eyes a cat's again, golden and split. "He's coming for you, Nathan Nathan. My kindred, my brother-brethren-breath-breathe. He'll be here soon—"

Someone slammed into them; Nathan's head struck the brick wall and rebounded; bright flashes of light exploded in front of him, and Seb was moving, moving—

Time looped around—Nathan was sure, later, that was what must have happened—because he was seeing it again, just as he had from his place in the circle during the séance: Logan, his face purple and furious, seized Seb and lifted him and flung him out of the shadows and back onto the stage, where he struck with the doom-crack of thunder but made no sound. Seb was smiling, Nathan thought dazedly; even though it must've hurt like hell, he smiled and stayed silent.

His eyes glowed yellow.

"Do not touch him!" Logan roared and kicked Seb in the stomach.

Derek cried out, but Nathan couldn't understand the words.

"You bastard," another kick, this time connecting with the side of Seb's head, then one final time, solidly with Seb's balls, and *now* Seb made a sound, *now* he howled, ferociously.

Nathan wanted to leap over to him and kick his goddamn ugly ape face in, but he loved him still, more than ever, and maybe someday this wouldn't matter, high school wouldn't matter; Nathan would call for him and Seb (Logan? no, *Seb*) would come and they could be together after all.

He lied to me, he never believed me, never.

Out of the corner of his eye, he caught a flash of movement from somewhere back in the wings where Seb had touched him with too many hands, and there Nathan saw a line of white faces grinning out at him from the shadows. Then they drew back sharply and were gone.

"Son of a bitch," Logan panted, bent over, exhausted. Beside him, Derek stared, gaping. Seb lay where he had fallen.

The dead returned, as Nathan knew. The dead were sentient, but there existed things worse than the dead, things that *touched*, and he shuddered at the thought of those terrible ice-cold fingers probing him, stroking the sensitive skin of his testicles. He glanced down and saw that his pants were still open, that his penis was exposed to the world, that Derek and Logan must have seen. Red-faced and nauseated, he stuffed himself back into his underwear and hiked up his jeans and buttoned and zipped and belted himself back together.

Nothing, nothing, nothing could be worse than this.

Seb looked up. His nose was bleeding; crimson streams trickled from both nostrils and ran over his lips and down his chin. A small puddle had collected on the stage. His eyes were dark and human again.

Logan watched him stonily; Derek moved toward Logan, but Logan didn't look at him and made no attempt to enfold him or touch him in any way. Nathan felt some ghastly, inhuman cheer rise up inside him at this; then he felt sick and ashamed: nothing should end, he thought, why does everything have to end? Logan and Derek, and Seb lying there. *Soon we'll be done with this place, but not soon enough; will we miss it? Will we dream about it? Once it's over, will it mean more?*

"I started a fire," Seb said in a thick, choked voice. He grinned up at Nathan, and his teeth were stained pink. "Again. Remember? I told you. I started a fire again," he sang, "and again and again and again."

11

ON THE VERY last day of summer vacation, when he hadn't seen Logan and Logan hadn't called him and they didn't spend their last amazing gasps of childhood together as they had planned to, staring out the passenger side of Terry's truck ("Why the fuck do I have to take you to fucking Target? She never takes *me* to buy shampoo and shit; Christ, aren't you at fucking college *yet*?") Nathan saw—or thought he saw—Seb, or someone who looked very much like Seb, standing at the edge of the sidewalk that allowed him passage across the Sprague Avenue Bridge, which stretched over the Royal River. Seb, if it was Seb, just stood there, gazing up at the sky and the ball of sun broiling in the west where it flared in streams of purple and orange. For a second Nathan felt a stab of something—jubilation? terror? desire?—but Seb didn't move, and Nathan didn't call out his name.

Is it Seb? Is it one of them? Or, and a blade of old terror razored at him, *has Seb become one of them?*

The truck's windows were rolled all the way down and he could have shouted something or waved, but he did neither of those things. Neither did Seb. He turned away instead and disappeared, that horrible green jacket flapping behind him, off the sidewalk and down the dirt hill that led to a tunnel below the bridge that was used routinely by bikers and where transients often waited or reclined or slept. *Billy goats gruff, trolls*; creatures in the darkness that waited to grab you and pull you out of your world.

Seb vanished, was gone.

"Tomorrow I have to help you move, too," Terry said desolately, shaking his head and sighing. "Goddamn it. You know what, Nathan? Life just isn't fucking fair."

II

LOST BOYS

Drink and forget, make merry and boast,
But the boast rings false and the jest is thin.
In the hour that I meet ye ghost to ghost,
Stripped of the flesh that ye skulk within,
Stripped to the coward soul 'ware of its sin,
Ye shall learn, ye shall learn, whether dead men hate!

Don Marquis, "Haunted"

1

HE DIDN'T SEE the boy that first day, when every room and building and face blurred into a watercolor, pastel-tinged smear in his memory; but on the second day, which was better, Nathan caught a glimpse of him where he sat at the top of the lecture hall that held Nathan's first class of the morning: Theo Smith-Kingsley, all red hair (with a single wicked little curl deliberately placed, Nathan was certain, in the center of his forehead) and a strong jaw and pretty smiling mouth and exceptionally long legs that moved him swiftly from place to place. And though ultimately he didn't remember the face of the boy who actually *did* sit beside him, trying to whisper something friendly and inconsequential into his ear, Nathan eventually recognized the name, "Adam Harris," called and answered at least twice each of those first two days; recognized, yes, but, sadly, too late.

When the face of faceless Adam Harris appeared on the front of the school paper, and then again in the town paper, suddenly, as if struck by a blow, Nathan remembered him at last, poor Adam Harris, and felt a sick drop in his stomach. MISSING WAXMAN STUDENT SECOND TO DISAPPEAR, *The Garden City Gazette* blared; HAVE YOU SEEN THIS BOY? pleaded *The Waxman Warbler*, and, its byline, in a slightly quieter tone, "Waxman Student Disappears; Parents Distraught." As well they might be, Nathan thought grimly, setting the paper on his desk; you don't send your kids off to a pricy place like good ol' Waxman U only to have them vanish within the first week. Any more time than that and the university gets to keep your money.

Second to disappear? Nathan wondered Friday morning, the end of his first complete week, while brushing his teeth. He hadn't heard about the first to go, a wide-eyed, scruffy young man with the unlikely name of Piper Collins, a graduate student in forestry all set to begin his career at Waxman (*just like me*, Nathan thought uneasily, *brush, brush, brush*).

Piper had told his new girlfriend he wanted to explore the rural areas surrounding Garden City, just outside its protective valley; he'd insisted on taking his ancient and only semi-functional car, which was subsequently discovered by another day tripper in possession of a more reliable vehicle off on a side road, the glass of its windows and the chrome of its fender glinting away in the late summer sunlight. Its unfortunate owner was not sitting inside of it, huddled beneath it, or trotting about anywhere within its vicinity.

"He wouldn'ta just run off," the girlfriend had sobbed on the nightly news, her mascara streaked and her nose red and rubbed. "I mean, okay, yeah, so he said that maybe he wasn't as ready for school as he thought he was. He could'a been having second thoughts, but he wouldn't just run off like that! He went on that drive to clear his head, that's all. He loved me." Her voice caught in her throat, and Nathan felt a stab of sympathy for her. "He told me he loved me," she whispered into the reporter's microphone, "he wouldn't just *go*, not without telling me that he was *going.*"

Oh honey, Nathan thought, turning away from the girl and her eyes, swimming with misery, *sometimes that's exactly what people do.*

What had he whispered into Nathan's ear, poor faceless Adam Harris; but Nathan couldn't remember. *He was weak*, Nathan told himself, staring out the window of his dorm; *I'm not weak. I'm here, aren't I?*

Because it was exciting, wasn't it.

It's an adventure. A road that's opened before you, and maybe those other guys couldn't handle it, that's all. They vanished because they wanted to, and they don't really want to be found.

I *want to be found.*

SEARCH WIDENS FOR MISSING STUDENTS, the *Gazette* proclaimed on Nathan's second Monday at Waxman, and reading that evening in the vast, silent expanse of the university's library, he found himself frowning first, then shuddering.

If it wasn't a choice, he thought uneasily, *if it wasn't something they chose to do . . .*

Behind him, a raucous roll of laughter boomed out. Nathan swiveled to find that it originated from that slightly ruddy, now familiar face with its exclamation of red hair, sitting at a table far away (Nathan noticed, trying not to feel petulant, *Not anywhere near me*); as he watched, fascinated, a librarian with a set expression and firm hands strode over to the table where Mr. Theo Smith-Kingsley sat and guffawed and disturbed the general peace. The boy who sat irrepressibly at Mr. Smith-Kingsley's side grinned as well, and he couldn't seem to help but snicker when the librarian began her quiet though expressive harangue, her hands, far less firm, now grown into flickering birds.

Nathan looked away, glancing back with distaste at the front page of the paper. He didn't really want to read it again, but the only other option was to return to his dorm; then he remembered that his roommate wasn't there and would never be there again, so he shook his head, stood, grabbed his bag, then strode right by Mr. Theo Smith-Kingsley, who didn't look at him, so amused and intense was his focus on the librarian as her scolding reached epic proportions. But Nathan looked into Theo's eyes as he passed, even if they didn't see him, (*or*, Nathan thought, *maybe they did; it's possible, anything, I've learned, is possible*) and they were green and glinted like the glossy emerald depths of an old 7-Up bottle.

The night was chilly, even for early September; the temperature hovered in the mid-fifties, and Nathan, grumbling, wished he'd brought the blue hoodie Logan gave him before he left for Washington, probably forever. But he hadn't; so, he scolded himself, you must remain cold because that is your penance for letting him go (or, worse, for not going with him); *you will remain cold until you find someone to warm you.*

Thinking of Logan still caused a slightly-less-than-bearable spear of agony to jab between his ribs. He felt it was the appropriate price you must pay when someone you love leaves, and that knowledge, forever, that you're going to be stabbed in that single place until you just finally forget about them and then it might as well be as if they never existed. Logan was never coming back, and why should he? Logan had already pledged a fraternity and was to be initiated this very weekend; Logan hadn't met anyone worth asking out just yet, but there was maybe a boy at work he could possibly just; Logan hated biology, but it was necessary for his major so of course he; Logan was so glad he brought his car, because some campuses just don't allow cars, and maybe he; Logan was; Logan did; Logan is *gone*, Nathan thought, and dammit, there was the prick of tears that followed the stabbing, and he lowered his head so no one would see his eyes sparkling when he passed by.

The problem was that Nathan liked Waxman. He was finally where he wanted to be, the adventure had begun: he liked all the trees that ringed the campus and the little woods that grew up stoutly within its northwestern quadrant and the ornamental lake in the southeast; he liked what the other kids called "the Oval," the direct center of campus, where four ancient cobblestone paths led directly, unerringly, to an enormous stone cap embossed with an interlocking W and U that reminded Nathan of some occult symbol. He enjoyed the shape of the buildings, most of them over a century old; he could sense the workings of the past within them, tumbling forever like the same old waterfall, then returning to the start just to fall once more. He figured that if he looked hard enough, if he wasn't so afraid to do it, he would see them, all those students and professors and even the Indians who had warred with each other in the valley, like Roger said, long ago: all the people who had ever dared to exist in this place, walking here and there or striking someone or something, laughing and running or falling from high windows, dashing down paths only to disappear into the dark woods, or hunting, hunting. They're all here, Nathan thought as he walked back to his dorm, still; all you have to do is look for them. But he didn't want to look; as he knew from experience, if he looked he might *see*.

The transition from high school to college hadn't been smooth, even though not a single deader had appeared in over a month, not since his encounter with Railway Mary. His mother finally succeeded in stimulating the packing process, which Nathan had resisted since long before graduation. At last she convinced him to throw the possessions he wanted to keep ("Because we're getting rid of the rest," she said firmly; "This house is not a storage locker") into boxes that he carried heavily from his bedroom to a truck his father had rented for the purpose of moving Nathan across town and into the dorm and up onto the seventh floor; "Are you sure you don't want this?" his mother asked him, holding up a book or a polo shirt or some stuffed animal from childhood, and, considering, Nathan always shook his head, and she would sigh and throw the offending item into a white garbage bag and he knew he would never see it again. *I will buy new clothes*, he'd told himself (but not her); *I will buy new shirts and jeans and better shoes and a colorful bag that I will fill with books and notebooks and three thousand pens and I will chew on the lids while I'm waiting to take down notes recounting what my professors profess; these,* he thought smugly, *are the things I will do, and soon.*

His room, at last, was pitifully empty the day he left it, theoretically, forever; only the bed remained, the bedding stripped and packed so Nathan could take it away to college. Now it was covered with an ugly brown quilt which looked like a giant brown spider crouching in the corner of this room that was no longer his. He wished he could just smash it to hell; he hadn't spoken to Seb all summer long.

We never fixed the cracks the dead guy left on my window. They'll be there forever. Evidence that no longer matters. Useless proof.

Fuck Seb. Fuck him to hell.

The drive to the Waxman campus seemed to take much longer than it should have. They had dined, the four of them, as a family, all together for the first time since April, at a truck stop café at the edge of town his father favored for a reason none of the rest of them could fathom. Nathan munched slowly on a grilled cheese sandwich, which he dipped from time to time in ketchup, but it didn't create taste, and the lump of bread and cheese in his mouth was thick and wet and tasted like cardboard.

The sky outside that day had been a deep and flawless blue, a beautiful day in early September that no clouds dared stain. He tried to eat his gluey sandwich, he tried to smile at his mother, who had begun to cry that morning and continued, off and on, through-out the rest of the day; his brother remained uncomfortable and exchanged constant uncomfortable looks with their father.

"He isn't dead," Nathan's father said at last, with considerable irritation, and loudly enough that the family at the table beside theirs stopped eating and looked at them, wide-eyed and bovine. "For god's sake, he isn't *dead*. He can come home whenever he wants to. If he wants to take the bus he can take the bus or we can even pick him up. Jesus Christ, you two, it ain't like he's *dead* or something."

"I'm not dead," Nathan had whispered to himself, but no one heard him.

They deposited him on the sidewalk outside his dorm where three boys were already loitering, their faces cruel and their eyes hard. Nathan swallowed, drew himself up, took the duffel bag his brother handed him expressionlessly, kissed his mother, and half-smiled at his father. *I don't even know you,* he thought, *Jesus; hell. Fucking hell.* Then he turned around and walked past the three boys, who silently watched him go by. He thought they must be smiling, and they had started laughing (hadn't they?) by the time he made it to the front door. But it refused to open, and then he remembered that he would be denied entry until he scanned his brand-new student ID card, so of course they laughed. Why wouldn't they? Nathan would have been the first to laugh at some dumb kid who thought he could just walk through any door he wanted to, like he had some kind of right; he'd laugh at him, too, if he didn't belong.

His room was small, but he had expected that. Logan, describing his time with the long-ago theatre major he'd dated, had spent some minutes elaborating on the size and shape of the theatre major's dorm room, among other, more interesting aspects of that now forgotten boyfriend. But how could Nathan have anticipated that a boy would be there already, spread out on one of the beds, not a giant but close to a giant, over six feet tall, shirtless (*oh god, why isn't he wearing a shirt?*), who looked up from his phone, blue eyes flashing. He offered Nathan a wide smile, leaped off the bed, and Nathan, unable to look away, accepted the enormous paw the beaming boy offered him.

"Hey," the giant said, "you must be Nathan. I'm Barry. We talked on the phone in July, yeah?"

How, Nathan thought weakly, *how was I supposed to know he'd look like* this?

"It's hot as hell in here," Barry drawled, some kind of accent, and he shrugged into a thin T-shirt, which only served to further heighten his beautiful tanned abs. "I gotta get us a fan, unless you got one." He paused, appraising Nathan. "You don't, do you?"

"No," Nathan said. "Sorry. I should've thought of that."

"No worries. I didn't either. I took this side of the room because I got here first," and his grin widened, "and just kinda hoped you wouldn't mind."

"I don't mind."

"Sweet. Then no worries. It's tiny, jeez, don't you think? I never lived in just a room before."

"There's the rest of the campus," Nathan said. "That's going to have to do. We can spread out."

We? he thought, and felt his face turning red. He remembered, vividly and with some grimness, the last time he'd used the word "we" with another boy.

"You musta moved everything in while I was gone." He cast a squinted eye over the small collection of boxes stacked neatly on Nathan's bed. "That all you brought?"

"My folks live in town," Nathan said inadequately.

"Not me." Barry beamed. "Minnesota. Twin Lakes. Far away, but that's what I wanted. That's how I *like* it. I wanna do stuff and I don't want my friggin' parents just showing up whenever they want. Your folks like that?"

"I don't think so."

"Good. Who needs 'em?"

"Right." He allowed himself a little smile, and thought that it was hot in there; little beads of sweat trembled on his brow.

"You got a girl?" Barry said. He arched his perfect eyebrows, waiting.

Nathan blinked. "Oh," he said at last. "No. No girl."

"We'll change that," Barry said, eyes sparkling. "We'll get us a coupla girls. I'll help you, bro. You look like you could use some help, no offense. That's what I'll do, is *help*." He dropped a heavy arm over Nathan's shoulders and grinned down at him. "We are going to be best friends," Barry drawled. "*Best.*"

That night, Nathan lay frozen, able only to watch as a figure, blackly silhouetted against the window, glided across the room. His throat closed; his eyes watered; the figure was part and parcel of the darkness made thicker by the late summer heat. But he could see the white glint of teeth in its mouth, and how *it* saw Nathan watching it and raised a finger to its lips. No, he tried to choke, as the thing (*what was it?*) turned to stare down at Barry's sleeping body. *What did it want with Barry?* he wondered through his paroxysm of terror; *they've never interacted with anyone before, only me, only* me. Then he heard the rasping of its laughter, and, for the barest hint of a time, he heard a delicate fluttering sound as the thing revealed that it held itself in a shroud made of its own giant black wings, thin and membranous, like a bat's. Nathan thought that maybe he was dreaming; there were no monsters, there'd never *been* monsters; why would there be monsters *now?*

Barry, he told himself, *it wants to hurt Barry.*

He forced a hand to rise; he forced a leg to fall over the side of the bed.

The thing turned to him and he felt blasted by an incredible awareness of his own body, nearly naked, only his habitual dark jockey shorts preserving his modesty; but in that blast of heat came a creeping feeling of sensuality as well, and he moaned a little, unable to help himself.

Why, it's me, he thought with wonderment; for just a blink, the thing allowed a glimpse of its face, revealed in a shaft of horrible orange light from the lamps in the courtyard below. The features gleamed whitely and the eyes were solid, glowing yellow. It wasn't a human face, nor recognizable, but then it *was.*

Me, Nathan thought, dazed, *it looks like me.* It did, then it didn't; did, then didn't. *It only wants me to think that it has my face; I won't be deceived so easily.*

It chuckled, eyes flashing like coins in the light, then turned back to Barry, prone in his bed.

Around eleven, Barry, shirtless again, had unselfconsciously pulled down his pants and padded to bed, wearing just his boxers,

and as he went Nathan saw his penis drop out of the slit in the front
of his shorts where it hung, long and slim, poised there perfectly
between him and Nathan. Nathan, cursing himself, hadn't looked
away, hadn't even tried, and Barry, who must've, Nathan thought
darkly, *noticed*, finally tucked it nonchalantly back into his shorts
and climbed into bed and gave Nathan an obscure look.

"Well, good night," Barry had said, clicking off his lamp. Nathan,
who had never turned his on in the first place, sat in the center of
his bed and stared into the darkness and must have eventually, he
thought now through his terror, fallen asleep, only to wake with this
winged freakish thing in his room. *Their* room. He shared the room
with another boy, a *handsome* boy, he reminded himself, mustn't forget that, the owner of a big cock that just *tumbles* out of his shorts.

I have to save him somehow.

The thing was naked and glowing and beautiful in a way
that Nathan never considered himself to be; laughing soundlessly,
it loomed now over Barry. Nathan tried to cry out, tried to warn
him. Time must have jumped again, he told himself later, because
he would've remembered walking over to Barry's bed; *I would've
remembered.*

The thing laughed and laughed, now inexplicably by the
window while Nathan stood in its place, looming over Barry, the
yellow-orange lights distant outside throwing strange, dreamy shadows around the room. No, he thought, confused, I have to *save* him.
But, frozen and staring, he found that he couldn't take his eyes off
Barry's perfect brown nipples. Nathan could reach out, and he'd
never notice. He could just touch one and he'd never know; and then
Nathan saw the glitter of one of Barry's pretty blue eyes watching
him in the darkness.

"I'm moving down the hall," Barry told him a few days later
when Nathan came back to their room after his second class on
Native American literature and found Barry's side of the room completely stripped and empty and it was only Barry standing there by
himself, staring awkwardly as if caught, with eyes like marbles.

Nathan, swallowing sawdust, could only nod. Barry babbled,
or so it sounded to Nathan: "I met this kid in my psych class and
he's from Minnesota, too." His eyes gleamed, overly bright. "His

roommate's a total burnout and he's already gone so we're gonna room together this year. Nothin' personal man, but it's something I gotta do. Sorry." It had seemed that, for a second, he was going to extend his hand so they could shake, but at the last second he pulled it back, and they just stared at each other until finally Barry smiled bravely and said, "Well, bye," and he, whistling, hands crammed into the pockets of his cargo shorts, went out. And so Nathan was alone.

He didn't see it; didn't hear its laughter, nor the sound of its wings flickering against the window glass. Only I heard it; only me.

"I wanted to save you," Nathan whispered.

"We warned you," the mermaid woman told him and handed him his Tarot cards. He was certain he'd disposed of them before he moved out of his parents' house; numbly, he took them. Only now, instead of her mermaid dress or in her guise as an admissions officer, she wore the weeds of a stern matriarch, a black dress that fell and flowed around her, her hair coiled serpents, a thousand delicate ringlets. "Warned you, and you didn't *listen*," she told him severely; her hand lashed out and struck him across the face.

He watched her, one eye watering; she grinned at him. "This is the world you're making, and you've made a place for *him* in it as well, and it isn't at all sustainable. All you have to do," she said kindly now, tracing patterns on his cheek, "is call, and we'll come. Look what he's done to you already! He wants you alone; he wants you all to himself. You saw him, didn't you? So you know. Better us than *him*."

"No," Nathan sobbed, "I don't want you, I don't need you, I never need you. I can do this, I can."

"But darling," she said, stroking his cheek, looking at him with something like sympathy, or sadness, or possibly love. "That's just the thing.

"You can't."

And that was his beginning at Waxman University.

2

"HE KNEW HIM," the boy Julian told him on the second Friday of the term; relieved, and even though he liked the campus itself, Nathan realized that maybe he didn't care for the classes part of college so much, certainly not as much as he thought he would when this adventure began. Now the second week neared its conclusion, and he was glad for its ending. Julian, who had plopped down on the other side of him on that initial Monday, the side poor missing Adam Harris hadn't occupied, was a thick-set boy with tiny, excited eyes and mousy hair. He seemed nice enough, Nathan assumed carelessly, or harmless at any rate, and this was the third day Julian sat beside him and so Nathan just kind of let him.

Native American Literature: the professor, a graying woman with a defiant mouth and trembling chin, appeared far below them, though her voice echoed effortlessly throughout the hall thanks to the microphone she held.

"These spirits," she intoned, "recur in several creation stories of my tribe, but you'll find them, here and there, popping up in similar tales in an entire host of other tribal lore from around the United States." Julian had turned and, embarrassingly, craned his head around so that he could peer at the red-haired boy behind them, and Nathan tried to look without looking like he was looking.

"That boy who disappeared, Adam Whatsis. He knew him, I heard. His name is Theo Smith-Kingsley," Julian whispered, "and he has more money than god."

"Out of the way, Brides of Jesus," Nathan whispered back, "I'm cutting the line." They giggled together. Below them, the professor frowned, but her lecture continued unabated.

Nathan cast another covert glance upward in time to see Theo Smith-Kingsley whispering into the ear of a girl with yellow hair and a smart green sweater that clung to her lovingly; he gave her what might be, Nathan assumed, his most wicked smile, which she returned with an equal share of wickedness. He was certainly handsome; maybe a little weak in the chin, and his mouth was set perhaps the slightest bit more cruelly than Nathan might otherwise have tolerated, and his face was spattered with brown freckles like tiny flecks of paint. But his eyes were, after all, that delicious bottle-green, and they flashed in the dim autumn light thinned by the clouds outside, and his teeth were perfect and maybe his chin wasn't weak after all; maybe his smile wasn't so cruel. Nathan relaxed.

"I've even met one or two," the professor was saying. The class chuckled en masse.

Startled, Nathan looked around. Were they talking about spirits? What had Roger called them? Something creepy; something with "skin" in it.

"Spirits are everywhere, and they're everywhere all the time. Maybe what they call 'daemons' in some literatures. According to a thousand myths, they watch us. They are hungry. Patient. They can wait a long, long time."

The redheaded boy's eyes settled suddenly on his and filled with amusement, and he stretched out his endless legs; blushing, Nathan whipped his head around to the front. Behind him, he heard Theo laughing softly, whispering something to the girl, who giggled, too, trillingly, like a delighted little bird.

"And," the professor added solemnly, "they will always, *always* come when you call them."

"You could come over," Julian said, walking quickly to keep up with Nathan after the class poured out of the lecture hall, the morning air slightly crisper, the trees ringing the Oval now tinged with veins of red and gold. "If you wanted to. My roommate is gone."

"Okay," Nathan said noncommittally. "But this guy . . . Theo?"

"We could play *World of Warcraft*."

"I'm not really into, um, video games. Now, this guy—"

"That's cool. I get it. It's just, that's what we did back at my old school."

"Your friends?"

"Uh, yeah. Friends. I had hundreds of friends. Thousands."

"Me too," Nathan said wistfully. "So Theo . . . what's his last name?"

"Or, actually, if you want, I could show you this comic I've been working on."

"Comic."

"It's more of a graphic novel, actually. I'm an art major. Didn't I tell you I was an art major?"

"You did not."

"Maybe you weren't listening." Seeing Nathan's face, Julian added with some swiftness and a flurry of hands, "Kidding, kidding. It's just this little thing we came up with back in school. Me and my friend Dave. Dave and me, we'd work on it after school. It was about this badass guy who fights zombies."

"Zombies," Nathan said distantly.

"Yeah," Julian said, his cheeks pinkening. "And vampires. He's this total nerd by day, but by night he's all leather and Kevlar."

"Black leather."

"*Black* leather. Nerdy high school kid by day, monster killer extraordinaire by night."

"Like Buffy."

Julian gawped at him, eyes wide, mouth slackening. "No," he said after a beat. "No, nothing like Buffy. Not even. I mean, Drake's a *guy* for one thing."

"Drake?"

"Drake La," Julian said, grinning with pleasure. He rubbed his tiny hands together briskly. "Drake *U.* La. The U is for 'Ulysses.' Get it? He's, like, a descendent of Dracula. We thought that was pretty cool. He's Asian, too. Dave's idea. Dave was Asian. He was the only one in the whole town. Maybe that's why we were friends, I don't know."

"Why," Nathan said carefully, and looked over his shoulder hoping to catch a glimpse of red amid the crowd behind them, a flash of Theo's autumn fire, "would his being Asian have anything to do with it?"

"Jeez," Julian said uncomfortably. "I don't know. 'Cause no one else seemed to like him and . . . and no one else seemed to like me." His voice had dwindled, and Nathan felt a pang of sympathy for him. Poor kid, he thought, poor miserable guy; came here hoping to change, and he's stuck tramping down the same old sad little path he always did.

Not me, Nathan thought, scanning the crowds they waded through; *not me at all; I'm a new person.*

"Maybe after lunch," Nathan said kindly, "I'll come over for a while."

Julian's entire face lit up.

I am different; I am new; the old Nathan would never have offered to hang out with someone so soon, not like this.

Smiling warmly, he found that he was, even now, looking over Julian's head to pick apart the ceaseless wave of students that passed by them, thudding endlessly along on the stone path they ground beneath their feet.

Some of the warmth fell away from Julian's face, and a kind of passive resignation replaced it. "I've only heard his name, that's all," Julian said, "I don't really know anything about him."

"Who?" Nathan asked innocently. He decided to be kind to Julian, and he forced his eyes to focus on the other boy as they walked.

"*Theo.* I don't know very much. Just his name."

"And," Nathan said playfully, "that he's got more money than god."

"That. Oh jeez," Julian wailed. "I wish I were rich. Don't you? Ever?"

Nathan shrugged. A wind came out of the mouth of the canyon where Waxman University sprawled and chilled them, burning Nathan's ears and eyes; then he remembered Seb and summer and heat and he quickly thought of something else. He reminded himself that he was in the middle of a conversation, because Julian was looking at him as they walked.

"I guess I never thought much about it. We weren't poor or any-thing," he said, finally.

"But to have whatever you wanted whenever you wanted it. Hell."

"Sounds easy."

"You can't just get something for nothing. Weren't you listening to Dr. LaCroix?"

"Only when I have to." Nathan yawned.

"You think he's hot," Julian said, jeering. "Theo."

Nathan allowed himself a small, mysterious smile. "Maybe. Also, are you making fun of me?"

Julian twitched. "Maybe," he said, and laughed.

"Internalized homophobia," Nathan said, wagging a finger at him. "So twentieth century."

"I don't even know what that is." He took a step away from Nathan, staring at him with some unease, as if, Nathan thought, now growing more irritated, he'll catch something infectious.

"I don't have time to explain human psychology to you," Nathan said, feeling bored and antsy and a rising desire to get away. "Or the mysteries of human sexuality."

"I knew you liked boys," Julian said, delighted. "I knew it."

"Big whoop. So you have eyes in your eyeholes. Anyway, you don't?"

"Not really," Julian said. He sounded sad. "No, I mean. I mean, I don't."

"I don't believe you." Nathan, trying not to sneer, failed, and so sneered.

Julian blinked. "Believe what you want. You don't have to be a jerk about it." Which, Nathan realized, was true, and he should know better. For a moment he felt a hot blade of shame in his chest and guts. But goddamn it, something about this kid irritated the shit out of him; actually, he was growing more annoying by the minute and Nathan couldn't quite put his finger on why exactly.

Is it because he's totally a thousand percent queer but doesn't know, Nathan wondered, *or pretends not to know; is it that simple?* Either way, it was nothing to be cruel about. If Logan were there he'd lecture

Nathan about the spectrum of human sexuality; he would tell him that there is such a thing as asexuality and bisexuality and there are pansexuals popping up all over the place. Maybe Julian was asexual; maybe he just hadn't learned yet.

Or maybe he's on his own adventure, you asshole, that's none of your fuckin' business.

Nathan smiled a little. Distantly, he thought he heard or sensed a familiar, tinkling laughter.

"But it's true," Julian was saying with a shrug. "I don't feel anything for anyone. Not even a little."

"Well, I do."

"It's probably real easy for you."

"Oh sure," Nathan said. "Real easy. Look. Most people have sex, or at least try it, chumly."

"I don't know," Julian said, shuddering delicately. "It just sounds so *gross*, all of it."

Nathan said nothing. He was thinking about how he could eat lunch alone without this poor, sad Julian disturbing him with his talk of comic book characters that already belonged to somebody else, and evincing a sexual identity that Nathan didn't truly believed fit him.

Why oh why, a sly voice whispered at him, *do you think it's your job to decide what fits him and what doesn't?*

He glanced sideways at Julian, struggling to keep up, and felt a wave of pity wash over him. Poor Julian.

What he wanted was to be alone; what he really wanted was to disappear into the crowd, to vanish there and break down, bit by bit; just a respite, a little reprieve from this smothering boy and classes and the routine that pressed around and down on him. So he allowed himself to be, once again, at the party, even though it felt dangerous and wrong, even though the mermaid lady herself, hostessing, seemed dangerous and wrong; ah, yes, the party, where he mattered and where they noticed him, his tuxedo impeccable, the air around him warm and fragrant with cologne and champagne.

"I owe you all so much," he toasted as they roared for him, as they cheered, and their animal heads didn't seem so terrible this time, not so terrible *really*. "All my friends. You don't know what you do for me, you have *no* idea."

"You're pretty," Julian said glumly, and Nathan could barely hear him over the crash of his party. "You have no idea how it feels to be *not* pretty."

3

HE HAD BEEN walking through the woods—though they couldn't seriously be called a *woods*, not compared with the wildernesses that lay just outside the little valley harboring Waxman and Garden City and their people; those were miles and miles of nothing but trees, one following the other, and would, Nathan knew, swallow you whole and you'd never be seen again—walking through the Waxman Woods that were really just thin aspens and poplars clustered together in that far corner of campus when he saw the first lost boy.

As he walked, Nathan reminded himself again to be kinder to Julian. There really wasn't a reason *not* to be kind to Julian, even if he did say awkward things and was the neediest little person he'd ever met. He'd be nicer to him. He knew Logan would.

The lamps that ringed the trees didn't penetrate the shadows as they spread, but they blazed in the distance; the woods themselves were already enfolded in darkness.

And there was the missing boy.

Nathan hadn't intended to linger past dusk. All day he'd inhabited a kind of haze since waking fifteen minutes before his 8:00 a.m. math class, in which, though still deadly dull, Nathan displayed a hitherto unforeseen aptitude. He had finally discovered the rhythm of the university, vaster and infinitely more complex than the idiocies of high school, but he'd adapted, and now he could walk without much thought from building to building until he at last closed the week like a neat circuit.

Waxman's campus made sense to him now, even the woods, where he felt compelled to go wandering during the empty afternoons (like a fairy tale he'd heard or dreamed, he couldn't remember which; "Once upon a time, there lived in the deepest, secret heart of the woods, an old old bear who was really a woman . . ."), and there he would meet a jogger or boys on bikes or the occasional couple lingering for a quick kiss. He'd never walked there after dark until now, but the day had dragged and felt, for some reason, more difficult than it had the day before.

He glided reluctantly through it all like a ghost, from dorm room to bathroom to class to class to class, and at one point, he remembered that he should probably eat something, but he didn't feel like pressing through the jostling masses of freshmen in the cafeteria (what they all laughingly called "The Food Zoo," but it wasn't so funny when you were actually *there*, everyone snorting and shrieking their laughter and devouring their food like snarling beasts, and it made him think of the party, which, though horrible, tempted him nevertheless) and, finally, turning away from the animals at the watering hole, he decided it was safer not to bother. Then *blink*: somehow he was back in his room with his head on his pillow staring at a blank white wall with no idea how he had come to be there. Finally, after an unknown length of time, he pulled himself up and slid into his sneakers and yanked on the blue hoodie Logan had given him and slipped like a wraith from the dorm. The sky was alive with plumes of red and purple; he aimed for the woods before he even really considered his options, hands crammed into his pockets and shoulders slumped, and no one he passed even looked at him.

Julian had tried to call him several times the night before, and Nathan steadfastly ignored each call. He didn't want to encourage him; *I'm doing him a favor*, he thought. *Encouraging him would be unkind.*

He received a text from Logan after 9:00 or so, and he'd answered immediately.

"Date tomorrow, wish me luck," it said.

"Good luck," Nathan dutifully replied, then he turned his phone off and watched old *Dark Shadows* episodes until he fell asleep sometime after midnight.

Waking at 7:45, he opened his eyes and found the room full of bright buttery sunlight that stung, and he observed without panic that he was in a bed in a small room with concrete walls, pressing and painfully white. *Where could I possibly be?* Then he remembered and smiled a small, dark smile and slid naked out of bed and looked at himself, unblinking, in the full-length mirror within the wardrobe Barry had abandoned and thought, *I am so pale; there's so very little of me actually left.*

But the routine, the machinery of school, pulled him into his clothes and to the bathroom to brush his teeth and then to math, where he listened dutifully and took notes; when he looked at the notes later, the numbers made sense and then they didn't, and there were doodles on every inch of the paper's margins, and the doodles were all the same thing: wide open eyes that stared, each slit down the center like a cat's.

As he passed from his final class that day, he realized he was bewildered because he couldn't remember even walking through the door of the building as he was now walking out of it, much less what had transpired within its walls, and suddenly there was Essie, pale-faced, dark eyes, as gothy as she'd been on the night of the séance. She saw him at the same instant, stopped, and a smile spread over her face like slow syrup. By then, it was far too late to turn and duck away.

"Oh my god!" Essie squealed and threw open her arms. "Oh my *god*, I didn't know you went here, holy fuck, *Nathan*," she bugled and embraced him before he could bolt.

He felt bewildered, compressed within the thickness of the absurdly heavy coat she wore.

"Nathan, you don't even *know* how *good* it is to *see* you!"

"Hey," he said weakly, released, looked around, but no one stopped or noticed, and for once he was glad. Essie seemed thinner than before, when Seb opened his mouth and spat that vileness at her (and that was before he was possessed by a demon), but she still caked on the makeup, black and clumpy mascara that clung in sodden chunks to each individual eyelash. He wondered, with some despair, if she had friends, *any* friends. Did she still see Mikyla?

Whatever happened to Mikyla? Didn't Essie have anyone to tell her not to do that to her eyes?

"This fucking place," she observed, and shockingly, spat on the sidewalk, then grinned at him. "It's *huge*. I had no idea when my mom finally made me decide where I wanted to go because I never even thought about it. I mean, right? And Mikyla isn't even going to school, lucky bitch, but no one told me there'd be all these people."

"There are," he had to say something, "people."

"And buildings. Have you even figured out where all your classes are? Because I haven't."

"It's the third week of school," he said.

"Yeah, but I don't go to *all* of them. No one makes me anymore. No one takes attendance or anything." She sounded disgusted, and the expression she made, beneath the white pancake makeup she wore spackled onto her face, was nearly ghoulish. "It isn't like school was before, so why should I go? Besides, all my classes start before nine and I just can't make myself get up that goddamn early."

"I have math at eight."

She screwed her face up even more tightly. "So gross. I can't even think about that. It makes me sick to even think about that. School. I mean, why even bother?" She giggled. "But I guess I am bothering because here I am! It's just, no one watches you anymore, no one pays any attention. Nathan, god!" She threw her arms up in the air. "Here we are! Just you and me and I haven't seen a single other anyone that I even know. It's the weirdest thing, like I'm a totally new person! 'Cept my roommate is a complete weirdo; you got a roommate?"

"I did," he said.

She arched one pierced eyebrow. "What happened to him? Shit, he's not one of those missing kids, is he? Because that would be totally—"

"He moved out," Nathan said quickly. "What's wrong with your roommate?"

"She's an art major," Essie said, shuddering. "All she does is smoke pot, and she isn't even subtle about it. *And* she doesn't share. Plus she has a boyfriend and the rooms in Windsor Hall are so little, and we're almost near the top, so it's not like I can just jump out the window because I'd *die*," and she giggled, "but I think I'm going to die anyway because they're just so gross about it. So much *humping*. What happened to yours?"

"He moved out is all." Nathan wished madly to be anywhere else in the world.

Logan would help me, Nathan thought desolately. *Logan would talk and I could just stand here and smile like an idiot and after she was gone he'd say something like, "Auditions for Thriller ended forty years ago, babe." And we would laugh together.* Nathan missed him, horribly, achingly.

"Homophobe, huh," Essie said sympathetically. "You know, I always used to wish that I could be gay. You're so lucky. Hey, maybe I'll try it. Give it a little taste." She giggled that mindless giggle again. "Isn't that what college is for? Experimentation?" She put her hands on her hips and spread her legs, sheathed as they were in black-and-white striped tights like the Wicked Witch of the Goddamn East. "I'm going to find myself a girl," she crowed, "and just stick my tongue right down her throat!"

Nathan, horrified, wanted to tell her that she'd never had a day in her whole life when she didn't know exactly who she was, even if she was just copying someone else. Suddenly he was overwhelmed with a vision: Essie as she would appear in ten years, maybe a little more; plain, no more hair dyed ridiculous colors; wide, sad eyes staring forward liquidly; hands encased in bright red oven mitts while a fat dog waddled between her legs. Children squalled and screeched somewhere behind her, and she tried to smile as she held out the pan of hot cookies she'd just released from the oven. Tears stood out in her eyes; Nathan heard again the horrible things Seb (or whoever had spoken through Seb, or what) said were in her future, dooming her, and a wave of sympathy washed over him. He wanted to help her wipe away her makeup, but gently, so gently; he wanted to aim her toward a bath scented with exotic oils.

"I dunno," he said. "I don't think so. Maybe."

"You're missing Logan, I bet," she said, and he blinked.

He knew Essie wasn't an intuitive person. *But maybe this isn't Essie at all. Maybe she really is somebody different who thinks she knows me and I think I know her but it's all a mistake and she just looks like this girl I used to kinda know but never liked very much. Maybe I should have been nicer to her,* he thought, and remembered Julian. *Maybe I should make sure that she never gets in a car again.*

"A little," Nathan said defensively.

Essie didn't pick up on his tone or chose to ignore it.

"He's dating some guy," she said, then added, "I saw it on my phone the other night. Of course he is. I don't know why you guys never hooked up in high school. I mean, he's perfect, right? And you're . . . well, you're just . . . Nathan!" She waited, and when he didn't respond, she smiled placidly. "I bet he'd save you from the homophobes, fucking Garden City, liberal my ass. You two would be such a cute couple, I mean, Derek's like still my best friend, but Logan was only with him 'cause there was, like, no other options, right?" Then, seeing his face, she added in a rush, "I don't mean it like that. Jesus, it's just, you guys were friends and all and—"

"Essie," Nathan said, "I really have to—"

"My mouth, Christ, I open it and everything I'm thinking just falls out of it. Mr. Ricketts used to tell me I didn't have to say every thought that stomped through my brain, remember that? But I just kinda do." She giggled mindlessly.

"Listen, I've got stuff I should—"

"Hey." She grabbed at him, her hands a white blizzard, flurrying at him. "Hey, Nathan, let's go get dinner, just you and me, we can head over to the Food Zoo and—"

He recoiled from the naked desperation etched deeply into the lines on her face and the gaping square of her mouth, flecks of waxy lipstick clumped on her teeth, and as he did, he felt a wave of unhappiness flare out from her. He turned away, aware that it was a horrifically awkward move and that forever afterward every interaction he shared with Essie would be tainted with that same horrific awkwardness, but his mind was filled with a sheet of white fire that blurred all thought. He moved back and away quickly through the crowd of other students passing to their dorms or the Zoo where cheap, shitty food awaited them. Essie actually cried his name, her voice echoing after him like the squawks of a big crow, and as he ran away from her, he caught the flash of a white face with that familiar shock of crimson hair atop it, but then the crowd shuffled again and he was left, gasping, a stitch in his side and his forehead drenched with sweat, against the back of a building he'd never seen before.

The brick felt cool and real beneath his fingers. He looked around wildly, but Essie was nowhere to be seen. He was alone. He retreated quickly back to his dorm room and huddled on the bed and stared at the wall wondering what was wrong with him.

The woman in mermaid green sat beside him, her ankles crossed delicately, her martini glass full to the brim, and she sipped around the olive floating and bobbing and said, "The next time you come, darling, idiot boy, you might as well just stay, and forever."

To shut her up he slid off the bed and left the dorm and found the woods ("—there lived a boy who once was handsome and who was maybe a prince and a wolf or both those things—") and then the blanket of dark enveloped everything, including him, and there stood the missing boy, pale in the dark, wide-eyed and watching him.

He recognized him from the paper and, hazily, that single day in class: Adam Harris, who had tried to whisper in his ear. But now he was flickering, glowing, his face perfect as if carved delicately from the most exquisite marble, his eyes white and luminous. His mouth opened and no words emerged. But his hands moved forward like angry owls, fluttering, and Nathan shrank back against a tree that supported him and held him with its bony branches. Watching him, standing there real and dimensional and yet, awfully, glowing and white, Nathan knew that Adam Harris wasn't just a missing boy now but a dead one.

For a moment he felt relief. He knew how to deal with dead boys, he thought; that wasn't anything new.

Then the skin of the boy's face rearranged itself, and the enormous head of a wolf sat on his shoulders, eyes piss-yellow, teeth stained and sharp. A pointed pink tongue flicked out from the thing's jagged mouth-cavern and lapped all over those delicate, deadly teeth.

Nathan, frozen, heard the mermaid woman whisper, "The hungry dead," but this wasn't the same at *all*.

Another hitch, and Adam Harris possessed a giant owl's head, with feathers gray and glossy. His hands groped at the air; his eyes remained yellow but had grown into round orbs that glared hideously.

The trees pressed closer; a gust of wind, hot and stinking, blew around and inside Nathan's mouth. He gagged on the meaty odor of death and rot that collected on his tongue and the insides of his cheeks. He choked. The world flipped so that the trees and the path lay before him, evil and white. The boy was wolf, was owl, was something horribly in-between. Branches clacked around them, and a furious roar emerged from the Adam-thing's gaping maw that grew louder, then louder, then *louder*. The air pressed hot and *stank*.

And he *reached*—

Then Nathan, whimpering, was alone. The boy-monster-thing was gone. So was the wind, but not that overwhelming stink of rotten flesh and hot, dead earth.

"I'm sorry," he whispered, swallowing his gorge, "for whatever happened to you, for what you are, god, who *did* this to you?"

He listened, but no reply came, only the sounds of insects hesitantly beginning their evening songs and, somewhere, what sounded like great wings tearing at the air.

Later, trembling on his terrible little bed, he continued to wonder what had happened to Adam. *He stared at me like he knew me,* Nathan thought, and shook; *like he knew me and hated me.* He was dead, but *different*; changed into a monster. A beast; a werewolf. A *thing*, infected.

Infected by . . . what?

Who—or *what*—had killed him?

Changed him?

And what, Nathan thought, staring wide-eyed into the dark, *does that change have to do with me?*

4

THE LAMBDA ALLIANCE, named, according to its student board leaders, for the Greek symbol of diversity, was Waxman's answer to the kind of LGBTQ group that most college campuses boasted. This one was allowed to flourish with weekly meetings and parades and big mixer dances held several times a year to accommodate those queer kids too young or unable to convincingly portray age so as to be admitted into the Pink Panther, Garden City's only gay bar.

A month of school had passed, somehow, and the dance the Lambda student board planned was Halloween themed. Nathan knew he would never be allowed through the doors of the Pink Panther, and so set his hopes exclusively on the dance, though it reminded him, uncomfortably, of high school.

Julian had told him that morning: "I'll go with you if you want. I don't mind. It's not like I'll find someone, but you should definitely go. But I don't want to go alone, so I'll just come with you."

Nathan, biting his tongue, had replied, "What the hell. But make sure you get a good costume."

Nathan had decided to go as a warlock; he'd already planned how he was going to stiffen his hair, grown longer than ever before over the past month, so that he could form it into twin horns to curve above his face, and the makeup he'd need to create convincing rope burns encircling his neck. He purchased a pitchfork, red plastic, which he thought a warlock would probably affect instead of a broomstick to soar through the October skies.

"It's getting weird out there," Keith Jackson told him after the meet-and-greet the Lambda student board held as their opening-of-the-year celebration at September's end. Keith, who was usually cheerful and always glowing, round in the face and stomach and carelessly handsome, was a senior and the president of the Lambda Alliance. The meeting took place in a too-large room in the student center carpeted in ancient, intolerable gold, nubby and wearing away in places. But Nathan found the sixty or so kids who gathered there warm and receptive, and it hadn't been as impossible to talk to people as he'd feared.

Keith proved instantly affable. He'd introduced himself and his boyfriend at the meeting's end; "A townie," the boyfriend said, grinning, "too old for him, and lecherous." He shook Nathan's hand. The boyfriend's name was Wallace; he was thirty-five and a teacher at a high school in one of the bedroom towns that grew progressively smaller the farther one drove from Garden City. They were perfect together; a couple from a magazine ad, one of the newly progressive ones, where two men could be seen romping giddily about on the balcony of a fancy hotel overlooking the ocean, or on a massive boat, sailing away together into a blissful sunset.

"It's hard to meet people here sometimes," Keith said. "I mean, in Garden City. Wall and I met online."

"Don't tell him that," Wallace said. "It makes me sound desperate."

"Wall isn't out in Burke," Keith said. "How can you be? You know Burke? You can't be out there."

"I could be," Wallace said. "Burke isn't as bad as you make it sound."

"He couldn't," Keith said confidingly, as if Nathan were the only person in the entire room. "And even if he was, who are you gonna date in Burke? So we've been together for a year and he's right. He's way too old for me." He took Wallace's hand and kissed it.

"I'm from Garden City," Nathan said. "Originally."

"That's better," Keith said. "I'm from a farm in central Washington."

"Seeing anyone?" Wallace asked, but Nathan, shyly, shook his head.

"You're a freshman, yeah?" Keith said.

"I finally feel like I know stuff," Nathan said, amused at how easily the words came, even as he was horrified by how unutterably stupid, how banal they sounded in his own ears. "Where my classes are and which ones I can skip and the perfect time to go to the Zoo so it's not packed with three million snorting wildebeests. Stuff like that."

Keith snickered and Wallace continued to grin.

"And they still haven't given me a new roommate yet," Nathan said, encouraged. "After Barry ran away with his tail between his legs."

"Pansy," Wallace said, and they all laughed together.

"Maybe he thought you were a serial killer or something," Keith said, then made a wry face. "Sorry, sorry. Too soon."

"The missing boys," Wallace explained.

"Of course," Nathan said. But I'm not him, he failed to add. *It's not me. Just in case anyone is wondering.*

"It's not really funny," Keith said. "I try to make everything into a joke sometimes. Three missing boys and that girl who was attacked." He shivered dramatically.

The girl in question, Emily Banks, was also a freshman. She'd appeared a few nights before, screaming, covered in scratches, at the front desk of her dorm, her hair streaming and mussed and the front of her blouse torn.

"He came out of nowhere!" she'd shrieked, over and over, first to the campus police and then, later, to the real police, after they'd taken her, trembling and unsteady, back to her room and given her a blanket and some hot cocoa to drink. "He had these big hands, these big *big* hands! He grabbed me with them, he had these hands, he *scratched* at me!"

Her statement included further details: the color of the man's hair (black), a scar on his face (below his right eye), and a windbreaker (blue, with a hood). Of course, everyone assumed that Emily Banks's attacker was the same person responsible for the disappearances of Adam Harris, Piper Collins, and, just last week, Will Pretty Weasel, a sophomore originally from the Flathead reservation to the north of Garden City. Every male on campus sporting a windbreaker, particularly if that windbreaker dared to be *blue*, was scrutinized with cold, narrowed eyes.

"That's what I mean about weirdness," Keith said. "Maybe your roommate—former, I mean—maybe that's what he's feeling. Suspicious."

"Maybe," Nathan said, and thought about Barry lying before him in the darkness, how his eyes had gleamed, half-lidded, and then widened.

"You going to the dance?" Wallace asked, and Nathan nodded. "We're going as the Scarecrow and the Tin Man."

"Cute," Nathan said. He tried not to smile.

"Look at him," Keith said. "Holding back his barf. Atta boy, Nate. And you're right: it is totally to barf. We're looking for a Cowardly Lion or a Dorothy. You in?"

"I'm going as a warlock," Nathan said.

"Sweet," Wallace said, amused. "The Wicked Bitch of the West."

"That's me," Nathan said, and they nodded at him approvingly. Warmth unfolded inside him like delicate petals.

It's happening after all. I don't need parties that aren't real, not when there are real parties and dances to attend. Friends, he thought, glowing. *I'm having friends.*

He sat, later that night and after the meeting's close, in the lobby of his dorm where orange Naugahyde couches were arranged in parenthetical shapes, each with a little coffee table set neatly within its sphere. He had chosen that place specifically to plow through the Hawthorne short stories due for American Lit the next class because, for once, the lobby was empty of its usual clientele whom he had begun to observe routinely with a mixture of scorn and longing whenever he returned from the outside world: boys in baseball caps and tight jeans and sweatshirts with hoods and sports teams emblazoned on their fronts or backs, and ponytailed girls in pink sweatpants or bejeweled shorts built of the thinnest material possible. They never actually studied, that crowd, but chose instead to strut and giggle or roar and demonstrate for each other.

Nathan, reminded tremulously of high school, usually avoided the lobby. But as he approached it after the meeting, he found it stood deserted, and so he retreated to one of the parentheses and sat gingerly, looking around as if he couldn't quite believe that he was alone, save for the R.A. on duty and an older girl with her tired face buried in a book roughly the size of her head. She shook her head disgustedly, lifted her book, and drifted out of the room to greener, more Nathan-less pastures. He smiled to himself as he sat, imagining he was in his own personal study, in his sixty-room mansion, where he went to be alone with his thoughts.

Just outside the room was the hectic hurly-burly of his everyday existence, his friends and family clamoring for his eye or just a single word in their direction. "Nathan," he could hear their voices echoing dimly in the halls of the great house around him. "Come out, we know you're in there, come out to us." And he smiled and shook his head sadly. *No smoking jacket for you, sir, not until you finish "Young Goodman Brown" and maybe a quarter of "Rappaccini's Daughter."*

The woods were lovely dark, he thought, pausing the story of young Puritan Brown. *Dark and deep.* Except they weren't *really* lovely, were they? He remembered Adam Harris and his monster's head glowing in all the darkness of the trees, and he shivered. The terrifying Black Forest of Germany, fairy tale famous, full of wolves and witches, yes, *yes*; dark and deep.

A shadow fell over the book and he looked up with dismay, but it was only a girl he recognized from lit class, and, lo! the same anthology that rested in his hands rested in hers as well. She looked at him and offered a hesitant half-smile, then both their eyes skated away from each other.

"H'lo," she murmured and took a seat on another one of the slippery couches, two away from his own. She immediately opened her book, revealing her own yellow highlighter and pen. He watched her, but he looked away before she could catch his eye. He frowned.

Dammit, he thought. *Goddammit, I won't be able to concentrate on anything now.*

Come out, come out, wherever you are; old sport, old bean; wilder music; the stroke of twelve! He shook the maddening siren-song away, shifting on the unyielding surface of the couch.

He studied the girl coolly, wondering how long until she came over begging the answer to some question or another. "Yes," he would tell her, "his wife *is* a witch. They're all witches, and evil. The man loses his faith for a reason, and then he can never trust anyone again because of that reason. Don't you know anything?"

But she didn't stir or even look up at him, and after a moment Nathan, cautious, rose carefully from the Naugahyde couch and drifted over to where she sat and looked down at her book until finally he was forced to make a quiet coughing noise, and then she peered up at him and gave him that awkward little half-smile again.

"Sorry," she said. "I'm really into this."

"No, I'm sorry," he said, and offered her back her smile, reflected. "It's me. I just had a question."

"I didn't hear you come up to me or anything."

"I move on little cat feet, like fog."

She cocked her head, still smiling, but confused, and he groaned inside. *Stupid, stupid.* "It's this class," he added, quickly, "I love it, I really do, but this older stuff . . ."

The girl rolled her eyes. "Hawthorne and Melville and Irving, oh my." She laughed and Nathan laughed with her. "I read most of this junk in high school, like, last *year*. What good is it to be reading it again?"

"Dunno," Nathan said. They'd read *The Scarlet Letter* in sophomore honors English, but he'd never heard of the rest, or ever been tempted to get anywhere near *Moby-Dick*.

"Exactly," the girl said, crossing her arms. "I think this is all a giant waste of time. I could read it on my own and have exactly the same experience. Don't you think?"

"Absolutely." He didn't.

"So then," relentless, she said, "what's the *point*?"

"But the professor, the teacher, I mean, doesn't he, I don't know," and Nathan dragged his hands through the air in useless patterns, "help, at least a little?"

The girl shook her head sadly. "Not *me*. I might as well be teaching myself. He's good with background information and facts. That's about it. I can find that junk in five minutes by myself. G. F. G. I." She barked a cruel little laugh. "Go fuckin' Google it."

"I guess," Nathan said, now unsure.

"He just stands up there in front of all of us and he doesn't want us to even talk or offer *our* opinions. He just wants us to write down whatever he regurgitates, and I don't seriously understand at all how it helps me. I can interpret this all just fine on my own, thanks."

"It's hard for me," Nathan said awkwardly, cursing himself for even standing up in the first place. The girl was gazing up at him now with some horrible sympathy in her eyes. "I just can't get into the words, the way they're arranged and everything. They're, um, they're thick," he said, inspired.

"But you understand it, don't you? What Hawthorne is saying?"

"Sure. We're all fucked, right?" He grinned, but she didn't grin. He felt, cursing himself ever more harshly, like a moron. Then she smiled politely, and finally she spilled her musical laughter again.

"You could say that," she said. "You could say *that* all right. Fucked, damned, evil, depraved." Her eyes drifted over his shoulder. Behind them, floor-length windows marched across the walls. During the day, they revealed the outside world in all its autumnal splendor, as Garden City's famous trees trembled and transformed under increasingly icy winds into fiery shades of orange and magenta and blithe yellow. Now they showed only darkness pressing its empty face against the glass; gibbering nothingness. Nathan and the girl saw their own dim reflections there, white oval faces and enormous swimming holes where their eyes should be.

"I'm afraid now," the girl said in a softer tone, "pretty much all the time."

"Of what?" Nathan asked, genuinely surprised.

"Things," she said, smiled a little, tugged on the frayed edge of her sweater's cuff. "Things in the dark."

"The lost boys."

"Not at all like the ones in *Peter Pan*."

"You're safe in here."

"Am I?"

He laughed. "You're safe from *me*."

"But that's the point. I'm not, though, not really, and neither are you from me. The evil is here with us. It's here all the time."

"And no one is who they seem."

"Or what."

"Monsters?" He remembered his beloved fairy tales from child-hood; *I am a wolf,* he thought dutifully, nostalgically; *I am a wolf and a bear and a witch and a boy and a bird who knows just where to fly.*

"If you look too carefully at yourself," the girl said, "you'll see it there."

"I don't like that idea."

"You're not supposed to. I'm Deborah, by the way."

"Nathan."

"I know. I heard Dr. Rossbach call your name the other day."

"I like to think," Nathan said carefully, "that *maybe* I'm not a monster."

She shrugged. "It's very possible. You heard about that girl?"

"The one who was attacked? I don't remember her name."

"Me either. Brittany or Malorie or something like that."

He grinned. "Those names are nothing alike."

She waved the words away and looked at him seriously. "She made it all up, *whoever* she is. The attacker, the attack, the blue wind-breaker, everything. The little scar, the big hands. She invented it all."

"How do you know that?"

"She admitted it. Blrgh. I hate that word: 'admitted.' Like the witch trials, when they 'admitted' that they were witches because they'd drown them if they didn't. There was an article today in the *Warbler.* Supposed to make us all feel better, I guess, but I don't. I'm just even more pissed. At her, at this whole goddamn sorry world. Y'know, when I go anywhere I carry my keys with me, especially if it's dark, and sometimes even when I'm not alone: I carry my keys between my fingers like goddamn Wolverine. Most of the girls I know do that. My guy friends tell me what I should do to prevent myself from being raped, but no one's telling the rapists not to rape."

Her face was frightening and fascinating, so bright did it blaze with her indignation, her disgust.

"Anyway, Brittany-or-Malorie burst into her faculty advisor's office yesterday and spilled the real story: that she'd made it up."

Nathan found he was gaping, but the harder he tried to not gape, the wider his mouth grew. "That's nuts," he said at last.

"Not as nuts as you'd think," she said, then added primly, "I did some research after I read about her in the paper today. This is really a common phenomenon on college campuses. It's awful, and it reinforces those horrible old ideas about the girl who cried wolf and blaming the victim and, Christ, no wonder no one reports rape. Just once I'd like to not have to worry about the possibility that I won't be able to jab my keys into some asshole's eyeballs in time, or at all, but still I'm wondering why she did it. Why make something like that up, really? For attention?"

"She was really shaken up," he said. "Was she faking that? She must have scratched herself, I suppose. To make it look more real."

Deborah was nodding. "I think she was lonely. No, I'm sure of it. And scared. Or maybe it was real for her. Maybe she believed it so much that it became real." She shook her head now. "I have a hard time believing that she's the evil one, even if she did cause this great big stir and every guy on this campus with a blue windbreaker had to hide it—boo hoo, poor them—or burned it and—"

"And we still have those missing boys," Nathan said. "No one made them up."

"Yes. The missing boys. I think we all just assumed that her attacker was the same one who caused those disappearances. We just assumed they were linked."

"But they aren't. Because she invented hers." Nathan's eyes skated back to the windows. "But whoever took *them* . . ." He looked back to Deborah. "Maybe she really just wanted attention after all."

"Nope. Too simple. I think if we talked to her, if we looked at her and her background hard enough, we'd find that she lives in a kind of fantasy world, at least some of the time. Or that she's under a great deal of stress. Hell, at this school, who isn't?" She laughed at herself, delighted. "I'm not usually an armchair psychologist. At least, not on purpose."

"Someone could say she was evil, that's what you mean. Or that there's evil inside her, maybe way deep down underneath where no one would even notice it. Maybe not even her."

"I think so. Because of this: What about all the girls who really are raped? Every girl you know, I guarantee, has a story. An *experience*.

And what about hate crimes? Did you know that a kid at this school last year told people he got gay bashed after Lambda's Halloween dance? He had tons of details about the attackers and the time and the place, was all kinds of specific, and they found out later, the police and the media I mean, that none of it happened. Not even a little. If it were me, if I were gay or if I'd ever been beaten up or attacked or something, I'd be pissed. Super pissed. Furious."

"Me too. Because then no one would believe you."

"Is that evil?"

He said immediately, "A kind."

"A kind." She nodded. "Right, a *kind.* No witches, no pacts with the devil that offend the Puritans' angry god. Little 'evil,' then. Evil with a small 'e.'"

"Pacts with the devil," Nathan murmured, trying to sound scholarly.

"I think I get the Puritans. They had all of America at their backs, those dark woods and long, long shadows. Look out there. Who knows what's outside? They didn't, and I don't either."

"Thanks, Hawthorne," Nathan said and grinned, "for a *lovely* evening."

"Heh. It's about control, though. They didn't have it. And neither do we. Not really."

"I wish I had more control. Jeez."

"So do I. So do most women."

"And gays," Nathan added. "Speaking on behalf of the gays who are me. I'd like more control. A magic wand," he said, inspired.

"Magic," she said. "Absolutely."

"I could believe in magic," Nathan said.

She smiled, really smiled, for the first time, open and friendly. "It's nice," she said with sudden warmth, "to talk to someone, *with* someone, about this stuff. I get tired of thinking about it all by myself. See? This is what I want from that stupid class."

"Yeah," Nathan said, then stopped because he had no idea what he was about to say next; he didn't really enjoy reading Hawthorne or Melville; he did believe that the professor knew more than he did. He caught, for a moment, a flash in Deborah's eyes of some incredible need, a void opening that he hadn't perceived at all during their conversation until just then.

Flustered, he took a step backward and said, "Hey, I just remembered—" and something closed up inside her, folded fast like petals that revealed a hint of what could have been beauty.

Now I'll never know, he thought. And that made him feel both relief and terror.

"Yeah," she said. That flash of something—despair or anger or longing or all of these—was gone as if it had never been, and she was merely polite. "Absolutely. It's heady stuff."

"Totally." He hesitated on his way back to his own couch, indistinguishable from hers, where his identical highlighter waited for him.

"Hey," he said, over his shoulder, "listen, thanks."

She blinked up at him, a stranger again, and he was a stranger, too, as if they'd never spoken. "Yes?"

He watched her for a minute. "If you wanted to," he said, "we could—"

They both jumped. Outside, somewhere in all that pressing darkness, rain rose up and beat itself in a fusillade over and over against the tall glass walls, which took its aggression but trembled delicately, nonetheless, against the force of the wind behind the rain. Nathan looked at Deborah and she looked at him, and then he took his book and his pen and his highlighter and walked out of the lobby and back to his room and looked out the window at the storm clouds gathered in the blackness, at the tiny white forms scurrying around below him, trying without success to avoid the sting of the rain.

5

"HERE'S THE THING," Julian said drunkenly and tittered a little.

Nathan felt a mingled wave of compassion and irritation in nearly equal parts wash over him.

Oh, Julian, you poor, poor fool. But I'll watch out for you; I swear I will. He'd recited multiple times this very litany since he'd met Julian that evening outside his dorm, continuing across the lawn, and all the way to Keith's room.

"Here's the thing," he said again, and waggled his glass. "I don't think I ever ever *ever* knew anyone as well as I know you guys." He exploded into little giggles again until tears squirted out of his eyes. "Which is to say," and he sighed, "which is to *say . . .*"

"Not at all," Keith said politely.

"Exactly," Julian said, and sipped from his cup.

Keith lived in what the university called Paladin Hall but what everyone else at the school referred to as "the Palace": only five floors, modest for one of Waxman's dorms, with sixty rooms total, but they were all single rooms and thus far beyond the means of most of the school's students, and therefore highly prized. The rooms themselves were vast. Keith had decorated his exquisitely, with colorful throw pillows adorning an expensive couch and tapestries instead of posters of popular bands; delicate crystal lamps posed proudly on tiny antique tables. Keith didn't bother to affect anything so gauche as humility, but simply handed Nathan a glass of wine held in a decanter made of the thinnest glass Nathan had ever touched, and gestured toward the couch, where Julian sat by himself. Wallace reclined in a plush chair the color of dark arterial blood with his legs crossed and a broad smile on his face.

"Listen," Keith told Nathan at the meeting the Monday before the Halloween dance. "You and your friend I-can't-remember-his-name have to come over for a few drinks after the meeting. I'm not even going to consider taking no for an answer. Just let me do a little tidying, half an hour tops, and when it's all over just show up and don't bring anything but you."

"They want us both," Nathan said to Julian afterward. "So look, you're going to have to be cool. Do you get what I'm saying? I don't want you to talk about comic books or the Buffy rip-offs you're planning or Buffy at all. Be cool, that's all I'm asking for."

Hey, didn't someone say that to you once? Maybe Seb, maybe Logan; don't talk about those horror movies, those fairy tales, werewolves, witches; don't; be cool, just be cool, Nathan.

And Julian, chewing delicately on his lower lip, had considered this request for a long moment, then said, "I'm not cool?"

"My father makes his own wine," Keith said after they were all sitting. "It's good, right?" Behind him, Wallace lifted a glass serving tray covered with tiny cheeses and slices of meat and a variety of different breads and offered them to Nathan and Julian with a droll bow of his head.

Nathan, who had shared several bottles of wine with Logan over the past few years, thought the wine was bitter, but he sipped away at it; Julian, meanwhile, took a hefty draught and his eyes watered. "It burns," he gasped.

Wallace and Keith exchanged amused glances. "It's potent," Keith said at last.

"I'm not much of a drinker," Julian murmured.

"I'm not, either," Wallace boomed good-naturedly. "In fact, I could probably get into some trouble, you two being as underage as you are."

Nathan, embarrassed, thought, *No one was going to say anything about* that; *Jesus, why does he have to ruin something so easily and so quickly?* He felt despair rise inside of him as he looked at Wallace's happy face and tried desperately to tamp it down.

"Shut up, Wall," Keith said.

"What did I say?" Wallace said, gesturing with his wineglass.

"Lots of people at the meeting tonight," Nathan said; someone had to say *something*. "More than last week."

"Thank you, Nate," Keith said with a pointed look at his boyfriend. "I thought so, too. That's how it always starts at the beginning of the year. We had a hundred people sophomore year, when I started thinking, really thinking, about running the whole shebang—"

"Stalin," Wallace observed into his glass, "Napoleon."

Ignoring this, Keith said, "—by myself, more or less, but a hundred people! Wow, I thought. Think of all that support, all those systems. Think of what you could *do*. But by springtime, we're lucky to have ten, fifteen people show."

"Five, last April," Wallace said with a sad shake of his head. "Including me and el Presidente here."

Julian, giggling, looked into the bottom of his glass and squinted.

"Here," Wallace said. He took Julian's wineglass and handed him a red plastic cup. "Just beer. But it's dark. Be careful."

Julian, sniffing, sipped, then giggled. "It tickles," he said.

"I think this is going to be a good year," Keith said with an obscure glance at Wallace. "There's some cool people showing up already." He smiled widely at Nathan.

"And the dance," Nathan said demurely. "How's that gonna go?"

"Go?"

"Are there, um, people?"

"Eligible bachelors?" Keith said, chuckling. "Glass slippers? Pumpkin coaches?"

"Something like that," Nathan said, blushing.

"Little mice," Julian tittered. "Little mice with horses inside them."

"Even if the meetings slow down," Keith said, stretching out his legs, "the dances are always big. Last year the line extended out of the Elks Club and all the way down the block."

"Happy homos," Wallace said, gesturing, "as far as the eye can see."

"Happy horses," Julian said, "just waiting to get out."

"You won't be single forever," Keith said, and he patted Nathan on the arm.

"Thanks," Nathan said. He wished that the veins and capillaries in his cheeks would freeze shut.

"He wants to know," Julian said, slurring, "if there will be a boy there."

"Julian," Nathan growled from between gritted teeth.

"One particular boy."

"Oh?" Keith said politely. "Who is it? Maybe we know him."

"Everybody knows him," Julian said to his beer. "Everybody."

"He's nobody," Nathan said quickly. "Forget about it."

"No, you have to tell us now," Wallace said, grinning. "We're intrigued."

"That red-haired boy," Julian said, swinging his glass. "That *red*-haired boy."

"Theo Smith-Kingsley?" Keith said, raising an eyebrow.

Nathan took a quick breath, squared his shoulders, then, smiling, said, "Yeah, kinda. Do you know him?"

"Julian's right," Keith said. "Everyone knows him."

"I don't know him," Wallace said.

"Everyone on campus," Keith amended. "He's rich, for one thing. Really rich. His dad invented something important. I can't remember what it was, but none of us can live without it, and his mom divorced his dad and then she wrote a novel or something—"

"Wait," Wallace said. "I know this. Marcia Smith-Kingsley?"

"She kept her maiden name hyphenated," Keith said to Nathan. "Even after the divorce was finalized."

"Marcia Smith-Kingsley," Wallace said dreamily. "She wrote that book about a girl who strikes out on her own and invents a cure for a disease that's wiping out everyone in the world, and she battles pirates, I'm pretty sure, at one point."

"They made a movie out of it," Keith said. "Last year."

"Or maybe vampires, maybe she battles vampires."

"I don't really know him," Nathan said desperately. "We just have a few classes together."

"Or vampire pirates. Vampirates. Ha!"

"He's adorable," Keith said firmly, as if that settled the matter. "That red hair isn't even ugly, and it could have been just tragic. He's lucky."

"Nathan," Julian said, "is going to leave his slipper behind and that boy will find it and they'll live happily happily happily . . ."

"We have an econ class together," Keith said. "Do we know anything else about him, though? Does he like, and this is only a for instance, say, *boys?*"

"I don't know," Nathan murmured.

"But you'll find out," Wallace said.

"I want to. But who says he's even going to be there? He probably won't even be there."

"Everyone will be there," Keith said, grinning and nodding.

"Oh, yes. Everyone goes, Nate. Everyone," Wall said.

"I saw him with a girl," Julian said somberly. "Poor Nathan, poor old Nathan. I saw Theo King-Smithsly with a girl at the library once." He hiccupped, glared into his cup, then held it out plaintively. "Empty," he said. Sighing, Wallace took it and refilled it from a bottle on the tiny card table they'd set up as a bar.

"I'm looking," Nathan said carefully, "for the one. It sounds stupid, I know. I'm a total cliché. But I want it."

Why are you talking? he thought fiercely. *Why are you saying these idiotic things? Have more sense.* The party hovered in the back of his mind, threatening, as always, to explode upward and out. He could smell ice-cold gin, that piney tang, hanging before him, just a whiff.

Desperately, he added, "Him. I want *him.*"

"The one," Keith said, and Wall continued to nod.

"Of course you do," Wall said. "We all do."

"Although some of us," Keith told him pointedly, "don't need to look anymore. Do we." He turned back to Nathan. "Besides, you never know. Maybe he's a serial killer or something. *The* killer."

"My luck," Nathan said.

"Rich, spoiled boy gets bored, whacks a bunch of people—"

"*Whacks?*" Wallace, horrified, gestured wildly. "*Whacks,* Keith?"

"Sure," Keith said, pleased with himself. "Hold my very full purse, you poor people, while I slit your poverty-stricken throats."

"Like Sweeney Todd," Nathan said, enjoying himself. "Only he kills the poor instead of the rich."

"I think Sweeney Todd killed indiscriminately. Or maybe that was Angela Lansbury. Her character, not the real Angela Lansbury. I mean, *probably.*"

"You guys," Julian said and burst into tears.

Alarmed, Keith's head whipped around and Wallace gasped and Nathan put a hand to his face and closed his eyes.

No, Julian; come on, Julian. You can do this. You can be one of them—we both can, we both can.

"You're my friends, my *best* friends," Julian sobbed.

"Julian is shy," Nathan said quickly, groping for words, for sense. Everything was skidding out of control, a car on an icy highway, *skidding—*

"But you *are!*" Julian wailed. He sloshed his cup, and beer overflowed in a dark froth and struck the carpet, where it fizzed balefully. "I never had friends like you before, not *ever!*"

"Julian," Keith said helplessly, reaching out then withdrawing. "Hey, Julian, listen—"

"We should probably—" Nathan said, white-faced and standing, but Keith shook his head and so Nathan sat back down again.

"People don't see me," Julian blubbered. "They walk right by me, and it's like I'm a ghost, and even Dave, I don't think Dave even really, you know, because I never even hear from him anymore. Oh god, oh Dave, even *him,* and then you guys—"

"Water," Wallace said, and rose swiftly.

"—then *you* guys, and here you are. Nathan," Julian said, and pressed his wet and working face against Nathan's shoulder. It was hot, and Nathan cried out, he couldn't help himself, and recoiled, and Keith looked at him reprovingly.

"Nathan," Julian said, "Nathan, oh, Nathan—" and Nathan felt helpless and trapped. *Kind. Be kind.* The chant, the litany.

Then Wallace was there with the water and Julian drank it sloppily so that it dribbled down his chin, and Nathan felt an unexpected stab of sympathy for poor Julian. They watched him, breathlessly; then he turned and opened his mouth and ejected a crimson mulch all over the carpet. Keith leaped up and Nathan cried out and Julian made a thick sound and hiccupped and then vomited again.

"He's never had a drink before," Nathan said miserably a few minutes later. "I should have said something."

"Maybe," Keith said quietly, "you should have."

Nathan bowed his head.

Wallace, scrubbing with a multitude of towels, glanced at them uneasily. "Is he going to be okay?"

"I don't know," Nathan said, still stinging from Keith's rebuke.

"I love you, I love you, I love you," Julian chanted. He drank messily the water Keith offered him.

"Hey, listen," Nathan said, later still, by the door, Julian wavering before him, his thick face pressed once again against his shoulder. "I'm sorry, man."

"Don't worry about it," Keith said, then offered him a brilliant smile. "No, really. Just make sure he gets home okay."

"I'm sorry," Nathan said miserably.

"I told you," Keith said warmly. "I already said. It's perfectly all right. No harm, no foul. I just wish," he said carefully, "that you knew him better, that's all."

"I'm . . . trying," Nathan whispered.

"He thinks you're his friend," Keith said quietly, forcibly. His eyes didn't blink. "Don't you think maybe he needs that?"

"Love," Julian said. His eyes were closed; a bubble of pinkish spit grew between his lips, expanded, then burst. "Love, love, lover."

"I'm just getting to know him," Nathan said desperately. "I shouldn't have let him drink. I would have stopped him if I *knew* what was going to—"

"I was going to ask you," Keith said, "if you would ever consider being the president. I'm graduating, you know, and I need somebody I can trust, who will take over and keep what I've built from washing away. Sandcastles," he said thoughtfully, "high tides." Then, briskly, "But I'm not so sure now."

"Who, me?"

Julian whimpered like a dog dreaming uneasily beside the fire.

"I'm just not sure, that's all." Keith smiled that brilliant smile. Only now did Nathan see how edged it was, how it could cut if he wanted it to. "Take him home. Make sure he gets there okay. Don't leave him anywhere, for god's sake. You don't want him to go missing, too, do you?"

Indignant, Nathan sputtered, "I would *never*—"

"This stain isn't coming out," Wallace called from behind them. "Sorry, babe, but I just can't get it to—"

"I'll try in a minute," Keith said sharply over his shoulder, then he turned back to Nathan. "We'll see you Friday night," he said, and his voice was cold. "At the dance." He opened the door.

Nathan, furious, felt dismissed. *Take the rabble with you, my friend, and even though we are friends, don't ever ever forget that you're the rabble, too. You can just go; hold-my-purse-poor-people indeed.*

Haltingly, Nathan said, "Thanks. I'm sorry, Keith, really. I guess I should've—"

"Yes, well," Keith said shortly then. "Good night." He closed the door in their faces.

Nathan stood there, blinking. A glissade of fury, fueled by embarrassment and loss, rose up inside him, and he considered lashing out at the door, hammering it with his fists; he thought about releasing a scream and a whole series of cleverly constructed slurs, an invective so potent the paint of the door would blister beneath his rancor. He did none of these things. He bowed his head instead, and sighed.

"Come on, you great idiot," he growled at Julian.

"I don't really think you hate me." Julian smiled blearily. "I think you must be a very good person deep inside, and that's why I love you."

Nathan considered this. Poor Julian, he thought mournfully, lost in the dark, all alone in the woods.

"No," he said quietly. "I don't hate you. Not even a little."

Julian smiled at him, a great dopy smile, and Nathan couldn't help himself; he smiled back, equally as dopy. He allowed his fingers to dance, for just a moment, across Julian's forehead, straightening his hair. Julian's eyes shone up at him.

"Try not to fall down," Nathan said, because he was going to be kinder to Julian. Stupid, dear, clumsy Julian, and he pulled gently on Julian's arm until, stumbling together, they made their way to the elevator and down into the lobby of the Palace and out into the crisp autumn night.

6

LEAVES FELL AND flew everywhere, flaming on the trees and then collecting in brown piles all along the sidewalks that criss-crossed campus. Nathan enjoyed kicking through them as he walked, enjoyed the crunching of their little bodies beneath his sneakers, enjoyed picking them up sometimes and crumbling them into dust in his fingers so that the wind could take it in a swirl and carry it away into nothingness.

The day after the disaster in Keith's room at the Palace, Nathan, knowing it was hopeless, left a voicemail for Keith: "You should call me back. So we can talk. I think we should talk so that we're all on the same page. Come on, man. Please." After he hung up, he closed his eyes and touched a hand to his forehead, knowing that every word had been meaningless.

He went for a walk after leaving the useless message; with most of the sidewalks deserted, he froze, balking at the sudden appearance of two boys standing directly in his path. They hadn't been there a second before, he was sure of it. Then he recognized them from the newspaper: Piper Collins, in the senior photo they'd taken from his high school yearbook, had grinned sunnily, eyes sparkling, while in his picture Will Pretty Weasel only glared out at the world, his mouth small but ferocious, as if to say, *Fuck with me. Go on and do it, sons of bitches, fuck with me. I dare you.*

Now they were faded, their faces washed out, completely leached of color, and their eyes held no luster. People passing by stepped around them without looking at their faces, and even though neither boy cast a shadow on the sidewalk, the leaves stirred nonetheless in the movement of their wake as they came relentlessly forward.

It's me, Nathan thought, frozen, *just like the mermaid woman said; they're here because of* me.

But these things (or boys; were they boys, still?) were different than the ones that had come before. Nathan didn't know what it meant; he didn't know what they would *do*; he covered his mouth with his hands to smother any screams that might escape. He tried to run, but they were just behind him, and now they were *three*, for Adam Harris, as terrifying as he'd been when Nathan last set eyes on him in the woods, had joined them. All three of their faces were covered in fine, thin dust, and this dust was laid over with spider-webs; Will Pretty Weasel's black, glossless hair was decorated with four dead leaves.

But even as he watched, the skin of Adam Harris's face twitched and bubbled, as if something beneath it pressed *up*; Will Pretty Weasel's furious, betrayed features shifted and bulged; Piper Collins grinned humorlessly, the bared teeth of a predator, and his lower jaw gaped, stretched, and Nathan cried out at the angry, swirling darkness he saw there deep in his gullet. A hand danced its way from the center of Adam Harris's forehead, fully formed, the fingernails ragged and torn and stained with earth, and it clutched in Nathan's direction; the multi-jointed leg of a spider, covered with fine, pulsing hairs, burst from Will Pretty Weasel's right eye socket. The eye sprayed out in clots of jelly, while the spider's leg pawed furiously at the air. All three boy-things whined eagerly, a dissonant, frighteningly canine sound that grew louder and higher. Nathan turned, tripping, to run; they reached for him; his legs tried to move, to poise him into forward motion. Then they were upon him.

Hands, so many hands, and *cold*; their faces, eager, writhing over him, *One of us*; darkness all around him and the thick stink of their rotting skin and the green-gray and moldy meat beneath it. It swelled up around him as they pressed ever closer to him and held him to themselves.

Then, one by one, they put their mouths on him.

He thudded back to his dorm an unknown time later, his body one massive ache, his head throbbing, his face dull and unable to move. His eyes stared forward and did not blink. He had returned to awareness, sprawled there on the path through the woods, with a curious young man and woman kneeling beside him, patting his cheeks, shaking him by the shoulder, and asking, their voices thin with fear, if he was okay. He shook them off, muttering platitudes, *fine, I'm okay, thanks, no, I'm fine, thanks, thanks.* Then, stumbling, he'd come out of the woods and back into the campus proper and eventually found his way, weaving, to his dorm. He knocked dully, repeatedly, a perfectly timed staccato until the R.A., red-faced and furious, opened the door and snarled, "Look, asshole, if you make me get up one more time, I'm gonna charge you," but Nathan ignored him, staring blindly forward instead, and stumbled his way to the elevator, which was, blessedly, empty. He supposed that was when he started to cry, hot tears, furious and blazing; he let them loose; inside he was glacial.

What caused them to go, he wondered, before they did whatever it was they had planned to do, those three dead and terrible boys? Did someone come along the path? He thought he remembered, just before the darkness enfolded him, a pounding, familiar sound, like carpets being waved through the air to free them of dirt and debris. It didn't matter, though; the lost boys hadn't completed their task. They hadn't hurt him. He didn't feel hurt.

Just inside. Just inside where no one can see. Where not even I can really see.

But they left teeth-marks behind. When he dared to look later, naked in the shower where he could cry and not be heard and where the water pounding against him felt almost holy, he found that his body was peppered with little red welts, on his throat, where his arms bent and flexed, on his inner thighs, and . . . on his cock. Somehow not even that had been spared.

You liked it. You wanted them to eat you all up, the mermaid woman chanted. *You even had a hard-on, my* god. Her chiming, lisping little voice sang these vile words directly in his ear.

He couldn't see her, but he smelled the gin in her drink, and the thickness of her perfume, which flowed around him in a serpentine fashion, a hint of delicious flowers.

I didn't, he told her, numb. *Please, you have to believe me. I didn't want them; they're horrible; I didn't; I don't want to go with them, I don't* really *want to die.*

Dully, he shuffled like a zombie (*don't think of zombies*, he growled to himself) and looked out the window. Far below, he could see into the courtyard, where three tiny forms moved back and forth, back and forth, pacing. Other students went out of their way to avoid them. They were looking up, he thought, and moved quickly away from the window. *Looking up at me.* The mermaid woman laughed her evil laughter. *Out there. Out there for now.*

He held himself, shivering. *But how long*, he thought, and his teeth chattered like bones, like terrible bones, *until they find a way inside?*

7

"YOU SAID YOU wanted some control, right?"

He looked up from his place at one of the long tables that lined the lecture hall where his American Literature professor held sway to find Deborah standing before him, her face calm and dispassionate. The bell would chime its delight at their captivity in a minute or so, and Deborah, he had discovered after the awkward end to their conversation the other night, regularly habituated herself in the front row, while Nathan slunk unerringly to the upper ones.

She probably thinks that Dr. Rossbach will gut her if she's not seated in the first row, he thought, feeling fiendish and quite enjoying himself.

"Here," Deborah said in that same passionless tone, thrusting a slim book into his hands. He squinted at the cover. It was a bland, navy blue for the most part, except for the letters, which were distorted and a jarring, jaundiced yellow proclaiming the title: *The Power of Witchcraft Today.*

"I thought," Deborah said, half-smiling, "that it might give you some insight into the Hawthorne."

"The power of witchcraft," Nathan said.

"Today," Deborah supplied helpfully. "That part's pretty important, I assume. Look at the shapes of the letters. They're just so big." Her lips twitched with amusement.

"I don't really know what to say."

"You could say thank you."

"I could." Now his lips twitched. He flipped through the pages but didn't really read them. "What about this—any of this—made you think of me?"

"I thought," she said carefully, "that you seemed like the kind of person who sees into things. Mysteries." She was blushing now and, empathetically, Nathan blushed back. "My boyfriend gave it to me. I think it was supposed to be a joke, but I really enjoyed reading it."

"Is it, like, spells or something?"

"Or something." She raked her fingers at her hair, wilder today than when he'd seen her last. "I don't want to offend you."

"I'm not offended."

"Oh? Well. Good, then. It was just an impulse I had this morning. I thought about what you said. How you might be a person who could use some control in your life."

"I might be that person," he said dryly. He found that wheels were already turning in his mind.

If I'd had this book last year, he thought, remembering the crystal he'd thrown out the window of Logan's car a few days after the séance in the auditorium, *if I'd known real words, real chants, real incantations, then maybe . . .*

He thought he caught a glimpse of the mermaid woman in a row far below him, but she turned her blonde head away so he couldn't see her face.

"I'm not promising that anything in here is going to actually work," Deborah said. "And I'm no witch."

"What makes you think that I am? A warlock, yeah? Isn't that the boy of witch?" He snickered. "I feel like I'm on an episode of *Charmed*."

A crease appeared in the center of her forehead. "Okay," she said, reaching for the book, "fine, I'll just—"

"No," he said, and pulled it back. "I didn't say I didn't want it."

She watched him warily, then broke into a full-fledged smile, which was sunny and rather likable. "All righty."

"I'll let you know if I turn anyone into a toad."

Below them, the blonde woman rose quickly and made her way, swiftly and smoothly, down the row until she reached the aisle, brushed by Dr. Rossbach on his way toward his podium, who gave her an irritated look, and then she was gone. Nathan watched her go, feeling icy cold as he did.

Deborah's smile grew broader. "Frog legs," she said. "They taste better than toad. Or so I'm told."

Exhausted looking, Dr. Rossbach cleared his throat and spoke indirectly into the microphone at his podium so his voice sounded uncertain and trembling.

"'Rappaccini's Daughter,'" he said, "is literally poisonous to the touch. Is Hawthorne being rampantly misogynistic?" Without waiting for an answer, he added, "No, of course not. And our titular character isn't even the stereotypical *belle dame sans merci*. She's just strictly off limits. The literal embodiment of 'be careful what you wish for.' Hands off, fellas. Even if she's into you, you must not, as Hawthorne tells us, dare to be into her." The class giggled, and Nathan, tuning out, flipped through *The Power of Witchcraft Today*. "But let's be honest," Dr. Rossbach said, chuckling. "Doesn't everyone want a demon lover? Someone dangerous, attractive, powerful? Someone imbued, by their very existence, with magic?"

"What happened to Mr. Smith-Kingsley?" Julian asked him after class as he plopped down across the table that Nathan managed to secure for himself amid the insane thronging bustle in the Zoo. He said nothing, only growled something noncommittal and continued to flip through the book's pages. "He isn't in Native Lit anymore, is he?"

"I haven't noticed," Nathan growled, and turned another page.

"I think you absolutely noticed."

"Well, I didn't."

"Okay. I noticed for you. And he hasn't been to class in over a week. Do you think he's, like, *gone* gone?"

"I don't have the slightest idea."

"I thought you'd be heartbroken."

"I don't even know him."

"Not yet. But there's the dance, right? And maybe he would've been there, right? And then you two, I mean, the *both* of you . . ."

Nathan looked coolly up from the book and said, "Look, Julian, don't you have an elsewhere to be, getting drunk and barfing on someone's shoes that aren't mine this time?"

Julian pinkened, then looked down at his sandwich. "Sorry," he said, and took a bite. "Sorry," he said again through a mouthful of bologna and Miracle Whip.

"Hell," Nathan said, softening. "It's fine. Just don't do it again."

"Oh, I won't," Julian said immediately. "I'm not going to drink anything ever again. Wine, beer, root beer, Coke—"

"You gotta keep some beverages, because, hey, necessary for living. Just take it easy next time, chumly. That's all I meant."

"There won't be a next time, I swear," Julian said, looking solemn. He chewed thoughtfully, then dared to look up to Nathan again, who had, by this time, rediscovered his place in the book. A crossroads, he thought. He wondered if that just meant a place where two roads meet. Was it that simple? Jeez, there were crossroads *everywhere*.

"Why did that girl even give you that book?" Julian said crossly. "You've been reading it this entire time."

"I'm interested."

Julian snorted. "In witchcraft?"

"I've been reading Tarot cards for years."

"Yeah, but that's not witchcraft. It's just," Julian said with glee, "*weird*. Like, weird with a beard, that's all."

"If you say so."

"You don't really think you can tell the future, do you?"

"They've always worked before," Nathan said.

"I wouldn't want to know. What if they tell you something bad? Like, that you're going to die of cancer or get hit by a car or a dog's about to bite you or something?"

"Then you could probably try to avoid dogs. Or cancer."

"That's stupid. If the future is going to happen, then there's nothing you can do about it." Then, as if struck, eyes wide, Julian said, "Hey. What if knowing about the future causes it to happen? What, then?"

"I don't do it that much anymore." Except that my cards came back to me, Nathan thought miserably, even though I threw them out. *She'd* brought them back; *she* wanted me to have them.

So you can know, icy lips had whispered next to his ear, *how completely you belong to us. The cards, the cards, the glorious cards will tell you that, if only you'd ask them.*

"But you're going to do spells now."

"Maybe," he said and waggled his eyebrows, miming satanic-looking glee.

"Conjuring? Is that what they call it?"

"A lover," Nathan said, delighted, and pointed triumphantly at the page before him. "If I can't find him by just looking around . . ."

"You should try Grindr," Julian said solemnly. "Or is it Tinder? I get those two confused."

"I've been waiting for him forever," Nathan said, idly tracing pentagrams in the crumbs Julian's sandwich left in his wake, then rubbing them out. "It's time I commanded him to come to me. And hey, would'ja look at that? Here's the spell to do it." He squinted. "Page ninety-three. 'To Summon a Lover.'"

"You'll probably get a demon."

Nathan raised an eyebrow. "Oh yeah? Once you figure out the difference between Tinder and Grindr, you can get back to me with your knowledge of demonology." Hierarchies, he thought, remembering the words of the mermaid woman when she had appeared outside the abandoned antique mall: the hungry, idiot dead, then Outsiders, and . . . what else?

And what about the lost boys? What have they *become? And why?*

Julian chewed thoughtfully. "Demon lovers," he pronounced. "It doesn't sound so silly now, does it. Not with the trees like that. Not with how the air smells. Halloween," he said, chew, chew. "Yeah, you could probably conjure up *something*, I guess."

8

HE DECIDED EVENTUALLY that, yes, the place where two sidewalks met did constitute a crossroads; "A multitude of cultures have believed since time out of mind," Deborah's little book proclaimed, "that the Devil can easily be summoned at this mythic juncture. A talented mage may command him, though he is wily and dangerous, and he will bring you whatever your heart desires. But he will also take what he wishes: always remember that sorcery turns easily on the sorcerer."

Nathan, who didn't actively *not* believe in the existence of the Prince of Darkness, felt his heart speeding up as he crossed campus at ten minutes to twelve, wrapped in his thickest, blackest hoodie, which, admittedly, helped him feel witchier than otherwise he might; a black hoodie, he'd decided, was *de rigeur* for someone about to attempt a solo seminar in spellcasting.

Midnight, he thought, shivering as he crossed the leaf-swept sidewalk. *Why must it be midnight?* Aesthetically, he supposed, it made sense. The absolute darkness, a ceiling without stars that pressed, lower and lower, drove home this point more than any other. Still, he wondered at those magicians of old, witches hovering over cauldrons or drawing charmed circles in faraway clearings, breathlessly waiting for the stroke of twelve. But now we have time zones, he thought with what he figured must be a certain kind of wisdom; smirking, he wondered, *Do demons even bother to consider daylight savings time when making appointments?*

In the right pocket of his hoodie lay a pack of matches; in the other, his hand wrapped around them still, he held four black candles, each about as thick as a pencil and no more than three inches long.

This isn't a love spell, he thought as he walked and glanced nervously around, *or a spell to make someone love you. It's to find love, him, the one.* Journeys end in lovers meeting; he'd read that in a book once. How had it turned out in that story? Happily? It must've. It had to.

Are you really stooping this low? Asking the devil for help? That voice sounded like Logan's, amused, a little exasperated. *I thought we decided the devil was, like, a metaphor or something. A symbol. The id, like Freud said.*

Shut up, Logan, he snarled in his mind. He felt a stab of loneliness and painful throbbing in the great hole Logan left in his absence. It wasn't getting better, Nathan thought, dismayed. He'd thought it would get better. His eyes burned, began to fill, and a sob caught in his chest.

I thought it would get better, but it's not.

He encountered no one, not this late and not this chilly. Why was no one sweeping along the path, hurrying back to their dorm or out to a bar? Where had everyone gone? He remembered, with the force of an icicle stabbing straight down his spine, the lost boys, and how they'd changed, their groping hands and their mouths and their teeth, and that was during the day; what would they do to him if he chanced upon them there, in the blackest part of the night, in these woods, in the so-still and secret heart of midnight?

Walk, damn you. Keep going.

Streetlights lined the paths and dropped down pools of pure white light, and he stuck to these gratefully as he hurried along. The closer he came to the woods the more anxious he grew, the more tightly he clutched the candles and the matches in his pockets, the more he cast frightened glances over his shoulder again and again. But there was no one behind him; he heard no other steps striking the concrete other than his own. The night spread still and absolutely silent and at last the path curved as he knew it would and there were the trees and the crossroads; he heaved an enormous sigh of relief and relaxed minutely.

The trees still held some of their leaves, but mostly they looked like tall, skeletal sentinels with bony arms that they positioned at the ready, now, the witching hour. Nathan looked upon them respectfully. *I'm not going in there, not again*, he thought, with one last glance around. He knelt carefully upon the frozen concrete and closed his eyes and smiled as the stone beneath him released its chill through the protective layer of his jeans and the skin of his knees and through the muscle into his bones where it froze all through him, branching out through his veins until it reached his heart and made it cold and firm and ready.

Seb kept the deaders away. That was true, I know it was.

If this worked, Nathan thought, moving uncomfortably on the icy concrete, he could get *someone* to come to him, to love him. Then maybe he could keep them away, too, whoever he turned out to be.

A lover. A champion.

Looking nervously around the darkness, Nathan knew those lost boys were just going to keep coming. And they wouldn't be content to stay in the woods, or to trot back and forth outside his dorm. They were different. They *bit* him. They'd get in. Sooner or later, they'd get in.

Their mouths. Their teeth.

"Please," he whispered.

They're different than the idiot dead, but they're hungry just the same, and they'll take you and eat you, devouring you until there's nothing left.

And he didn't want to die.

I don't want to die.

"I don't *want* to go with them," he said aloud, and his eyes stung with angry tears. "I came here to *belong*." And then he thought, glancingly, of Seb, and even of mysterious Theo Smith-Kingsley, and of the photography class he'd tried to sign up for that was already full, but, the professor had assured him in an exhausted-sounding email, would most likely have a few spots opening in the spring. A career, Nathan thought as he looked up at the sky, visible in all its

vast blackness through the crooked branches of the trees, something
to do that he could call his own, something he could *be*.

And somebody to love.

He laughed at himself and brushed away the foolish tears. He
felt like a goddamn Disney princess, the Little Mermaid perched on
the rock, singing her fishy, inhuman heart out about finding a place
to belong.

Well, what the hell is so wrong with that?

"Nothing," he growled ferociously, "absolutely *nothing*." He
shook his head, fumbling with numb fingers in his pockets until he
removed the candles and the matches. He regarded them curiously.
Sacred objects, yes. Then he tried to set them up so they formed a
square. But they resisted him and tipped, falling, over and over again.
He glanced at his watch and saw that the minute hand trembled just
before the twelve, and a wave of panic overtook him. The streetlights
threw down their white light furiously over him so that he could see
too clearly how the candles fell and then fell again and then *again* as
he tried to set them up and keep them up; how the matches refused
to light and stay lit, blown out each time by the breath of a questing
little breeze that danced its way out of the mountains.

Time, time, time, whispered by his ears, the voice of the breeze,
the hiss of the skeletal tree branches rubbed together, violins making
music for the dead, and he didn't want to think of the dead, not *now*.
What did Young Goodman Brown see in the woods, he thought hys-
terically as he regarded his last match, what did he *really* see? Then
the matchhead flared into flame and, heaving a sigh of relief, Nathan
used the wax's black drippings to anchor the candle and its brothers
to the icy, unyielding concrete. They flickered up at him, offering no
warmth.

He stretched out his hands. His mouth had gone dry; his tongue
cleaved to its roof; no words came because his mind was empty.

The wind ruffled his hair, danced over his skin, laughed in
his ear.

"Satan," he said clearly. "Beelzebub. Ba'al." He smiled; he
couldn't help himself; the words were so ridiculous. "Lord of Flies.
Donald Trump." He snickered; the wind licked at his ears and his

smile faded. His eyes flickered back and forth, but the only sound was the sound of the gods, spirits, demons, their breath held, their attention captured; perhaps their attention had been captured . . .

Spirits will hear you. They will always hear you. And they will come when you call.

"Come to me," he whispered, and his voice was very loud in his ears. "If you can hear me, wherever you are, *what*ever you are, hear me and come."

The wind hesitated; something unseen moved before him in the forest and made a sly, deliberate sound, and Nathan felt terror and an exhilarating joy rising, huge and dark and glorious.

"Come to me," he said, louder. "I want you, come to me," and the candle flames straightened, *lengthened,* and all the streetlights went out at once and closed him in a circuit of darkness broken only by the flames as they flickered their golden light.

The light of the candle flames blazed up and turned an icy cold blue, the color of dead skin, the fingers that had, once upon a time, scratched nightmarishly against his bedroom window.

There was no sound, not even the wind; whatever had moved inside the woods was gone or holding itself very, very still.

Nathan waited, shivering, anticipation dancing over his skin like electricity.

"Find him," he said. "Let him hear me." He took a shaky breath. "I want you. I *need* you. Be my champion, hear me. I want you."

He swallowed; he took another breath; he froze. Everything around him was held and silent and perfect.

Someone was listening to him. He would remember this later, when he was lying in his narrow bed, alone and shivering and grinning up into the darkness, this feeling that an eye had opened somewhere, that a face had turned massively to gaze down upon him. Someone was listening.

"I don't want to be alone anymore. I won't, do you hear me?" he said loudly, and his voice rang with power. "So find him and send him to me because I'm tired of waiting. Come to me, whoever you are, wherever you are, come to me and *be my own.*"

Somewhere he heard a sigh that might have been the wind, small and quiet and gentle and resigned.

He waited.

He trembled; every hair on his body stood up. His flesh knurled into hard little knots that vibrated with secret electricity.

Finally, after an endless, empty time: *No one is here*, Nathan thought. He relaxed by inches. He hadn't realized that every muscle in his body felt tense and bunched. Later, he would ache, even standing for nearly half an hour under the scalding water in the shower, his muscles would throb terribly.

Icy beads of sweat stood out on his forehead. *No one is here*, he thought, shaking his head, *no one was ever here, stupid*.

He saw that the candles glowed minutely with ordinary golden light. With one swipe of his hand, he knocked them all over and was plunged into immediate darkness. The moon, if indeed the moon sailed through its pattern in the sky, was hidden by the thickness of the clouds.

He snorted derisively. *Come and get me, devil, why don't you; come and get me, monsters; come and get me, dead boys*. He decided to leave the candles and the blackened and bent matches where he'd dropped them. Let someone else figure out what they meant, he thought with sardonic humor. He stood, his knees protesting and a muscle screaming in his back and he walked the way he had come along the path.

I am a fool, he thought distinctly. His hands balled into fists inside his now-empty pockets. The sound of the wind whispered through the eaves of the buildings as he passed them, rattling the corpses of leaves, and he bowed his head and gritted his teeth. *Deborah and her stupid book*. But he was the one tromping out into the darkness and the cold; he was the one who called out into nothing. Then he remembered that feeling of being watched, of being *seen*, and the possibility that someone, something, had heard him after all, and he thought again, *I am a fool*.

As he came up the path to his dorm, he saw there was a figure outside after all, tall, and though he couldn't see his face, he recognized that flare of red and gold hair under the lights and the crimson eye of a cigarette butt glaring at him in the dark. He went absolutely cold, as if he'd been thoroughly doused with a bucket of water.

"Are you waiting for me?" he said. He felt immediately inadequate and clumsy. The boy wasn't alone after all, Nathan saw with a flash of heat. He stood outside the doors of Mickelson Hall beside a young woman with dark hair who Nathan knew, in the moment before she turned her face to him, dismayed at his interruption, could only be Deborah. So it was. She smoked a cigarette just like the boy at her side; smoking with Theo Smith-Kingsley, just like they were the very best friends in the whole wide of this world. Nathan felt bile rise in his throat.

Theo's hand rested on the small of her back; their faces were flushed; her lipstick, Nathan noted, as if checking a list, was smeared.

She's with him. Betrayal; close; intense. *She used a spell, maybe, or, hell, maybe she didn't even have to do that. Don't be an idiot; straight people find each other inevitably, if that's what they want.* They *don't need spells.*

Blood rose, endless oceans, into his cheeks. His eyes throbbed in their sockets.

Straight people don't have to worry about that, do they, because odds are usually in their goddamn favor. Hey, if you're straight and I'm *straight and I'm into you, you're probably into me, too.*

He gritted his teeth. He wouldn't even think about how goddamn *fucking* unfair it all was.

He isn't the one. It isn't him. You should never have even thought it might be him.

Still, Nathan's hands remained clenched into fists. He could feel his nails digging into that soft, sensitive meat of his palms. He enjoyed the pain. He needed it to remain firm and cold and stoic.

"Sorry?" Theo said. His eyebrows, as red as his hair, were both raised. He sounded surprised. "Sorry, what did you say?"

"Hello, Nathan," Deborah said evenly. She was attempting, he was certain, not to smile.

He wished he'd never met her. He wished she'd never given him that book. "My boyfriend gave it to me," she'd said. Was her boyfriend, then, Theo?

As he opened his mouth to say something, anything, just as before, when he had knelt on the hard concrete sidewalk outside the woods, he had no words, so the three of them simply stood in their places, a tableau, temporarily frozen: Theo watching Nathan with calm, amused eyes, Deborah smiling, her lipstick smeared, and Nathan, with his mouth agape and his hands shoved into his pockets. Then, behind them, there came a soft purring sound as a chilling and delicate autumn rain began to fall.

9

THE NIGHT BEFORE the dance, Nathan dreamed that he was a witch flying high above a little town that he was certain had to be Salem, but of old; Salem, dreaming Nathan decided, was the only place for a witch to fly. He didn't soar high on a broom or even a pitchfork, which, now that he fully considered it, sounded a little silly. Without pitchfork and without broom, he simply flew, his arms spread before him, the wind chuckling in his ears, his hair grown long and luxurious and whipping around his face in that forbidden midnight wind like wild ribbons. Far below him, a patchwork quilt of tiny model trees and large, perfectly geometric yellow circles that were fields, the countryside spread out before him: it was his, and it belonged only and forever to him. They can't have it back, he thought darkly, soaring, waggling his fingers and marveling at how they weren't even a little numb despite the dark wind he cut through neatly like a shark knifing inevitably through ebon waters.

He wished for lightning and the satisfying crush of thunder that would follow; he thought of their hateful faces and their harsh words and the lies they told each other in the light of day, and how they gave and how they took. He wished their blood would boil in their veins and he wished their butter to turn rancid in the way he was sure witches thought about cursing as they flew, and their cows' titties would dry up and their children would be born with curling tails and the cunning buds of horns; he wished.

It's so, so *easy for them, isn't it? Just so damned easy.*

Then, suddenly, there were hands all around him, cruel fingers digging into the meat of his shoulders and the mutter of angry voices, and somewhere a rook was screaming with laughter. His face was filthy with mud and blood, the prickles of a hemp noose driving into his neck, and the hands forcing him down, down, down . . .

He woke, gasping, and rose from his bed to stumble weakly to the window. He looked out and saw a figure down in the courtyard staring up at him, but the light from the streetlights and the waxing hook of the moon hanging in the sky wasn't enough to reveal his identity, if indeed that solitary figure belonged to a man. Nathan thought it did, but he couldn't tell.

"I could stop by sometime this weekend," his mother told him over the phone the next morning. Nathan rolled his eyes, then felt guilty about rolling his eyes, reminding himself that she cared, that she loved him. "I could pop in if you aren't too busy. Just to say hi."

"You could," Nathan said. He hadn't showered yet. It was Friday and almost noon and the dance was that night and he couldn't move from the bed where he'd been sitting, perched on the edge, since he woke from his dream of flying and hanging, sometime after sunrise.

"We don't hear from you near often enough."

"I know."

"It's like," and she laughed, a jagged shard, "you don't even live here anymore. It's like you moved somewhere else, far away, after all."

"I'm not, Mom. I'm still in Garden City."

That unpleasant shard of laughter again. "Still. That's how it feels."

Silence then between them. He wanted to rise. He could do it if he wanted to. He wanted to stand up and go to the bathroom and piss and shower and brush his goddamn teeth. But his eyes moved around instead like captured animals, to the door and then to the window and then back to the door again and then back to the window.

Get out of this bed, he thought. He wished desperately for the voice of someone, anyone; he would take even the dulcet, wicked purr of the woman in the mermaid dress, but she wasn't going to appear then. No one was going to save him. No one was *there*.

I am alone. I always have been.

And I always will be.

"How's Logan?"

Nathan blinked. Outside, in the hallway, raucous, simian laughter rose, and the thundering of feet. The music of teenage boys, loosed upon an unsuspecting world, free from the chains of their high schools and their parents' houses. Groups of boys, he knew, unsupervised, left to their own devices were the worst of all the monsters. "Oh," he said. "Fine."

"Haven't you talked to him?"

"Mom, I really have to—"

"I spoke to his mother the other day."

"You did?"

"In the grocery store. She didn't recognize me at first, but then she did. She didn't tell me that I look tired, but I could see it in her eyes. She thinks I look tired. You'd think so, too, if you saw me."

"What did she say? About Logan," he added.

"That he's having the time of his life. Good grades, of course. How are your grades, by the way? That he loves college. That he isn't coming home for Christmas."

Nathan opened his mouth and closed it. Something inside him felt heavy, pressing. He wanted to lift his hands, but there were shackles encircling his wrists and he wasn't dreaming. They were cold and heavy and they smelled of wet iron. He closed his mouth until it became a thin white line.

Blithely, his mother continued, "Some kind of exchange, I think she said, or he'll be working more or he'll be out of the country for a while. I thought you of all people would know. But he loves it, she said, he just loves it."

Nathan closed his eyes and saw a midnight countryside below him, far away, the perfect circles and the black snaky lines that were rivers and streams.

"Good for him, I said. Don't you think? Sweetheart?"

"Sure," Nathan heard someone say, and he supposed it must have been him.

"I could bring your brother with me when I swing by. Wouldn't you like that, sweetheart?"

"Hmmm?"

"Terry. Your *brother*. I could bring him with me when I stop by. Maybe today, maybe tomorrow. Wouldn't you like that?"

"Yes," Nathan said and opened his eyes wide. "Absolutely."

"Nathan," his mother said sadly. "My little love, the world doesn't hang squarely on you, you know." He heard irritation in her voice, and it was so rare and so unexpected that he actually sat up and listened. "The world," she said, and she sniffed. "Little man, it isn't all about *you*."

10

HE HAD TO rely, finally, on egg yolks stirred together with three copious spoonfuls of sugar and half a bottle of cheap hair gel to convince his bangs to stay standing so they appeared, he *hoped*, to resemble the great curving horns a warlock should affect. The pitchfork was red and plastic, and he'd decided that, though silly, it was practical in the sense that it gave him something to do with his hands if they grew too out of control, as he feared they might. The rope burns encircling his neck were purple and glaring and below them hung a tiny noose composed of silk threads colored the most delicate, the loveliest shade of cerulean that Julian had handed him with a shy smile just before they left together for the dance.

"Found this mixed with some stuff I brought from home," he'd said. "You can have it."

"Thanks," Nathan had replied quietly, equally shy. The concept of passing gratitude to Julian seemed appropriate now, fresh and new.

"Come to my dorm before the dance," he'd said to Julian, inspired, at the end of class on Friday. "We can go together." And of course Julian's face lit up and he'd clapped his hands like an excited child, and Nathan felt a spasm of guilt for all the irritation he'd suffered for the other boy since school began, for the way he'd snapped at him again and again. He isn't Logan, Nathan thought wearily, but who is? It wasn't fair for him to expect to find any bit of Logan inside him. Maybe it was time he'd stopped running from anyone who wanted something from him, even if was only his attention, a crumb of affection. No one was going to hang him from a gibbet; his magical protector had yet to materialize. It was time to move forward, away from the things that scared him.

I'm afraid of them, he wanted to whisper back. *I'm afraid of everyone, and afraid of being alone.*

Don't be so melodramatic, the voice sniffed, and for once he thought that it was really and truly his own, and no one or nothing else's. *Time to grow up. Time to stop being afraid.* And so he'd used the beautiful cerulean rope to fashion a noose, which Julian himself dropped duly over Nathan's head, avoiding his newly formed hair-horns.

They decided to walk to the Elks Club in downtown Garden City, which lay just over the bridge that crossed the Royal River and separated Waxman's campus from the town proper. It was long after dark when they finally left Mickelson Hall; Julian chattered as they went, dressed in a lion costume that was far too big and hung lankly around him, yellow and limp, making him appear even pudgier than he really was.

Julian was determined to allow nothing to spoil his evening.

"I've never been to anything like this before," he said cheerfully as they walked. It had rained earlier in the afternoon and the streets were slick and gleamed under the bone-fragment of the moon that made the trees look pale and skeletal, most of their leaves stripped away. "I'm so excited," Julian said, nearly skipping.

You should call your old friend, Nathan, wicked, wanted to say, *Dave, yeah? You should call him and see if he wants to meet you there.* He forced himself to take a breath; instead he said quietly, "Yeah. Me too."

He's a friend, he scolded himself, *and right now he's your only friend. Remember friends? Remember what that was like? Knock it off, for fuck's sake.*

Nathan liked this new voice. It was so *butch.*

"I hear there'll be a thousand people there," Julian said.

"That sounds excessive."

"But it's what I heard. Do you think there will be? That there can be? I mean, how is that even possible?"

"Halloween," Nathan said wisely.

"Not just that though. There's nowhere else to go in Montana. That's what I heard. What else are you supposed to do?"

"Who?" Nathan said wickedly.

Julian thought for a second, pausing, caught. The road beneath their feet was black and the trees over their heads reached for each other as if to join hands.

Finally Julian said, "Oh, you know. People. You never came to these, um, dances when you were in high school?"

"No," Nathan said, realizing that they hadn't, none of his friends. "No, we didn't." *It never even occurred to us*, Nathan thought, dismayed. They were there, all the time, just waiting. *But we never went.*

"I would've."

"Oh? You would've?"

"For the fun," Julian said quickly. "My town was so small. There was nothing to do, not even a little. And it wasn't like I had a ton friends like you, or even—" But he cut the words off and, after taking a breath and waiting through another chunk of silence, Nathan merely nodded and said nothing. "I don't know anything," Julian said quietly. "You know?"

"Yeah," Nathan admitted. "Me neither."

"That isn't true. You do."

"You should stop thinking that I wrote the homo handbook. There isn't a homo handbook."

"Maybe not. But wouldn't it be cool if there was?"

Nathan laughed softly.

"We're going to meet people," Julian said, clapping his paws together. "We're really really really going to do it."

11

IT'S LIKE THE whole world exploded, Nathan thought, and nearly turned back at the door. *Don't be stupid*, his strong new voice hissed at him, *get in there*.

They climbed a flight of marble steps littered with glitter and orange-and-black confetti and cigarette butts, most stained with lipstick, until they reached the main floor and a lobby where, through a single door, music blared and thumped, mixed with the excited babble of a thousand twenty-somethings.

Julian had been right; Nathan was astounded. The door bled darkness and occasional, intermittent flashes of light.

"Jiminy Cricket," Julian breathed. He took Nathan's hand with his costume-paw and squeezed it; surprised, Nathan squeezed it back.

A thin boy with spiked black hair and silvery, sharp piercings mapping his face waited, bored, by himself at a long table decorated with plastic Halloween pumpkins and pamphlets that prescribed the most assuredly safe ways to practice sexual intercourse. As a bonus, it gamely offered directions to the weekly Lambda meetings. This angular, complicated boy looked up at them haughtily and raised his eyebrows, drawn thin and black and rounded above his kohl-lined eyes, and said, "Singles or couple?"

"Singles," Nathan said. He hastily dropped Julian's paw.

"Right," the black-haired boy said, grinning at them. "I seen you before at the meetings, yeah? I seen you both."

"We go," Nathan said, more defensively, perhaps, than he intended, but the boy only nodded, grinning still.

"I seen you outside," the boy said to Julian, "waiting."

Julian blushed.

"Singles, yeah. Five dollars each." He held out one bony hand.

Fire in emerald streams flared out of the door beyond him; the whole world, Nathan thought dazedly, the whole entire world exploded just inside there; Julian was pulling on him and together they walked through the door and into that darkness and fire.

Nathan would attempt, later, to piece together the evening, to stitch it back into sense from the fragments that he could actually recall. The darkness felt so *thick*, with the bodies of the people and with the darkness itself. A DJ booth at the far end of the dance floor was raised high on a dais where white and green and blue lights flashed from their strobes; above the floor a mirror ball shed silver fragments like stars onto the revelers below.

Squinting, Nathan could make out girls in black, girls with witch hats and cat ears, and an endless number of muscular boys who had already discarded their shirts or tucked them securely into their back pockets. Three boys grinding against each other wore only miniscule slips of underwear to cover themselves, the better to show off how completely their bodies were covered in paint that caused them to appear elemental: one was painted a green-blue and decorated in darker blue lines like waves; the second was all over fiery orange and yellow with flames composed carefully around his mouth and eyes; the third was wound all around in dark brown and green lines that Nathan supposed were branches and leaves. They gyrated and giggled and kissed and then gyrated some more.

Nathan scanned the crowd. Where was *he*? But the dancers were thick and jostling. He realized that Julian was no longer at his side, that he was alone.

Later, he remembered wandering through the crowd and attempting to dance and then, finally, feeling foolish, slinking away again until, at last, he leaned against a bare space on the wall and merely watched.

They're so beautiful, he thought achingly. He longed to be one of them and so, after an endless time, he thought, *This is it; this is the place where I can belong.* He forced himself away from the wall and back onto the floor and no one watched him or looked at him or noticed him at all and he hated that and was grateful at the same time, so he raised his arms over his head to imitate the boy whirling around and around beside him. He wondered, fleetingly, where Julian could be, and then, with a nasty sort of shock, realized that he was looking directly at him, that Julian had found someone, a *boy*, Nathan realized incredulously, but it was true, and the boy had Julian pinned tightly against him and they were kissing, sloppily and with an excess of spit, in the very center of the floor. Nathan's face blazed even under the cover of the dark. He turned quickly and moved away, allowing the swirl of people to pull him into their tide and wash him from the sight of Julian kissing the boy he'd found.

He wandered dizzily through the crowd. There were tables lined up against one of the walls; some were occupied, but others sat, squat and empty, although their former occupants had trustingly left their drinks behind so they could join the other dancers.

Nathan smiled. Smooth and sly, he lifted one of the plastic cups, then another, and moved swiftly away where he could sniff the contents of the glasses far from the scene of his crime. One contained rum and Coke, and this he drained eagerly and tossed the glass over his shoulder; the other held something clear he recognized immediately, that familiar smell reminding him of the forbidden party where the mermaid woman and all his animal-headed friends waited for him. Grinning, he drank it down, then squeezed the cup until it cracked and dropped it onto the floor, where it lay like a giant, damaged insect.

"Horny," a boy told him and stroked his cheek, "horny little devil." Nathan recoiled and moved away from the boy, who stood behind him and roared laughter, and;

Nathan took another glass from an empty table and slurped at the contents, then, gagging, spit them out and grabbed another and drank deeply of a dark ale, and said, "Daemon? Daemon?" and a pretty girl with the face of a skeleton smiled at him kindly;

and the music roared around him and carried him on its shoulder and swirled him around until he started to laugh. He couldn't stop laughing and smiling and he thought, *This is the best night of my life*, and;

"Daemon?" he called into the crowd, then, cautiously, "Seb?" but no one heard him, and;

the music roared and the beat drilled into his head and he found Julian and thumped him on the back and Julian grinned and said something but Nathan couldn't hear it and then it didn't matter anymore because the music and the crowd whirled him back into the giddiness of the dance and he was lost to it;

and the elemental boys allowed him into their circle and skipped mincingly around him, their arms linked, singing and chanting, and Nathan reached for them but they were elusive and wicked and did not allow him to catch them; "I just want a kiss," he cried out at one point, "just one kiss, please!" The green-blue boy said, "They aren't *free*, you know," and Nathan howled joyously and took the boy's hands and led him in a series of merry steps;

"More wine!" someone cried nearby. "More music!" and;

"Wilder women!" a thick girl with bleached hair cut screamingly short shrieked and her friends took up the cry; "Wilder women! Wilder women! Wilder women!" and Nathan joined them until the words made no sense and then he was pressed against a wall of wet and pulsing naked flesh where the light blazed like fires;

"More wine!" someone cried in a voice grown warbled and cracked. "More music!"

and then, without any awareness of the passage of time or the separation of space, he found himself sitting in the lounge across from a handsome boy with crimson plastic devil horns perched atop his head. The boy smiled into Nathan's face and said, "You may be the most adorable demon I've ever seen," and Nathan said, "Old devil. I'm not a demon at all, old devil horns. That's you. I'm a *warlock*." He reached out and took the boy's hands and the boy allowed his hands to be taken and then squeezed them reassuringly. "Your costume is better than mine," the devil-boy said shyly. "I didn't know what to do, so I ran out today and bought these. I only have one red shirt and so I put that on but I don't think it's, you know, a great costume or anything."

"You are pretty," Nathan said solemnly. "You are very pretty and so it doesn't matter what you're wearing because you're so very pretty."

"No one ever told me anything like that," the boy said. His eyes held no color, Nathan thought, and he leaned forward to see for sure. His hair was sandy and deliberately unkempt, and Nathan recoiled because, for just a second, he was certain that it was Seb sitting across from him, that he'd come all this way just to find Seb again, which was miserable and unfair, just when he'd so recently moved on, left him back with the old Nathan of Royal High. He pushed his chair back and tried to stand but his legs wouldn't hold him and the boy reached out a sure hand and gripped his arm and pulled him back down and said, "What's the matter? What's wrong?" and he wasn't Seb at all, and Nathan relaxed and allowed relief to wash over him.

"Nothing," Nathan said. "You aren't him so it doesn't matter."

"Him who?"

Nathan tried to smile, but he could feel tides of darkness rising up around him, waiting to fall and crush him. "Old devil Seb," he said, and tried to sound suave and dismissive. "I don't know."

"My name's Kyle."

"I'm Nathan." He sighed. "Thank you for not being Seb."

The boy Kyle smiled. "I do what I can."

"Whooo," Nathan breathed. "I stole all these drinks."

"Do you want another drink? I'll buy you another drink."

"Another?" He sat up, blinking. He felt cold and tried to seize the few remaining shreds of his sobriety, thinking, *I can just be* not *drunk, can't I?* The room was spinning, he was spinning around in circles; he tried to will the dizziness away. He choked and said, "Another?"

"Uh-huh. I bought you a rum and Coke. You said you wanted it. You just pounded it back."

"Jesus," Nathan exhaled. "I don't remember."

"So maybe not," Kyle said. He pushed a red cup at Nathan. "This is water. Drink it instead."

Nathan did as he was told, slowly, trying not to slop, trying not to embarrass himself.

"I don't want to embarrass myself," he said carefully, sipping, and peered at Kyle over the lip of the cup. "This is my first time doing something like this, you know, and so I don't want to embarrass myself."

Kyle made a table out of his linked fingers and rested his chin charmingly upon it. He watched Nathan with his colorless eyes. "Doing what? Having a drink?"

"Nah," Nathan said. "I did that a lot in high school. Oops," he said, and offered him a half-smile. "You'll think terrible things about me. I don't drink all the time, but sometimes. I'm not my friend Julian who can't hold his liquor and barfs all over nice apartment carpets. And my shoes. I'm not Julian at all, but maybe I should be. He came here and found a boy right off the bat and they're off somewhere now kissing."

"Lucky Julian," Kyle said. "You a freshman?"

"Yup," Nathan said, then winced. "Oh. Is that bad?"

"Not really."

"Then I," Nathan declared grandly, "am the only freshman in the whole wide world."

"You're pretty," Kyle said, "too."

"Pretty is a stupid word."

"It was yours."

"Yeah. I remember that. But you are." He hiccupped. "Cute."

"Okay. You're cute, too."

Impulsively, Nathan reached out and took Kyle's hand. "I like this. We can be cute together."

"But you're very drunk."

"Only for the moment."

"But what happens then? What happens after you're not drunk anymore?"

Nathan considered this. "I don't know," he said at last. "I don't want to think about it. I want this to go on and on, that's all. I don't want tonight to ever end."

"It has to," Kyle said sadly.

"Not for yet," Nathan said, whining. "Come on. Promise me that."

"I promise you that," Kyle said obediently.

"I was looking for him, you know," Nathan admitted.

"Him who?"

Nathan shrugged. "*Him.* I called him up. But maybe," and the dark tides swelled, "maybe no one is coming."

"I'm here."

"Very true. I said, I told Julian, or maybe Julian told me, but somebody said that I'd be lucky to get a demon."

"Look at me. I'm a demon."

"You are," Nathan said gravely and touched Kyle's face. Kyle allowed this. "You really really are." He sighed happily. "So long as you're not one of the deaders or the Outsiders or the serial killer—"

Kyle's eyes widened. "Serial killer?" he said, then laughed his charming laugh. "Oh, right. The lost boys. That's what the paper's calling them. Someone's seen too many vampire movies."

"No," Nathan said mournfully into his cup of water. "They weren't vampires at all. Or they weren't *just* vampires. But they did bite a little."

The boy Kyle laughed softly. "Listen, I'm no serial killer. I'm not even really a demon."

"That's disappointing. I thought that seeing a demon would be kinda cool. I mean, what's a demon even look like?"

"I can be as bad as you want me to be. Badder than any demon."

"I thought you'd say something about being your average horny little devil."

"That too," Kyle said gravely.

"Do you have any brothers or sisters?" Nathan asked dreamily. Kyle laughed, and Nathan pleaded, "No, I want to *know*."

"I don't," Kyle said. "I'm an only child."

"Me too," Nathan said. "Just me. All alone. All alone for my whole life."

"No one," Kyle said, and Nathan found that they were still holding hands under the table and that the party whirled and crackled around them, and it was a real party this time.

Really and real, real and really.

"No one should have to be alone."

It's him. I found him, I did.

His heart ran like a rabbit in his chest.

"Are you from Garden City?" Kyle said. He didn't wait for an answer. "I'm not. I'm from this shitty little town," and he gestured with that same ferocious disdain, "over by Prairie Rose. You know Prairie Rose?" He sighed. "It's this terrible place with an asteroid belt of shitty little towns full of shitty little people all around it. I couldn't stand them growing up, and I thought if I could just get away, then everything would be better. And I did get away, finally, but turns out it isn't any better because people are shitty wherever you go."

"People are the *worst*," Nathan said. "I keep trying and trying to fit, you know what I mean? To fit?"

Kyle nodded gravely. Nathan sipped delicately at the water and felt salvation in its coolness, in its lack of burn.

"But I end up messing it up somehow. I'm always afraid to talk. Are you ever afraid to talk?"

"Only sometimes," Kyle said. "I can talk to *you* though. Come on," he said, standing, and held out one hand. "Let's get out of here." Nathan, with no hesitation, reached out and took his hand and Kyle pulled him to his feet and they stood together, laughing and swaying. Holding hands, they left the lounge and tripped quickly down the filthy marble stairs and through the door, which exhaled them out onto the street where a few people stood in groups, smoking in their Halloween finery, their cerements of the dead and the macabre, and Kyle, suddenly sneering, said, "Nice costumes, shitheads," and one girl heard him and flipped him off and he laughed and pulled at Nathan and then they were running into the darkness.

"Where are we going?" Nathan asked.

"Let's walk around campus," Kyle said. "I'm a senior. Did I tell you that? I'm almost done here. I'd like to look while I still can."

The fresh air revived him; Nathan drew in a deep breath and felt cleansed. "It smells good out here. But I'm cold. I think I left my coat back at the Elks Club. And my pitchfork."

"We'll go back and get them tomorrow," Kyle said. Nathan, shivering, smiled at Kyle's choice of pronoun. "I can't believe you don't have a boyfriend."

"I haven't ever. Not really."

"Seb?"

"Seb?" Nathan was frightened. How did Kyle know about Seb? He wasn't really Seb after all, was he, deep down underneath that face and those bones? Did Seb live and lurk inside him even now? "There isn't any Seb. Seb is gone."

"Okay," Kyle said neutrally. They had come over the bridge and, stepping over a curb, found themselves back on the Waxman campus. Shouts and giggles echoed through the darkness, the sound of running feet; white shapes flitted from place to place; Kyle grinned at him and his teeth were very white in the darkness.

"We—" Nathan said, and Kyle leaned down and kissed him.

I've never done this; is this how you do it? Nathan thought as Kyle's tongue found his and began a ferocious battle. *This isn't nice,* he thought, dismayed, *this isn't right, this isn't what I—*

Then Kyle broke the kiss and grinned down at Nathan. He was panting and Nathan was panting, too.

"The woods," Kyle said, all white teeth, sharp teeth. Nathan's hand was frozen in his. "Let's go there."

"It's dark," Nathan said inadequately. He wanted the words to come but they wouldn't. His head spun and he thought it would spin right off the top of his spine. But Kyle held his hand with such insistence that there was no resisting.

"You aren't afraid of the dark?" Kyle said teasingly. It didn't matter what Nathan might say; Kyle was pulling him and they were running again and there was no one else, not anywhere, as if the campus were completely and absolutely emptied of all inhabitants. Not a single light burned in any of the buildings or dorms as they sped by.

Nathan thought his heart would burst; his head. What would happen when they got to the woods? What would happen to him there, in the trees?

Then they were there. The path had carried them that far, or Kyle had followed it unerringly.

Has he come brought boys here before? Nathan thought with a tiny prickling at the back of his neck; then he realized that they had left the path and stood, instead, in a cold little glade, made silver by its flood of moonlight pouring down upon them through a break in the trees.

"Here it is," grinning Kyle said. "This is my place."

Fright fluttered, a terrified moth inside him, tickling his throat, its tiny antennae and feet and eyes pressing up against the soft meat of his esophagus.

"Dude," Kyle tittered. "You look totally freaked out."

"Seb?" Nathan whispered.

A crease appeared above Kyle's eyes. "What's the matter with you? I'm Kyle. I told you. What's the matter with you?"

"Where are we?"

"I told you. My place. I like to come here. Sometimes I come by myself. Sometimes," and he chuckled, "I don't."

"I don't like it here."

"C'mon babe, it's really cool. No one to disturb us. Just you and me." He dropped to the ground and nestled down amid the leaves, some of them damp, some of them crunching into colorless dust as he crushed them. He patted the ground at his side. "Lie down."

The moth battered the meat of his throat as he lay down beside Kyle, who put his arm around Nathan's shoulder and pulled him close. They kissed again and Nathan thought, *This isn't so bad, not really; Seb never kissed, never.*

Somewhere nearby he heard a small voice that whimpered and cried, "I just want to go home."

"That's not so bad," Kyle said in his ear. "Is it?" His breath was hot against Nathan's cheek and Nathan recoiled from the smell of something dark in there, like cold meat. Kyle's teeth nipped at Nathan's earlobe and sent slivers of sensation down his spine; he moaned despite himself and Kyle chuckled again. "I like you, babe. I like you a lot."

"Please," Nathan whispered. "Oh please."

"You've been with guys before."

Nathan swallowed. "Yeah, but—" He stopped. He didn't know what else to say. What was happening? *Fast,* he thought. *It's all so fast. Seb? Seb, where are you?*

"I want to touch you," Kyle whispered in his ear. His hand crept down Nathan's thigh and dropped onto the crotch of the black-and-gray pin-striped slacks he'd purchased at the mall that afternoon because they seemed like the kind of thing a warlock would wear; the hand was insistent and pressed against the mound of flesh that lay just beneath the surface.

Nathan moaned again. It felt familiar, but still it was too, *too* fast.

No; let it happen, he thought dreamily.

Kyle's mouth on his mouth.

Just let it all go, let him do what he wants.

"You want this," Kyle groaned, pressing himself against Nathan so he could feel the other boy's hard length throbbing against him. "You want me. I could see it." He kissed him. "I could see it back there at the dance. I can always tell, I can *always*."

They rolled together over the leaves, and as Kyle went down, Nathan opened his eyes wide and stared up into that place where the trees broke and the sky was just there, a midnight tear, but so black now that even the stars were obscured and there was only the light of the moon resisting its prison of clouds, barely breaking through to show off streaks of silver.

Kyle struggled with his zipper and Nathan sighed.

"Seb," he whispered.

"Stop saying that *name*," Kyle growled. And Nathan was free from his pants. He nearly cried out at the pinch of cold, but Kyle's mouth was hot and shockingly wet and enveloped him absolutely, and Nathan knew it couldn't be Seb, because Seb didn't go down on him, never had, never would, he said. "Do it yourself," Seb would growl. "Christ, can't you just finish yourself off?" But there were good times, too, Nathan wanted to wail, that wasn't all; Seb could be kind; he could be gentle; he knew Seb really had loved him, in his own way, somehow.

Nathan arched up off the ground and cried out because the pleasure was exquisite and terrifying.

"Seb!" he cried. "Seb! Seb!" He sobbed. "Seb!"

Three marble faces peered down at him, ringing him, and he froze in horror. Below him, Kyle continued his ministrations. The faces of the missing boys became bats, furry and sharp, their eyes round, red, furious globes; their teeth were needles and clicked in the caverns of their mouths. *It's him!* Nathan thought in a perfect ecstasy of terror, hardly aware that he was coming, that Kyle was slurping and nuzzling and growling down there.

It's him, Nathan tried to scream. *Oh my dear sweet Christ, oh my fucking god it's him, he's the one.*

Then the lost boys were gone and Kyle's hands were rough and uncaring and they flipped Nathan over onto his stomach. Nathan cried out miserably and Seb said (*no, no, not Seb*), *Kyle* said, growling, "Shut up, I told you, shut the fuck up."

Nathan heard the angry buzz of his zipper and then the hot wet as Kyle's cock slapped against him. Nathan cried out again, but his face was pressed into the leaves and his mouth was filled with their dried bodies and icy slime. He choked on the mud and the leaves; he gagged. "No, no, no," he cried, squirming away on his belly.

"Stop it," Kyle said. "Just hold fucking *still*."

"No," Nathan screamed into the leaves and the mud. Kyle roared and Nathan threw his elbow back and felt it connect solidly with Kyle's shoulder, a glancing blow, but enough to make Kyle cry out.

"Dude, what the fuck?"

Nathan, squirming still, managed to pull himself to his knees. He spat mud out onto the ground; his hands clenched into fists. "Get off me," Nathan croaked. "Leave me *alone*." He pulled up his pants.

Kyle stood, swaying, rubbing his shoulder where Nathan elbowed him. "What the fuck," he said again. "I thought you wanted to."

"Seb," Nathan whispered.

Kyle's eyes narrowed. "Look," he said reasonably, "I did you, yeah? You owe me, even if you don't like me, dude; you *owe* me now." His pants were still down around his ankles, and his cock jutted forward, smaller than Seb's, thinner, like a little thumb, and Nathan couldn't help himself: he laughed. It wilted as he watched, poor little thumb. "Come on," Kyle said, wheedling, creeping forward. Nathan's laughter dried up in his throat. "Why are you afraid? What's wrong with you?"

"I don't want to, all right? Just go away."

"No," Kyle said. "Hell no. Come on, dude. Nathan? Was that your name? Come on, Nate. Just suck me off. Huh? How about that? Just suck me off. We'll call it good."

"Stay away from me," Nathan said. "You're *disgusting.*"

"Hey," Kyle said, his face going dark, "fuck you. You came to me. You came with me. So fuck you."

"It's you," Nathan whispered. His back found the hard press of a tree trunk and he flattened himself against it, staring. "It's you, I know it, it's you."

"You're batshit." He sounded frightened now. "You're fucked, you're *fucked.*"

"Seb!" Nathan screamed. "Seb! Help me, help me, please!"

Kyle launched himself across the glade, absolutely silent. Nathan tried to dodge, but Kyle's weight struck him in the chest and knocked him to the ground and they rolled together in the leaves. Gasping, Nathan pulled himself up and began to run. "Come back here!" Kyle screamed behind him. "Come back!"

The woods were darker than ever and the branches reached down and clutched at him. The moon was gone; white faces flashed out at him as he ran, the lost boys glaring with their own faces the color of fish bellies, baring saber teeth. He could hear Kyle roaring behind him, could hear the thunder and the ripping branches as he came.

This is a nightmare, Nathan thought, running. *It has to be. How did I come here? How did I get to this place?*

Nathan burst through the trees and found himself in what he thought was a different glade; then he saw the places on the ground where the leaves were disturbed and where the mud held the grooves of his body when Kyle had forced him down.

No, he thought, trembling and sick. *No, no.*

Kyle cried something out behind him and Nathan whirled around, raised his fists.

I can do this. I'm not a weak person, I can do this.

Then all sound stopped and the night was empty and cold and absolutely frozen with its silence.

A stitch burned in his side. His eyes bulged in their sockets.

He waited.

His breath emerged, a tattered ghost from his mouth, and hung before him in the autumn air.

He waited.

Someone was coming.

He whimpered. "No," he said firmly, "no." He drew himself up and forced his hands to become fists again (*or claws*, he thought distantly; *they could be claws, too, if I want them to be*). He stood there, ready.

The branches rustled. Then they parted.

A shape entered the clearing.

"Oh god," Nathan whispered.

The clouds raced away and the moonlight fell over them, silver, and it parted Theo Smith-Kingsley's red hair and turned it black. He was smiling kindly, hands resting comfortably in the pockets of his slacks. He wore no Halloween costume; his eyes flashed in the moonlight.

"I know you," he said. "Right? I've seen you before."

"You," Nathan said.

"Outside Mickelson Hall. What's wrong? I heard yelling. Sounded bad. You okay?" He took a step farther into the glade. His face flashed concern. "Hey. Are you okay?"

This is the way the world ends, Nathan thought clearly. He went forward and Theo Smith-Kingsley reached, and Nathan, breathing and then ceasing to breathe, fell. Theo caught him and held him and Nathan looked up and there were no monster boys, no white faces glaring at him, no one but just they two. He closed his eyes and thought, *It's him*, him, *it's really really really him*.

III

THE HOUSE IN THE WOODS

Then my heart it grew ashen and sober
As the leaves that were crispèd and sere—
As the leaves that were withering and sere,
And I cried—"It was surely October
On *this* very night of last year
That I journeyed—I journeyed down here—
That I brought a dread burden down here—
On this night of all nights in the year,
Oh, what demon has tempted me here?
Well I know, now, this dim lake of Auber—
This misty mid region of Weir—
Well I know, now, this dank tarn of Auber—
In the ghoul-haunted woodland of Weir."

Edgar Allan Poe, "Ulalume"

I dwell with a strangely aching heart
In that vanished abode there far apart
On that disused and forgotten road

That has no dust-bath now for the toad.
Night comes; the black bats tumble and dart;

The whippoorwill is coming to shout
And hush and cluck and flutter about:
I hear him begin far enough away
Full many a time to say his say
Before he arrives to say it out.

Robert Frost, "Ghost House"

1

"WORMWOOD," THEO SAID carefully, deliberately, and frowned down at the book that lay open before him on the rumpled blue and pink comforter covering Nathan's dorm bed. Squinting, he leaned forward and read, "Vervain. Two pinches. Or valerian." He shook his head. From his chair, near but at a safe distance, Nathan looked up and smiled when he saw the expression on Theo's face. "Maybe it says valerian? No. Can't be valerian. That's wrong, absolutely." Theo looked to Nathan and shrugged. "Why would you mix valerian with wormwood?"

"I couldn't say," Nathan said with some wickedness. "*I* didn't write that book."

"Somebody did. Do you ever wonder who?"

"Lost to the ages. Who cares, anyway? I want to try all the spells."

Theo smiled mischievously. "All of them? Eye of toad, wool of bat."

"For knitting sweaters. That girl—I don't remember her name. Do you remember her name?"

"I don't remember her name."

"It was her book. She gave it to me."

"Forget all about her; she doesn't matter. We'll use it for our own purposes."

Nathan nodded firmly. "Yes. I've got to know."

"And I suppose," Theo said, flipping another page, "you can't just ask them."

Nathan shuddered. "I don't want to even see them again if I can help it."

"Poor baby," Theo purred, and he sounded, Nathan thought, genuinely sympathetic. When Nathan looked at him, though, he saw that Theo's gaze lingered on a crack in the wall above the space where Nathan's head rested nightly on his pillow. He turned sharply to the window and saw nothing, but heard, instead, the eerie and somehow compelling whine of the mid-November wind.

He hadn't seen that Kyle boy since Halloween; not that he wanted to, but he was curious, a little. There was something about him that had called out to Kyle; he'd looked at Nathan at the dance when no one else had.

And he tried to rape you, a voice snarled. This one was new, different from the mermaid woman's or any of the others he'd heard off and on throughout the entirety of his life. It was sexless, ageless, raspy. He had tried and failed to imagine a consistent face to match its dreadfulness: sometimes he pictured a perfectly bald man with a gray rubbery face and hollows where his eyes should be, and sometimes a melancholy young woman with long white arms. He tried to keep himself from giving it a face, to keep himself from imagining anything. That's how he'd ended up with the mermaid woman and all the rest of them, he reminded himself.

No matter where they were when these thoughts intruded, Theo would stiffen and look over at him sharply, and Nathan would warm, wondering if Theo could hear him. Perhaps he could.

You weren't her boyfriend, Theo? That girl Deborah?

Two weeks, Nathan thought now, looking out the window and forcibly reminding himself not to care about Kyle, whoever he really was. It had been two weeks since that awful night; he held the thought and smiled over it secretly. The most wonderful two weeks of his life.

There's only us. Me and Theo. Just the two of us.

Theo's eyes moved away from the crack in the wall and fixed on Nathan. "Mission the first," he said, raising one long, slim finger. "Find out why these lost boys are so different than your other deaders." Theo's immediate and unquestioning belief in Nathan's ability to see the dead had flooded him, initially, with relief; so far, Theo had evinced no signs that he was anything but firmly in Nathan's camp, which meant his faith in Nathan and his belief in the seen-unseen world was sound.

"Mission the second," Nathan said, raising his own finger. "Find out who took them. Who . . . changed them."

Theo hoisted himself up on one elbow. As Nathan watched, he slammed the book and grinned. "Henbane and hellebore and mandrake," he declared. "Or is it mandragora?"

"Languages," Nathan said obscurely.

"True, true. The mixing of tongues. Look, I cannot abide a roof over my head for one more goddamned minute. You feel that?"

"I feel that."

"And I certainly can't read *this* anymore."

"At least it isn't literary theory." Nathan slapped his palm against the twenty-five-hundred-page textbook assigned for the class he loathed the most, and that, to be honest, he hadn't actually attended since the day before Halloween. The pages were onion skin and stuck together each time he attempted to flip them. But he had to read them, he knew, prodding himself as he had been prodding himself with regards to the class and—tell the truth and shame that devil—most of his classes over the past two weeks. Or all of his classes. When was the last time he'd attended? He couldn't remember.

"Literary theory at least makes a kind of sense," Theo said. He smiled his little wry smile and shook his head. "Anyway, that's what the tutor I had when I was thirteen said. He swore by it. Said he wrote volumes and volumes all by himself, just on literary theory. But witchcraft? I don't get it."

"Good for dispatching demons."

"Is that what they are, these lost boys?"

Nathan frowned. "They change. Sometimes they're animals, sometimes things come out of their faces." Theo raised an eyebrow. "Spider legs," Nathan said, grimacing. "Giant, bristling spider legs. Claws. And their eyes . . ."

"Spiders. Yick. No, thank you," Theo said daintily. "Witchcraft it is, then." He rolled over and placed one hand on his tummy, guarded by the thick sweater he wore, a vivid crimson interspersed with zigs of orange and zags of dark indigo. "But here's what I'm thinking," he said, scowling up at the ceiling. "Who decided that grinding together vervain and mixing it with belladonna and adding a crystal and the tears of seventeen and one-half virgins and then chanting over it in Latin or Aramaic would have any effect on the world at all?"

"If I had to guess," and Nathan chose his words carefully, "I would say that magic or witchcraft isn't a science, shouldn't even ever be thought of as a science, and that you just try—like give and take maybe—and you add this and you mix that and you hope and hope and hope . . ."

"And maybe nothing happens at all, even a little."

"Maybe not," Nathan conceded. "Or maybe something does."

"Trial and error, you mean." Theo chuckled. "*Witch* trial and error."

"Maybe not everyone can be a witch."

"But *you* can," Theo said, winking. "Okay, you convinced me. Magic is real. Spells work. Henbane, hellebore, mandragora. And so we're going to solve the mystery, you and me."

"But first," Nathan said, closing the hated book of literary theory, "we take in a mid-autumn stroll."

"Should you be shucking your responsibilities so easily?"

"Should you?" Playful.

"Touché. People have always just kind of let me do what I want, whenever I want to. No one has ever held me down."

"Nannies."

"Governesses. Tutors," and Theo yawned, then shook himself lazily. "I was always so curious about public school, normal kids, what they did, whatever 'normal' meant. But I read all the time because I could. I could do whatever I wanted. They just let me."

"Lucky."

"Yeah," he murmured, seeming small and quiet and a little lost. "Real lucky." Nathan resisted the urge to reach out and touch him; *maybe*, he reasoned, *he doesn't want to be touched, or maybe he doesn't want to be touched by you.*

Theo reached out and his fingers slipped between Nathan's, linking them together, and he lifted their hands.

Twins, Nathan thought, wide-eyed, *except his is so much bigger than mine, honestly, like a paw.*

Theo leaned forward until their foreheads were nearly touching and said, "We'll figure it out together. You and me. Magical detectives. Solving crimes with vervain and valerian and the tears of seventeen and one-half virgins."

"And chants," Nathan smiled, "in Aramaic."

"Or Latin."

They sat like that for an endless time, a minute or an hour, Nathan wasn't sure; the moment stretched, and Theo's eyes in all that ocean of time were unblinking, and they searched Nathan's so intently that Nathan grew uncomfortable.

I can't read him at all, Nathan thought. He swallowed awkwardly. He couldn't tell what Theo was thinking or who he was, didn't know what he wanted. Then the moment ended, and Nathan saw that he wasn't sitting on the end of the bed with Theo, that their hands weren't linked at all (*had they been*, he wondered breathlessly; *did he really touch me like that?*), their foreheads far apart.

But Theo's eyes remained locked on his.

It's happening again, Nathan thought, dismayed. *What is reality? Why is the noise in my head getting out again?*

Suddenly, Theo leaped off the bed with liquid, somehow uniquely feline grace, and thrust his arms into the storm-gray peacoat that was his favorite (and expensive, too, Nathan had thought with a cynicism he tried to repress; he'd seen the tag the first time Theo took it off; Burberry, of course, and cost a grand at *least*); he held out one enormous hand, eyes gleaming. "Come on, Sixth Sense. There's autumn air to be inhaled."

Nathan didn't hesitate, but came immediately out of his chair and donned his own black hoodie, and they left the dorm together and no one looked up as they passed and no one saw.

The trees that lined the campus avenues were gray and bony and Nathan thought uncomfortably of Halloween, Kyle and the monster-boys staring down at him, but then he forced his mind to skate away from that memory.

Theo watched him, eyes narrowed. "You're thinking things better left un-thought. The lost boys," he guessed, and Nathan nodded, wincing. Somewhere a bird screamed, causing them to jump, but it was just a crow grown fat on garbage left out behind the cafeteria in the student center. Its black eyes were beady and scanned its kingdom below.

It sees us, Nathan thought, *even if no one else does.*

"You do believe me," Nathan said, trying not to plead. "Don't you?"

"Of course I do," Theo said instantly. "God, why wouldn't I? This world has way more unusual things inside it than someone who sees dead people and monsters." He lifted his arms and spun around in a delicate circle, beaming up at the sullen sky. "To misquote James Whale, the air itself is *filled* with monsters!" He lowered his arms and looked seriously back at Nathan. "And maybe that's why I was drawn to you."

"You were drawn to me?"

Theo waved a hand dismissively. "You see things. I see people who see things." He shrugged. "That's my special talent."

Nathan smiled a little to himself, and they walked together in companionable silence. Glancing around, Nathan, surprised, realized they hadn't even left campus. He looked at the street sign and confirmed it: University Drive, the inanely named street that ran parallel to the western border of campus, busy night and day with cars that drove too fast; but there it was, empty, oddly, of all cars, and the cobblestones beneath their feet were a hundred years old and trodden by over a century of college-bound feet. Now they were alone, just Nathan and Theo; somewhere, distantly, muffled by the fog that shifted and hovered around them, came the clopping of what could only be horse hooves—*pulling carriages?* Nathan wondered. *That isn't, shouldn't, can't be possible*—and the lights trying valiantly to pierce the murk were too soft to be electric. Gas lamps, Nathan realized; beside him, Theo was whistling softly and gently.

The world is empty, he thought breathlessly, wishing he could reach for Theo's hand.

Where are we? Or when are we?

What if there's something out here watching us?

His internal temperature plummeted. Theo whistled; if the lost boys returned, would they attack Theo as well?

"I will always protect you."

Nathan turned gratefully to the other boy, but he was whistling still, hadn't said a word. What felt like a blade pierced Nathan just behind his eyes, and he blinked. The fog swirled; their footsteps were muffled and there was no other sound. They walked; the fog; Theo whistled, smiled, whistled. Everything was white, god, so *white*—

And something began to shriek in the fog behind them, then to roar—

They stepped together then off the curb and into the street that Nathan thought must have rushed up from nowhere, all at once.

"Magical protections," Theo said; they were off the Waxman campus and walking deliberately into the university neighborhood where the houses were lumbering, century-old monoliths, much prized. Nathan had often imagined himself living in one, creeping from room to room, perhaps holding a candle in one trembling, veined hand, perhaps using that hand to flutter against the disintegrating lace curtains, perhaps glaring hungrily out into the actual world at the students who passed by him with his black eyes and razor-sharp teeth . . .

Nathan laughed shakily. It still felt difficult to catch his breath, and his heart thundered angrily in his chest.

"So, Elphaba," Theo said cheerfully. "What's our first step, now that we've left our magical tome and the handful of mandragora back in your dorm?"

"I think we should find Kyle," Nathan said, then added quickly, "Even though I don't want to see him again, obviously. But he seems to be prime suspect guy, don't you think?"

"He certainly possesses the violent tendencies of a demon murderer," Theo said gravely.

"I don't think the killer is necessarily something like *that*. He's probably just a regular guy."

"And the lost boys?"

Nathan shrugged. "Maybe I'm just, um, growing into my powers. I feel stupid saying 'powers' though," he added sheepishly. "But maybe I am! And if the lost boys were killed violently or unexpectedly, maybe their ghosts are, um, *manifesting* as horror movie monsters, undead, zombies, vampires, and werewolves . . ."

Theo smiled affectionately and tousled Nathan's hair. "You've got that psychic investigator vibe down cold."

Warmth glowed up inside him. Quickly, he said, "So maybe we should ask around. See if we can find him."

"You haven't been to class in a week. Any of them."

Frowning, defensive, Nathan said, "Don't you think stopping a murderer is more important than writing pointless short stories for a creative writing class I don't even really give a crap about?"

"I'm a bad influence," Theo murmured, but his lips twitched, trying to become a smile.

"I don't need influences. I can mess my life up all by myself, thanks."

They started to walk again, silence a wall between them. *Dammit,* Nathan thought, and he wanted to smack himself. *Way to go, chumly. Way to mess everything up like you always do, you stupid shit, you stupid, stupid—*

"How would you feel about that?" Theo asked carefully. "I mean, really? If Kyle were our mysterious, murderous friend? Or even just another victim? Not to sound casually ruthless or even ruthlessly casual, but—"

"I don't want him *dead*," Nathan said uncomfortably, "if that's what you mean."

They stopped and Theo looked wordlessly at him. "I don't," Nathan insisted.

"Just checking," Theo said. "Because here's the thing."

Nathan frowned. "What?"

Theo shuffled awkwardly, looked up to the sky, down to the ground, anywhere, Nathan realized, but at him.

"He's . . . gone," Theo said at last.

Nathan blinked. "Kyle?"

Theo nodded almost imperceptibly. "Yeah. Kyle Matthews."

"I didn't know his last name."

"It was in the paper this morning. I didn't want to tell you."

"You should've," Nathan said, more sharply than he had intended.

"He hasn't been back to his dorm since Halloween. His parents are pretty frantic. Not surprisingly. I guess even an asshole has parents who love him."

Nathan sucked in a deep, hissing breath of sharp autumn air. "So he's one of the lost boys."

"Or he's on the lam."

"What does that even mean?" Nathan said, surprised into laughter.

"I always picture a guy standing on top of a sheep," Theo said innocently. "Riding him like a surfboard. Don't change the subject. Either Kyle is our killer or he's another victim. Both pretty bleak options."

"Which means we're back to square one."

"The square where we don't know anything."

"Yeah. That one."

"But we have your Tarot cards."

"And spellbooks."

"Spellbooks, henbane, mandrake." Theo gestured with one black-gloved hand. "Look. We've come out of the forest and into civilization."

"The forest," Nathan said and snorted. "Yeah, sure. We've been lost there for years."

"We thought it was a sanctuary. We thought we needed it."

"We've been wandering unattended through the woods for months—"

"Years," Theo said somberly, nodding.

"We have starved and learned quite a lot about ourselves, including the truth of who we love—"

"Who we *really* love," Theo said, correcting him.

"Home," Nathan said and made an expansive gesture that encompassed the whole of Garden City's downtown, its twisting labyrinth of streets, some broken, some cobblestone, winding and crossing each other and twisting back around; some became one-ways with little warning, just to entrap the innocent. Trees were now completely denuded and sheltered nothing and no one but glimmered under their false finery of cheery plastic Christmas decorations that glowed with secret, inner light. The specialty shops and tiny boutiques held to themselves the people of the town as they bustled in and out, looking warm and healthy. Here was Garden City, the place Nathan had known all his life, but it was like he was seeing it *really* for the first time. Now he could love it. He could show it to Theo, and they could see it together.

I won't be afraid anymore, not when I'm with him.

"We have come through the woods," Nathan said in his normal tone of voice. "Now we are home. Where we belong."

Theo clapped him companionably on the back and, grinning, said, "I'm starving. Aren't you just starving?" Nathan laughed, and they went together into the streets and blended seamlessly with the people on their holiday shopping missions, just two more ordinary young men who smiled and laughed and looked at each other with something, someone observing might think, that could have been the beginning of love.

2

"FAGGOTS," ONE OF them said, jeering, and Theo lifted his head like a surprised deer. As Nathan watched, fearful, he seemed to grow taller, and then even taller than that, and he was still only sitting. But his face was calm and watchful, curious maybe. Nathan licked his drying lips and Theo sipped, delicately, at his mocha. One of the other boys who sat so near to them said something under his breath, and the third, the one who hadn't spoken yet, giggled uncomfortably; his face was pale and troubled, and he looked like he wanted very badly to run.

The air in the coffee shop they'd chosen—The Spark, naturally— was thick with the heat of the weekend shoppers and gawkers; mostly college students, but a few townies, too. Theo was fearless, as Theo was always fearless, and strode through the masses to the end of the line, which was longer than Nathan had anticipated and wound like the coils of a snake through shelves displaying little Japanese figurines and pint glasses with superheroes printed upon them, back to an entire alcove devoted to locally brewed beers and bottles of wine with colorful and exotic labels.

"I've never been inside here," Theo told him as they approached.

"You'll love it," Nathan promised.

"If you do," Theo had said, smiling, and Nathan felt warmth spread through him.

Theo paid for their coffees and the simple sticky bun devoid of nuts but coated nevertheless with caramel at least two inches thick and darkly, secretly brown. Theo enjoyed sugar immensely, consumed great amounts of soda and candy bars and cookies and cakes, more than anyone Nathan had ever met; "I'm the poster boy for the future of diabetes," he'd said once, grinning through a mouthful of Hershey's Kisses.

They sat at a table, and Nathan hadn't noticed until it was too late that it was positioned only a few feet away from three familiar young men, two wearing flat-brimmed baseball caps and the other bareheaded, though his hair was long and shaggy and bleached and curled around his ears. If Nathan had been paying attention, he would have noticed immediately how the boy with the bleached hair craned his head on his long, thin neck when Nathan and Theo sat at their table, and how his eyes had widened with recognition, and how he had turned to his friends and elbowed them and, sniggering, said something low and vile under his breath, and then they'd all laughed loudly and coarsely, which Nathan heard but paid no attention.

"Did you come here a lot when you were in high school?" Theo asked him and Nathan, opening his mouth to answer, was interrupted by another dark tide of laughter from the boys behind them. Theo, arching an eyebrow, turned to look.

"Faggots," the bleached boy said loudly, and Nathan felt the world sink away beneath them.

"Did you say something?" Theo asked politely. He held the mug that contained his triple shot mocha in both hands and sipped nonchalantly at the sweetness inside. Nathan felt his cheeks burn.

"Yeah," the blond boy said. "I said your names. I thought you heard me."

"Yeah," the first boy with the cap said, the one whose face was bestial, leering, not nervous at all. "We thought you heard us."

"You guys are all out and proud," the blond boy said. "Isn't that a thing? Got parades and all kinds of shit?"

"Parades and shit," the first hatted boy said, laughing moronically. The second hatted boy looked down at his hands.

"I remember you." The blond boy smirked. "You remember me? Know my face?"

Nathan said nothing; he drew his shoulders up instead and locked his hands together tightly.

"Yeah, you do," the blond boy said. "You were a little bitch back then and you're a little bitch now. Nothing changes."

Nathan opened his mouth to say something, anything, but no words emerged. His throat felt locked, held in the jaws of some terrible trap.

"Fuuuuuck," the blond boy said. "You make me sick."

"Sick," the first hatted boy agreed.

"Is that so?" Theo asked politely. He sipped, sipped at his mocha.

A wall of darkness passed over the blond boy's face; his eyes thinned and his teeth gritted together. "Fuckin' sick to my fuckin' stomach, bro. You think you can just come here in public and be all faggoty and shit, where normal people can see you?"

"Normal people," Theo said, musing, and put his hand on Nathan's shoulder; Nathan's head jerked up, and he looked directly into Theo's shining eyes.

"Fuck," the blond boy groaned, "they're gonna kiss."

Theo's eyes. Smiling.

"I remember you," Nathan said, and looked directly at them, these monstrous boys, these goddamn animals. His voice wasn't loud, he didn't think it sounded loud, but it carried easily across the distance between them, and he did know them: the blond one was named Rory Brannigan and the first boy with the baseball cap was named Dylan. But it was the third boy Nathan could definitely place, a boy whose face he'd seen only two weeks before, part of the crowd as he veered drunkenly through the crash of the lights and the heat and clouds of pheromones at the Elks Club on Halloween. He hadn't recognized him then, but he did now. His name was David, and his face was so pale that he looked gray, and so thin that he was nearly gaunt.

"I remember *you*," Nathan said again. David shrunk into himself while Rory and Dylan seemed not to notice and instead roared their simian laughter.

"Good for fuckin' you," Rory said. "I remember you, too, bitch. You and your faggot friends. Hell. You thought you were such hot shit. Better than us."

"Maybe we did," Nathan said. "Maybe we *were*."

"You aren't better than me," Rory said darkly. "You aren't better than shit. Faggot."

"You should be careful," Nathan said conversationally, and his eyes flickered to poor scared little David, pissing himself as he sat there, hands warring helplessly, praying his friends wouldn't look at him, wouldn't notice. "You should be really careful, you know."

"Fuck you," Rory said clearly, "Succubitch."

Theo sighed, shook his head, opened his mouth to say something, then thought better of it; instead, he sipped, sipped, sipped at his mocha.

"There's something happening in this town," Nathan said softly. The place where Theo had touched him burned pleasantly, as if his hand were still held there, blazing away with tremendous heat. "Didn't you know that?"

Rory's eyes narrowed. "What the fuck are you talking about?"

"It's like a fairy tale," Nathan said. "An *evil* fairy tale though. Little boys going into the woods and never coming out again."

"Oh fuck," Rory said. His face paled, but two red circlets blazed in his cheeks, and his eyes threw out sparks. "Oh my fucking Christ. You goddamn perv!"

"Little lost boys," Nathan sang, "who go into the woods and never come out again. Eaten up. Guts chewed and bones crunched: slurp slurp slurp."

"Shut your mouth," Rory said, grinning, but there was no laughter in his eyes, no amusement, just shards of fear crystalizing there.

"What got them, do you suppose?" Nathan smiled perfectly; his eyes met Theo's and their smiles echoed and their eyes flashed and grew brighter. "What met them there? Or brought them there maybe? Was it the big bad wolf? The wicked witch? Like Hansel and Gretel inside that candy house? Touched them, killed them, ate them? Was it—"

"Faggot homo *freak*," Rory snarled and stood up so quickly that his stool fell over and clattered against the hardwood floor of the coffeehouse. No one noticed, and no one looked or moved or came over; Rory moved forward with his hands clenched into fists and Theo stood up but Nathan remained still.

"Go ahead and hit me and you'll see what happened to them. It'll be you next, you and your friend over there," Nathan said clearly, lifting his chin. David's eyes widened and filled with tears of terror. He rose and moved quietly away, but Dylan noticed and growled something and so David stood there, frozen with fear, a rabbit about to run as far as its legs would carry it. Rory also froze, his fist in mid-air.

"You can't hurt me," Rory whispered, though he sounded unsure, and his fist remained, floating before Nathan's face.

"Oh sure," Nathan said. "Sure I can." Then he grinned. The grin was teeth, all teeth, a broad grin that simply *jostled* with teeth.

Rory's eyes locked on his. Beside him, Theo laughed, a small, chiming sound, but it shivered around them, sweet but with such dark menace beneath its silver veneer that it muffled the little whimper that fell from poor damned David's mouth, and Nathan threw his head back and roared evil laughter, gale after gale, because oh my god it was so fucking *funny*. Rory dropped his fist; his eyes grew wide and so did his mouth, and he backed away from that onslaught of terrible laughter. They were both howling with laughter like big bad wolves, and the boys backed away, toward the doors that led to the sanctuary of the outside world.

Rory looked back one time to spit, tearfully, "You should be dead, you faggots. You should all be *dead*." Then they were gone, as if swift eddies of water carried them away.

"God," Nathan said, wiping tears away from his eyes, still gasping and choking. "Oh Jesus, I have never done anything like that before, not even once in my life."

"I have," Theo said, wiping away similar tears. "Once or twice."

"You're bigger than me. All imposing and stuff."

"Size," Theo snickered, "has got nothing to do with it."

Nathan snorted again.

"Don't give me that look. You know what I mean. It's funny is all. What was all that stuff you were saying?"

"About the woods?" Nathan shrugged. "HellifIknow. No, really. I don't. It just kinda came to me."

"You were scary." The laughter died away now. "A little."

"Scary in a good way?"

Theo considered. "I don't know," he said at last. "I'll have to think about it."

"Listen," Nathan said, feeling real fright for the first time. "I didn't mean it. Okay, I guess I did, with those assholes, but it's not me."

Theo narrowed his eyes. "What's not you?"

"It's not me. I didn't do it. I'm not the one. I'm not." He swallowed. "I could never—"

"I don't know what you're talking about," Theo said. He tossed his titian bangs out of his eyes. "Half the time, I have *no* idea. Hey, look at that. This mug is empty. I drank all of my mocha while you were waging your little war."

"Little?"

"Or maybe it was a battle. A skirmish. Fighting to save our souls."

"I couldn't just sit there anymore. But it doesn't mean that I'm the one who's been . . . who's been doing all of this . . . this . . ."

"Shhhh," Theo said, putting one finger against Nathan's lips; his eyes danced with merriment. "Just shhhh. Incantations. Spells and chants. You called something into being. Right? That's what you told me, and I think, no, I'm absolutely positive that I could see it then. You were fierce. Like a champion. Just be quiet for a bit. Finish your coffee, champ."

So he did.

3

THEY FINALLY FOUND a body, which the murderer had considerately propped against a tree in the deepest center of the campus woods so, unlike those of the lost boys, it would actually be discovered. The Sunday paper proclaimed it the morning after Theo and Nathan's venture into the city: the face was unmarred, the eyes staring, but the stomach had been opened and the guts strewn about the clearing, and the heart had been removed and was nowhere to be found.

The campus was, naturally, in a panic.

Nathan and Theo, lying on Nathan's bed and listening to music, not saying a word to each other because they didn't have to, had not read the paper or looked at computer or phone screens or talked to anyone; it wasn't until the following day, Monday, and only after Nathan pulled himself from his bed in the early afternoon, eyes red-rimmed and blinking in that dreadful hard white light, that they'd found out.

"Theo?" His voice cracked with disuse. But he was alone, and so he padded, shivering and barefoot, down the empty hall of his dorm, which stretched on and on with each step. As he walked, he thought about the dream he'd just woken from, where he'd been running through the trees and something flew through the shadows behind him, but when he looked back, all he saw was a vast, amorphous shape—living, liquid darkness. He'd screamed, and he heard a sound like the beating of carpets; wings, big black wings, and cat's eyes that glowed hot yellow and the flash of teeth in a vast mouth.

He'd screamed himself awake.

He looked, looked, looked around.

There had been no one in the room but himself.

The thing before, that's what it was; the one that tried to get Barry, only then it looked like me. Who will it look like now?

He'd looked fearfully to the window, but no monster's face glared inside, no beast hovered there with enormous inky bat wings.

He showered in the washroom, alone again, and thought about the classes he should probably be attending. He remembered the email he'd received a few days before from Jimmy Weston, the grad student who taught Intro to Creative Writing, not-so-politely requesting an audience. He could vividly recall reading the syllabus on the first day of class, and how crudely betrayed he'd felt, jolted by the realization that he was being taught by people who weren't teachers at all; they were students themselves, not much older than he was. But at least Jimmy was handsome: curly hair, maybe in his mid-twenties, surely no older than that.

"Jimmy," Nathan said out loud to himself, smiling into the pounding spray of water as it drove relentless spears against his face. "Jimmy Jimmy Jimmy." Then he thought, as was his habit now, of Theo, and how fearless he was. "This card," Theo had said last night (last night?), considering as he prepared to lay it down on the bed before them, "*this* card, now, must mean good fortune. Oh, oh no, it's reversed. Hell. So it must mean bad, yeah? But," and he'd winked, "bad fortune for who, I wonder?"

After he finished his shower and left the dorm, Nathan passed a girl on the quad with red eyes and a running nose who immediately averted her gaze and quickened her pace as she rushed by him. Overhead, the grim ceiling of sky grew darker, and he remembered that Thanksgiving was looming and the days were drawing tighter around everyone. He cursed himself for sleeping so late (again, he thought, snarling at himself) and felt a strange pang of something that couldn't really be fear at the thought of the darkness, could it? Then he was at Jackson Hall, a twisted edifice of multiple floors designed sometime in the late 1960s by an architect Nathan figured must have been insane when he imagined this particular building into existence, with its hallways that jolted jarringly in one direction and then simply ended, classrooms within classrooms, sub-hallways that connected to others above and below with strange stairways fading into shadows, never lit well enough to be found easily. Nathan wondered as he entered the building, blowing heat into his hands, if he would really be able to find Jimmy's office, or if he would wander the shadowed corridors of Jackson Hall until he died, and then, as was the case in cursed Garden City, after that . . . long after that. He thought of the lost boys and tried to shiver away the rime of ice that crept up and over him.

I will never *be like them, never.*

"Come in," Jimmy Weston called. For nearly five minutes, Nathan had hovered outside the door to what he was a little startled to realize was actually a honeycomb of offices and not a single suite, until the jingling of his hands fingering the keys in his pocket alerted Jimmy within.

Jimmy's smile, wide and without a hint of tooth, faded a notch when Nathan stepped across the threshold and came into the light. "Right," he said. "Nathan. Hi. You can come in." A frown creased his brow, and he made an impatient gesture. Then he smiled wryly. "Sorry. Day before the day before Thanksgiving break. Everyone is gone. So, of course, I'm here alone reading student stories by the light of my hundred-watt desk lamp. Which, according to my wife, will make me blind soon. Sit down."

Nathan glanced around the office, which seemed sad despite the efforts of its occupants to work their respective personalities about the space: framed pictures of people Nathan assumed were loved ones, printed quotes from authors he'd never heard of, cutouts from magazines of actors and rock stars, weirdly. At one of the desks, a vivid-turquoise Japanese lantern was affixed to the ceiling and occupied by a single light bulb; Nathan, watching it for longer than he supposed he should, wondered why he found it so sad. What about it, besides the fact that it was the only thing at all in the entire god-damn place like it, made it look so alone?

Jimmy smiled his wry smile and watched Nathan's eyes. "I share this office with six other people," he said. "As you might have noticed, we have vastly different tastes in décor."

"It's not so bad."

"It does all right," Jimmy said and sighed. "Considering I spend most of my time here, I should just set up a cot in the back and call it home sweet home."

"That would be weird." Nathan had begun to sweat, despite the chilly temperature that caused the entire building to feel like one big tomb. His armpits became a jungle, and they itched.

"Meh," Jimmy said. "I brought it on myself." His eyes were dark green behind the thin spectacles he wore. Nathan couldn't remember ever having looked at them before, at least not up close. They weren't kind, even though he was trying to be kind; Nathan guessed they'd be cold and hostile all the time in a few years. He already looked at his students like they were insects; he'd already begun to hate them. Nathan was forced to close his own eyes and command his hands not to scratch at the growing wet beneath his arms.

"So," Jimmy said, leaning forward and smiling widely, "tell me why you haven't been to my class for over three weeks."

"Has it been that long?"

"It's absolutely been that long," smiling Jimmy said. "You have missed, by my very scientific calculations, fifteen classes. Which means you're failing."

"Oh," Nathan said. He thought he could hear the wind wailing, but he was too deep inside the darkness of that terrible building to hear anything outside.

No one knows I'm here.

"Oh," Jimmy said, then he leaned back in his office chair—yellow fluff peeked out of a hole in the back that opened and closed like a mouth every time he shifted his weight—and folded his arms authoritatively over his chest. "Oh, indeed."

Nathan forced a smile to match Jimmy's. "I've had a lot of stuff going on."

"I can imagine," Jimmy said pleasantly. "You're a freshman, yeah?"

"Yeah."

"I was a freshman once," Jimmy said, shifting his eyes somewhere up and to the left of Nathan's shoulder. "Not even that long ago, but it feels like a million years. I went to Waxman, too. And I wasn't even this pretentious back then." He chuckled, an invitation for Nathan to join him. Nathan didn't.

He's practiced this, Nathan thought wisely, forcing his hands to remain still in his lap. *He knows exactly what he's going to say and when he's going to say it. He isn't real; none of this feels real.*

"And I have classes of my own. Bigger assignments. A novel to write. A thesis to write. I'm supposed to graduate in the spring. So, I get it, buddy. I really do. Miles to go. But the point is, you gotta keep going."

"I guess."

Jimmy's pleasant-not-pleasant green eyes narrowed the tiniest bit. "Why did you sign up for creative writing?"

"I don't know."

"Sure you do. Unless you scrolled through the course catalogue at random and just stuck your finger out blindly."

"Sure. Yeah. That."

His eyes narrowed another degree. "I have fifteen other students. All fifteen are passing the class. You are the only exception."

"Sorry."

"If you fail, you'll be on academic suspension."

"Okay."

"Jesus Christ!" Jimmy exploded. Nathan flinched. Jimmy leaned back in his chair with such violence that the wheels holding it to the floor screamed in protest. He pressed the palms of his hands against his eyes and ground his teeth together. "I thought I would help you, kid! I thought I would give you a chance!" He lowered his hands. The eyes that glared at Nathan now were red-rimmed and the green in them flashed out. "I want to give you a chance," he said more calmly.

Nathan thought about it for a moment. "Why?" he said.

"I don't like being punitive. Do you know what that means?"

Nathan shook his head. *Idiot man, idiot child*, he thought, then, chilled, realized it wasn't his voice at all, nor his thoughts: it was that *other* voice, the new one, gray and low and wolfen. *Careful*, that voice whispered to him. *Careful of this idiot boy, this man-child. Careful careful, take steps, careful. It could be him. He could be the one.*

Nathan eyes widened.

The one what? Nathan's own voice answered. *Could it be my lover? Conjured from the darkness by my call? Not likely.*

But still: the possibility remained.

Or the other. Killer. Monster.

Which is he, then? snarled the gray and grating voice. *Both? Neither?*

Nathan didn't answer it.

"It means," Jimmy said tiredly, "that I don't like to punish people. College isn't like high school, Nathan. You understand that, don't you? Now that we're a month out from finals? No one is going to stand over your shoulder making sure you pass all your classes. No one is going to wake you up if you sleep through your alarm clock." His voice had taken on a slightly despairing edge. "You get that, don't you?"

"Of course." He watched Jimmy carefully, as one might watch a madman. It had never occurred to Nathan; he'd never even considered that Jimmy . . .

"Then you have to change," Jimmy growled. "The money—do you even understand how much *money?*"

"Sure," he said. He didn't.

"And there are other people who *want* to be in my class. It's capped, which means that you've taken the spot of someone who really wants to—"

"Listen," Nathan said, "I'm sorry. All right? Is that what you want me to say? Then I'll say it. I'm sorry."

"People say that," Jimmy said wearily. "All the time. Especially freshmen."

"I mean it. I took creative writing because I thought it sounded interesting. Because I thought it would help me."

Because Intro to Photography was full.

Jimmy watched him carefully, arms still folded, but said nothing.

Desperately, drawing his fingers through the air as if to clutch the words that might help him, Nathan said, "I thought I could get a lot of this stuff out of my head, and I was starting to, I was doing it . . ."

"I agree," Jimmy said quietly.

"And it was helping, but now . . ." He stopped, unsure, and a little frightened. Clarity rose up and smote him and he wondered what he was doing there. His stomach gave a little hitch and acid splashed into the softness at the back of his throat and scalded him.

Where have I been? Why am I lying to him, throwing all this bullshit at him? God god, where am I, where have I been?

Somewhere far away a door opened and slammed shut. Nathan shivered, but Jimmy didn't move or blink.

"But now?" Jimmy said softly, patiently.

"And now," Nathan started. "Fuck." He released his breath in a whoosh and sank into himself. He found he was on the verge of tears, and he tried to swallow them back.

"It's okay," Jimmy said. He reached out and touched his shoulder. It was instantly electric. Nathan allowed the feeling for a second and then pulled back with more of a jerk than he intended. Jimmy drew his hand back and looked at it, then back at Nathan uncertainly. "It's okay, buddy," he said.

"But I'm going to fail."

"Not necessarily. Why do you think I called you in here today?" Nathan shrugged.

"I'm going to make a bargain with you."

The devil, that gray and flabby voice whispered into his ear. *Deals with the devil.*

"You owe me one short story and a revision. Those things you can do on your own. But you've missed out on class critiques. That's an experience you can't replicate."

Only half-listening to Jimmy, Nathan was distracted by footsteps somewhere in the honeycomb of offices. Was someone coming? He wondered idly where Theo could be.

"Nathan," Jimmy said sharply, and Nathan started. Jimmy was glaring at him again. "You have to listen to me. I want to help you."

"Of course," Nathan said.

Lover murderer lovermurdererkiller?

He was itching again; he wanted to vault out of his stupid chair and away from this stupid man-boy and his words and his bargains. Sweat beaded at his hairline, and he swallowed. He desperately wanted to find Theo.

Jimmy closed his eyes. "Fine," he said, before opening them again. He leaned forward, and in the dim, chancy light, he seemed menacing, unstable. One eye bulged while the other squinted, and Nathan was reminded of the vulture-eye from Poe's "The Tell-Tale Heart," which exhausted, unfunny Professor Rossbach had attempted to teach them just before Nathan ceased attending American Lit. "Fine," bulgy-eyed Jimmy growled. "We'll just have to—"

The door to the office opened and they both jumped.

The little woman framed in the doorway glared at them. She was a little taller than Nathan, her blonde hair pulled back into a high ponytail. Nathan thought her exquisite, somehow, breathtaking.

"I've been waiting for ten minutes," she said. "I'm sorry to interrupt," and her cold blue eyes flickered to Nathan's, "but it's not safe these days for me to wait out there in the dark all by my lonesome."

"Oh god," Jimmy said, grinning. "Liz, you scared the hell out of us."

"Hi," Nathan said.

"Hi," the blonde woman, Liz, said. "You a student?"

"Creative writing," Jimmy said hastily. "This is Nathan. He's missed some classes so we're helping him catch up. Liz," Jimmy said, gesturing, "is my lady friend."

"Lady friend," Liz said, snickering, then looked directly at Nathan. "He's being cute. We're married. Freshman?" she said with sudden unpleasantness.

"You got me," Nathan said.

"It's always freshmen," Liz said. "I don't know why any of you bother to take this class."

"Liz," Jimmy said, but gently.

"I'm sorry," she said, and Nathan knew she wasn't. And she knew he knew. Her eyes flashed prettily. She was dressed nicely, a bright blue pencil skirt and matching heels. Were they going out? What were their lives like? Nathan was immediately wildly curious about them both. "Jimmy's time and attention," Liz told Nathan, "are often eaten up by freshmen who don't take his course seriously enough." Her arctic eyes drifted back to Jimmy. "Plus, he's a *writer*, you know."

"I've heard."

Jimmy stood up quickly. "Gotta use the john," he said, then smiled deprecatingly at Nathan. "Pardon me. The appearance of lovely Elizabeth has caused me to forget everything I once knew about professionalism. I shall," he said, bowing at Liz, "return in just a minute. You'll be safe with Nathan until then."

"Hurry," she said flatly, and, chuckling, Jimmy disappeared into the hallway.

Nathan and Liz looked at each other.

Liz removed a pack of cigarettes from her purse and offered one to Nathan. Wide-eyed, he took one. "Atta boy," she said, lighting her own with a delicate blue lighter, then his, before returning the lighter with magician's speed into the depths of her purse. She inhaled deeply and blew a perfect ring of smoke into the air. Nathan tried to imitate her, though it had been a long time since Seb had taught him how to blow smoke rings. Still, what emerged from his lips was recognizably round and hovered in the air between them before spinning away to dissolve into nothing.

"I know," she said. "You don't have to say anything. Smoking is outlawed on campus. So sue me. I'm a bad influence."

"Wasn't going to."

I'm a bad influence.

Theo had said that, hadn't he? Nathan felt uneasy.

Why are you questioning your memories? Sly, gray, inhuman nasty voice. *Why now? Are there moments, points, elements to your memories, the stories you tell yourself, that don't quite fit together the way you think they should? Are you missing time? Minutes? Hours? Days?*

The voice started to laugh. Soft, evil laughter.

He took another hasty drag on the cigarette and allowed the smoke to fill his lungs. His heart raced and sweat broke out on his forehead again, but he felt calmer. *No missing time*, he thought. *No missing minutes, hours, or days. Everything is fine. Everything is just the way it's supposed to be.*

Liz narrowed her eyes in just the same way her husband did. "You really here because you skipped class?"

Nathan decided it was safer to use as few words as possible, and so he nodded instead.

"Seems like a waste of time," she said. "Listen, you think he *likes* having these meetings?"

"Yes?"

"Actually," and her eyes glinted as she exhaled another blue wreath of smoke, "you might be right."

"Time kinda gets away from me," he said awkwardly.

She raised a perfect blonde eyebrow.

"I've been busy lately," he added.

"Of course." Relaxing, she sounded almost kind. "You think I didn't go to school? I did. Just finished last year. How do you think me and handsome Jimmy met, after all? I used to skip class, too." She shook her head ruefully

Baffled, Nathan said, "Why?"

"Why do you?"

"I forget about them."

"So why are you here?"

"I'm supposed to be. He asked me to come here."

"No, braintrust. Here, at Waxman?"

Because I belong here. And who even are you?

"Because," he said evenly, "that's what you do."

"Do?"

"College. You go to college. That's what people do next."

"Do they?" Her lips curled into a smile. "Everyone you know?"

"I guess," he said, then he remembered Seb. He felt a pang. *I called out for him,* he thought, *in those dark woods, all alone in the night, and he didn't come.*

Theo came instead.

Where is Theo? Where is he now?

Hours. Minutes. Maybe even days. Gone; just gone.

"Fuck," Liz said. She crushed out the end of her cigarette delicately with her thumb and forefinger. "You guess? Don't be stupid, kid. Sorry. I forgot your name."

"Nathan," he said helpfully.

"Right." She snorted. "*Nathan.* Don't be fooled. College is just a big fucking waste of time. But you know that already," she said wickedly, "don't you. Otherwise you wouldn't be in Jimmy's hot seat."

"I just slipped a little," Nathan said desperately. "I'm going to be better."

"No, you won't. I'm sorry to say it like this. But Jimmy shouldn't've left us alone. Or maybe he did it on purpose. I never thought of that. Good cop, bad cop, y'know? Maybe he thought I'd scare some sense into you."

"I'm not scared."

"You should be. There's something wrong with this place. Can't you tell?"

For the first time, Nathan saw the fear in her face and heard it crackle in her voice; it was in the lines around her eyes and her mouth and the way her hands jittered just the tiniest, slightest bit. "It isn't . . . good. This isn't even a good town." She sounded on the verge of tears. "Shit like this doesn't happen in good places."

"Like what?" But he knew. Another boy, he thought, and his stomach felt cold and tight, and his testicles drew up and felt full of ice shavings. *It's another boy; another boy has been lost; it's another boy, all right.*

"You haven't heard?" Her lips pursed together. "How is that possible?"

"Who was it this time?" he whispered.

"I don't know her name."

Nathan sat up straight. "Her?"

"Some girl, a smart girl. She was a member of the Harrelson's Honors College, but they cut her up anyway, just cut her all up like meat. A goddamn sack of meat."

"A *girl?*"

She laughed jaggedly, a snarl. "Why is that so surprising?"

"Because . . ." His voice trailed off. He didn't know what he wanted to say.

"Right," Liz said sharply. "Exactly right. And she's the only one they've found so far. Cut wide open." Her voice hitched, and he realized that there were tears in her eyes. "Propped against a tree in the direct center of the campus woods. Her stomach," Liz whispered. "Her *heart*."

"God," Nathan said. He felt sick. His skin broke into prickling rows of gooseflesh.

Is that what he'll do to me?

Liz opened her mouth to say something else, but Jimmy entered the room, smiling, his voice booming with good cheer, "Lord, who died?"

"Not funny," Liz said. Her voice was still brittle, but any hint of tears was gone. "Not funny, *James*."

"Sorry, sorry," he said. He held up his hands blamelessly. "What's the topic of convo?"

"That girl," Liz said.

Jimmy's smile faded. "Oh, right."

"Did you know her?" Nathan asked.

"No, but I recognized the name when I heard. She was an English major."

"Deborah," Nathan said, the word a chip of ice that had condensed in his mouth, burning his tongue, so he spat it out. He didn't know how he knew, but he did. He wasn't at all surprised when Jimmy nodded.

"I don't remember her last name," Jimmy said, "but you're right. Did you know her?"

"We have a class together," Nathan said. He felt numb all over.

"Had," Liz said nastily. Her eyes gleamed. "No one has a class with her *now*. She doesn't get classes *now*."

"Elizabeth," Jimmy said, but absently. "They found her in the middle of the woods. Faculty, actually, a husband and wife in the history department, out for an early morning walk. Stumbled over the body. *Her* body, sorry."

"Jesus," Nathan whispered.

"I'm surprised you didn't notice the police on your way over here. They've been crawling all over campus since yesterday."

"I didn't see them."

"Well, that makes four disappearances and one actual murder," Jimmy said. "Quite a run for a school like Waxman. But the boys are just missing. The latest—I'm the worst, I can't remember his name for the life of me; Kyle, maybe, that sounds right—but all his stuff was still in his apartment. He hadn't been to any of his classes or his job since Halloween."

What about your classes? What about your job, silly old Nathan? When was the last time you talked to Amy? Can you remember? Silver, metallic laughter, and hateful. *Can you remember even one simple thing?*

Liz nestled closer to Jimmy, her eyes never leaving Nathan's face. "I want to get out of here," she said. "I don't feel especially safe, even with you two strapping gentlemen here to protect me."

"I think you should protect us," Jimmy said, kissing the tip of her nose. "If there really is a serial killer, you'd kick his ass, I have no doubt." His eyes darted to Nathan; shockingly, he offered him a quick little wink.

And Nathan, equally shockingly, found himself winking back.

4

THEO, IDLY RUNNING his hand through his hair, looked up at Nathan, smiled widely, and said, "Do you believe in werewolves?"

Nathan blinked. "I suppose," he said slowly. "I might as well. I see deaders, I see Outsiders, so why not werewolves?" He wanted to sit on the edge of the bed beside Theo; he wanted to touch that fiery hair. He did neither of these things. Theo, waiting, only smiled. "Why, do you think it's a werewolf?"

"A whole pack," Theo said lazily.

"Why are you thinking about werewolves?" He kept his voice light, amused. Outside, the sky was dirty gray and smudged as if by ash; the light that filtered through the clouds was also gray, the color of brains, or what Nathan imagined brains would look like. *Brain-light*, he thought, and shuddered. *That's not what those lost boys were, though; they only* looked *like wolves. They're . . . something else.*

"I was thinking about the world," Theo said, but slowly, as if he were unsure of the words. "All the worlds. This one and . . . others."

"Are there others?"

Theo rolled onto his stomach so he could look up more easily at Nathan's face. "You know there are. You must. You're the one who sees everything."

"Maybe it isn't real at all," he said, and, turning slightly away, ran his hand uneasily over the cheap wooden railing at the foot of the bed. "Maybe I'm just crazy." He thought about how dreadful the dorms were, how they were thrown together so inexpensively. *How long have I been here; when was the last time I left or saw the outside world?* He wondered, idly, about the time, about the day. *I don't even know*, he thought, and smiled.

That girl Deborah had been killed, but by who? By *what*? Time meant nothing; when had it even happened? He felt his eyes burn. He didn't want to think about Deborah, who had been gutted, or Kyle, who was only missing.

Why did they find her body but not the others? And why hasn't she appeared to you?

Why hasn't Kyle?

That was his own voice for once, and he felt a cold arrow pierce him, run up his back, through his guts, directly in the center of his forehead.

I should be going to classes.

I should be out in the world.

But this was easier.

So much easier.

Don't think about it, Nathan's very own voice said reasonably. *You're warm, aren't you? And safe. Theo is here, as he always seems to be, for you, only for you. You don't hate anyone . . .*

But what turned the lost boys into monsters?

And you don't wish anyone ill . . .

Who killed Deborah?

And the only person you want to be with in this whole world is right this very moment lying on your bed.

WHO? WHO? WHO?

So just . . . enjoy it.

"Crazy? Hmm. Maybe you are," Theo purred.

Nathan watched Theo watching him, and his skin broke into ripples and rows of goosebumps; warmth exploded over him, and he wanted to luxuriate, wanted his mouth to gape open, wanted to moan and to laugh. *Be careful, be careful,* he thought laughingly; remember ol' devil Seb.

Theo hadn't said much about himself; who was he? Who loved him?

Werewolves. Shapeshifters. Creatures without form or definition; mirrors for the rest of us. We look into them and see, not ourselves, but something like *ourselves; uncertain of form, of shape, something in between, something horrible, vile . . .*

But that wasn't always true. There must be something intoxicating, Nathan thought dreamily, about being able to shed your form whenever you wanted, to become whatever you wanted, shift your skin and bones, your very molecules, forming and reforming yourself into something new, your soul, your *essence*—

"Crazy, crazy, crazy," Theo sang. "As the proverbial loon. You *could* be crazy, but we know better." His eyes flickered, gleamed. "Don't we."

"Werewolves."

"Vampires."

Don't make him into something he's not.

Nathan's hand hovered at his side.

"I like this world," Theo said. "We've got witches and dead-boy-seers and werewolves and vampires. Yes, I have to say, this is as interesting a world as I've ever seen."

Amused, Nathan said, "Have you been to many other worlds?"

"Oh, yes," Theo said mildly. "Hundreds. Hundreds of hundreds." His eyes flickered. "It's exciting, don't you think? At least a little bit?"

"You don't mean the murder."

Theo lifted his eyebrows.

"Oh," Nathan said slowly, "I don't know."

"You like horror movies."

"I like my horror *in* the movies. Ever since I saw that woman in the antique mall—"

"Was she the first?"

"The first I can remember. Logan used to tell me not to talk about horror, that people would think I was weird, and I guess they did, I—"

"There are worse ways to cope." Theo flipped onto his back and looked up at Nathan with wide and patient eyes. His sweater, riding up, revealed a pale hint of tummy, blond-gold curls of hair. "You could be nursing a serious drug addiction instead."

"I could have founded an opium den."

"You could have founded an entire city of nothing *but* opium dens."

"Booze."

"Clear liquors."

"An ocean of clear liquor."

"Vast oceans of liquors so clear you can see the bottom. What kind of sand lies at the bottom of an ocean of clear liquors? You could," and Theo raised a wicked eyebrow, "be carving up co-eds."

Nathan shivered, wrapped his arms around himself. "Not funny."

"Too soon?" Theo grinned.

"Yes, it is, and you know it."

"I do," Theo said, mock-sadly. "Dammit, but you're right. I'm a scoundrel, a villain. A beast and a rake."

"I don't even know what that means," Nathan laughed. "A rake?"

"I read it in an old book, maybe. Probably in my grandfather's very big, very stuffy library. The one in Boston? Or maybe the one in the Hamptons. I can't be expected to remember everything." Nathan gawped and Theo smiled a tight, pleased little smile. "So, we won't talk about missing boys and monster boys and murdered girls, all right?"

"You knew her," Nathan said quietly. "Deborah."

Theo watched him patiently, kindly. "Only a little. Just that one night. That one smoke. I wasn't her boyfriend." He sobered. "Something got her."

"Some*one*. Werewolves," Nathan said with a brisk shake of his head. He leaned forward; Theo looked at him expectantly with those shining eyes; their faces were very close. "Where were you before?" he said unexpectedly.

Theo blinked. "Where?"

"Before Waxman. Where were you?"

"Oh," Theo said vaguely, "around. Here and there."

"But *where*?"

"Somewhere else," Theo said, dropping his eyes, and his voice sounded quieter, as if all the playfulness had drained away, and Nathan, against his will, felt a pang of fright.

Tread lightly, he thought. *Theo could fly at any second, go back to wherever he came from and leave you absolutely alone; you just don't know.*

"Somewhere else," Theo repeated dreamily. He let his eyes drift to the ceiling of Nathan's dorm, where, just yesterday (*Was it yesterday, though? Can you be sure?*), Theo, laughing, had placed an entire galaxy of green-white stars that glowed in the dark when Nathan turned off the light. It wasn't until later (*How much later?*), when he was lying alone in his bed, hands laced together behind his head, staring up into the darkness, that Nathan saw the stars spelled a word, and that word was "YOU."

"Somewhere else. Somewhere far, far less pleasant than here."

He won't tell me, Nathan thought wisely. *Be careful, be wary.*

What is he afraid of? What scares someone like Theo; do we have the same fears?

Theo put his face down into the crook of his arm and his shoulders trembled. Nathan, alarmed, thought, Now you've done it; "Hey," Nathan said, frightened. "Theo?"

Theo's shoulders trembled, but as he lifted his face and displayed his ruddy cheeks and dry eyes, Nathan saw that he was laughing.

"It's okay," he said. "It's okay, Nathan. It's fine, Nathan. I like it better here, that's all," but his face shook. There seemed to be an argument beneath the skin, that the bones, those beautiful cheekbones, struggled with their stability, refused to keep their grip on existence, that the muscle over the bones threatened to shake itself into nothing, even though Theo's eyes shone brightly, lovely as trapped fireflies. Theo trembled so hard that Nathan feared he would shake himself completely into nothing.

Are you gay, Theo? Bi? Queer? Does it matter; can't you just love me no matter what?

Ol' devil Seb; Nathan could never ask *him* those questions; they refused to dance off his tongue. His eyes flickered up to the ceiling, where Theo's green stars waited for darkness to shine.

Theo hauled himself up, crossing his long legs so that he could rest his elbows upon them. He wasn't trembling anymore, and he looked at Nathan and smiled and nothing was scary and he wasn't

about to blow apart, there wasn't a golden light inside him that
blazed furiously, some kind of ferocious starlight. And there wouldn't
be, Nathan told himself, there *wasn't*, and it wouldn't come blazing out of him and render him into absolute nothingness if Nathan
didn't stop asking questions. A little personal supernova, all because
Nathan had poked and prodded.

"It's okay," Theo said again, his voice his usual deep baritone.
He reached out and put a hand on Nathan's knee and squeezed it.
"Really. It's . . . hard for me to get close to people. I'll tell you things
someday, I promise. I just need time."

"Good," Nathan said, a reprimand he didn't mean. "Because I've
told you everything about me."

"I know. I will. I promise. I *promise*." Beaming, he picked up the
book of witchcraft poor dead Deborah had left behind.

Outside, the wind rose into a shrill scream and beat its naked
skull against the window.

"I'll keep you safe," Theo said.

Or did I say that? Or will I?

"From the lost boys?"

"From *everything*. And if they ever ask you—"

"Ask me?"

"If they ever ask you, or try to take you," Theo said, "you just say
no. You stay away from them."

"I want to."

"You have to." Theo sounded serious enough that Nathan felt
frightened again, and then he broke into his typical bright and sunny
grin. "Hey," he said, inspired. "I suppose what you *really* need is
someone to protect you. Knight in armor, shining or otherwise. A
boyfriend."

Nathan's mouth opened and then closed again.

"You'll catch flies," Theo said primly. "Okay, so after we catch
the killer, we'll rustle you up a boyfriend. A nice guy, I promise. I'll
have to give him my seal of approval, of course, before I let him anywhere near my Nathan." He furrowed his brow and squinted down
at the page of the spellbook before him. "Here," he said, pointing.
"This one. For drawing back the veil. That certainly sounds promising, don't you think? Nathan?"

A boyfriend.

"Let's try," Theo continued eagerly. "Come on. Revelation. *Exposure.* Goodbye secrets, goodbye veils! Draw 'em all back, I say!"

What you really need is . . .

"Sure," Nathan said, but his throat was too dry and the word didn't come out and so he cleared it and tried again. "A spell. For revelation. Why the hell not?"

5

"YOU WERE SO good to come," Liz called from the kitchen. The house closed in around them; Nathan shifted his weight on the thin cushions supporting him on the cheap little couch and thought that this was the kind of house that wanted to claim a person because it was too small and too lonely otherwise; *this* kind of house opened its doors like a pitcher plant and held on tight to whatever it could catch. The clinking of spoon against glass jangled unpleasantly in his ears as he looked around the Weston living room. He shivered, remembering how he'd come to be there.

"Nathan!" Liz Weston had called with the force of a rifle-shot across the quad an hour earlier, freezing him, his hands curled into little fists; he wished madly, as he always seemed to be wishing these days, that Theo were with him. He had turned, already knowing fully well who he'd find, and was thus absolutely unsurprised to observe lovely Liz, coiffed and perfect, striding briskly toward him across the frozen grass in her delicate blue heels. "I saw you," she'd said, not at all out of breath, "from the window of our little house," and she pointed back in the direction from which she'd come. Nathan, following her gesture, saw a small dark house of indeterminate color directly across the street; its windows reflected the last dying light of the sun. There was no yard that he could see, only a flagstone path, where those same flagstones had come untethered and looked like an idiot's smile with stumps for teeth.

"Your shoes," he'd said, groping for something intelligent to say, "are very blue. Pretty," he added quickly, and shuffled his weight. She smiled back and said nothing. He looked around, then jerked his head in the direction of her house. "Do you ever think that the path to your house looks like a grin?" he said, unable to stop himself. She blinked, smiling still as the words continued to trip out over his tongue. "A big, idiotic grin, where the stones are like big stumpy teeth?" His bag, hot and heavy, pressed down on his shoulders. "Scary," he added weakly.

She continued to smile as if he hadn't just expressed such an inane absurdity; he supposed, in light of the recent arrangement of time and events and his inability to place them in any semblance of actual chronological order, that there was a very real chance he hadn't said anything at all.

"Are you heading to class?" she'd asked brightly.

"Back from it. Going home. My home. To my dorm, I mean." Why did he feel the need to explain? He shouldn't, he thought crossly; she didn't need to know *everything*.

"The dorms. Oh, how I remember the dorms."

"Right. You went to school here."

"I was in Mickelson."

"I am, too."

She'd laughed, a pretty, tinkling sound, and he watched her without expression. She seemed different now, he thought stonily, than the woman he'd met the day before (*Had it been the day before?*) in Jimmy's office. "What a coincidence! That I should see you just now. Or maybe I have, a million times, and I just didn't know it was you. You actually go to class today?"

"I promised I would." So it *was* yesterday, he thought, tapping his upper lip.

"Holiday begins tomorrow. I would'a skipped."

"I promised," he said uneasily.

"Promises are meant to be . . ." She trailed off; he saw little dimples at each side of her mouth the same instant he noticed vicious little lines cut in tiny crisscross patterns at the corners of her eyes.

"This place," she whispered, glancing around. The campus was almost deserted; half the student body had begun their vacation early.

They were afraid, he'd thought wisely, and they probably should be. She shuddered, but it seemed she could make even shuddering a pretty act. "Look," she said, brightening, "are you done for the day?"

"With learning. Nothing else. I plan to keep on breathing and stuff." Stop talking, he told himself fiercely.

"I'm bored. Jimmy won't be home for hours. I should be prepping for Thursday," and her face darkened a notch, "but *he* makes the entire meal. Won't budge even a little, the jerkface. All I get to do is sit and watch the parade on TV."

"Everyone loves a parade. We're a parade-loving people."

"People?"

"We gays. We're, um. A people."

Is your husband a murderer?

His eyes widened.

I didn't say that out loud, did I? He was beginning to panic.

I didn't, did I? I didn't. I didn't. I'd know if I did. Wouldn't I?

Is your husband a stone-cold killer of women? A kidnapper of sleek and sexy college boys?

She squinted at him, then her face broke into a broad smile. "You're funny. Come on," she said and took his arm to pull him. "You can keep me company."

"I should—"

She laughed, cutting him off. "Just for a little while. We can get to know each other."

So there he was, suffering the springs digging into his ass beneath the cushions of the terrible Weston couch; Liz was somewhere in the kitchen preparing drinks.

I shouldn't be here, he thought, shifting.

What are you afraid you'll see? the gray voice said with evil, scraping laughter. *An earring? A baseball cap? Will Pretty Weasel's pretty head?*

Nathan's scalp had begun to itch the minute he'd stepped over the threshold and hadn't stopped since Liz ushered him to the couch and announced her intentions to make them both a cocktail. And there she was, two drinks in plastic cups, both blue, the same shade of her beautiful shoes and her eyes, and the cups sat on a tray and two little paper umbrellas sprang from between perfect square ice cubes. "Sex on the beach," she said. "My favorite."

He took one. "Thanks." He raised it and said, "Here's to your, um, health. And happiness. And your . . . husband. The three H's. Heh." He sipped. "There. 'Heh' makes four."

She giggled and touched the lip of her glass to his. They made no sound as they connected. She sipped, then daintily wiped the corner of her mouth. "Thanks for coming over. I hate to be alone, especially now."

"You're so close to campus."

"I know," she said wryly. "Makes it real easy for the big hero." She smiled, small and pointed and thin. "There's five."

"He's not so bad."

"He's really not." She stirred her drink with the umbrella. "Mmmm. These are pretty good, huh."

"The goodest," he said, then, apologetically and smiling, added, "I'm not an English major." The drink was overwhelmingly sweet; he had no idea what ingredients went into the creation of a sex on the beach, but he remembered Essie making him one at a party last year or the year before. It hadn't been as sweet as this one though, cloying, thick, like syrup. But he sipped at it nevertheless, thinking, *Theo would enjoy this; he's like a big hummingbird.*

"I drink too much," she said conversationally, and he understood that *that* was the difference he'd sensed on the quad. She was drunk, or near enough, and she hadn't been drunk in Jimmy's office; if she had been, it was a different kind of drunk than this. She giggled, watching his reaction. "Isn't that a terrible thing to tell someone you barely know? But I feel," and she put a trembling hand on his knee and leaned forward and said sincerely, "I feel as if I do know you. You're an old soul, Nathan, has anyone ever told you that?"

"Some monks, once," he said.

"You are," she said and leaned back and closed her eyes, "an old, old soul. You must be as exhausted by this place as I am."

"Coffee does wonders for your ability to not sleep at night ever."

She cracked one eye. "I feel like I was just here, just you. Not so long ago. Jimmy taught the writing class every idiot at this school has to take, and I waited until the very last minute to be one of those idiots. Lucky me, huh?"

"He was your teacher?"

Did anyone disappear from campus when you were busy basking in his great teacherly-ness?

"Oh yes. I loved him from the moment I saw him." Her voice was brittle-sounding, but her smile was sharp. Her eyes, unfocused, wandered somewhere along the line where the ceiling met the wall, which was white and dirty. Light brown smudges crawled all over it. Over *all* the walls, he saw; Nathan's head swam. "Do you believe in that bullshit? I never did. Even in high school, I never did. It wasn't so long ago. *You* know." She laughed and touched his knee again. His muscles thrummed, bunched and tight, to keep him frozen in his seat, to prevent him from flying out of that dreadful room and the clutching house with its clutching occupant and down the street, back to the relative safety of his dorm. "No," she said reflectively, "I never believed in love at first sight or true love or any of that shit. But here I am." She sounded bewildered and looked at him closely, so closely that he recoiled the tiniest bit. "How am I here?" she whispered. "Do you know?"

You married a murderer.

"I don't," he said.

Might have married a murderer. Maybe murdered a marrier.

She made a face and sipped at her drink. "Of course you don't. Who are you? You're new here. You don't really know."

"Aren't you from Garden City? Montana?"

"No. I'm a lost princess from a faraway land. Illinois. I came here on a scholarship, but I cheated." She laughed. "My best friend wrote the essay. *And* she filled out the application. Isn't that funny? I never even wanted to go to school. I worked at a nice restaurant. I'd be a manager now if I'd s-stayed."

"It's all I thought about," Nathan said, surprising himself. "It consumes me." Melodrama, as the mermaid woman would say; where was she, these days, anyway? His head felt full of light, exquisite. He didn't need her, he thought, pleased with himself; he didn't need any of them anymore. He was sorry he'd allowed them to exist in the first place.

"I hate this place." Her lower lip trembled. "I hate this school, I hate this town, I hate this filthy fucking state and all its filthy fucking people. This isn't how the world is, not really. Where *I* come from—"

"You're afraid," he said.

"Yes," she said immediately. "Aren't you?"

"Not really."

"You should be." She smiled slyly.

"The missing boys."

"I suppose they don't have to be dead."

"They are."

"You sound sure."

He swirled his drink around and around; it seemed, somehow, to have refilled itself while he wasn't looking. "I do, don't I," he said, smiling a large and loopy smile.

"Maybe they ran off together."

"All four of them? Please." He made a dainty gesture, his wrist intentionally limp. "Where are they holed up? You have to feed and water them. Growing boys and all that."

"So why change your M.O.? Why go from boys to girls? Why suddenly leave a body? I'm no expert, but it seems logical to me that you wouldn't just change your entire operation, the way you do things. And it's a big change. To gut someone," and her voice hitched and Nathan could hear the slight tinkling sound of the ice cubes trembling in her glass. "To take out their heart. That takes effort. Commitment." She looked vaguely around the living room again.

Outside, the last of the daylight trembled behind the mountains. She stood up and walked to the window and yanked open the curtains and stood there, bathing herself in those final red rays. "It's always so dark," she whispered. "You don't even know how dark it gets in here." She sighed, and he thought it was the saddest sound in the world. "Look at those mountains. I hate them. We don't have mountains where I come from. And you know why I hate them?"

"Why?" he said dutifully.

"They're so big and far away and *dark*. They could be hiding just about anything."

"You shouldn't be afraid," Nathan said. "Just don't go out there alone."

"But I'm always alone." Her back was to Nathan, but he knew what her face looked like. He could clearly see the expression set there, hardening by years of preparation: the twin grooves above the point where her nose met her forehead, the deepening line dividing her forehead and the top of her skull. "I am. And you are, too. I know it."

"No," Nathan said, startled, "you don't."

"Have you made any friends since you started here? Be honest."

"I—"

"*I*," she said mockingly, throwing the word back in his face. Swaying unsteadily, she loomed over him. "No boyfriend, no girl-friend, no *friend* friends. I'm right. I know I'm right." She leaned down, only inches from his face, and her terrible red mouth exhaled a sickly sweet odor barely masking some foulness like garbage mixed with vodka mixed with maple syrup; it floated over him in a cloud. "*You. Are. Just. Like. Me.*"

"Christ," Nathan snarled and set his drink on the coffee table, scarred and chipped and haunted by the ghosts of a thousand wet glasses laid down without coasters; smiling, Liz returned, somewhat unsteadily, to her place by the window, her back to him. "You don't have to sound so pathetic." Glaring at her, a terrifying possibility occurred to him, and he froze in the glaring.

Is it you? Or you and him*? Do you do it together? Do you take them down like hunting lions? Lionesses . . . they're the hunters, aren't they . . .*

He realized then that he was drunk. His stomach twisted unpleasantly. He wished for Theo again; Theo would save him from Liz.

"Brave boy," she said, laughing harshly. She redirected her gaze out the window where the sky glowed a dark and secret purple; the final swords of sunlight had disappeared back into their sheaths. "Stupid, brave boy. You don't know how this goes. This stupid god-damn machine. Or your place in it."

"I have friends," he said defiantly. He didn't want to say Theo's name for some reason; it seemed imperative that he not mention Theo's name. "Julian," he said, "and, and my friend Logan—"

"Right." She sounded tired, dropped her head. "Sure you do. I believe you."

"I don't get you," he said, studying her.

She's no killer. She's too weak.

His head throbbed; the world swam.

Why do you think Jimmy is the killer in the first place?

Because we cast that spell. Drew back the veil. We did that, Theo and me, and there he was; his face appeared in the candle flame, like something in a movie, just hovering there—

Liz heaved herself back into the ancient easy chair across from him that did not, of course, match the sofa. "I don't get me, either. Neither does Jimmy. Neither does anyone. That's my curse. Do you know what I'm supposed to do? What *he* wants me to do? I'm supposed to be friends with the faculty spouses, go to lunch with them or get drinks, ol' Geddrich's weasel-faced wife, and Vincenzo's husband. He's this ancient, miserable queen; god, they're both so *old*, old," she chanted, "old queens, the both of them. And Straub's wife. Venetia." She shivered. "Ugh. They're vicious. They really are like weasels, and of course Jimmy isn't faculty, he's a student, so they'll be sooooo nice to my face, but they can't *wait* to chew on my ankles the very moment second *milli*second I turn to leave."

"You shouldn't feel so sorry for yourself," he said, disgusted. He managed to wonder if the drink was loosening his tongue or if he would've said these things to her, bald, naked, regardless.

"I don't usually. But it starts to add up. You'll see," she said narrowly. "One day."

"I," Nathan said, tossing his head back, "am going to live to be a thousand. *Ten* thousand."

"I could tell the second I met you. You're like me," she said again, swaying where she sat. "Just like me. You want and you want, and before too long, you want everything, and you wish harder than you've ever wished, and then when you get it and you hold it in your hands you're not sure anymore but it doesn't stop you from wishing. Hungry," she said, blinking in the growing dimness of the room. "You get so hungry, and then you're hungry all the time."

"That's not me." He thought of the words of the mermaid woman from back in August, and felt a cold wave pass over him. He could feel it writhing around inside, like thin hands rising out of tar.

I'm not like them, not hungry like they are. That isn't why they want me, is it?

"Sure it is. You've got someone right now, don't you? But where is he? He isn't really yours at all." She laughed. "You can't lie to me. You are me and I am you and you'll see." The drink fell from her hands and ice cubes washed across the dirty carpet and Nathan cried out, he couldn't help it. He stood up and set his drink on that cheap coffee table and said wildly, "I have to go, excuse me, I have to go though."

"You can't," she said darkly, swaying where she stood. He saw that she was going to fall, so he went to her and put an arm around her and that was when the door opened, of course, and Jimmy Weston stood there, framed against the deepening darkness without, and he smiled at the tableau before him and said, "Here's one campus mystery solved: What does the beautiful Elizabeth Weston do with her day?" Then he laughed heartily to show, Nathan supposed, that he was joking.

"Darling," Liz said, shrugging Nathan off. Weaving, nearly done in by those beautiful, treacherous heels, she crossed to her husband and put her mouth on his. Nathan watched, fascinated, as Jimmy didn't recoil or react or do anything, even with Liz's sharp mouth and garbage breath all over him. "Welcome home," she said, trying to laugh, but it came out a sob.

"My wife enjoys company," Jimmy said, shrugging out of his coat and dropping it unceremoniously over the arm of the sofa.

"I'm by myself," she said petulantly, but her eyes sparkled and were bright, "all goddamn day."

His eyes remained on Nathan. "They tried to give you a job in the office at the English department. I've reminded you a thousand times: they try to give you a job and you always say no."

"I hate them," she whispered. "All those people. And they hate me."

"That's not true." He saw the puddle on the floor, the ice melting, the drink soaking into the carpet. "Do you want help cleaning that up?" he said quietly.

She turned away from him and crossed her arms. "Let me. You go somewhere else."

"I'll help you." He put his hands on her shoulders and massaged them gently, then kissed the top of her head. She relaxed against him; Nathan, watching, was fascinated. "I always do, don't I?"

"Bastard. Smug prick."

"Not at all," Jimmy said, and he winked, again, at Nathan, who dropped his gaze. His face burned; he wished madly that he had taken a different path back to his dorm.

"I should go," he said. *I'm sure you have more college boys to ravage*, he considered saying, but decided, wisely, to swallow back the words before they could fall.

Magic, he thought, recalling once again the spell for revelation, for drawing back the veil that he and Theo had performed together, hands clutched, a candle burning between them, eyes locked on each other, sweat dripping effortlessly from both their brows. Eyes gleaming; Theo's eyes were the greenest Nathan had ever seen; eyes, lips, lips moving at the same time, the *exact* same time, chanting, again and again: "Aletheia, hear our prayer, Aletheia, grant us aid, Aletheia reveal, draw back the veil, we beg you, Aletheia, we call. *Veritatem, veritatem, veritatem.*"

And there, and there, and there he was: Jimmy's face, like a dream, hovering before them, just above the candle flame, misty and indistinct, but definitely Jimmy, the green of his eyes, the golden curls on his head. That little smug smirk quirking the corner of his mouth.

The spell had revealed him, as commanded.

What did we intend to reveal, Nathan wondered, *with our silly spell; did I really see Jimmy's face?*

Who is Jimmy? Lover or murderer?

"You don't have to," Jimmy said. He released his wife and moved effortlessly into the kitchen; he returned a minute later and handed her a dirty blue kitchen towel. She bared her teeth for the smallest of seconds, kicked off her heels, and knelt on the rug. Nathan felt his stomach roiling. *Gotta run*, he thought; *out, out, gotta get* out. He squared his shoulders and aimed his brightest, most ferocious smile at Jimmy. "I do have to go, though," Nathan said. "It's dark."

Lover? Murderer?

"This place," Liz said, squinting at the rag.

"You could turn the lights on," Jimmy said reproachfully.

"Would it matter?" she whispered.

Both or neither.

Nathan shrugged on his coat. "It's going to snow."

"Probably," Jimmy said, but he was noncommittal and did not move from where he stood by the chair. Nathan found himself admiring his fingers, how long they were, how strong his hands seemed. They fixed on the back of the chair and squeezed, but gently.

"Take him back to his dorm, for Christ's sake," Liz snarled. She was trying to stand; she nearly made it, but then she weaved again and laid her hand flat on the floor to steady herself. "He can't go alone."

"I can go," Nathan said. He thought, *Theo thinks I should have a boyfriend, does he; that's what he wants for me, is it;* his eyes crawled over Jimmy, his shirt, his khakis, pressed flat and neat with the creases sharp and crisp. *I'll know then, won't I, either way; either way, I'll know.*

Veritatem, veritatem, veritatem: truth, truth, truth.

He saw that Jimmy was watching him watch; he smiled back, small and mysterious.

Killer or lover. Lover or killer.

You're being a child, Nathan told himself severely, but it didn't matter; *you're behaving like a spoiled baby,* he thought furiously.

"Maybe," Nathan said slowly, "I could use the company after all."

"The walk won't hurt me," Jimmy said.

"Not even a little," said his wife, standing now and still weaving, weaving. Jimmy put a hand on the small of her back to steady her. She laughed once, a jagged and bitter sound.

6

"OH CHRIST, OH *fuck*," Jimmy said. Droplets of sweat fell from his forehead and pattered delicately, like spring rain, onto Nathan's upturned face. He wanted to recoil and he wanted to retch, but he finished, swallowed (every last drop, he thought, and remembered Seb; every last goddamn drop), then, trembling, heaved himself up off his knees. They throbbed dully, and he wiped away bits of lint and carpet fibers.

I suppose what you really *need is a boyfriend.*

The office was dimly lit by the single lamp perched at the edge of Jimmy's desk, and Nathan bumped it with his hip as he stood. The shadows nesting in the remainder of the room danced and slithered. He wiped his mouth with one trembling hand.

Is it him? Double, double; incantations, a charm to cause a powerful trouble. Did I summon him?

Theo thought Nathan should have a boyfriend; sure, okay, great; a Theo-less boyfriend he would find.

You're acting like a sullen, spoiled child.

Jimmy dropped his hand onto Nathan's shoulder, and he nearly screamed but bit it back and continued to stare wildly into the darkness. "That was awesome," Jimmy said quietly, and brushed his lips against the back of Nathan's neck. "Hey. You can look at me. It's okay."

"It's dark in here," Nathan said.

"Yeah." He could hear the smile in Jimmy's voice.

Now, he thought. *Do it now.*

"You like it dark."

"Sometimes."

"You like me," Nathan said.

"I do. I have since I first saw you."

So it had been Jimmy all along; Nathan had been led to him. It had to happen that way; he'd *asked* for it.

"I think I knew," he said to drown out the crash and thunder of his idiot thoughts. "Liz knows."

Stop him. It's time. You can do it. You know how.

Stop him, Nathan thought dreamily. *Yes . . .*

"She doesn't." Jimmy sounded alarmed.

He should be alarmed, Nathan thought. *After he does it, after he tries, after it's all over . . .*

Where are these thoughts coming from?

Panic, but only a flare, dim now and far away.

Someone else lurked in his mind.

Stop him. No matter what. No matter how.

"I think so."

Provoke him. Make him see.

Nathan's breathing grew quicker, heavy. "She knows everything. She's a smart woman."

"I love her."

"Sure."

"I do." He was defensive.

Nathan placed a hand below his own belt to feel the throbbing there; Jimmy hadn't touched him, hadn't even offered to reciprocate. *Like Seb*, Nathan thought darkly.

"But we haven't been together. You know, lately." He didn't sound bitter. Just pensive. "She changed after we were married."

"I hear that happens."

Jimmy laughed. He put his hands on Nathan's shoulders, and Nathan didn't pull away. He thought of Liz, of Jimmy's hands on her, only minutes before.

"Hey," Jimmy had said, snapping his fingers as soon as he'd closed the front door of his house on his wife's hateful face. "Do you mind if we stop by my office on the way? Stupid of me. I left some papers there and I'd like to pick them up. You don't mind, do you?"

"It does," Jimmy said now. "Oh boy, it does."

"You've done this before."

It's him, it's him, it's him, Nathan thought deliriously. His erection pulsed and throbbed.

Maybe he wants to cut your throat. Maybe he'll try to take you into the woods so he can devour you.

You've got to get him first, and you know it.

The knowledge bloomed in him, naked and blazing: the eagerness he felt wasn't his own. With a sick thrill of horror, he thought, *Oh my god my god, it's one of* them, *an Outsider, there is an Outsider inside me* right now.

They wanted to feel, Nathan remembered, horror filling his mouth like thick wet sand; they wanted to touch, to crush, destroy. They wanted to know what it felt like to crack a neck under their vile fingers, and they couldn't do it without Nathan.

"I have," Jimmy said, and he didn't sound the least bit ashamed. "But you're my first student." That was a lie; they both knew it.

They want me to kill him oh my GOD.

Jimmy's face was shadowed, but his eyes glinted in the darkness. His eyes were human, not at all like an animal's; Nathan wondered at the disappointment he felt. But he took a step toward the other man, nevertheless.

"I'm not going to return the favor," Jimmy said kindly, taking a compensatory step backward. "Sorry. I'm not queer. I want you to know. I don't mess around like that."

Nathan stared; Nathan blinked; his mouth came open and then closed.

"Look," Jimmy said, still kind, "I'm sorry if I led you on. I like you, yeah, but I'm not gonna suck your dick." He laughed gratingly. "I'm not a cocksucker."

"I don't understand," Nathan said, bewildered. His hands clenched and unclenched.

Yes, yes. Use your hands. Do it that way. It won't be hard; use your hands.

"What's to understand? I'd fuck you. Hell, I will fuck you next time if you want. In a few minutes, give me a few minutes, I'll fuck you in a few minutes if you want. But I won't kiss you, so don't even ask. And I won't suck your dick. They ask sometimes," Jimmy said, apologetically, and shrugged a little.

His hands clenched. Unclenched. Clenched.

"You're not him," Nathan whispered, astonished.

Somewhere, far away, came the explosive, scraping sound of evil laughter.

Jimmy frowned. "Him? Him who?"

"Oh god." Nathan could feel the slime of Jimmy's semen still mired on his teeth, at the back of his tongue. He backed away and covered his eyes. "Oh *god*," he said, and it came out a screech.

"Listen," Jimmy said, alarmed, moving his hands through the air. "I'm not going to push it if you don't want me to. But I want to be clear."

"You're not him," Nathan said, and his chest hitched. "You're not him at *all*."

"Don't freak out." Jimmy started to laugh, but the sound fell apart, shattered like glass. "You gotta be an adult here."

"You're neither. You're nothing."

"No one will believe you," Jimmy said. His voice was rising, becoming thin and boyish. "If you try to tell. Just so you know. No one will believe you."

Nathan moved away from him, stumbled blindly through the dark, struck a chair, and cried out. The cry became laughter. He'd been so wrong; *we've been so wrong, me and whoever came to life inside me*. Nathan tried to drag in breath through the jags of laughter. "You poor, sad human," Nathan said, pausing in the doorway. "Sad man, just a man."

"No one will believe you!" Jimmy said, and his voice followed Nathan as he ran from the office, the childish shriek of a young, dumb crow, and it followed Nathan down the hallway, running and laughing. "Do you hear me?" Jimmy cried. "Do you hear me?"

7

"OH, I COULD'VE told you *that* would happen," Theo said, and turned to glance at Nathan before returning his eyes to the road. He didn't sound serious or upset or hurt, and Nathan was glad and embarrassed.

"You know why I did it."

"Of course." Amused, charming as always.

"You don't have to laugh at me." Nathan turned to glare into the darkness as it rushed past the car.

"Oh baby, I'm not laughing at you."

"It sounds like you are."

"I'm just driving the car, driving the car," Theo sang. The trees beside them, twisted and gnarled, were black bodies against a blacker darkness, pressing in around them. The road was rutted, unused, barely a road at all, and yet there they were, and they traveled down it swiftly, together in Theo's little car.

"My mom gave it to me on my twelfth birthday," he'd told Nathan when he pulled up to the curb in front of the dorm and gestured for him to get in, Nathan, for god's sake, it's freezing out; look, it's starting to *snow.* "Or maybe I was thirteen. I've got six more. But I never use them. Just this one. I love this one, it's my favorite, so I wanted to drive you around in it. Take you places. Look, I know what you're thinking. I tried to give them away. I did! Who needs six cars? But my mom wouldn't let me. Get in already, would you?

Your hair's all soggy." The car, though small, was sure and fleet of foot; the arms of the trees lining the little road made them look like slim white bodies, sad women, frightened men, huddling closer and closer together until they all looked the same, white and glowing amid the falling snow.

"You told me to go for Jimmy," Nathan said now, furiously. "You practically pushed me at him."

"I did?" Innocent. "Me? Good god."

"Then why—" Now Theo *was* laughing, and Nathan joined him, couldn't help himself. "I'm sorry," Nathan said at last.

"Shut up," Theo said cheerfully. "You apologize way too much." He reached over and snapped on the radio and a burst of static caused them both to cry out and the car to swerve; then the static cleared, replaced with the meaningless chanting and rhythms of a pop song Nathan had never heard before. "That's more like it," Theo said. He turned up the volume. "I love this."

"One of *them* was there."

"In his office?"

"Inside me."

"Oh. I was afraid that might happen."

"You were?" Nathan stared.

"It sounds like something they'd do, doesn't it? Sneaky."

"I thought that Jimmy was . . . you know." He shivered.

Theo drew a finger across his throat, then pretended to choke. Nathan stared at him, but he only smiled back, pleasantly, and said, "Of course you did. Because, ultimately, the killer could be . . . any-one. Right?"

"It wasn't him."

"No."

"But I thought it was."

"Or *it* did."

"It. The Outsider."

"I fucking hate these *fucking* Outsiders." Real anger now.

"Me too," Nathan said. His voice hitched in his throat. He looked fiercely out the window.

"So," Theo said carefully, "what did it tell you to do?"

Near tears, Nathan whispered, "It wanted me to . . . to . . ." He drew a shaky breath. "To stop him from making more . . . like the lost boys. It's what I wanted. What *it* made me want."

"The Outsider."

"But I don't," he said in a rush. "Theo, I don't want to die, I don't want to kill myself, and I don't want to kill other people. I swear it. I know that's not a normal thing to think or to say, but I don't." The words came in a rush; his eyes blurred and burned. "I don't," he said, choking back the tears. "I don't want that."

Theo sighed, then he laughed a little. "You know what?" Then, very clearly, he pronounced, "Fuck 'em. They don't mean anything. Stupid, idiot ghouls. Stupid, mean-spirited, sneaky monster assholes. Just say: fuck 'em. Can you do that?"

"I don't know." Small. Whispered.

"I think you can," Theo said firmly. "The idiot deaders," he said, shaking his head. "I'd almost prefer them to these motherfuckers. At least they're not encouraging you to strangle your professors with your bare hands."

"*It* made me feel that way," Nathan said darkly. "I didn't want to."

"Let's blame the mermaid woman and her merry troupe of jag-off animal-heads. Like the backward gods of Egypt," he said, disgusted. "*So* derivative. You'd think they'd have more imagination. They don't have imagination."

"What about Jimmy?"

Sneering. "He doesn't mean anything either. You'll go back to his class, and he won't even look at you. It'll be just like it never happened."

"I don't know if I want that."

"Why wouldn't you? Like it never happened."

"I'm an idiot. Like *them*." But he laughed.

"Yes," Theo said fondly, and he reached out and touched Nathan's face. His fingers were hot, but the heat felt good. The heat felt right. Nathan couldn't help it; he rubbed against those fingers like a cat. "Sometimes you are."

They drove for a while with contented silence between them, the cheerful blaring of the pop music on the radio.

White flakes of snow like a surprise hail of meteorites filled the air, making flat, dramatic splatting sounds as they struck the glass. Theo turned on the windshield wipers and they slapped at the glass; faster, faster, slapping louder, as Theo turned up their speed.

"Ugly night," he said, grinning. "Hey. You know what I used to want to be when I was a little boy? A meteorologist. That's the first thing I wanted to do. I could'a predicted this." He uttered a wild laugh. "And then I changed my mind; I told my mom, 'I'm going to be an archaeologist,' even though I wasn't exactly sure what that was, but I liked how the word felt in my mouth, against my teeth and my tongue. I knew that I wanted to dig up the past." The words were coming faster and faster; slap, slap, went the wipers. "For a while, I thought that meant dinosaurs, so then I told people I wanted to be a paleontologist, but one day I realized I had grown out of lizards, and I just wasn't that interested anymore. But bones and ancient civilizations fascinated me. My family tree fascinated me. Still does. I used to spend hours in my grandfather's library, looking at his books."

He stopped, watching the snow fly at them like white ghosts. Nathan hesitated, then said, "Is that what you're studying?"

"No," Theo said. His smile was bitter, then just sad. "It isn't. Because I grew out of that, too. My mom and dad didn't even want me to come to Waxman. We're from Massachusetts, well, Dad still lives there, Mom's in L.A. They aren't married anymore, but who is these days? They didn't want me to come here, and they didn't want me to become an anthropologist."

"I thought you said archaeologist."

"Words," Theo said evenly. "Just words. Hell, you think *I* even knew what they meant? I knew I liked books and I knew I liked history. So now I'm a history major, but tomorrow I might decide to be a librarian, which would make my folks crap themselves, but who cares? Day after that I might decide to become an airplane pilot or a spaceman, which, by the way, I also once upon a time very much wanted to be." His eyes flickered over to Nathan for the barest breadth of a second. "What about you?"

"Me," Nathan said.

"Photography."

"Supposed to be."

"But?"

"I haven't done it for a while. That's all."

A beat of silence, just the slapping of the windshield wipers.

"Tell me why," Theo said quietly.

"Where are we going?" Nathan asked again. He'd resisted the urge to wonder aloud since they left Waxman. "Trust me," was all Theo had said when Nathan climbed into the car, the nighttime sky glowing tarnished silver and the streetlights reflecting off the shelf of cloud hanging over their heads. Nathan had supposed he didn't have much of a choice at the time. He sighed, more heavily than he had intended.

"You don't need to make big dramas," Theo said, and for the first time he didn't sound pleasant or charming; *he's irritated with me*, Nathan thought, and shrank back against the seat and his eyes widened and Theo was watching him out of the corner of his eye. "Don't sigh and carry on. Trust me. Would I let anything happen to you?"

"No," Nathan said in a small voice.

"Oh, for god's sake. I'm not *angry*. All I want is for you to trust me."

"I will."

"Good." He relaxed, silent again. The snowflakes had grown larger and the sky spat them down relentlessly into the face of the car; the frightened trees pressed closer still, sometimes scratching against the metal roof, and tendrils of mist wended their way out of the forest and across the road.

"What was that?" Nathan cried, craning his neck desperately backward until it hurt, but there was only blackness at the windows.

Theo didn't turn to look. "What was what?"

"Something beside the road. I don't know. Tall. Or big. With eyes."

"Lots of things have eyes."

"Could it have been a deer?"

"Could it have been a deer?" Theo smiled softly, secretly.

"It didn't look like a deer."

"I've seen deer when I've come through here before," Theo said noncommittally. "Bastards jump out and smash against your grille. Never hit one though, myself."

Nathan squinted into the darkness; trees and snow; the road was white with it, if it really was a road anymore. Perhaps it was a trail; perhaps it was nothing but solid, frozen ground. Was it a wilderness? An endless dark forest? Perhaps they had sailed backward in time. Maybe there were no people anymore; Nathan closed his eyes so he could enjoy the hum of the engine. The car bumped and jostled along.

"You promised you wouldn't be afraid," Theo said.

"I'm not."

"Your voice says you are."

"I'm not."

"Why don't you take pictures? I've never even seen you with a camera."

"I didn't bring it with me."

"You left it at your folks'?"

Nathan glowered down at his hands.

"Tell me why," Theo said. His voice was low, gentle, musical.

"Because . . . the last time I tried . . . the last time . . ."

"Was it one of *them?*"

Nathan shook his head. "No," he said quietly. "I mean, yes, before. That happened. But I tried again. After. Just to see. And." A breath. It hurt. "It was just nothing. I mean, there were trees, and a dog, a golden retriever—because golden retrievers make me feel better about the world—and one with a house, but they weren't . . ." He screwed up his face and glared out into the darkness, at the black trees that fled before the light of Theo's headlights. "They weren't good. They weren't bad. They just weren't *anything.*"

Silence. Long ribbons of silence.

"You don't think you could get any better?"

"I've thought about it. But I doubt it."

"Isn't that what college is for?"

College is for you, is what Nathan wanted to say, and he nearly reached out to take Theo's hand. For a moment he thought he had, but he blinked, and Theo's hands were both planted firmly on the wheel.

Theo was smiling. Just a little.

Nathan took a breath. "I don't know anything about you. Not really, not very much."

"I just talked your ear off. Not literally, because gross, but you know what I mean."

"Okay, so I know a little more. But—"

"You know all there is to know. More than anyone else does. You think I tell everyone I meet I wanted to be Spaceman Spiff when I was six?"

"Your mother is a writer."

"She is?"

"A famous writer, don't be dense, don't make that face, she is. And your father invented something."

"Is that so."

"For Christ's sake," Nathan exploded. "You know everything about me! I've told you absolutely everything! I don't know your middle goddamn name; I've never even been to your dorm or your apartment or wherever you live; I—"

"I know," Theo said. "We're here." The car stopped abruptly; Nathan's seatbelt dug into his collarbone, and he grunted with the pain. He looked up. They were in a clearing of sorts, and the moon broke through the clouds overhead and spilled silver effulgence onto everything, including the hulking black house that erupted from the place where the road ended before them. Nathan gasped, couldn't help himself.

"Oh my god," he said.

It was three stories and gabled, and whatever color it had once possessed was faded, or the paint had chipped away under a constant onslaught of seasons, so that the boards comprising its skin were dark gray, Nathan, peering, saw, and not black after all, and weathered and warped. It was so large that it loomed over them, with a multitude of windows that looked out and beyond the boys below with a kind of practiced indifference. Nathan, shivering and holding himself, felt it was watching them and pretending not to; if they looked away, the boards and windows would move and the door would shift in its frame and something inside would come running out . . .

"Indeed," Theo said mildly. He killed the ignition, and turned, beaming, to face Nathan. "Shall we?"

8

WHEN HE WAS six, Nathan was bitten by a dog. Not a terribly big dog as far as dogs go, but its teeth certainly looked big enough when Nathan faced it; and they *felt* big enough when the dog planted them into Nathan's arm and gave it a ferocious shake. Later, Nathan supposed that the dog had meant to break his arm or tear it from its socket, as his father would tear the drumstick from the turkey on Thanksgiving. It was a big yellow dog, bald in places; Nathan remembered that the hairless patches were pink and raw looking, like muscle. Its eyes had locked immediately on his, and they were as yellow as its hide, yellow as piss, yellow as the teeth it bared, sabers all. It loomed over him; the shadow it cast just before it lunged enveloped him; its snarling filled the world. Nathan screamed and an older girl and her brother, who had been playing down the block, came running. The dog still had Nathan quite firmly by the arm and blood sprayed in amazing freshets.

"Hey!" the boy had screamed, and the dog flattened its ears back and growled with crystal clarity even over Nathan's shrieks of pain. "Hey!" the boy cried again, and the girl, who said nothing, seized the length of a branch that had fallen from the tree in front of Nathan's house. She threw it with the intention of striking the dog and, perhaps, convincing it to let go of Nathan's bleeding arm. Nathan's brother, Terry, was nowhere in sight; his mother and father were at work. Years later, Nathan finally wondered why he'd been left all alone; why had no one been there to prevent this terrible thing from happening, this apocalyptic thing?

The javelin-branch missed, but the dog, jaws snapping, dropped Nathan and backed away, and Nathan collapsed onto the grass.

"Come on," the boy said, taking a step forward. "Come on, kid, we'll—" but the dog, roaring now, lunged forward, and the boy darted backward with a little shriek.

Nathan forcibly chased away the grogginess and the intense desire to simply faint with three quick, brisk shakes of his head. Something inside him opened; he had the dim impression that there was a man standing in the direct center of the nearby street, but Nathan couldn't tell who he was or why he was just standing there and not coming to help. And there was the dog, after all, to be considered.

It tried to eat me, he'd thought.

Nathan found himself standing; he didn't know how. Didn't matter.

Blood had spattered all over the lawn, the sidewalk, splashed nearly at the man's feet. Hot and wet and red; it glittered in the weak sunlight overhead.

The man in the street was old and bald, and he had glowing yellow coins for eyes. He was smiling. His teeth were perfect, white and straight, and very long, like piano keys.

You're one of us. You are us and we are you, the man had said.

The dog growled, baring its enormous teeth.

Nathan's eyes flicked from the man and back to the dog.

You are us, boy. We are you.

The dog took a menacing step forward.

Nathan didn't blink; he took a step forward as well. The world held its breath. Somewhere, he heard the dry, rasping sound of the man in the street laughing, laughing.

The dog stopped growling, froze in its place.

You've got something, boy. You know that? You?

No, he said, tried to say, shaking his head; *no.*

The man was implacable; the man grinned; Nathan felt an answering grin curl across his lips. Something began to build inside him. The dog roared and snapped.

The yellow-coin eyes glittered. It's okay, those eyes said; this is inevitable. Light; power; strength.

Show us.

Nathan felt an explosion up and around him, a sure and shining sense of light that flew out of him, invisible, or maybe just the tiniest hint of a flash, and the dog recoiled and whimpered before it turned and tucked its tail between its scrawny legs. It ran away fleetingly, whimpering. Nathan never saw it again. He never learned where it came from, or why it attacked him.

He turned to look for the old man in the street, but there was no old man.

One of us, a voice whispered.

Nathan felt his stomach twist and knot itself. That feeling of sureness, of certainty, of strength and power, vanished, if it had ever really been there.

He remembered his arm and looked down at it, at the slick rivers of blood that pulsed from the punctures. His skin looked very white in contrast to all that pulsing red.

So much blood, he thought musingly.

Then he fainted.

He thought of that dog now as he followed Theo out of the car and into the wintery night, their breath hanging white in the air just before their mouths, the fat flakes of snow thick and somehow exotic, continuing to dance lazily down from the sky. For the first time in forever, the scar, small now, pulsed, not painfully exactly, and he wondered whatever happened to the dog, which was surely a skeleton now.

Maybe that happened, he thought, *and maybe it didn't. I was a child; what did I know? What do I know now?*

Theo was smiling up at the house, his hands on his hips.

Or I sent it away, he thought, awed. *All I had to do was look at it and it went away.*

Was that possible? He smirked, shaking his head. "Possible," he was beginning to understand, was a deeply stupid word.

Where has this power been since then? Was it a once-in-a-lifetime thing? Did it abandon me when I started seeing the deaders?

He wanted the power back. He wanted to send away threats with a glance. It would be easy, so very easy.

And that man. He just stood there in the street. Watching me. He wasn't one of them. He wasn't a deader. Was he an Outsider? I never saw eyes like that before, and I thought they were solid, completely, solidly yellow, but they weren't. I remember now. They were split down the center, like a cat's eyes.

"There's a hierarchy," the mermaid woman had said.

What did that even mean? There were the deaders, Nathan thought, counting, and the Outsiders like the mermaid woman, and the lost boys. What else? What else could there be?

Did he have wings? Oh, dear god, did he? Big wings, thin, membraned, black, like the end of the world, stretching and reaching. Wings like that thing in my room, the night with Barry; did he have wings, that old man? Did he?

He said I was one of them. But I'm not. I'm not. I'm not I'm not I'M NOT—

"No werewolves here," Theo said happily, then tilted his head up to the moon sailing through the tears in the clouds, parted his lips and howled quietly, gently. After a beat, Nathan joined him, and they howled together, then laughed. Theo slapped him companionably on the back and laid his enormous arm over Nathan's shoulder.

"This," he said grandly, "is my place."

"This."

Theo nodded. "This," he said, and sighed his contentment.

"No one lives here. It's a wreck."

"I didn't say I lived here," Theo said, thinning his eyes, "I said it was mine."

"That road is hardly there at all now," Nathan said with sudden understanding.

"Once, maybe, but not now."

"Jesus." He crammed his hands into his pockets. It was colder than he thought; the snow grew thicker. "How'd you find it?"

"Driving," Theo said vaguely. "Up and down old back roads. I had time, once. Lots. So I went exploring."

"It's creepy."

"I thought you'd like it."

"I do." He did; he didn't. It was horrifying.

I love it.

"I knew you would. That's why I brought you here. I've never shown it to anyone else, not ever."

Nathan felt warm, despite the chill in the air. His eyes flashed, and he turned to Theo and looked up into his eyes and said, "Are we going inside?"

Theo grinned. "There's nothing in there," he said. "No dogs to bite you," and he began to run. He turned back and called, "Come on, you are *much* too slow," as he danced up the steps, which looked old and black but held him perfectly well. Nathan followed, laughing delightedly. He put his hands on the veranda that looped around the entire house, then he ran into Theo, who had stopped short at the door and was gazing at it solemnly. It was thick, despite its age and the fact that the house had been abandoned long ago, though it looked to Nathan as if it might stand for another century, or a century of centuries. There was a face, he saw with a chill, a knocker, glaring with frozen eyes and grinning stupidly at them; its tongue flopped out from between its useless teeth. "Gives it character," Theo said, "charm." He punched Nathan lightly in the arm. Laughing together, they threw open the door and dashed like little boys into the foyer.

The smell of the house struck Nathan instantly, and he stopped, recoiling, and said, "I can't."

Theo turned to look at him, honestly puzzled. "What's the matter? Floors are firm. No worries about that. This house was built to last even if no one will ever live here again, so don't get any ideas about rotted floorboards or dungeons below."

"The smell," Nathan said, trying not to gag. *Like cold meat that has gone over bad.*

"Imagination," Theo said, but the flicker in his eyes had gone. Was he afraid? "This is my castle," Theo said. "I am lord of the manor."

"It's old."

"Totally old. I don't know anything about it; I just found it like this."

"Sitting out here, all by itself, all alone out here in the woods like this."

"I call it the Black Forest," Theo said, grinning wolfishly.

"Like in Germany."

"Where all the fairy tales come from. Forests as far as the eye can see, oak and beech and fir, so thick and so dark they might as well be black."

"You've been there."

"Of course." Theo smiled. "I go wherever I want. I've always gone where I wanted to, done whatever I wanted to." He closed his eyes and whispered, "Witches and werewolves and ghosts dwell there. *Die hexen. Die Weriuuolf.*"

"Is that what *they* are, do you suppose? The lost boys? I thought that they couldn't possibly be—"

"Werewolves? Could be, could be. Or that could just be a word." Theo stroked his chin, mock-scientifically. "But I think *that's* what Little Red met in the woods. Those whacky Grimm brothers were very clear about that. Not an ordinary wolf at all. *You* know; you like those fairy tales. You always have. The scarier, the better."

Nathan glanced around at the ceiling high above their heads. Giant black circles of mold or rot or both spread out like ink blots.

"There are castles in the Black Forest, just like this one," Theo said. "Many castles. Ruins, sprinkled throughout the hundreds of miles the forest spans." He sighed.

"You miss it, don't you?"

Theo nodded.

"Let's go," Nathan said. "Right now."

Theo raised an eyebrow.

"Seriously. Fuck school. Fuck our classes. Fuck our teachers." Theo laughed, and Nathan joined him. "Fuck it all! Let's just go. We can backpack or stay at hostels and eat lots of bread and sausage and drink gallons of beer and chase deer and run from the wolves and find a witch to enchant us and then turn us back into whatever we really are, and then—"

"Whatever we really are," Theo said quietly. "Whatever it is we're supposed to be." Something glistened in his eye in the silver light that poured through the giant windows. Nathan only then noticed how they had remained curiously untouched by vandals or by time; they were whole, complete, beautiful. Theo put his hands before his face, and when he removed them, it was gone, that sparkle or that shine, whatever it had been. "Why do we need to find a witch? Let's just change ourselves."

"Deal," Nathan said. He moved around the room, marveling at the carpet gone thin and nubby, peeling in some places and, in others, gaping with holes as if touched by acid, but those holes revealed a beautiful hardwood beneath. Nathan kicked aside a tumbleweed as he made his way to the mantel. A fireplace dozed beneath it, long unused, but the mantel itself was lovely, and he touched it, hardly daring to breathe. Not a speck of dust. The wood was mahogany and topped with real marble.

"Carrara, as a matter of fact," Theo called after him. "I checked."

"Whose house was this, I wonder?" Nathan glanced up above the mantel, where a portrait hung of a sad-faced woman in a long white dress, dark of hair and eye, gazing down at them solemnly and, maybe, he thought, with some benevolence. Her hands were made up of long, sensitive-looking fingers that she had clasped together: *Here is the church, here is the steeple.* Her cheekbones were high and noble-looking, giving her face an aristocratic look, but her eyes were sunken and nearly lost among the shadows. Still, they gleamed with some avidity, but what kind? Maybe it wasn't benevolence after all; was she lonely? Cruel? Vengeful? Her eyes glittered. He looked to Theo. "Is it hers?"

"Could be," Theo said, joining him. He gazed up at her without interest. "She looks like a sparkling conversationalist."

Nathan gave him a reproachful look. "Now, now. This is your lady, undoubtedly, if you really are the lord."

"Oh, I am."

"Then you must be kinder to her."

"But it's so hard. She *isn't* a sparkling conversationalist; not even a little."

"Maybe she's lonely. Sitting up there all this time while you're out and about, plundering and burning down villages—"

"Sacking," Theo said mildly. "We call it sacking."

"—and all she can do is wait and sigh and grow more bored, sadder and sadder and—"

"Stop," Theo said, laughing. "You're making her too real. Next thing you know, she'll step down out of that damned frame and onto the floor here with us."

"You don't think that would be cool?"

"Listen, you're the one sees dead people; not me."

Nathan shivered. "I hope there's no one here with us. This place wigs me out just sitting here doing nothing all by itself."

"You said you liked it. *I* say it's glorious." Theo spun around, softly and slowly, and performed a delicate pirouette.

Nathan applauded. "Look at you go. I had no idea you could do that."

Theo cracked one eye as he spun around again. "Lot about me you don't know. As you've pointed out so recently. Maybe I wanted to be a dancer one time *and* an archaeologist. Maybe I was good at it, even if I am way too giant-sized. Who's to say?" He stopped. "Look around. What do you notice?"

Nathan scanned the room. "No dust," he said at last.

Theo nodded enthusiastically. "Right-o. What do you suppose that means?"

"You've been out here with a Swiffer. Compulsively."

"Guess again."

Nathan's smile faded. "I don't know."

"Me either," Theo said, shrugging. "That's part of the fun of this place."

"In an Addams Family kind of way."

"We could live here instead of running off to Germany."

"Then you really would have to get a Swiffer," Nathan said. He glanced up, squinting critically. "Plus, the ceilings could use some work."

"I have money."

"So I've heard."

"As much as we need."

"Theo," Nathan said, shifting his weight awkwardly from foot to foot. "Look, I don't know what you think. I mean, I don't know exactly what to say. I never know what I should say—"

"Shut up," Theo said mildly and took Nathan's face in his hands and kissed him. Nathan, startled, nearly pulled back. But he didn't. Theo's lips were soft, as he had expected them to be, but the kiss was quick and it was over before Nathan knew it. Theo danced away, smiling down at him because he was so tall, and said, "Come on, let me show you the second floor," as if nothing had happened.

And Nathan, blinking and disoriented, followed him.

"You know what I hate most about Disney movies?" Theo said as they reached the landing. He paused, one hand gliding along the balustrade (which, Nathan noticed, was also curiously free of dust or cobwebs or detritus of any kind); his brow furrowed and he half-smiled. "They always have those cheap-ass happy endings."

"They're Disney movies. That's their *raison d'etre*."

"Ooh, French! Be still my heart. But the fairy tales," Theo said insistently. "The originals. You know them."

"All of them."

"Then you know," and they continued up the stairs, "there is some fucked-up shit that goes on. Red Riding Hood gets eaten by that wolf—"

"Werewolf, you said."

"Excuse me, *were*wolf. Birds attack the eyes. Iron boots for witches. And the Little Mermaid turns to foam after she walks on knives because that's the price for being human. Sick shit, I'm telling you."

"I don't think that would sell," Nathan said wryly.

"You're right. But that's why I love those stories. They're real, or more real than fucking Disney."

"The Grimm brothers collected them. Well, not the Little Mermaid. That was Hans Christian Andersen. But they didn't make them up. Or at least, not all of them."

"I think you're right," Theo said as they moved down a long hallway that had, once upon a time, been papered with what Nathan thought must've been blue and gold; now, it was peeling off in strips, a victim of the elements, or it had turned black in big patches the same way the ceiling downstairs had. Under the peeling paper in a few places, something had dug the plaster away and exposed wooden slats like ribs.

He kissed me, he did it, Nathan thought breathlessly; then, doubting himself, *Didn't he?* Nathan felt moving through this house was like a dreamworld. Nothing was real, or everything was.

Who owned it? Who owns it now? It must belong to someone; does Theo really—

But Theo was still talking, Theo was saying, "Going from village to village, collecting, collecting, always collecting. The . . . oral tradition." He snickered.

"Pervert."

"Fellow pervert. It was all about transformation. That was the seed at the heart of all those stories. Good and bad, those are just words. Even the good guys aren't *really* all good guys. And the bad guys especially could change on a dime. That's what I love about them. You can't expect anything. You never know what's going to happen next."

He kissed me he kissed me, Nathan thought. *Everything is real.*

"Check this out," Theo said, leading him through a door that hung half off its hinges and into a shadow-swept bedroom surprisingly well lit by the moonlight spilling through its high windows.

"This was her room," Nathan said.

Theo's eyes widened the slightest bit. "I believe you," he said at last.

"That's big of you."

"Shut up. You see, that's all I mean, and I believe in what you see."

They looked at each, and Nathan felt absurdly touched. He was having a hard time remembering what had happened downstairs: *Did he put his lips on mine? Did we howl like wolves? Did he grow wings and the beak of a raven and fly away into a cut in the air?*

"I wonder how long she lived here," Nathan said.

"She might not be real," Theo said. "Even now. Could be she's just the subject of a painting someone bought in an antique store and shoved up there on the wall."

"You know better." It came out in a whisper; the upstairs air was hard to breathe, stale somehow, and colder than it had been on the ground floor. He began to shiver.

"I told you to bring a hat," Theo said, frowning, then draped his arm around Nathan's shoulders. "There. Better?"

Take me home with you, Nathan whispered, or thought he did. The weight of Theo's arm felt good. He *did* feel warm, and Nathan closed his eyes and laid his head against Theo's chest and nestled there. "Don't be afraid of her," Nathan found himself saying, and Theo moved away from him and took back his arm and peered at him in the darkness with wide eyes.

"Who was she?"

"Is."

"Okay, is."

"She came here a long time ago," Nathan said dreamily. "This house is older than you think. That road we drove up is nothing but vague, yellow tracks in the grass now. And the woods grew up all around it."

"That's impossible."

"Sure, it is. But it's true. She was a bride, and *he* brought her here, took her from all she knew, just like a fairy tale, and he locked her up in this house he built for her and never let her go—"

"Princess in a tower," Theo said, staring.

"Just like that. This house in the woods, miles from anywhere, no friends, and the painting was her gift to him—"

"Narcissistic. I dig it."

"—and she hung it up there high, so he could never take it down. He allowed her to wander through the woods, and she hoped that the portrait would grow old and she would stay young, because after he died—"

"How did he die?"

"When his horse bolted and threw him and trampled all over his head. She wasn't sad, though she tried to be. She kept the house and never left again because the world had changed so much around her, and even she wasn't the same. She would come to that room every day to gaze upon the portrait with a hatred that grew fiercer with each passing year, until finally she died, and the portrait did not take her spirit, which faded away. She was gone, wherever people go when they die and stay dead. But what no one knew was that the *portrait* had taken on a life of its own. It looked out on the drawing room and saw whoever came before it. It had become something different. Alien. But it was still," and he swallowed thickly, "*alive*. It can't do anything but sit and stare. Watching. All it can do is watch. And now it hates everyone. Including us."

He stopped and opened his eyes; he had scared himself. Theo watched him with some kind of expression, but in the dimness, Nathan couldn't tell what: appreciation? fear? disdain?

He's the one who kissed me, Nathan thought petulantly. Then he laughed and said, "You're right, it's nothing. I made it all up."

"Weirdo," Theo said, but warmly. Nathan saw that he was smiling, and for a moment he felt weak with relief. He was warm all over. He took a step forward, but Theo put a hand on his shoulder to stop him, and, horribly, said, "Nathan."

"What?" Nathan growled. He wouldn't be frustrated, not now.

"It could be me, you know."

Nathan froze. His eyes grew wide in all that dark. "What could be you?" he whispered.

But he knew.

Theo only looked at him. "You don't know everything about me. You said so yourself."

"I know that you aren't a killer."

"Do you?"

"You'd just *tell* me?"

Theo laughed, a cold, heartless sound. Then he dropped his head. His hands clenched into fists. "I don't know," he said, and the coldness was gone as if it had never been. He just sounded sad. "I'm tired."

"Of what?"

"Pretending." He met Nathan's eyes.

I can't breathe, Nathan thought, *I can't*; "What are you pretending?" he said, his voice cracking.

Tell me it isn't you; please.

Theo stared down at him, unblinking.

"Hell, it could be *me*," Nathan said. He hated the anger he heard in his voice, how sharp and buzzing it sounded. "You ever think of that? It could be. Why not, huh? Why couldn't it be me?"

Theo grew silent, watching. He's thinking, Nathan thought, afraid; what is he thinking about? How he brought *me* out to this empty, deserted place, an impossible distance from home? That no one knows *we're* here? Is he wondering, even now, why he might have done such a thing?

Theo licked his lips.

"What would you do," Theo said slowly, considering each word, "if I told you that I have a boyfriend?"

Nathan watched him through a wall of ice that grew up between them.

He was pleading, his eyes large in the dim. "Or a girlfriend? Or both? Or none? What would you do? What would you say?"

"I—" Nathan began, but then closed his mouth with a snap.

They watched each other. Theo's eyes were inscrutable, unblinking. They searched Nathan's face instead. Nathan opened his mouth.

Below them, the front door flew open, loudly, explosively, and then it crashed shut again. Glass tinkled; they heard it fall from an unseen window.

Their eyes met and they came together without sound and held each other and shivered, and that was their only movement. Theo held up a finger to his lips; his eyes never left Nathan's.

They listened, but they only heard the hollow hooting of the wind, which rose every few seconds into a pantherish scream before dying away. They held each other and listened, and the house rocked under the pressure of that ferocious wind.

"I think—" Nathan started to say, then, directly below them, footsteps began.

Theo giggled madly. He put one of his hands in his mouth and bit down on the soft meat of his palm to quiet the sound. Tears collected at the corner of his eyes and ran down his face. Nathan could feel them, hot, scalding, over his fingers.

You brought me here, Nathan thought, feeling his eyes dart around wildly in his sockets. He wanted to shout accusingly, *Is this what you wanted?* But he dared not speak.

The footsteps moved around downstairs like a whirlwind, ferocious; a giant cat, perhaps, or a bear, enormous, grown hideously large out in these abandoned woods.

Nathan had to pee; Theo must have seen something of it in his face, for his eyes widened, and he shook his head firmly. But the pressure in Nathan's bladder only grew, as if a fist inside him, bearing down, clamped with strong, cruel fingers.

I won't, he thought. He bit his lip. *I won't, I won't.*

The footsteps were climbing the stairs.

Their eyes jumped to the door through which they had entered the room. It stood open, inviting anyone out there to follow them.

The urge to pee became overwhelming, a demand. Nathan tried to cross his legs, bit down on his lip until he tasted metal, but it did no good.

The air around them grew colder, and they pressed closely to each other, cheek to cheek, hands clutching and holding.

He is so very warm, Nathan thought distantly. *Am I coming apart?* His fear was consuming him, making all of him fly away as if nothing could be held together any longer. He could melt like mist into the walls, right into the molecules that made up the wallpaper, soft pink and green, like heather. He would let that happen.

The footsteps stopped.

A woman walked into the room.

She was big, taller than Theo even, her hair cut so screamingly short that pink scalp showed through in places. Her eyes were hollow and shattered, and she wore the clothes of a man: an oversized flannel shirt partially tucked in, revealing the midnight moon swell of her gut, and cowboy boots thick and clotted with black mud. She saw them immediately.

"Thought you could get away," she said, and her lips split like twin livers to reveal perfectly white straight teeth. "Thought you could come here and go up the stairs and touch everything and hide from me." She sneered, then roared, "From *me!*"

"We didn't mean," Nathan said, but his teeth were chattering and he thought that his bladder would simply explode, and the words didn't come out so he tried again. "We didn't mean to."

"Leave us alone," Theo said. His voice was firm and ferocious at the same time.

"Come here to steal things," the woman said. She breathed deeply so that her giant breasts expanded under the flannel shirt. Trembling, Nathan saw that it was only buttoned in one or two places; he could see the nipple of the left breast, which was long and sagged down toward the white swell of her belly. The nipple burned dark purple in the chancy light of the room where she had found them, unerringly. "Come into my house to steal what belongs to me?" She laughed, big and booming. Her eyes were round and silver as the moon.

"We didn't come here to steal anything," Theo said.

"Liar," the woman said immediately. "Oh, you filthy liar." Her livery lips were wet with spit. She took a step forward then, and Nathan's eyes bulged as she came, for he could see now that she cast no shadow on the floor.

"Theo," he tried to say, tried to point; *she's one of them*, but the words were splinters and they stuck firmly in his throat.

"Get out of here," Theo commanded. "There's no place for you."

"Theo, don't," Nathan wheezed. And then he had the paralyzing realization that Theo could see her, too.

Theo drew himself up firmly. "We'll knock you down. How do you know we won't? We could kill you, if that's what we wanted to do. Now let us go."

The woman laughed her wild laugh. "Girls, girls," she said, jeering, and put her fat fingers before her mouth to stifle the sound, which came out in a spray of stupid, horsey laughter. "Coupla faggy girls, holding each other tight like that." The laughter stopped as abruptly as it began, and she glared at them with those terrible eyes, blank and silver. She removed her belt with delicate, precise smoothness. "Won't do you no good. Come into my house to steal. Don't you know what I do to faggy little girls who come into my house in the dead of night to steal?" Her breathing grew heavy; she was nearly panting with excitement. She started to slap the folded belt against the thick meaty palm of her hand: *crack*, it went, *crack*.

"Leave us alone," Theo said again. But he sounded uncertain now.

"Can't," the big woman said, growing taller as she came for them; she swelled until she filled the room, all wrath and eager anticipation. One hand darted forward with animal speed and slapped Nathan across the face so that his head rocked back with dreadful force and he fell away from Theo, out of his arms. Dimly, he heard Theo call his name, but he could do nothing but fall, forever it seemed, until at last he stopped and struck the floor. His face held no feeling at all. In a daze, he thought that maybe he'd broken his neck; he couldn't move from where he lay.

The woman, seeing the wetness at the crotch of his jeans, laughed her dreadful, bestial laugh. "Baby," she sang, "baby oh faggy baby! Look at you! Disgusting! Foul!" She punctuated this last word by lashing out with her foot so that the toe of her enormous boot connected solidly with Nathan's calf. It seized immediately, and he opened his mouth to scream, but the pain swallowed the world. He couldn't get any air, so the scream hung silently.

The dog, he thought, absurdly. *Oh god, the dog is back, and this time it won't stop. It won't just bite my arm; it will tear out my throat and lap up my blood with its long pink tongue. The dog will tear off my head and devour it.*

But no. She wasn't a dog. He looked at her and saw what she was.

Reality warped and shivered around him; he tried to sit up, and the woman, laughing still, was a bear, huge and hideous. She drew back her arm to hit him with the belt, but Theo threw himself forward with a ferocious shriek and tackled her, driving her against the wall. Nathan sat up in time to watch as puffs of plaster-like miniature mushroom clouds rose from the walls, which had rotted beneath the pretty paper. The whole house, the entire place, was rotting away.

It will fall down on us, crush us, and it will bury us here forever. With her.

The woman threw her arm out and backhanded Theo, who flew across the room, but too far, it wasn't possible. Then the terrible, gobbling woman turned her empty eyes back to Nathan, grinned with long teeth, and came for him again.

Nathan thought she'd bite him, bite him like that dog had, because the dead people were hungry all the time. The mermaid woman had been right: he only saw the hungry ones, the horrible hungry dead.

She will tear out my throat and drink my blood as if it were water.

Theo threw his arms around her neck with the foggy bellowing of an angry bull, and she echoed him with her own bear's roar. She spun around with deadly speed and latched her hands, the size of shovels, around Theo's throat. His eyes tried to close but were unable, not with the pressure of the woman strangling him with those shovel hands, so they bulged, wide, then *wider*; his tongue protruded from his mouth and tears rolled down his face. It began to turn purple on its way toward eternal nighted black.

The dog. You sent it away, remember?

Theo's face darkened, darkened; his eyes bulged; his nose and mouth leaked fluids.

Do something! Turn it against them. They encouraged you, now turn it against them!

Nathan didn't think. He flew across the room, became a bird, raven or rook or crow, no, an *owl*; furious and silent and full of that sense of power. He struck that silver-eyed woman with his elbow at the side of her neck, drove it into her, thought icily, *Break* your *neck now, dead undead or whatever, break your goddamn neck break it like a tree branch.* She made a thick squawking sound and loosened her hands from Theo's throat and fell over backward, landing first on her enormous butt, then on her head, which struck the hardwood floor with a crack as loud as old ice on a pond gone black and rotten just before it breaks apart for good on the first warm day of spring.

Theo gasped and clutched his throat and hawked and spat a wad of blood onto the floor. Nathan reached out, eyes shining, grinning despite himself.

"Run!" Nathan yelled. "She's dead or she's a bear or she's *something*, but she'll kill us now unless we *run!*"

Theo, wide-eyed and white-faced and grinning, too, said, "Lions and tigers and werebears, oh my," and seized Nathan's hand. Nathan yanked him up with all his strength just as the woman planted her shovel-hands against the floor and heaved herself up onto her knees. She lifted her head and her silver eyes found Nathan and widened, marking him. She came for them, crawling on her hands and knees, fast and crab-like, but she grinned and growled and slobbered. Her teeth were stained pink.

"GET BACK DOWN," Nathan said in a voice like thunder, and she did, scooting backward as if struck by an enormous, invisible fist, and she roared out her fury.

They ran; bolted together down the hallway, threw themselves down the stairs, struck the balustrade, and cracked the newel post. They could hear the woman scrabbling behind them, but they made it down the stairs and Theo slammed the door shut. The doorknob instantly twisted and turned and the woman inside was howling and screaming; they leaped down the steps as she threw open the door. She was enormous; she filled the entire doorway, a grizzly sow, furious, running at them in that terrible rolling way specific to grizzlies, her tiny beady eyes silver and red, their faces captured within, but they were safe in the car with the engine ignited.

She struck the side of the car with a sound that was the end of all the worlds.

"Drive!" Nathan screamed in a delirium of terror.

And Theo screamed back, *"What do you think I'm trying to do, take her out for a chicken dinner?"*

Nathan threw back his head and shrieked crazy laughter, and the woman's bear-face filled his window and glared in at him. She showed her butcher knife teeth in a slobbery snarl; then they were driving away and she was left behind, roaring impotently and running with that ursine roll. Snow filled the air, blinding them, and she was gone and the house was gone, lost behind them. But no matter how fast or how far they drove, they found themselves still locked deep inside the secret heart of the forest.

9

THEO DIDN'T REQUIRE an invitation; they came silently with chests that heaved and dripping brows into Nathan's dorm room. They passed Barry, long-forgotten, in the hallway, and his eyes widened as he took Theo in; there was, after all, between they two a certain resemblance in body size and facial structure. But even though Nathan didn't acknowledge him, didn't even see him as they passed, Theo's head swiveled on his neck like a mannequin's so he could offer Barry an enormous, crazy grin, all white teeth and lupine eyes, and Barry backed away until he was flat against the wall.

Then Nathan's room, and Theo's hands were on him.

"I wanted you from the moment I saw you," Theo said, and he pulled Nathan's belt off and Nathan couldn't talk, could only nod, and Theo kissed him again, harder, then ferociously, until their teeth clashed; Theo had his cock out and then Nathan's, too, and he pushed them together like kindling so they could *feel* each other, and he knelt down before Nathan and engulfed him completely, down to the base of his erection, and Nathan *screamed*, the heat, the wet, the burning.

"Fuck me," Theo said, and "Fuck me fuck me kiss me," said Nathan, and they kissed and they fucked, back and forth and back and forth; "Love you love you love," Theo growled in his ear, thrusting; Nathan's back arched in a bow until he thought it would break; Theo, teasing him, fingering the slit of his cock, *tasting* him, and staring at him with wide and knowing eyes. Somehow there was music blasting, and the snow had become sleet outside and hit the window again and again, relentlessly, and the wind gibbered and then shrieked until its throat was too full of snow so it could only choke.

"Love fuck love me," Nathan said; and Theo threw his head back because he was finally coming, it was love love was coming, on Nathan's fingers and his face and in his mouth and it was cold, it was all freezing cold, Theo's semen was like ice that burned and Nathan loved it and lapped it up, every icy drop.

10

AT SOME POINT in the night, though he wasn't sure when, Nathan opened his eyes and reached out his hand. The beds were twins, and even though he'd pushed them together, they were still achingly small. The spot where he'd left Theo sleeping as he himself fled down the corridors of sleep was empty.

I'm dreaming, he thought, smiling. *The whole thing was a dream, or all of it is a dream and I'm somewhere else. I'm in my bed back at home, or I'm in Seb's bed and he finally let me spend the night. Seb, at last; Seb loves me and I love him.*

He sat up then, blinking, his naked chest cold from the currents of air twining around him. He could see the ugly orange light from the lamppost in the courtyard down below; he was in his dorm room, and he was alone. He began to tremble, so he lay back on the lumpy mattress and put his head on his pillow and closed his eyes, and as he did, he put one hand over the spot where Theo had lain. It was flat and so, so cold.

But when he moaned out loud some hours later and his eyes fluttered because the light streaming in through the window was hard and white, he heard rustling beside him, felt warmth blooming, felt the naked skin of a body; he opened his eyes and Theo was looking down at him, his expression wry and amused.

"You sounded like you were in pain," Theo said. "Or scared."

"I dreamed," Nathan said.

Theo nodded, as if that was what he'd expected. His shoulders were so round and so white, scattered with freckles. Nathan touched one, slowly, lovingly.

Theo smiled. "Can't sleep all day," he said.

"Why not?"

Theo considered this, then shrugged. "Okay. Maybe we can."

"I don't know what day it is."

"*I* don't know what day it is."

"Or the year."

"Nope."

"I thought," Nathan said, slowly and shyly, "that maybe I dreamed it all."

"If you did, then so did I."

"It was scary."

"It was."

"You believe me now? About *them*?"

"I always believed you."

"Don't go."

"Couldn't pay me." Theo leaned down until they were eye to eye, then he winked and kissed the tip of Nathan's nose. "You're mine now."

It's not him, Nathan thought, relieved, *and it's not me. So who?* Nathan felt a surge of confidence. *We'll find him; we did that spell, we can always do more. We can always, always do more.*

Later, as they showered together in one stall, alone in the vast washroom, Nathan, allowing Theo to scrub his back and, teasingly, run his hands over the curved globes of Nathan's buttocks, said, "Theo?"

"Yes?" He was amused, aroused. Nathan could feel him, hard again and growing ever harder, pressing up against the cleft of his ass.

"What you said. Back there."

"About what?"

"About . . ." Nathan bit his lip.

Say it, that gray and withered Outsider's voice spat in his mind. It screamed bits of laughter, mocking him. *Say it*, the voice hissed and gibbered. *Say it and be damned!*

But I have to, Nathan thought, dismayed. *If I don't, I never will.* "About boyfriends."

"Yeah?" He didn't stop his ministrations.

"You said, 'What if I have a boyfriend? Or a girlfriend?'" Nathan swallowed. Theo's mouth was on his throat, his arms came around both sides of him and his hands, slick with soap, went lower and lower, his teeth were nipping. Nathan closed his eyes; Theo's hand found him, and it was so *insistent*; Nathan opened his mouth to moan, but said instead, "You don't, do you? You wouldn't do this, *this*, with me, would you, if you really had a . . ."

Theo turned him so that they faced each other, and Nathan was afraid. But Theo's face, though thin and white, held tenderness. "I told you. Didn't you hear me? Last night. I loved you the moment I saw you."

"Oh," Nathan said inadequately.

Theo sank down onto his knees, and his eyes never left Nathan's. "I thought you believed me," he said, and took Nathan into his mouth.

"I do," Nathan said. He put his hands into Theo's tangle of thick, wet hair. He closed his eyes. "God."

When it was done and the water striking them made them feel pruned and logy, Theo kissed him and said again, "You summoned me. Didn't you know that? There was no one before you. Never." He laughed his wild laugh, and there was something dark in his eyes, but Nathan didn't care anymore. He felt instead an answering darkness inside himself that flowered and grew and twined. They made love again back in Nathan's room, and afterward they held each other as the wind shrieked and whooped outside and the world grew white and cold and then even colder with snow that cried relentlessly, *Winter, winter coming.*

Later, Theo slept beside him, his head on Nathan's chest. Nathan's fingers stroked his hair absently. He stared up at the ceiling, but every few seconds his eyes moved, as if drawn by magic, back to the window, which showed nothing but white. *You summoned me*, Theo had said. The wind wailed, the wind *screamed*. He tried to keep his eyes from the window, but back they went, circling again and again. He could feel Theo's breath on his chest, warm.

He's real, Nathan thought with panic, gently putting his fingers against Theo's throat. There was a pulse. *Oh thank god; he's real, he's real.*

You summoned me, he'd said, and, *You are mine.*

Nathan's eyes went back to the window where the snow swirled and seemed to become faces with eyes that thinned and glared in at him accusingly.

You are mine, you are mine, you are mine.

Theo smiled in his sleep and continued to breathe deeply and gently, and, watching the faces at the window, Nathan felt that old familiar ice rime over him again, black and thick in terribly recognizable patterns, chilling him and freezing his heart.

IV

THE BLACK FOREST

"I AM SURE, Carmilla, you have been in love; that there is, at this moment, an affair of the heart going on."

"I have been in love with no one, and never shall," she whispered, "unless it should be with you."

How beautiful she looked in the moonlight!

Shy and strange was the look with which she quickly hid her face in my neck and hair, with tumultuous sighs, that seemed almost to sob, and pressed in mine a hand that trembled.

Her soft cheek was glowing against mine. "Darling, darling," she murmured, "I live in you; and you would die for me, I love you so."

I started from her.

She was gazing on me with eyes from which all fire, all meaning had flown, and a face colorless and apathetic.

"Is there a chill in the air, dear?" she said drowsily. "I almost shiver; have I been dreaming? Let us come in. Come; come; come in."

"You look ill, Carmilla; a little faint. You certainly must take some wine," I said.

"Yes, I will. I'm better now. I shall be quite well in a few minutes. Yes, do give me a little wine," answered Carmilla, as we approached the door. "Let us look again for a moment; it is the last time, perhaps, I shall see the moonlight with you."

J. Sheridan Le Fanu, *Carmilla*

1

LAST NIGHT.

He stood, abruptly, at the epicenter of the party, that grand curl of a staircase rising before him so familiar, still white and gleaming. He tapped the slick-smooth balustrade with one firm finger and wondered if it ever existed in the actual, outside world. *Reincarnation?* His mouth twitched, amused. He wondered what Theo thought about that possibility. Had Nathan existed in this world before, only to remember it now? Had he created it all by himself? And if he had, had he drawn from some impossible pool of memories, of real places and real things and real times? Somewhere in the vast swell of the room he heard, inevitably, the chiming, lisping laugh of the mermaid woman in her dress of sparkling emerald.

"And, of course," a bright-eyed young man said directly into his ear, "you just *know* he won't come. He won't dare show his face at all, I mean, how could he?" The boy, for he seemed younger even than Nathan, sipped at his cocktail, releasing an unpleasant giggle, a bubble of gas. "We don't want his kind *here*."

"What about my kind?" Nathan said, and the boy took his hand and squeezed it. His fingers blazed.

"But it's your house," said the boy slyly. "On this night, always this night, in your house, we're here for *you*, handsome. She's already told you. I know she has."

"The midnight hour is close at hand!" the mermaid woman called to him from across the room, over the heads of the throng who lifted their glasses and cheered, all hale and robust. "The witching hour, for all the witches here!" She trilled merry, evil laughter.

"What do you want from me?" he asked the boy.

I know him, he thought. Those dark, sad, horrible, broken eyes; *I know him; from where?*

"What we've always wanted," the boy said, frowning and staring into his drink as he swirled it around and around. Instead of an olive, Nathan saw the furry head of a rodent, dark and drowned, bobbed there, and he looked away, repulsed. "You should stay this time," the boy said impulsively. "We've wanted you for simply ages. We've been telling you and telling you."

"I know you," Nathan said, but his voice was lost over the rising cheer of the group of men and women surrounding the mermaid woman, who, it seemed, had just shared a salty riposte with them; they howled in joy, loving her.

"You're going to have to choose." The boy raised his voice. "Him or us."

Nathan narrowed his eyes. "That isn't a choice. There's no choice to make *there*."

"School is meaningless." The boy laughed. "A dream. You can't go back to the way things used to be. They won't have you; you must know that by now."

"Stop it." But he felt that familiar chill of ice in his guts and he knew the boy was right.

"I can't. It's for your own good."

"I won't choose."

"You'll have to. The world won't take you back, so you can come with us and stay here at this party forever . . . or go with him. And you'll see," the boy said, spitting laughter, "what kind of a choice *that* would be."

"I *know* you," Nathan insisted.

The boy smirked. His eyes glowed, hot and full of challenge.

"Tell me," Nathan said, "about the hierarchy."

The boy raised an eyebrow. "What a lovely, exquisite kind of word."

"She used it and you know it. She said there was a hierarchy. There's the deaders—"

"The idiot dead," the boy said, gently correcting him, then considered. "The *hungry*, idiot dead," he added. His face glowed cold and blue, his nose a hole, his eye sockets empty except for the *worms*—

Nathan looked away, his anger growing.

He's trying to confuse me, he thought, furious. *I won't let him; I can't allow that.*

"Is that what the lost boys are? And that terrible woman in the woods?" Nathan said through clenched teeth.

"Oh, we have nothing to do with *them*. He made them, probably. Like an infection." He shuddered. "Aren't they just the worst? Infection. Ghouls! Loathsome."

"And there's you—"

"Us," the boy simpered. "And what did she call us?"

"Outsiders."

"Lovely. Simply divoon. I love that word, don't you? Divo*ooooooon*."

"Focus," Nathan snarled.

I am wandering in a dream, he thought. *I have always been here, will always be; when I die . . .*

"'Outsider.' A little on the nose." He tapped his own, then reached out and tapped Nathan's. "But it'll do. And it makes sense. We are outside. But we watch. We just want to feel, that's all! It's so simple."

"You won't be able to," Nathan said, "if you kill me."

When I die . . .

"Kill you?" the boy exclaimed, horrified. "Nathan, darling, whoever said anything about killing you? We're not monsters, you know!" His brow crinkled. "Actually, I suppose we are." His laughter was chiming and childlike and wicked. "If you join the party, then the party goes on indefinitely! You'll be one of us. You have all that power; you even used it recently! Felt good, didn't it?" Nathan only stared at him, stone-faced. "You want to feel that way again. Hey, chumly, stay with us and you can! Always and forever you can!"

"I don't want to."

Don't you?

"But you invented this." He swept his arm out in a slow arc. It stretched as it went, housed within the crackling black fabric of his immaculate dinner jacket. But Nathan saw that it ended in the claw of a panther, ebon-furred, the nails needle-sharp and gleaming. "This?" the boy said. "This is all *you*, old chum; don't blame *us*. The party, the costumes, even the champagne and those pink and gold balloons. They all came from your very own *cabesa*." He reached out to tap Nathan again with the tip of his panther claw and Nathan recoiled.

"Stop trying to distract me," Nathan growled. "I want to know. There's the dead, the Outsiders, the lost boys and . . . what else? Who is doing the infecting? She talked about it, but she talked in circles, because that's all you morons are capable of doing; you're as bad as the deaders; hell, you're worse!"

The boy was glaring. "Call us morons then, you beast," he said, deadly quiet. "The truth is . . . the truth is . . ." He sighed and dropped his eyes. When next he spoke, his voice was nearly inaudible. "We don't actually know." He folded his arms over his chest and drummed his claws against his shoulders; his face drew together in a sullen pout.

"I hurt your feelings?" Nathan gasped with laughter. "Oh, that's rich. That's delightful in its richness! Hell. So you don't even know what you are?" The boy's lower lip trembled furiously. "You might be spirits of trees and rocks for all you know. Or maybe you are just deaders after all, but it's been so long that you've forgotten and so you think you're something special." Horror broke through the paroxysms of laughter overtaking him. "There is no answer. Or you don't have it. So it's all just nothing."

"That's bleak," the mermaid woman called from where she stood surrounded by a group of things that squealed and belched from the pink and hairy tentacles writhing in the centers of what passed for their faces; at least their evening gowns were chic, Nathan thought, laughing and dazed with horror.

"That isn't true, though!" the boy said. "Listen. We're here because we felt your light. We're like moths in that way. You glowed so bright and fierce that we came to you. We learned that you gave us shape and form. And we can *feel* when you're here. Stay with us," the boy said, small and sad, and he touched Nathan's cheek with a hand that had become human again. "Please," he whispered.

Nathan ground his teeth together. "What about the hierarchy?" The boy only shrugged. "You aren't innocent. You may be stupid, but you aren't innocent."

"Don't call us stu—"

"The *hierarchy.*" With deadly speed, he seized the boy by the shoulders and gave him a brisk shake. "What did she mean?"

"Let me go," the boy whined. "You're hurting me when you do that; it hurts, okay?"

Nathan gave him another shake; the boy's mouth gaped open, wide, too wide, and he shrieked, an inhuman, hurt, animal sound. But Nathan shouted over the screaming, "What else is out there? What else have I seen? Or will see? Tell me!" Then, quieter, more intense: "Is it a demon? Is that it?"

The boy's screams stopped abruptly. "Demon isn't the right word," he said sullenly, trying again without success to extricate himself from Nathan's grip. "And spirit isn't the right word either, because there *isn't* a word right enough. You're the stupid ones, with your useless language. Your words that are too complicated or not complicated enough. Vampire, werewolf, demon; upir, dybbuk, loogaroo. You have no idea! Ancient things. Do you really want to know? They are a part of your world. They can be whatever they want, form themselves however they want. They think you're interesting. They're playful. Sometimes they even trick themselves into thinking they love you."

Nathan stared, horrified again, and released him before he realized he had done so.

"Skinwalker is the term your clever friend Roger used. His grandmother's grandmother's grandmother might have spoken thrillingly of '*Naap*': a troublemaker, a trickster. A shapeshifter. Or," he said, relenting, "I *suppose* you could say demon. Or daemon, with that extra a. That's rather charming. Demons. Devils."

The creature before him was, Nathan realized, shrinking as he spoke, growing younger; his voice piped high and shrill.

"Your kind has always been sooooo afraid of the devil, and that's probably good! He has horns, or does he? He has cloven hooves, or does he? Do his eyes glow gold and hot? Are they split like a cat's? Is his semen icy cold?"

"I *do* know you," Nathan said through numb lips. He saw him clearly now, cleaned up nicely in his fancy tuxedo, but the face was the same: the pale, unhealthy skin color, the damp black bangs hanging like crooked fingers above his dark brows, and those terrible, broken eyes. "The boy from the antique mall. I saw you that day with Railway Mary, before I knew she had a name. I knew you were different than her—"

"You don't know *anything*," the boy said in a voice like the shriek of a blizzard; his jaw muscles locked, his eyes were the red-rimmed eyes of a great cat. He whirled away, and the crowd devoured him.

Nathan stood stock-still, staring after him, whispering to himself, "Maybe I don't."

Deaders. Outsiders. Demons.

So that was the hierarchy. *Beings that, through the shitty, bad luck of the lamp that shines out of me—that I can't feel or see, that I don't want or need—brought all these things into my orbit.*

Fuck, he thought wryly, me.

The lost boys are infected. What does that mean? Who infected them?

Shift, and he found himself nodding stupidly at a woman with the gray and leathery face of a rhinoceros perched upon her pretty neck. Her eyes were tiny black dots, and the horn above her mouth, which formed idiocies he couldn't follow or understand—but he nodded moronically, nevertheless—jabbed at him constantly, only inches from his own face.

These are my options. He moved away to avoid being skewered, and the rhino woman laughed merrily as if that were the best possible of all jests. "Theo?" he whispered. "Theo, where are you?"

He could stay with Theo. Wasn't that an option? Couldn't it be his choice? As soon as they figured out who the killer was, they could banish the lost boys and any other deader that wanted a piece of them. And after that . . . ?

"Just Theo and me," Nathan said, and the rhino woman recoiled as if he had spat upon her; harrumphing with indignation, she vanished into the crowd.

Nathan smiled to himself.

I could try college, he thought. *Actually give it the old college try, ha ha; I could go to my classes and study and figure out what the hell I want to be, try to find whatever the hell I'm meant to do.*

The path through the forest; decisive action. With Theo, I can do anything.

The mermaid woman had mounted the staircase and was standing five or six steps up so that she towered over the others. She lifted high her glass and called out in a voice that cut through the crowd like the clever blade of a knife: "Let us raise our glasses to our host, our very favorite, our darling, our Nathan, who brought us here so that we may share in his light, just as he always has, just as he always will!"

No, Nathan tried to say aloud, *this is idiotic*; but he was frozen in place, couldn't even turn his head. She stared emerald icicles down at him; he felt the cruelty in her smile, the way only one corner of her mouth lifted, how little lines like jagged cracks marring the earth after rainwater dried ran roughshod all over her face. She loathed him, and she knew he knew. Yet she raised her glass ever higher and called out, "To Nathan!"

"Theo," he whispered, "Theo, please."

"To Nathan!" the crowd responded.

To his horror, Nathan's own hand rose as well.

A dark shape appeared in one of the tall windows that were more like walls, rising twenty, thirty feet high, up and up, behind the mermaid woman. A shape that grew darker and darker and *thick*—

"Nathan!" she cried, and "NATHAN!" the crowd echoed.

"Nathan," he whispered.

Nathan, he heard. A smile. *Hello.*

The window behind the mermaid woman exploded. Everyone screamed, the mermaid woman ducked, shrieking; they tried to scatter as something burst through the glass, a thing with glowing golden eyes and enormous black wings lined with scarlet veins and a flash of a salt-white face; a black slash for a mouth writhed, studded with butcher knife teeth. It was grinning and laughing, the invading thing, reaching out with long, white fingers, each tipped with a curved yellow claw that reminded Nathan of the foot of an eagle he saw once perched on a telephone pole along the highway. With a single swipe of the monster's claw, it tore through the mermaid woman, who opened her mouth to shriek, fell forward, twisted in the air, and was just . . . gone.

The thing, the thing, the shadow-winged monster *from my first night in the dorm. The one I was so sure was coming for Barry, but it was me, me, and it came for me, and it's here for me now.*

Nathan blinked; the beast roared dreadful laughter, moving too quickly for Nathan to catch a glimpse of its face. It launched itself into the crowd. They attempted to run; shrieking, they bolted like rats, and yes, some of them wore the heads of rats, some were nothing more than pink and bulging monstrosities with too many eyes or none at all, just mouths and screaming teeth; Nathan watched as the thing tore through each Outsider just as it had the mermaid woman, swiping, ripping with its monstrous mouth and jagged teeth, tearing and tearing and tearing.

I can feel the chill of the wind on my face, Nathan thought. *I can hear it howling, and I don't think this is a dream, no dream, no dream.*

He looked down at the floor and saw, for the first time, that it was composed entirely of the tiniest, most delicate arrangement of bones. And he understood, crushingly, that it always had been.

Later, when he tried to tell Theo about it, what was surely a dream and not, he insisted, an actual place he'd visited, he found that the words wouldn't come, though Theo allowed him the attempt with a polite smile.

"Maybe it means you have a champion after all," Theo said after Nathan had given up. "Maybe they got a good thrashing and now they'll go into retreat."

"A monster?" Nathan said weakly. "You mean, I conjured up a demon?"

"Better than *them*. Isn't it?"

"I don't know," Nathan said quietly.

"At any rate," Theo said, "I bet you're done with that woman and her mermaid dress and chignon that's sixty years out of date. I bet," and Theo's eyes sparkled with merriment, "you'll never see *her* again. Hey, c'mon. Let's watch an old movie on your ridiculously tiny TV."

2

"I'M NOT GOING to stay the entire time," Julian said happily; around them, bodies bustled through the Student Union, festooned as it was with garlands of silver and crimson and metallic emerald green and clumps of poinsettias, all thrust together in their pots and arranged, irritatingly, with no discernable pattern. Nathan had been glaring at his Native American Lit notes for half an hour before Julian plopped himself down in the seat at the little study table across from him; he glanced up with something like despair and didn't bother to smile or offer the other boy anything resembling a word of welcome.

Julian's face was round and red with holiday humor. "At my folks' house. For winter break, I mean. Jeepers, have you even thought about how long it is? Really?"

"Five weeks," Nathan said.

"Five weeks," Julian said, nodding and smiling his pleased little smile. "Five amazing weeks. In high school, we had a week and a half if we were lucky." He closed his eyes and shivered pleasantly. "And you know what I'll be doing."

"I can't imagine."

"Well," Julian drawled, "I'm coming back the day after Christmas. I can't stay in my dorm, of course, but that's okay, because I get to go home with Bradley." He added, with a lecherous little wink, "*He* has his own apartment."

"Bradley?"

"Come on, Nathan, *Bradley*." Nathan made an uncomprehending face. "My *boy*friend? The one I met at the dance? The one I've been telling you about for the last half hour?"

"Oh. Right. That Bradley."

"You don't have to be jealous," Julian said wickedly. "Just because you're going to die a lonely old spinster."

"Men don't become spinsters."

"Then whatever the man of spinster is. You don't have to be *jealous*, hon."

"Hon."

"Darling. Sweetie darling." Julian beamed. "God, the past month has been di*voon*, you don't even *know*."

"Divoon isn't a word." He thought of the party—the dream, dammit—and the dark-eyed boy, but wouldn't allow himself the privilege of a shiver, even if he wanted to.

"Bradley says it all the time."

"I'll bet."

The past month, as far as Nathan was concerned, hadn't been at all divoon, not counting the times he spent with Theo. Thanksgiving came and went, and that was nightmarish, the day after their experience in that terrible house, the day after they made love for the first time (and that was how Nathan thought of it now, not in curlicues or with little cartoon birdies flittering about, and not clinically, with tiny typewriter font, but in his very own handwriting with gray graphite pencil; he loved Theo, and Theo loved him), and he was amazed at the thought, as he continued to be amazed. They watched movies on Nathan's tiny television or on his laptop, lying side by side on the two dreadful twin beds, still pushed together, took walks in the early morning along the Royal River, by the ash trees that lined the trail in the park; they had their sex, and it usually happened several times a day and was always, Nathan thought with a trace of smugness, exquisite. But thoughts of Theo and all the magical things they did together lay over every moment of the Thanksgiving break he'd spent at home, so that, finally, none of those memories felt real. Sometimes he was certain that he was just fading away, inch by inch, that there was so little left of him, that whatever it was that could be called "Nathan," memories, experiences, individual thoughts, was all nearly gone.

Even his search for the killer had grown dim and unimportant. And that term, "killer," was rather dramatic, Nathan thought dreamily as Julian droned on and on. Really, a killer? Maybe those boys just ran away; maybe they couldn't handle college. It wasn't for everyone, was it; it was even possible that Deborah had tangled with an animal of some kind, or that she had simply killed herself. The details he'd heard about the state of her body could have been exaggerated. Didn't college kids gossip just as badly as anyone else? Nathan's thoughts of the killer were fading, growing misty. Besides, it was probably Kyle Matthews.

There did seem to be one other possibility, but it was too far-fetched to even consider, too far on the side of complete nonsense, idiocy, and so he'd pushed it readily from his mind. No one else had disappeared; no one else had suffered at the blade or claws of a killer or an animal or a killer animal; it just didn't seem to matter anymore, that was all. So little seemed to matter these days.

Except for Theo.

"The dorms are going to close," Julian was saying, and Nathan nodded as if he'd been listening all along. "Soon. You know, Nathan? You know?"

"Oh," Nathan said, "yes."

The dorms were indeed closing soon, which was going to be an issue. They had also closed on Thanksgiving, no exceptions: if you wanted to stay in Garden City that Wednesday through the following Saturday, you'd better have friends or family in town or enough cash to rent a hotel for a week. Most of the kids Nathan had overheard were leaving campus and the city and wouldn't be back until late Sunday night. Nathan, of course, had returned home. His *real* home, and he always thought of it that way, even if he didn't want to. "It won't be so terrible," Theo told him after yet another enjoyable afternoon spent alone together. "It isn't like you've never done Thanksgiving before."

"Come with me," Nathan said for the millionth time, and for the millionth time, Theo closed his eyes and smiled and shook his head sweetly, *no.*

"Out of the question," he said, "absolutely. I have my own holiday drama to deal with, believe me."

"Then take me with you. It'll be fun." He heard the tinge of desperation in his voice growing more cloying, but he was powerless to stop it. "I won't even have to be your boyfriend. I can be your roommate, or just some guy from school."

"What makes you think I'm not out at home?"

"Because I don't know anything about your home or your family," and Nathan's eyes narrowed, as they always did when they broached this particular subject, "or your life at all before now."

"You know all you need to know," Theo said with his customary head-toss.

Nathan knew he couldn't accept that answer for much longer, as he'd been doing all month; but he kept this knowledge to himself. "I don't even know how you're getting there. Wherever it is."

"Broomstick," Theo said, and his eyes sparkled.

"Baboon's blood," Nathan replied, swatting his arm, and then Theo laughed and Nathan laughed and Theo snuggled his head against Nathan's chest and kissed him and they didn't talk about it again. The next day, Theo walked away, whistling, with his hands shoved into his pockets, out of Nathan's dorm. Nathan watched him until he was gone, alone again, faced with the inevitability of home.

Terry stared lifelessly, squinting occasionally, as if Nathan were a ghost or an image on the television, a show about a brother he once had or someone who looked like his brother; they didn't speak, not really, and his father smiled and clapped him on the shoulder, but Nathan couldn't feel the weight of his father's hand, his touch. They asked him all the right questions, or the questions that each, privately, thought they should ask, and since Terry wasn't going to college ("Not ever," he told them repeatedly) it was as if Nathan had returned from some foreign land. Dorothy, perhaps, after her silver shoes carried her over the sands of the Deadly Desert, or Alice, fresh from her jaunt through the Looking Glass. His mother was the only one who studied him carefully, with eyes that were over-bright. Too often he caught her staring at him while he watched television or concentrated on the screen of his laptop or his phone, her eyes full of a strange kind of light, sparkling too much; he knew that any second she might cry, and he could not abide that, absolutely not.

"You comfortable in your old room?" she asked him on Thursday morning. She didn't cook the Thanksgiving meal; traditionally, and through mutual agreement, that role went to Nathan's father, who would be up before dawn to gleefully slide the turkey into the oven after a good night of marinating in a brine in their garage. But his mother made them coffee and sat beside Nathan on the couch after she handed him his, prepared in the mug he'd used throughout high school and subsequently forgotten until he held it once again in his hands, staring at it with something like wonder. A splash of cream, and he smiled, inhaling it, the way he liked it.

It was strange to hear her refer to his room as "old," for her as much as for him; he could tell by the expression on her face after she said it, that weird light in her eyes, the downward tilt to her lips, as if she'd made an off-color joke in front of her boss. "It's fine," he said. He didn't want to sound like some stupid emo teenager, some sullen idiot who couldn't express himself; "It's nice to have a big bed again," he added awkwardly.

"I hated the dorms in college," she replied. "My roommate was furious the entire year because the sorority she rushed didn't accept her." Her lips pursed. "You're lucky you don't have a roommate."

"I have this awful feeling that they're going to try to place some-one for the spring semester. I'm hoping I'll fly under the radar."

"Haven't you made any friends?" she said, tracing idle circles on the side of her own coffee cup. "Someone who wouldn't mind moving in with you?"

"I don't want to live with anyone."

"You're going to have to, someday."

"Not necessarily." He sounded sullen, couldn't prevent it.

"What," she said, and even though he knew she was teasing, the tone of her voice and the words he knew were coming made him shrink against the cushions of the couch and stare furiously at the screen of his phone, "don't you want to marry some nice boy, give your father and me some grandchildren?"

"No," he said shortly.

"But you could."

"Yeah."

She opened her mouth and then closed it again, hesitated for a moment longer, then decided to change tactics. "How are your grades?"

He sank lower into the couch. "They're fine," he said.

He had attended Native American Lit because Theo laughingly insisted but that had been it. Even more than he had in high school, Nathan was struck by the nearness of these almost-twin winter holidays; "You've only now figured this out? Really?" Theo had said to him. "That Thanksgiving is just Christmas without the presents? Oh baby," staring at Nathan with sorrowful eyes, "I have so much to teach you!" It was idiotic. Nearly a week off school, then another two weeks, and then finals, and then they were off again for more than a month. What was the fucking point?

So you have exactly what you want, then. Is that what you're saying? You've found your happy home, your successful little life with your red-haired mystery boyfriend. Adventure over? Story over? Or, do you ever wonder . . . ?

That little gray voice was back, and had grown, if not a face, then at least a pair of eyes, jaundiced and pale, glaring at him from the far corner of the room; in the kitchen, he could hear his father humming tunelessly and the scraping of a metal spoon against a metal bowl as he stirred the stuffing.

It isn't as if you have to go back, the voice said. *Do you even want to?* The eyes stared, for there was no mouth to actually form the words; unexpectedly, Nathan felt a pang for the mermaid woman and his friends from the party. But Theo, per usual, was right; he'd neither heard nor seen her. Or any of them; not even the lost boys. Nothing until now, and that terrible gray voice. The eyes did not blink.

It isn't as if there was anything worth having there, and don't you dare say Theo. What is Theo? Did he hold your hand in the dark? Did he save you from that bear-woman? Did he laugh at your stupidity and joke and touch your nose? Who's to say he'll come back to you or even be the same if he does? You don't know. And you never will. What's happened this past week, Nathan? Where have you been? Where haven't *you been? And could you ever show anyone that dark and deserted house in the woods? What* is *Theo; why go back?*

Nathan dismissed it as just another Outsider, but with some unease (*Weren't they all destroyed? Or was that just a dream?*); they were tragic, and they said horrible things, but they couldn't actually do anything. They just talked and talked; he could ignore that.

You're weak. The voice.

Shut up, he thought fiercely, refusing to say the words out loud. *Just shut the hell up right now.*

Weak, the thing taunted nevertheless. *Weak, weak, weak. Tell me about Theo. Tell me what you know.*

I won't say it, he thought stubbornly. He felt his lips coming together tightly in an unconscious imitation of his mother. *You want me to say that Theo isn't real, that I made him up, that none of it has been anything. But look:* you're *the one who isn't real; you're the one who comes out of me, out of the stupid fucking worthless hole that is my mind, and I can put you back there any time I want. Maybe instead of exorcising you or letting you eat me, I'll eat the fuck out of* you.

But the unblinking cigarette eyes burning holes through him contradicted this thought, and the voice chuckled, an ominous, humorless gray sound like the rasp of metal against metal. *Scrape,* went the spoon against the bowl in the kitchen, his father's firm hands; *scape, scrape.*

"Are you happy?" his mother said unexpectedly, and Nathan, startled, jerked up from his slouch.

"Sure," he said with as much nonchalance as he could muster. The warmth and sincerity in her voice, in her face and her eyes, made tears rise and sting him and he looked away quickly. "Why wouldn't I be?"

"College can be a scary place."

"It's not." His laugh was harsher than he intended; they wouldn't talk about the disappearances or about Deborah, he knew. Was it possible they hadn't heard? "It's high school with no bedtime."

"But you made some friends?"

"Sure I did."

"I'm sorry Logan isn't here."

"I haven't talked to Logan in weeks."

"Still. You need friends, Nathan. I worry about you."

"You don't have to." He dared to look at her out of the corner of his eye, then flickered back to his phone.

"I do." She reached out and touched his hair, brushed his bangs out of his eyes; they had grown long and wavy and he supposed he should cut them at some point. Theo had suggested that he dye his hair or bleach it or some charming combination of both. He'd do it after winter break. Theo would help him; he could choose the color. "It's a mother's prerogative to worry."

"Worry about Terry."

"I do, believe me." She brushed his hair again. He almost pushed her away, thought better of it, and tried to force himself to relax, inch by inch. But his muscles felt bunched, coiling as if preparing for flight. "I want you to be happy," she said, and her chest hitched and he looked away from those wounded eyes and scowled. She felt like a stranger to him now. Maybe he'd loved her before, but he didn't recognize any part of her. *Nothing*; and she didn't know him either.

Slipping away, inch by inch, moment by moment. Dissolving.

She opened her mouth, but then thought better of it.

His father's voice boomed, "Anyone out there like to lend a hand? Turns out I only have two!"

"You fucktard," Terry snarled in Nathan's ear after dinner, punching his arm with all his strength. "They want me to go now, too, fucktard, because of you." Terry, agonized, transformed all feeling by his own special brand of alchemy into rage. His face was red, his teeth bared, and Nathan, reminded of some furious horse, realized he knew absolutely nothing about his brother.

Poor, sad, angry Terry; who loves you, Terry? Who knows any single thing about you?

"Don't you think that I'm happy here?" Terry said. "That I would leave if I wanted to?"

"I'm sorry," Nathan said, rubbing the place where Terry lashed at him. "Really, I am," but Terry was already gone, back into his own world, wherever it was, because Nathan didn't know. Nathan had no idea what special contours or pathways or monsters his brother's private world held.

That was the rest of the week, on repeat.

"I really should say I'm sorry," Julian said now, peering at Nathan through his eyelashes. "For going on and on about not being queer, when it was obvious to everyone who ever met me that I totally am. I'm sorry," Julian said, patting Nathan's hand. "Sweetie darling."

"So now you've embraced being a giant stereotype instead."

"I have not." Julian pulled his hand back. "These are things I want to say and I'm saying them how I want to say them."

"Sure."

"I think you're the one with the closet problem."

"You do."

"Yes. I think you came to school thinking you could do whatever you wanted whenever you wanted, that the boys would come flocking to you, and instead you're alone and you don't do anything anymore and you're only getting more and more bitter." He giggled. "You'll get crow's feet and one of those terrible frown lines, right," and he reached out quickly and tapped Nathan's forehead before he could stop him, "*here*."

"You've gained all this insight," Nathan said angrily, "now that you're out and proud. Is that it?"

"It's been very eye opening." Julian puffed his chest out. "Bradley and I are running for prom king and king."

"Where? Back at your old high school in Butt Fuck Egypt?"

"You don't have to be crude. And you're an idiot. *Queer* prom, dummy."

Nathan dimly remembered hearing about prom from Keith and Wall before they iced him out; thinking of them now gave him a strange pang, and he realized that he hadn't spoken to them in over a month, since before Halloween, and that he hadn't been to a Lambda meeting in longer than that. Then the pang faded. It didn't matter. He felt a feline satisfaction, thinking, *I don't need* them *anymore*. He wondered if Theo would be up for something like queer prom, and he decided to ask him later. They'd rejoin the real world. Eventually.

There was a trace of unease at the thought of something like the "real world."

What other worlds are there, Nathan dear? that flabby voice simpered.

They could do all the things you're supposed to do in college: dances, hanging with friends, maybe even take in a class or two. They'd do it all once they were finished with . . .

Finished with what, *Nathan dear?*

Hibernating, he thought, and that felt right. Yes, they'd been hibernating, like bears, wrapped up in the warmth of each other. But they couldn't do that forever, of course; of course, they couldn't. And they wouldn't. Nathan was positive.

"Aren't you going?" Julian asked. "Oh right. Probably not. You'd have to go stag, and besides, it isn't like anyone has seen you in ages, like a billion years."

Nathan frowned. "Why would I go stag?"

"Come on, Nathan. You're *so* transparent. You've been mooning over this unattainable boy since school started, and you'll never be able to have him, and so you've decided to hide away and be Mr. Emo Guy. Which I'm half-tempted to allow you to do."

"You know so much about me," Nathan said dangerously. "Did you take Bradley to your dorm to show him your comics? Are you still working on the 'been there, bitten that' adventures of Dracula, excuse me, *Drake U. La*?" He shook his head. "You aren't, are you. Bradley wasn't interested, so you stopped. And you loved doing that, but you gave it up. For him. Don't tell me about me, Julian."

"Theo Smith-Kingsley has a girlfriend," Julian said after a long, icy moment. "They're, like, the king and queen of Waxman. Sorry to just say it like that. But you have to know." He leaned forward. "Nathan. You *have* to."

Nathan shrugged. He saw the world now through pane over pane over pane of ice, each a little differently swirled, distorting this face, reshaping that body, each transforming the world of the other, warping it differently. Not horrible, necessarily, just . . . different.

So he told himself.

"Look, it isn't like I don't want you to be happy," Julian said. "I do! But you can be so *mean*, Nathan. Like just now. Can't you hear it? Bradley says you're unhappy and that's what makes you so cruel sometimes, and I think he's right." His eyes grew wide. "You're smirking. That's a smirk, I know it. Wait. *Wait.* Are you hiding Theo Smith-Kingsley away somewhere? Do you two hole up together? Do you have *assignations*? Nathan! Is it like the *down low*?" He was nearly squealing now with excitement. Nathan traced idle patterns of a mystical sort that he might have recalled from Deborah's spellbook on the tabletop in front of him. "Is that where you've been?"

"I've been trying to catch up on all my classes," Nathan said primly, tracing. "Turns out I want to pass my finals."

"You haven't been to Native American Lit in a month."

"I was there the Monday before break."

"If you say so. Hey. If you and Theo were, like, really, um, doing it," and Julian's face, Nathan noted with some satisfaction, despite all his brand-new bravado, began to burn a rather spectacular shade of pink, "you'd tell me, wouldn't you? Right? Wouldn't you?"

Nathan peered into Julian's eyes, desperate with need and want and hunger.

Poor Julian. He has no idea what's out there waiting for him.

"You're right," Nathan said, offering him his most brilliant smile. "Theo Smith-Kingsley is as straight as a very straight arrow." He forced himself to reach out and touch one of Julian's soft, pink hands. "You are the best friend I have, and I would absolutely tell you if I had him squirreled away somewhere. I would tell you anything." And they laughed together. Ice, Nathan thought; different worlds, all so far from this one.

"You need to find a boyfriend to protect you," Julian said at last.

"Protect me?"

"Don't be dense, Nathan."

"I'm not dense."

"You sound dense." Julian leaned in. "There's still a killer out there."

"Maybe."

Don't think about the killer. There is no killer. And even if there were . . .

"Sweetie darling. You need a boyfriend. You told me you wanted one. You told me that college was where you were going to be free and more yourself, and that you'd finally, *finally* find a boyfriend."

Did I say that? Nathan wondered. *It certainly sounds like me, doesn't it? What a silly thing to say, to base your entire existence around. I'm not that boy. I'm not.*

"I know it sounds stupid and old-fashioned, but I think we need protecting, you and me. We're the kind of boys who can't protect ourselves."

"Protect me from what?"

"Jesus, Nate, we were just talking about it!"

"Don't call me Nate."

"Sorry, *Nate*. The missing boys. And that girl. The one who was gutted. There's got to be a killer, you know."

"Maybe they're unrelated."

"The police don't think so. I don't either."

"So what happened to the other bodies?"

"Who knows? I'm not a serial killer." He chuckled. "You know, for a while, I thought it could be you, that you were the one."

Nathan started, planted his hands angrily on the table, half-stood. "I'm not!"

"Don't make a scene. Sit down, Nathan, people are staring. Look at you. Your face is all red. I don't have any reason to think you're not, that it's not you. Wait. Yes, I do have a reason."

"What is it?" His face was flushed with embarrassment now and his head throbbed.

"You're not going to like it."

"Just tell me." He was tired. He wanted to go back to his room and wait for Theo.

Theo, who does not have a girlfriend.

I'd know if he had a girlfriend.

I'd know.

Throb, went his headache. *Throb, throb.*

"You're too weak," Julian said kindly. "Too weak to do anything like that. You couldn't kill anyone. Please. You'd be too scared to do something so awful."

"That's a good thing."

"Is it?" Julian squinted at him. "No, really. Not in the killing people way. In the life way. You're afraid, and you've always been afraid, and you'll always be afraid. Forever and ever."

"One month as a card-carrying gay man," Nathan said furiously, "and now you sprouted a backbone. Suddenly *you're* not afraid anymore."

"That's right." Julian was solemn now. "It's what I needed. I'm glad we went to that dance. Even if I hadn't met Bradley. It was like there was this whole world that existed all my life and I was outside of it. But I could sense it, even if I didn't understand it. This whole amazing world. And I came here and I met you and I knew right away what you were. Why do you think I sat by you that first day? It was like I found a magical door, like that wardrobe to Narnia, but it was only open just the tiniest, teeniest crack. And I didn't know how to make it open any more than it already was. And you," Julian said with unexpected scorn, "I thought you could help me open it, but it turns out you were just like me, hiding away, pretending, living in this fake world, like me, just like me, and the door wasn't open for you either."

"You're wrong." Nathan's hands were clenched into tight fists; he knew that if he could see his own face, it would burn deadly white, like salt.

"I'm not. When we went to that dance everything fell away, and I knew that I'd been lying to everyone and to myself my entire life. Even before I met Bradley, as soon as I saw those lights and smelled those people and felt that heat, the door opened all the way and I'm just so pissed that I never tried anything like that before. I've wasted all this time and I'm fucking furious about it."

"You fat little faggot," Nathan said distinctly through clenched, gritted teeth. "*Faggot.* How do we know it's not you, huh?" Those two words, near twins, the most dreadful ones, seared his tongue. Instant shame fell over him, clouding him and burning at the same time. Tears, somewhere back in his eyes, burned, but they burned cold. He hated that word. *Hated* it. Had he said it; had he *really* said it? Twice? He felt numb.

Julian shook his head sadly. "Oh, darling," he said. "I guess you don't."

Nathan watched him carefully. He swallowed and heard a tight click. He couldn't force his hands to relax. *I'm not a monster*, he chanted to himself. *I'm not a monster, I'm not.*

"I feel sorry for you," Julian said softly, looking down. "That's the thing. You told me you've always known what you were, you had this weird clandestine relationship with some douchebag who was probably really straight in the end, this weird messed-up relationship all through high school, like it's this amazing thing for you to be proud of, that this guy let you suck him off for two years, and poor little me, so lost, so confused, when *you're* the lost one, *you're* the confused one, because you have more fear inside you than anyone I've ever met. You can call me names. You think I haven't heard them before? Please." Julian stood up. Nathan watched him, tight, trapped, invisible lines of force like chains holding him so that he couldn't move. "I feel sorry for you," Julian said again.

They looked at each other.

Behind them came the sound of one of the campus choirs warming up before they burst into melodious, joyous paeans to Christmas, Christmas, Christmas. Nathan's stomach lurched and he doubted that he'd be able to keep down his lunch. The feeling passed but left him trembling, nauseated and weak.

"Have fun on your break," Julian said at last. "I hope I see you again in the spring. I really do." He drew a breath. "But I don't think I will. I don't think you'll be able to come back here. They won't let you."

Nathan said nothing.

Julian waited, smiled, shook his head, and began to move away. Then he saw something. He stopped and jerked his head to the right.

Look, Nathan.

Nathan looked.

Nathan opened his mouth, but no words came, no stinging retort.

A flash of red, someone tall, someone with sparkling eyes, bottle-green, familiar and well-loved, his hand locked with the hand of a willowy young woman. They were close, they were laughing, and their laughter was so *loud*; the crowd parted magically for them as they moved deliberately through it. He was handsome as always, resplendent in the expensive white sweater he wore and a long, caramel-colored trench coat. Nathan had never seen that coat before.

Theo doesn't own a coat like that. I'd know.

Julian smiled at Nathan sadly; Julian shrugged. And, moving away, vanished.

"No," Nathan said, shaking his head. But there Theo was, still holding that girl's hand, now leaning down (because he was so tall, *much* taller than Nathan was), lips close to hers, lips on hers. Nathan felt himself stand, heard his voice erupt from his mouth, nearly a roar, a sad, ferocious, hurt sound, "Theo!" he cried. "Theo!"

The boy broke the kiss and looked around, and the girl at his side looked around as well. Her eyes were the wide, frightened eyes of a doe, sensing danger in a deep, dark wood. Theo's eyes found Nathan's, then moved on from him, skating away with no sense of recognition, no acknowledgment.

"Theo!" Nathan cried miserably.

He blinked, and Theo and the girl swirled away, lost in the crowd.

Nathan's legs were rubber; his knees refused to hold him. He sat. His mouth opened, his breath came bubbling out of it like a fish. It was hard to breathe. Like a fish.

Betrayal. The closest, the most unexpected.

He thought. Looked down at his notes. He couldn't read them; his eyes blurred and he rubbed at them furiously; he was scalding inside, he was frozen. He wanted to scream and snarl and go tearing through the clot of students who filled the Center like stupid, staring cattle, but he couldn't move. The choir sang in earnest. He imagined their faces flaming, melting like tallow, their clothes sending up black billows of smoke.

I'm crazy I'm crazy as a loon I am *a monster I'm crazy I'm*

A shadow fell over his notes.

He looked up.

Theo smiled down at him kindly. He wore a dark-blue peacoat (Burberry again; Nathan recognized it) and a matching navy watch cap, like a sailor would wear. His hair would not be contained, and it came frothing out in a delectable mass of red curls. Nathan wanted nothing more than to put his hands under the cap and sink his fingers into that hair as he had a million times before, pulling and pulling. "Babe," Theo said. "Wanna get out of here? Leave the studying to the students?"

Nathan swallowed; it hurt, but it was manageable. He could swallow it all down.

"Are you real?" he whispered.

Theo threw his head back and laughed. A girl at a table behind Nathan turned her head and glared at them with a pinched bird's face. "Could you guys try to be quieter, please?" she said in a bird's pinched voice. "Some of us are trying to study."

"Boogedy boogedy boogedy," Theo said, making a monster's face at the girl, who recoiled, then sniffed haughtily, and turned quickly back to her own notes.

He looked back to Nathan and grinned, broad and sunny.

Nathan was trembling.

"Are you real?" he said again.

"Come on," Theo said insistently. "Let's go downtown. Try that fifties diner we've been talking about. I'll even buy you a frosty chocolate milkshake."

Theo held out his hand.

Nathan stared at it.

"Don't worry about *him*," Theo said softly. "*He* doesn't matter; he's no one."

How could you be? How?

"Come," Theo said, "along with me."

Held out his hand, held it—

crazy monster looney tunes

"Sure," Nathan said firmly, briskly. He closed his notes with a slam. "Why not? I got nothing better to do."

He stood. He shouldered his backpack. He drew a breath.

And took Theo's hand in his.

3

ONCE UPON A TIME, when we all lived in the forest—
What is that? Who said it?
I'm not sure. You did, maybe.
Or you.
Could be, could be. But that's where we started, don't you think?
That's where the fairy tales began.
This is more than a fairy tale. You know that now.
No.
Yes. Yes. And yes.
They scare me. They always did.
Shhhh. Just listen. Once upon a time—
Yes, once upon a time—
—when we all lived—
—in the forest—

"Oh, the forest is vast and very dense," Theo said with the utmost seriousness, but Nathan caught the wild sparkle that flashed customarily in his eyes, and the world cracked open and Nathan could see an endless looping circle of darkness lined with chalk-white faces, staring at him with punched eyes and smiling blue lips. He tried to tell himself that it was just his imagination, that he didn't actually see them, *I don't see them I don't*, but the fact was that he did. He blinked and they were gone.

"Very dense indeed," Theo said. "They call it the Black Forest, *Schwarzwald.*" His voice turned guttural and spitting, but he smiled anyway. "Which means it isn't the home of laughter and light. The trees are practically crying out with the melancholy of their existence, knowing, and they *have* to know, don't you think, about all the terrible things that have happened right there before their wooden faces: witches and Sabbats and werewolves that sometimes put on clothes and suits of skin and faces to fool you. To eat you. And nymphs who wait to pull innocent people into ponds and lakes, way down into cold darkness to drown them there."

Outside Nathan's room, the wind hissed and teased the little drift of snow that had quietly accumulated on his windowsill, and together they watched the white face of the blizzard form and then reform itself, gibbering in at them.

Theo boomed his customary laughter and put his arm around Nathan's shoulder and pressed against him tightly. "There's nothing out there that can hurt you. I'm the big bad wolf, and I've left the forest and you let me in. Here I am now. To devour you," Theo said. Nathan, watching closely the marble lines of Theo's handsome, open face, thought with wonder, *He is the most terrible person in the world.*

You don't really have a girlfriend, do you?

He hadn't asked. Hadn't dared.

You aren't a murderer, are you? I'm not, am I?

I didn't see what I thought I did. Julian is wrong, per usual, that's all.

"You scare me sometimes," he said later, after Theo's talk of black forests was long over. *Or was I the one to say all that?* he thought sleepily. *Was that me all along? Who told those stories?*

Theo lifted his head from where it had lain in Nathan's lap for the last half hour or so and turned to look up at him. There hadn't been any talk of woods, or witches, or fairy tales; they hadn't talked, Theo hadn't talked, hadn't said anything. All they'd done was lie there.

I made it all up, just like I always do. Or we did. We talked all night. Or he did, or me?

Theo's eyes were sleepy, and he was smiling a little, confused, the
farthest expression from terrible Nathan had ever seen. His hair was
mussed from Nathan's constant petting of it.

"I do?" he said at last, blinking. "I'm sorry," he said, then, horrifically, "You were telling me about Seb."

The wind howled; another goddamn winter storm, the second
day of finals, and Nathan had managed to blunder through each one
he'd taken so far. He'd tried (he told himself he'd tried) his hardest,
Theo helping him study late into the night, ignoring all of Nathan's
questions about his own finals (*Did he even have any?*), and he had no
idea now if he was close to passing one or two or all or if he'd failed
each and every one. For Jimmy's class, he'd read, duly, an excerpt from
a new work, though he didn't remember writing it, suspected, dimly,
that maybe Theo had. His reward was a brilliant smile from Jimmy
and half-hearted applause from his classmates, who didn't recognize
him. Even Liz had been there, sitting in the front row, alabaster legs
shod in those familiar electric blue heels crossed prettily at the ankle
(*did she only own the one pair? Pathetic; so pathetic*), watching him
with avid, intoxicated eyes. After the reading, Jimmy had clamped a
hand onto Nathan's shoulder and, beaming, said, "Good job, buddy,
damn good job," before moving on to the next student.

Made it up, made it up, that gray and greedy Outsider's voice
chanted in his mind. He'd looked around wildly to find its owner,
some awful little old man or woman, but there was no one. *Made it
up*, the voice chanted nevertheless; *none of it real.*

But that wasn't possible: he *knew* he had gone with Jimmy to his
office after that excruciating conversation with drunken Mrs. Jimmy
in their grim and depressing living room, and there he and Jimmy
had . . .

. . . he had . . .

. . . *they* had . . .

Hadn't they?

Now, with Theo looking up at him expectantly, he remembered again that awful moment, there in Jimmy Weston's classroom,
when self-doubt crashed over him in a wave so heavy he crammed
the knuckle of his right hand into his mouth and bit down to stifle

the scream building in his chest. His eyes burned; *I sucked him off,* Nathan had told himself, standing there miserably with no one looking, and he prayed for Liz to crane her head to pierce him with flinty eyes and a self-deprecating smile, or for Jimmy to evince the slightest bit of discomfort, but there was nothing. It was as if they were enacting a scene from a play, one that occurs early in the narrative, before all that melodramatic bullshit about illicit extramarital sex with teachers who are supposedly straight while their wives booze it up back in their home-hell-hovel. The three H's, he thought crazily. Or were there four? He snorted.

Because that's exactly what it was: bullshit, soap opera melodrama.

He felt horror dawning again: the thing with Jimmy had been just like Seb, sucking off a straight guy who wouldn't reciprocate. Like he'd taken this great, big important thing from his previous life and altered it, but only a little, switched one straight boy for another, changed the location, swapped the depressing run-down bedroom for the depressing office, but it was the same scenario; how was that possible?

Because you don't belong here, Nathan. That proves it. It isn't any different than it was before. You don't belong. Choose us. You can bring us back; you can make us real again; you can bring the party back. We're waiting. Give us your light. Heal us, real us. Give us your life.

"You're thinking bad things," Theo said softly. The sleepy look in his eyes, tinged, Nathan saw, with flecks of gold and full of dark longing, hadn't changed; his hair was still tousled, sexily. "You shouldn't think those things."

"How do you know what I'm thinking?" Nathan teased, but an icicle brushed against his heart and chilled him, and the entire room turned cold. Outside, the wind shrieked in its witch's voice.

"You should talk about him." Theo drummed his long fingers against the bedspread, the cheap, terrible bedspread that Nathan loved, despite himself. Nathan, watching him, noticed that two of his fingers were exactly the same length.

Am I seeing that? "Tell me," Theo said, softly, insistently, "about Seb."

"You know his name."

"Only because you've mentioned him."

"There isn't that much to tell," Nathan said, drawing a breath.

Theo stared at him without blinking until finally Nathan collapsed. "Fine," he said. "I . . . loved him, I guess."

"You guess?"

"I did." Nathan closed his eyes. He didn't want to feel the pain. Couldn't they just go back to kissing or wandering around downtown; couldn't they just go into the forest and never come out again? "I loved him," he said, and the words felt like stone blocks being forced out of his chest, where the pain began, and up into his throat, and then out of his mouth. They were too heavy and too square and they didn't fit, dammit; he wanted to vomit them up, because Theo was looking at him and he could never resist him. "I loved him. Yes."

"What happened to him?"

Nathan shrugged, wandered across the room, stood by the window. It was a dream, he thought, that demon golden-eyed white-faced thing tearing through the Outsiders, ripping them into ectoplasmic pieces or whatever substance made them up. Just a dream, he thought firmly.

"I don't know. It seems funny to me, all that time we spent together, and I don't know if he ever knew me at all, or if I ever knew him."

"You were kids."

Nathan offered him a wry smile over his shoulder. "It wasn't that long ago."

Theo picked at one of the threads on the comforter, studied it, finally said, "Were you sad when it was over?"

"Yes," Nathan whispered. "But also relieved, I think. Yes. Relieved. Because deep down I knew that it wasn't . . ."

"Real?"

Nathan nodded, miserably. He didn't think he'd ever see Seb again, and if he did, it wouldn't be the same, because *they* weren't the same. They'd be strangers, and that's all they ever could be.

"All you could ever be," Theo murmured. Nathan looked up sharply at the other boy's reflection in the window, but it blurred, moved, shifted, crimson and gold and white white white, shifting, melting. "Would you ever want him back again?"

"Oh god," Nathan said. He pressed his head against the glass.

"Is that a no? A yes?"

"No," Nathan said.

Yes, that awful gray voice whispered in his ear.

"We'd be strangers," he said as forcefully as he could.

"Yes."

"Strangers."

"Strangers, yes."

Take me with you, Nathan thought. He wanted to shriek it out the window, but it wouldn't open; he wanted that arctic wind roaring out of the canyon's mouth where the school hung like a tongue to carry him away and rub him out entirely; would there be peace then in that void?

He could see only the woods, the shadows, and the sweet, sweet darkness that lay there in the trees: no classes, teachers, assignments, parents; nothing but the uninterrupted blackness of the woods.

No. No. Hold on. This is what you wanted, this—

"Maybe he'll come back someday," Theo suggested.

Nathan closed his eyes. "I don't think he will. I wouldn't want him to. I don't even want to see him again. I wish . . ."

"You wish . . . ?"

"I wish that I'd never met him."

"Is that all?"

"No. I wish he'd never been born. I wish he'd never even *existed*."

"Because of me?"

"I'm tired. I'm sorry, Theo, but I'm so tired."

"I'm not really the big bad wolf."

"I know."

"Or hell, maybe I am. I'll eat up all your bad thoughts. Chomp, chomp, chomp."

"They aren't *all* bad thoughts."

"You think I'm horrible."

"No."

"That's what you were thinking."

"No."

"Because I scared you."

"Not really."

"But I did scare you."

He hesitated. "A little."

"I love you, Nathan."

"I love you, Theo." They'd said it before now, a hundred times since that first night in the woods, with the house, with the bear-woman.

Theo reached up and touched Nathan's face gently. "You aren't crazy."

Nathan, frozen, said nothing.

"The voices, the deaders, Outsiders, dreaming of the past or the future. It makes you interesting, not crazy."

"How do you know?" Nathan whispered.

"That woman at the house: I saw her well enough." He laughed and touched his throat, where the bruises left in the wake of that awful ursine woman's crushing hands had finally faded away entirely only a few days before. He winced. "I mean, I see them in *you*." He sighed and stretched luxuriously, a giant ginger cat.

"I haven't, though," Nathan confessed, blushing. "Not since her. Not that I know of. I guess they could be anywhere, or anyone, just wandering around. But I don't think I have."

"You'd recognize them, wouldn't you?"

"Yes." He sighed and toyed with the curl of Theo's bangs above his forehead. "I'm sorry I said that thing. It was stupid."

"It wasn't." Theo rolled over and lay on his stomach, his chin pressing against Nathan's thigh.

"I love you, Theo."

"I love you, Nathan. I'm the only one," and he sighed happily. "I'm the only one who does."

Fear bloomed in Nathan's stomach and rose in coppery bubbles up through his throat. He could smell copper in his nostrils. *It isn't too late to go back, to just* go—

"I'll go," Theo said softly, his voice nearly obscured by the scream of the wind. "I'll just go, if you want me to. I would do even that for you."

No, Nathan tried to say, but the word stuck inside him somewhere and refused to shake loose.

He couldn't see Theo's face, his eyes. But he was tracing his finger along the inside of Nathan's thigh; his cock stiffened at that blazing touch.

"I," Theo said, "would even go back to the forest if you told me to."

Nathan's breath hitched and locked inside him. *Can't breathe*, he thought. Theo's finger stroked and stroked.

"Read the cards for me," Theo said, laughing. "Tell me my future." He lifted his head so Nathan could see his face. "The *future*," Theo insisted.

Nathan studied him carefully.

"What the hell is real anyway? What does it even mean? It's a stupid word. You knit up your own realities, Nathan my old Nathan, remember, and I am here because you wished it. If I scare you, it's because you're afraid that I'm not real, and I'm telling you that *it doesn't matter*." He chuckled. "Now. Read me the cards. Then I'll give you something extra nice."

Trembling, Nathan dislodged Theo's head from his lap, and walked unsteadily across the room to the dresser, where the cards lay, hidden beneath his jockey shorts and balled-up socks. His erection throbbed and pressed forward like a lance.

Behind him, Theo pursed his lips, closed his eyes, and howled: "Owwoooo," he said. Nathan found an answering howl leaving his own mouth, and, as they had before, and would again, they howled together, howling against the outside world and the monstrous shrieking of the wind.

4

"I'M SORRY I won't be there. It sucks."

"Sure." He tried not to let the sadness creep into his voice. Before him, Logan's image was the only bright thing in the darkness of his room, the curtains at the window drawn against the storm that continued to roar, unabated. Logan's smiling face flickered up at him on the screen of his laptop. His hair was cut shorter than ever before, but stylish, his face was thinner, and his cheeks were peppered with stubble. It made him look older and, naturally, even handsomer than ever.

"Don't be a sad panda. I'm taking a class during winter session, which starts the day after New Year's. And I have a job. Hey, what happened to your job? Do you even have one anymore?"

"Just the kind we call blow," Nathan said, and they chuckled at this stupid, childish ribaldry, like old times. Amy had left four or five messages for him after Thanksgiving, each one more confused, more hurt-sounding than the last, but Nathan hadn't returned any of them, and eventually she'd just stopped. He ached at the thought of her, but then he wouldn't allow himself to ache.

"My mom is super pissed," Logan said. "I told her that the roads would be shitty anyway, but she said that was beside the point. Said she'd buy me a plane ticket. Which is exactly what I want: to die in a plane crash somewhere between Cheney and Garden City. You know how those little planes are, right? People die in them all the time."

"I've never heard you talk about death before."

"Maybe I've just begun to consider the possibility of my own mortality," Logan said seriously, but even though the picture on the screen was pixilated and fuzzy, Nathan could see the sparkle in his best friend's eye. "Or it could be I'm just looking for excuses not to head back to the ol' GC. Man, getting out of there was the best thing I ever did."

Nathan didn't allow his expression to alter.

"I love it here, Nathan, you don't even know. I'm dating a couple of guys, maybe three, maybe four, because why not? I'm only eighteen; why should I settle? And the bars here let you in even if you are only eighteen, you just can't drink, and there's this awesome spot me and my friends all go on Saturday nights and we pre-game in my friend Jason's dorm room and head over totally wasted before we even get there. It's hilarious, you don't even know." He laughed, delighted with himself. "And I still have my job at American Eagle and I'm getting a 4.0 and it's everything I always thought it would be. I look back at Garden City and think, Jesus, how did we do it, I mean, how did we *do* it, you know? We were lucky. And poor Derek," he said without missing a beat, "I think of him, still stuck at Royal High, and we don't talk at all anymore. That was so ugly, that was such ugly shit, but it doesn't mean I don't feel bad for him, and Christ, Nathan, how are *you* doing? I haven't even asked."

"I'm good," Nathan said cautiously.

"Yeah? Well, there's the Lambda Alliance, right? And the Pink Panther? I bet you'd have to sneak in, huh. Are you seeing anyone? Your mom didn't know."

"You talked to my mom?"

"She sent me an email. I didn't think it was so weird. Hey, don't make that face. I've known her as long as I've known you."

"Yeah, yeah."

"So?"

"So?"

Logan heaved a heavy sigh and shook his head with mock sorrow. "Jesus, Nathan, you don't need to be so mysterious. Are you seeing someone or not? And I'm not even sure what I mean by 'seeing,'" he added philosophically. "Going out on dates? Just fucking? Long walks by the river? Heh. All of the above? That's what I'm doing."

Nathan felt as if he were floating, as if he were watching someone else barely hold up their end of this conversation. He wanted Logan to dim, become unimportant, a character in a movie or a book someone had told him about once. *Where was Theo?* It was getting dark. Tomorrow was the last day of finals and Nathan would have to make up his mind about what he was going to do.

Who is the killer? Kyle? Jimmy? Julian?

Finding the identity of the maker of the lost boys had, just the other day, begun to seem important again; one last thing, he thought carefully, one last knot to unravel, then he'd be free. Draw back the veil. Reveal, reveal.

Veritas, veritas, veritas.

When will this hurt go away? I just want it to stop.

"Your mom," Logan said, carefully now, "says she doesn't hear from you much."

"I guess not."

"That's kinda weird, don't you think? You're still in town; couldn't you just—"

"Hey," Nathan said, "you're the one who was just trumpeting the virtues of the world outside Garden City. You're the one who left. You're the one I haven't spoken to in three months." He drew in a horrified breath because he realized he hadn't said any of those words, not a one, and Logan, staring back at him from the tiny screen before him, was watching him expectantly; he'd finished his sentence and Nathan was expected to offer a rebuttal. Sweat sprang out on Nathan's brow.

"Remember that time we went down to the river when we were kids?" Logan asked; he would say anything now, Nathan thought wisely, to break the spell. "Like, little kids? Remember?"

"Which time?" Nathan said, relieved that he had spoken aloud (*Did I, though?* he thought; *how can I be sure?*).

"We were seven or eight, and I was spending the night at your house, and we got up way earlier than everyone else. I remember I could hear Terry snoring in his room across the hall. But it was summer, so even though it was early, it was still, like, a thousand degrees outside, and bright, holy hell, every little detail was just heightened. And you said, 'Let's go down to the river,' and even though it was only three blocks away it felt so far, like we were setting out on a trek. Some long journey, just you and me. So we went, and we took Terry's canteen and filled it up with water, because you said, 'Just in case,' and I remember I thought that was so funny, just in case of what? And we picked up these sticks that were at least twice as big as we were and we set off, like *Lord of the* goddamn *Rings*. The grass was so green, and it was quiet and still, no one in town was even awake yet but you and me, and we found the river trail and we followed it—"

"I remember," Nathan said, and this time he heard his voice, cracking with disuse.

"We went down where the trees were thickest, by that little sand bar, and we started using our sticks like swords and we were fighting—"

"Magic spells," Nathan said. "We were having a wizard's duel."

"Or casting spells, maybe? Were we casting spells? I think we were. Anyway, we were screaming and hollering and making a big ruckus until this raggedy-ass bum, like, *appeared*, with hair that stood out like *this*," and, chuckling, Logan demonstrated with both his hands, "like he'd been struck by lightning; it was just gray and he was *filthy*. Remember, his face was smeared with grease, and he started screaming at us, sounded like this big fat crow? And he said, 'You kids,'" Logan cried in the cracked, warbling voice of that long-ago derelict, "'you kids got no respect for decent people trying to get a good night's sleep!'" He broke off in peals of laughter. "Oh Jesus, Nathan, *decent* people, remember that? Decent people!" He laughed again, merrily. "And we ran away, but we were laughing, and by the time we got back to your house, your mom was up for work and we made ourselves some cereal, something terrible, one of those cereals that's based on a movie or a TV series. *Tangled* maybe? I think there was a Disney princess on the box, and then we watched cartoons until noon. I was just thinking about that the other day. It's one of my clearest memories from childhood. Because I do miss you, you know."

"I love you," Nathan said. "I miss you so, so much."

Logan smiled. "You're awfully quiet. Too much memory lane? I'm sorry. Seriously, Nathan, you have to tell me what's going on with you. You haven't said two words this entire conversation. Dude, I want to know what's *happening* with you."

"Nothing," Nathan said cautiously. "Absolutely nothing."

"I'll bet that's not true," Logan said fondly. "You always want to be in the spotlight, even if you pretend you don't."

"The spotlight."

"Center of attention," Logan said, smiling. "That's my Nathan." He laughed, and Nathan joined him and thought, quite concretely, peaceably even, *I will never see him again.*

5

HE SHOULD HAVE known that seeing Kyle again was just the beginning—a portent, a signal—but he simply didn't *know*; Tarot cards or not, it wasn't like he was psychic, as he had told Theo once with a grin.

Nathan had dozed after Logan signed off; "Got work in the morning," he'd said cheerfully. "Not that you'd know anything about that, lucky duck." Nathan allowed his mind to drift back to the day Logan had reminisced about. Of course he remembered that morning, loving Logan as he had never loved him before in that fortunate time before hormones and puberty and the turbid, festering bloom of adolescence complicated every stupid relationship he'd ever tried to forge. Loving Logan and his long, tan legs; loving Logan, who always knew exactly the right words to say when another kid was cruel to Nathan or when he fell and skinned his knee; loving Logan's ideas and his bravery and his imagination. Of course Nathan remembered that morning, and it was exactly as Logan had described it: sharp, every detail, and vivid, colors exploding above them in the sky and below in the grass that tickled their feet, the houses that lined the streets they danced across. Summer was limitless; they were charmed idiots greedily eating each day. Nathan moaned then, thinking of those days, lost now, and it was the moan that brought him back to wakefulness and caused him to open his eyes.

To find Kyle Matthews peering down at him, his face only inches away from Nathan's.

Nathan's breath froze inside his chest, and he held it, and held it, and held it until he thought he would explode.

Kyle was smiling.

"How did you get in here?" Nathan said, or tried to say; maybe the words escaped the vacuum of his chest, or probably they hadn't. He couldn't move.

Sleep paralysis, not real, just a dream.

"Did you come to kill me?" he tried to say.

Did you come to kill me at last? It was you. All along it was you, and I'm your latest victim. Nathan tried to scream, but he couldn't move at all.

I will not be your victim!

Kyle chuckled, a bare whisper of a sound.

"Get . . . off . . . me," Nathan managed.

Kyle's grin grew.

"You can't do this," Nathan said, stronger now.

Kyle's eyes danced with gleeful merriment.

"I'll . . . kill . . . you," Nathan said through gritted teeth. He tried to move, tried to move, *tried to move.* "If you . . . hurt . . . me . . ."

His eyes widened. He realized he could smell the other boy, the fungoid, worm-white stink of something that has lain a long time, decomposing, in cold, wet darkness.

Kyle's colorless eyes now blazed silver, and white veins stretched over the entirety of their surface. They were already sinking, those blue impossible eyes, back into their sockets, falling in. His cheeks grew hollow; his hair, now missing in patches, revealed naked skull the color of old butter; the skin of his forehead cracked. His chest neither rose nor fell.

A skeletal snout burst grotesquely from the center of his face, and his teeth became fangs. All of them. Like quills, sharp and deadly; his new snout-mouth *bristled* with them.

Abruptly, it gaped open, farther than any snout-mouth had a right to gape.

Nathan opened his own mouth to shriek, then closed it as fast as he could. There were living *things* nesting in Kyle's hair: wiggling maggots and black beetles with shiny, opalescent backs, some with wings. If he opened his mouth to scream, and one of those maggots or beetles or flying things fell into his mouth, Nathan knew that would be the end. He wouldn't even be able to scream. He would be lost forever.

He closed his mouth tightly until it became a thin white line.

"You," the Kyle-thing croaked, the word distorted by the shape of his horrible new mouth.

Nathan's eyes bulged. *They'll simply burst*, he thought, *all over Dead Kyle, and he'll be the one with something gross in his mouth, not me.* Wild, hysterical laughter flowered inside him and wanted to rise through his belly and out of his mouth, but he wouldn't allow it.

"All," Kyle said in his grating voice. "All." Those filmy silver eyes didn't blink; his mouth worked with terrible, fierce determination, fighting his new fangs. "Because," that mouth said. "Of. You. You. All because of you."

No, Nathan thought, *I will not accept this. This is not my responsibility. I will not.*

But the thing was nodding its head in jubilation, and as Nathan watched, horrified, skin flaked and then *slithered* off Kyle's face and skull. The hair blew away as if from a great gust of wind in thin, white drifts; the skin was pushed by liquid that gushed beneath it in yellow and white rivers; the eyes fell in; the snout-mouth juddered open in a silent roar and the tongue reached and disappeared into meaningless pink dust that came spiraling down. Nathan writhed beneath the thing above him, but it had planted its skeletal claws on either side of him, and its weight pressed down in a terrible parody of copulation. Just like that night in the woods the Black Forest Theo was always talking about.

That's it, then, isn't it, he thought dimly. *That's the real Black Forest; it isn't in Germany at all; it was here all the goddamn time.*

Kyle's skull was naked, glaringly white in the darkness of Nathan's dorm room. The canine jaw opened and closed without muscles or ligaments to make it work; it gaped, and foul breath floated across Nathan's nose so that he gagged on its dreadful stench.

Bastard, he thought. *Oh you bastard, you tried to hurt me; I wished you dead, and now you are. You are.*

"All because of you," the wolfen death's head sang at him. "All of it, you, Nathan, all because of you."

"No," Nathan whispered, but the word never made it past his lips.

"Yes," Kyle said anyway. "Dead because of you."

"No," Nathan said, and now the word was real. His terror and disgust and the fury growing in him had made it real.

"Suck me off," the horror chortled. "Come on, you owe me. Just suck me off, dude. Come on, you owe me. Just suck me off suck me off suck me off—"

"*No*," Nathan shrieked, and he lifted his hands from the mattress and shoved and the Kyle-skeleton-thing flew backward with a cheated howl. "I'm glad you died," Nathan cried, his fury overflowing. He shook his fists at the wolf-bone-thing crouching on the hard tile of his dorm room floor. He turned his hands into claws and advanced threateningly. "Do you hear me?" he snarled. "You sonofabitch, I'm glad you're dead I'm glad you're dead *I'm glad you're dead!*"

The thing threw its naked skull back and echoed cold, inhuman laughter, singing as it did, "Give it, give it, give, give," fading now, like mist, "we see you, we see we," evaporating, turning to nothing, gone, as if it had never been.

Nathan stared furiously. His hands clenched again into fists. They turned to claws, then back to fists. Claws. Fists.

I imagined it.

It was possible. But not true; evidence of the thing's existence was everywhere. The room was icy cold, and the nauseating stench of it remained, rot, decay. His mouth opened and he retched, but he put a hand on his stomach and thought, *I will* not, and he didn't.

He wanted to cry. He wouldn't allow himself.

It isn't too late. A voice, horribly familiar, resounded throughout his little room, and even when he pressed his hands against his ears, he could still hear it, whispering, hissing, inhuman. *You can still make a choice. It isn't too late. You know us. You want that peace, yes? You want to let it all go, don't you? We can do that, Nathan; we.*

He listened to that terrible, seductive voice, and thought, *Why, yes, of course, it's me; my very own voice.* He looked up at the ceiling, where the stars Theo had placed, so carefully, so meticulously, glowed down at him, and they read YOU and Nathan laughed giddily. *It is me,* he thought. *I'm the one they want. I'm special. I belong with them because I make them real, the living dead, the woman in the antique mall, the monstrous woman in the abandoned house held deep in the heart of the woods, and the lost boys, the missing boys, the dead boys, and now Kyle was one of their number, and he'd appeared here tonight because he blames me for his death. Is that why? Why would that be? What do I have to do with it?*

YOU, said the stars on the ceiling.

His head throbbed. He traced his temples with the tips of his fingers, which seemed to vibrate and thrum with a secret power. The room stank and swam; his vision blurred, and he turned from the bed where the Kyle-thing had hovered and saw that his Tarot cards were no longer on the top of his desk where he'd left them after he'd read them for Theo, and Theo, as promised, had given him something very nice. Pain spiked him between the eyes. He moaned. There they were, scattered on the floor, and not just scattered. *Shredded.* He knelt beside them, moaning. They'd been torn into pieces, each card, by wicked, gleeful hands, Nathan was certain. They were spotted with streaks of black: mud, icy, slimy to touch; fragments of dead autumn leaves, crumbled, clung to the rotten earth.

The lost boys want you. The Outsiders want you. But they don't care about your life; they don't care about your future. And what about you, *Nathan? What do* you *care about?*

His own voice now, his alone. He moaned again.

Do you care, Nathan? About school? About your life, your future? You used to. Can you see beyond now? Beyond tomorrow? Next week? You can't, can you.

"Shut up," he said, voice creaking, as if he were an old, exhausted man. "Let me just think for a second."

Who was that thing at the party? Or what? A demon? A monster? Is that what you want? Is it?

He was missing something; something didn't make sense. The room pressed at him, *stinking,* the cold driving him back until his knees struck the bed frame and he collapsed upon it. He curled up in the center, drawing his knees to his chest and holding himself. He shivered. It was a puzzle with missing pieces and none of it made sense.

He wished that it made sense.

And then it did, the very next day, when Seb Candleberry knocked on his door.

6

"OH," WAS ALL Nathan could say when he opened the door and there stood Seb, sandy hair grown shaggier, like hay thrust down over his ears by the army-green beanie he wore pushed back, his stubble now bloomed into a full blond beard with a matching blond mustache. Had he filled out more, even in the six months since last they'd seen each other; had he, impossibly, grown handsome?

"I wanna come in," Seb said. "I mean, I'd like to. If you let me."

"Um," Nathan said, and looked beyond Seb's shoulders, but the hallway was deserted. Most of the students in the dorm had flown; today was the last day before break and scurrying was mandatory by eight the next morning. And Nathan still hadn't made up his mind about where to go or what to do.

"Maybe not for long," Seb said. "Please? I been thinking and I wanna talk. Doesn't have to be for long. Please."

He needs an invitation. Why does he need an invitation?

"All right," Nathan said, unsure until the words popped out of his mouth what he was about to say. He moved aside. "Come in."

Seb stepped across the threshold.

"So, this is a dorm room," he said, marveling. "Cool. I never been in one."

Right. Seb had never even intended to go to college.

He glanced at Nathan, still hovering by the door. It remained open. "Where's your roommate? Wait. Dude. Are those beds pushed together?"

"I don't have a roommate," Nathan said carefully.

Seb's eyebrows rose comically. "I thought that was mandatory."

"I had one. He moved out."

Seb grinned. "Couldn't handle Nathan raw. I get that."

"What did you want to talk about, Seb?" Nathan sighed.

"That's not very polite," Seb said, faux-pouting. "Or hospitable even. I wanted to make sure you hadn't forgotten me. Something wrong with that?"

"I didn't forget you."

"Now that's obvious. How could you? Christ. It's empty in this place. Where are the smarty-pants? I thought everyone went to college."

"Today is the last day of finals." His voice was maintained and even. He made sure of it. "Everyone has to be out of their dorms by tomorrow morning."

"You included."

"Me included."

"Seems weird," Seb said, shrugging. He wandered around the room, peering out the window into the courtyard below, running his finger along the edge of Nathan's pillow, opening and closing desk drawers. "Forcing people to live together like this. My house is a sad ol' shanty shack and my goddamn bedroom is bigger than this. They expect you to *live* with someone? Another dude? That is fucked up."

"I kinda thought so," Nathan said, still by the door.

Seb opened up the wardrobe and made a face. "Hoo! Dude, you need to wash your towel. It's all mildewed and shit."

"Said the guy who never washed his any piece of clothing. Or his sheets."

Seb grinned. "I should'a, huh? I got no idea how my mom never figured out what I was doing all through high school. Or," and he waggled his eyebrows lasciviously, "who. All that dried jizz on the sheets? Yowza."

Nathan's face flamed. He dropped his eyes and carefully closed the door behind him, then leaned against it with his arms folded over his chest. "Is that why you're here? To reminisce about old times?"

"I heard you were having some problems up here," Seb said. One hand disappeared into the pocket of that same old green coat Nathan remembered so well. Disappeared, and began to play with something inside. Moving it about. Grabbing it and releasing it. Grabbing it again. "Murders and shit like that."

"Just one murder." Nathan's eyes were locked on his pocket. Was there a flash of something within, a hint, a *gleam*? Something sharp?

Grabbing. Turning it over. Releasing. Grabbing.

"You don't think one is one too many?"

"I don't remember you having such a social conscience."

Murder.

"Well," Seb said, hand in his pocket, "I was worried about you."

"You were worried about me." Nathan couldn't keep the edge out of his voice, the dry disbelief. *This is the possibility*, Nathan thought slowly, his thoughts huge and glacial but moving, nevertheless. *This is the possibility that seemed so impossible, because it is impossible.*

"It isn't just murders, though, is it? People have gone missing. Guys. Dudes. All dudes. Like four or five, right?"

"Four." Nathan couldn't blink. "And one dead, um, girl. Young woman."

"So, I thought about you, all by yourself up here—"

"I saw Essie a few weeks ago." *Run, hide*; he had to say something, anything. What words, he wondered; what spells, which incantations?

Julian thinks I need protection, that I can't defend myself; oh my god, is he right?

Seb made a face. "*That* bitch. Please. I haven't said two words to her since graduation."

"Or Mikyla?"

Seb grinned his grin. Hand in his pocket. Took a step forward. "Off and on."

Nathan felt icy fingers trilling up and down his spine. "I thought she was gone. California or something." He tried to move closer to the door.

"She is, she is. Don't get your panties in a twist." Another step. "I ain't talked to her either, since she left." His grin faded. "To be honest, I ain't talked to really anyone. Not in months." Hand, hand, hand in pocket.

Not possible. It couldn't be—

"Until now."

"Until now. You're it, my friend."

"Yeah?" Nathan took a breath. "So why me?"

"Well," Seb drawled and closed the distance between them. "Maybe I miss you."

Nathan stared, wide-eyed, breath trapped inside. "Yeah?" He made his voice as casual as he could. "I missed you, too."

Grin, flash of white teeth. "'Course you did."

"Cocky."

"Super cocky. One of the things you love about me."

He'd never hurt me. I mean, more than he already has, or ever did. He wouldn't.

I wished he'd never existed. I said that.

"Did you ever become a photographer?" He could smell Seb's breath. Sweet. Peppermint.

Nathan laughed, but it felt false. "It doesn't happen that fast. Plus, no."

"Why not?"

"The class. Um. Was full."

Seb waved a hand. "Not an excuse. Maybe," he said, considering, "you ain't a photographer after all. Maybe we're not any of us what we thought we were. Maybe—"

"Why are you here, Seb?" Nathan said, cutting him off.

Which was the moment, of course, when Seb kissed him.

And then backed away; or Nathan backed away; or they both backed away at the same time. Before it happened, though, memories sprang immediately to Nathan's mind: the yellow-hazy sky above the park the day Seb ran into him, like a sepia-toned photo, with the smoke of distant forest fires hanging heavy over the valley; the gray-blue wall where Seb had shoved his mattress and the place where, inevitably, Nathan's eyes would go when he was under Seb and Seb was fucking him, the hairline crack that zigged and zagged its way toward the ceiling; the shadows stretching across the walls of the auditorium like evil hands, that last night they were all together, the real end of everything, long before graduation day finally came, and the terror and hatred in Logan's eyes as that wicked voice croaked from Seb's throat; then, and at the last, the first time they ever really talked, when Nathan peered into the alcove and there crouched Sebastian Candleberry, weeping alone as if his heart were broken, would always be broken.

Because he is *broken.*

He saw all these instances of their history in a flash, some overlapping; when he opened his eyes as widely as they would go, he and Seb became separate creatures once again. He told himself he didn't feel the pang of loss, that old familiar serpent's sting; he wondered if Seb didn't feel it, too.

Maybe he's more broken than you even ever knew.

"Christ," Seb said miserably. "I'm sorry. I'm so, so sorry."

"Yeah," Nathan said, unblinking, unmoving. "Me too."

"No," Seb said, and his eyes, crimson now and flushed with tears, flickered up to Nathan's. "I mean it. I never should'a come here."

"Why did you?"

Seb stared at him without answering, his face a mask of anguish. His hand grasped at the thing in his pocket.

Nathan shifted his weight uncomfortably. "Come on," he said at last. "Give me something. You're freaking me out."

"Maybe that's a good thing."

"You were never cryptic like this before."

Now his anguish shifted to that familiar sullen look Nathan recognized. "I don't know what that means."

"It means that you're being mysterious for no reason. And it's bullshit."

"Aw, fuck," Seb cried and pressed one hand against his eyes. "I feel like we're back at the beginning, you and me. Like I'm just starting this again and no time has passed at all."

"It has passed," Nathan said quietly.

"Yeah. I know it. Fuck, don't I know it." He peered at Nathan from between the bars of his fingers. "Do you remember the beginning?"

"I remember all of it."

"But the beginning. That old dance you and me used to do; we were so good at. We did that dance for a long time. I thought I was tired of it. Shit, what did I know?" He reached out, slowly, tentatively, and put a hand on Nathan's shoulder. "I missed you. I *miss* you." The hand traveled down to Nathan's, the fingers brushing Nathan's, until they linked. Nathan's moved as if pulled by strings, magnetized, as if he had no choice, and hell, maybe he didn't; but that was too easy. *I called out for you,* he wanted to say, *I called your name when I was being chased by a monster in the woods; I called for you to save me and you never came.* He didn't say it, but their fingers linked nevertheless.

Is it you, Seb? Could it possibly be you? Savior, monster, murderer, lover; all those things and maybe more; could it be you?

He was destructive; Nathan knew it. He reveled in chaos. He liked to fuck shit up. It was the only way he could deal, the only way he knew how. So he just embraced all that dark anarchy inside himself and *went.*

Murderer. Maker of monsters.

Seb kissed him again with that same tentativeness, so unfamiliar to Nathan, so unlike the Seb he had known all his life.

We never kissed. We never kissed before, not ever.

"What are you doing?" Nathan whispered, but he didn't pull away.

"I don't know," Seb whispered back. "I never know." He touched Nathan's jaw with the tip of his finger, then ran it down the line of his neck. "I'm all fucked up. No job. My mom kicked me out. I don't got a place. I could only think of you."

Nathan watched him. "You can't stay with me. *I* can't stay with me. We have to be out of our rooms by tomorrow. I told you that."

"Yeah," Seb said uncomfortably. "Sure, but . . . I thought that . . . maybe—"

"Maybe what?" Nathan backed away. "Maybe you could come home with me?"

Seb shrugged.

"You need a place to stay," Nathan breathed. "You need a job. And you're suddenly gay."

"I'm not gay."

Nathan raised an eyebrow.

"Or maybe I am. I don't know; I've never known. I don't understand, don't you get that? But you're warm and I'm cold and I need to be warm, Nathan, I just need to be warm." He tried to kiss him again, clumsily, and Nathan took another step backward. Seb stared at him reproachfully.

"I don't understand," Nathan said. "I don't hear from you in months, I haven't seen you, and it was like you just cut me off, cut me *out*—"

"I didn't know what was going on," Seb said. "I didn't understand myself—"

"Bullshit," Nathan said cruelly. "I think you knew *exactly* who you were. A guy who liked getting his dick sucked, a guy who liked having his prostate milked every few days. Didn't matter who did it so long as it was done. You didn't love me. You were a hyper-hormonal teenage boy and that is all."

"That's too simple," Seb said darkly, furiously, "and you know it."

"Maybe, but there's truth in it, too." Nathan's grin was savage. "And *you* know it.

"So: say it."

Seb stared.

"Say it, then," Nathan said furiously. He felt dark winter swirling up inside him, trying to coalesce, to *thicken*, and he forced it away savagely. "Say that you love me."

"I love you." His eyes were wide and guileless.

Nathan sneered, leaned forward. "I. Don't. Believe. You."

Seb scowled, said nothing.

"So here we are," Nathan said, "back at the beginning, just like you said. The only difference is that I'm kicking you out of here. Out of everything. Forever."

"You can't," Seb said. His face paled.

"Tell me that you were in love with me. Tell me that you are in love with me right now. Not like friends, if that's even what we were. Like boyfriends. Like lovers. Tell me and *mean it.*"

"I love you," Seb said again.

Nathan laughed. It was a harsh sound; it reminded him of the sound that Dead Kyle made the night before, just before he faded into nothing, and how the bear-woman in that abandoned house laughed. Grinding crockery, shattering stone. *To make my bread I'll grind your bones.*

Seb lifted his fists. "Goddamn you. You don't know how hard this is for me."

"Fuck that. You don't know how hard it is, period."

"Fuck you, Nathan."

"You pretended like none of it happened. You told me that it was better, easier, because you ended up feeling embarrassed."

Dark color rose to Seb's cheeks. "So what if I did? You think I liked feeling that way? Confused like that? Shit. Confused ain't even the right word. I told you already, and I mean it, and I want you to believe it: I am cold, and I always feel cold, and nothing makes me warm. You're the only thing that ever came close."

He flew at Nathan, crying again.

Now, he'll do it now. Nathan prepared himself for the reveal of the shiny sharp inevitable thing in Seb's pocket, but instead, Seb locked him in his embrace, kissed him, then again, then again, each kiss growing hotter, faster, gripping Nathan's skull with both his hands, his cock hard against Nathan's thigh.

"Fuck me," Seb said, panting, "come on, if that's what it takes; you like that; I didn't want you to before because I thought," and he laughed and fumbled with his belt, "fuck, it don't matter *what* I thought," and heaved his pants and underwear down, then planted his hands on Nathan's bed and lowered his head. His erection jutted out ferociously before him. He looked over his shoulder. The sun outside had abandoned Garden City and left it with the swirling shadows of winter dusk. "Come on," he panted. "You always let me do you; now *you* do me. Come on, come on. Do it, Nathan, come on, *please.*"

Nathan closed his eyes: Seb in the park, Seb beneath him, Seb's eyes red from crying; "Seb!" he'd cried that night Kyle came for him in the diseased forest that formed the dark heart of Waxman, but Seb hadn't come. *A choice, a choice, you can come with us or go with him, and that's all*; and Nathan opened his eyes and turned away.

The thing fell from Seb's pocket and thudded to the floor. Small. Nearly square, not sharp at all, not razor, not knife.

The lighter. The silver lighter that had belonged once, he'd explained bitterly to Nathan four years ago or a million, to his father.

Just a lighter. Harmless now, on the floor. It gleamed slyly up at him, blinding him.

"Go," Nathan whispered. "Get out of here."

"Nathan." Seb's penis was wilting like a flower.

"Get out of here!" Nathan roared.

Seb's mouth worked, then he jerked his pants back up; his belt jingled cheerfully. "You faggot motherfucker," Seb snarled. He raised a fist. It was huge; it ate up the world. "I should beat the shit outta you."

"I thought it was you, you know."

Seb froze.

Nathan grinned. "Just now. I thought maybe you'd taken those boys. Killed that girl. Killed them all."

"You . . . you thought . . . ?"

"I did."

"You thought I could do that?"

"I did. For, like, a hot second. But you're weak. Someone said the same thing to me recently, and it pissed me off. But I get it. I am weak, and you're weak, too. That's why we were drawn to each other. I saw you reflected in me, and you saw me reflected in you. It was my weakness to . . . to . . ."

"You loved me!" Seb howled. "I know you did! I saw it!"

"I did," Nathan said, and he showed his teeth in a wolfen grin, "but I don't anymore."

"Faggot motherfucker."

"You don't even know what you're saying."

"You want me to hurt you."

"Or what you want."

"Fuck you!" Seb howled. "You don't get to tell me who I am! You don't!"

Nathan took a breath. "No," he said quietly. "You're right." It was like a hole had opened in the world and a light shone out of it, blinding, iridescent. He understood. He finally saw it clearly, shiningly; *oh my god, I do, I do.*

"You don't even know who *you* are," Seb said.

That light grew brighter, kinder. "I do, though. I finally do."

"Faggot. *Faggot.*" He was sobbing.

"Just go, Seb." He lowered his head. This was exhausting.

"I love you, Nathan," Seb whispered, and in the face of that unde-niable brightness, Nathan saw with perfect clarity that Seb meant it. "And I want to burn it all down—you're right about that—but that doesn't make me a killer! I just want to be warm, dude, that's all. I just want to be warm." But that fist still hung heavily between them, an anvil in the air.

Nathan inhaled, the slightest gasp of ice; the room, he noticed, was growing colder, then colder yet.

It would be easy.

So easy.

"Go," Nathan said warmly, kindly. That light burned from inside him; he had never felt gentler than now, in this moment. This tender, deadly moment. "I never want to see you again."

Seb hesitated. His eyes filled with tears and his mouth worked. He lowered his fist by inches, slowly, slowly, and then it was just a hand again, but reaching out for Nathan.

"Nathan, I—"

Nathan's window and the entire wall framing it blew in with a thundering, apocalyptic crash. White dust and the roar of the wind filled the room; Nathan flew backward, narrowly avoiding shards of glass and concrete that arrowed at him with deadly aim. His mind wasn't, wouldn't, *couldn't* process what was happening. Where there should have been a wall in a far saner world, there was none; dazed, he peered stupidly through the dust.

Why isn't the wall there? What happened to the window?

Then he saw, and he screamed.

Seb hung suspended, seemingly in mid-air, four feet above the tiled floor, his face marble-white with shock, his eyes huge and swim-ming. "Nathan," he said.

Two enormous hands composed of long white fingers held him; each finger ended in a vicious yellowed claw like the talon of a bird. Nathan recognized those hands and the claws gripping Seb Candleberry by the meat of his shoulders. Behind Seb's tortured, terrified face and trembling head, enormous, inky black wings unfolded, but Nathan couldn't see the face of the creature to which they were attached. They beat the air, those wings, stirring up dust and allowing inside a flurry of snow caught in the bone-cutting gale from the storm that had brewed above Garden City all week long.

"Help me," Seb said. He reached out for Nathan tentatively. But Nathan didn't move; he couldn't.

Their eyes locked.

"Seb," Nathan croaked.

Then he was gone.

"No!" Nathan screamed, reaching.

The wall was whole.

The window was closed.

The room roiled with the cold. Nathan could smell the snow; he took a step forward and screamed again, because the tile was wet where the snow had fallen and melted, though the wall was whole, unblemished, and the window was closed. He screamed again, with fury this time. Not all the snow had melted; some of the flakes danced and spun in the air, others whirled in giddy circles before they, too, lost their grasp on their shapes and delicate individual patterns and disappeared forever.

"Where is he?" Nathan whispered. The dim ghost of the mermaid woman shrugged; the gray voice said nothing, but there was a sigh, almost tender, and a rushing sound beside his ears. The party was silent, though Nathan could hear them breathing.

Make a choice: stay with us or go with him and be eaten. You'll see. We did.

"Where is he?" Nathan shrieked.

No one said a word.

He slid his arms into his coat before he even thought about donning it; the door opened, and he was running. He thought as he went, so fleetly, about Deborah and her book on witchcraft, the book he had used to call forth . . . *what?* The wall was whole, the window unopened, but the snow was there and Seb was still gone; where had Seb gone?

Campus lay deserted in the growing purple gloom that spread across Garden City like a bruise. He encountered no one as he sprinted down the slippery sidewalks, through plowed and shoveled berms of snow, and the blue and green and red holiday lights cast shifting, colorful shapes on the sides of buildings and the glaze of ice on the sidewalk and on the piles of snow as he passed. Somewhere, not too far ahead, he heard his name screamed once, Seb's voice for sure, shrill with terror and pain. He heard the flapping of enormous wings, carpets being beaten. He lowered his head and ran, then ran faster, then faster.

He looked up.

The woods. Of course. The trees grew before him, black, twisted shapes made menacing by the purple shadows of twilight.

He ran. Ahead of him he could just make out the shape of something impossibly enormous, blacker than the shadows it crossed, and it flew unerringly toward the forest.

"No!" Nathan screamed, but it disappeared into the trees with its victim.

I don't accept that, Nathan thought grimly; he pumped his legs, forced them to move harder, faster.

He barely felt the change in light and temperature when he entered the clutch of trees that signaled the opening of the woods, but leaden darkness met his eyes when he lifted them. He shivered, despite the exertion; copious rivers of sweat ran down his forehead and back and under his arms. It was much colder than any woods had a right to be, and darker than he remembered. He stopped, panting, trying to breathe, trying to see. He forced his eyes wide, but the blackness was impenetrable.

It took him. It came through the wall. The thing that scared away Barry, that took the lost boys, and, yes, probably killed Deborah. The thing that hurt the Outsiders and loosened their grip on me. It came through the fucking wall and just took *him.*

His teeth were chattering. But there were other sounds in the dark, and the clicking of his teeth couldn't drown them out: sly sounds, the rustle of fabric, half-whispers, smothered giggles, and the stealthy, creeping crackle of branches and dead husks of leaves that accumulated after fall faded into winter.

He jerked his head to the right: something had gone crashing through the underbrush, something big. He jerked his head to the left, because that carpet-beating sound had begun again. And something else: the sound of a person moaning, muffled by . . . ?

He took a final step and saw; his eyes widened, and he clapped his hands against his mouth. Water instantly filled his eyes. He shook his head three times, a denial, even as he absorbed the full horror of what lay before him.

The thing had hooked the claws of its feet onto the lowest branch of a large ponderosa pine and crouched there; its wings pulsed with the pleasure of the act it now consummated. Seb's head lay back against the branch, farther than it should have, because his throat was open and his head was pushed so far back that it looked ready to drop off his spine completely. His glazed eyes were wide with the horror of his situation; his mouth gaped, and blood ran in twin rivulets from each corner and down his chin. And even this wasn't the worst: the worst was the head of the monster itself, buried in the enormous red and black hole it had opened in Seb's sternum, a gaping slash that ran all the way down to his groin. The thing continued to dig, relentlessly, with its yellow raptor-claw-hands, into the cavity it had created, snuffling and delighting as it ate.

"Seb," Nathan whispered.

The thing raised its head. Its eyes caught a stray ray of light coming through the ceiling of flora overhead; the light flashed, golden coins in the darkness. It made a purring, questioning sound. The thing's white face was mostly a vast, wet mouth; its teeth stretched far back, working and champing, lizard-raptor-vampire-werewolf, black with Seb's blood and the chunks of vital organs glued to its lips and between its enormous teeth, twice the size of piano keys. Nathan opened his mouth to beg the thing to reconsider, to turn back time and undo its terrible will; then the thing, with a squeal (*of fury? triumph? delight?*) beat its wings against the icy darkness and launched itself off the branch, carrying its prize away with it. Nathan stumbled backward. Squealing still, the thing burst through the tops of the trees and vanished.

Nathan drew harsh draughts of breath that stung the tender flesh at the back of his throat and ached within his lungs. Dazed, his mind drifted back to those first days on campus: the lazy heat that lay over Garden City and made him feel like a young lion too exhausted to lift its head as a gazelle passes dancingly near; the whirl and rush of the students, marching along, and he, marching with them; his mother's voice, aching through his phone, the slur of her words; sparks of terror ricocheting in his stomach that first morning, towel in hand, toothbrush, razor, shaving cream, and the explosion of sound from the men's bathroom, the raucous, animal joviality of the rest of the boys on his floor, already knowing each other; Barry's eyes skating away from his when they passed in the hall, fucking high school all over again.

Now, staring at the empty branch before him, he forced himself to steady, to take a step forward, though his hands clenched into fists and then unclenched, though his bowels felt hot and prickly and loose, though his breath was coming in short little pants. The forest darkened around him again, the veil unpierced by any dagger of light. There was no sound, as if every creature within held its breath for this single, unending moment. He took a step; even the action of crushing the crust of snow and discarded branches beneath his sneaker caused no sound.

His mind drifted to his mother's sad, gray face;

Barry's eyes open beneath him, just a crack, then widening with recognition and realization, with shock, with betrayal, as Nathan and Nathan alone reached down to touch him;

Julian's damp hand grazing his as it rested on the table they shared;

Elizabeth's lipstick, like gore, clumped perfectly against her right incisor;

Piper Collins, Will Pretty Weasel, Adam Harris, Kyle Matthews, their faces made monstrous, horror-movie masks, their eyes sparkling with a terrible and focused avidity, while their hands, marble claws, reached and reached;

and he was one step closer to the branch of the tree.

"No," he moaned. "Oh no, oh no."

There was no sign that anything violent had occurred. That awful image of Seb's head, hanging on by a literal thread, flashed before his eyes; *this entire clearing should be splashed with gore.* But there was nothing, and the place on the branch where the beast's filthy yellow talons clung was blameless, utterly unmarked. The snow beneath the branches gleamed softly, innocent of blood.

He put his hands over his face and held them there for a long time. The mermaid woman hadn't the strength to appear at all now; there was no party. For once, that awful metallic voice didn't scrape in his ear.

Where am I? His own voice. *Somewhere I am sleeping in a great big bed; somewhere I am three or four or five; somewhere there is music playing on a radio and the sound of Mama moving around in the kitchen downstairs and I will wake up and the world will be new because I have dreamed everything and nothing terrible has happened. And nothing terrible will* ever *happen.*

Nathan opened his eyes.

It was me. All along, it was me. I'm the one.

The woods grew full of sound; a bird called out, shrill and forceful, and a squirrel chattered noisily directly above him. Somewhere, not too far away, something rustled branches aside, making sounds like cracked bones. Nathan shook his head to clear it and looked over his shoulder at his own tracks that came in wide leaps, zigzagging through the snow. It was a miracle that he hadn't clotheslined himself on a branch, or been decapitated, or pierced through the heart, destroyed like a vampire. He didn't want to think of vampires; the thing was all wings and long white fingers and a marble face, gaping mouth and gnashing, endless teeth; he certainly didn't want to think of vampires *now.* He giggled a little, but that was a crazy sound, so he stopped giggling and wiped his face. It was wet with icy sweat. He stared at the back of his hand, which shone under the moon's little light. He closed his eyes so he could decide what to do next; when he opened them again, he stood in the lobby of his dorm.

"No," he said; safe behind his desk, the R.A. on duty lifted his eyes from his phone-screen and glared. Nathan looked around, but the lobby was deserted, save for himself and the boy behind the desk, who shook his head and sighed heavily and retrained his gaze back on the screen. Nathan wandered about the lobby, staring at the walls with fixed interest, as if he'd never seen them before.

Everyone is gone. It's just me. The R.A. is angry because he's only here because I'm here; if I were gone, he'd cease to exist; he wouldn't occupy that chair at all anymore, never again. The whole world is white and new because the snow covered it all, every single blemish; I could go out there now and sing and dance and throw myself around in crazy looping circles and there wouldn't be anyone to see me.

"Good night," Nathan called foolishly to the boy behind the desk, who didn't deign to lift his head again, but simply raised a hand and made a gesture, half-shooing, half-waving.

I am real, at least; I exist, Nathan thought happily; *this whole world is mine, it belongs to me, there is no one else in all the world except for me.*

Nathan giddily danced down the hallway to the elevator, and rose, singing softly, until he spun between the doors at his floor.

Laughing, he called, "Goodbye, goodbye," and danced, danced, danced through the hall, eyes closed, spinning; YOU, Theo's stars had proclaimed, and, "You," he whispered, then grinned. "*Me.*"

Let them all hear because there is no one but me.

"Everyone," Nathan sang, "oh, thank you all for coming. This has been such an honor, and the party was only a success because of you, all of *you,* but now," and he stood outside his own door and slapped it playfully, "*now* I'm afraid it's time for all good boys to say good night, good night, night." He waved and smiled and then vanished back into his own room. It was dark and cold and, standing there with the safety of the hall and the light at his back, he thought, foolishly, *It is the wardrobe, the one that leads to Narnia, and behind me is the real world, and there are people in it somewhere, beyond this empty campus and all these empty haunted buildings and the woods that are, of course, full of ghosts, just as it always was and always will be; behind me is the real world but before me is all darkness. It's my last chance. I can still go back; it's not too late.*

Then he saw that the room wasn't empty after all. Icy waves, rippling fingers of cold came at him, and there, against the window, darker than the darkness, stood four solid figures, waiting for him.

They stepped forward into the light.

Their heads were skulls. He tried to scream: animal skulls, horses, goats, no eyes, empty sockets; their shoulders were shaggy with hair, and their *teeth, their* TEETH—

Nathan turned and fled from them. It wasn't the woods that were haunted after all; he ran, ran, ran from those monster boys and their animal-skull heads and relentless empty eyes and jagged mouths and hands that were cold and longed to touch him, to take his warmth for themselves, stupid monster boys, *his* warmth couldn't help them *now*, but it wouldn't stop them either, and they'd take him back to wherever they dwelled and drain away all his everything until he was a lost boy, too.

The time for choosing has come.

"No," Nathan whispered. He looked over his shoulder, and there they were, empty eye sockets, bodies sheathed in coarse clumps of hair; things of the forest now; they wouldn't let him get away that easily. "But I don't want you," Nathan said. "I don't, please, and even if I did, I—"

Where will you go? Who will take you now?

Deborah appeared before him, flickering, there and then gone, and she said through her mouth, wet and stained with red, "I know I shouldn't have given you the book. That's why *he* came to me, that's why he killed me. He took me there, into the woods, the deep and the dark of the woods, and he used his hands and his mouth, Nathan, his hands had claws, you saw, and his *teeth*, he used his teeth on me, because, he said, 'You are a sorceress,' but I'm not, 'you are wicked,' he said, but I'm not, 'you wanted me,' he said, but I never did, not much," and the words came faster, and Nathan was powerless to prevent them, "and I didn't know how you felt, okay, I did, I thought, *I'll take him for myself*, I thought, *no one's ever looked at me like he looks at me*, I thought I thought I thought *I'll care about myself for once*," and she shook her head and blood flew in red-black freshets. "I'm sorry if I ever hurt you; I didn't mean it. I'm not well, I'm not," and an owl's beak burst in an explosion of fleshy gobs from the center of her face. One eyeball slithered down her cheek while the other glared at him, yellow; she reached out her hands that were the reptilian claws of a bird, reaching for him, she reached—

No, and he ran.

He didn't take the elevator, choosing, instead to pelt madly down the stairs. Were they behind him, even now? Did they pursue him, plodding with their heavy legs and their hooves? *I saw their hooves*, he thought madly, *instead of feet*; the stairs went down and down until at last he burst out of the door and found himself back in the lobby. The R.A. lifted his head and stared, his nostrils flaring like a startled horse, but it wasn't the R.A. after all. Nathan pressed his hands against his mouth to hold in the rabbit scream of horror he knew would shatter all the glass in the place, because it was Seb behind the desk, Seb with red-stained shark teeth and blank silver eyes. Seb the undead boy; Seb the lost one; Seb, who was one of *them* now.

"Fuck me," Seb said, but there was no life to his voice; it was mechanical, a sigh. "Come on, if that's what it takes. You like that. I didn't want you to because I thought," he said, "I thought, I thought, I thought—"

"Oh, Seb," Nathan whispered.

"Yes," Seb said, and something flickered in his eyes and rustled in his voice; recognition? Life? The last vestiges, the last gasps? "Yes. Seb. It isn't too late. You think it is, but it isn't. Nathan, I, we—we could, we could—"

Nathan's mouth worked, but no sound came out. He shook his head, a denial, and then more words came from Seb's mouth, but they didn't match its movements.

"I could love you, I could; you could love me. It isn't too late."

His hand, winter-white, reaching—

Nathan felt his own hand lifting, rising despite himself.

Seb grinned, and his smile was red. "I started a fire," he said. "Again. We could burn it down, Nathan, just you and me," his voice rising into an inhuman scream, a *squeal*, "we could burn it all down, *all down*—"

Nathan dropped his hand.

I can't choose this, he thought, his mouth full of sweet horror. *I can't choose him.*

He fled.

It was a machine, he understood as he ran through the winter dark. The machine didn't need him as one of its cogs; the machine would see that another Nathan occupied his old room, that another Nathan accepted praise from Jimmy and sipped cocktails with Liz and rolled his eyes at Julian. *Another Nathan,* he thought dreamily, *another boy, someone else to take the classes that need to be taken and to kiss the mouths that need kissing.*

There was someone ahead of him at the end of the path.

I understand it now; this is where I've been heading my entire life. This moment.

"I've been waiting for you," Theo Smith-Kingsley said. "Feels like forever. Took you long enough; where have you *been*?" Theo wore a dark blue sweater beneath a dark blue peacoat and his beautiful dark blue knit cap that didn't quite conceal the froth of titian curls spilling out from beneath; they fell languidly over the creamy ridge of his forehead.

"I ran," Nathan said inadequately, gasping. "I ran all the way."

"Of course you did," Theo said. He laughed, but kindly, and put his hand on Nathan's shoulder. It was white as alabaster, and the fingers ended in long, curved yellow talons. He couldn't take his eyes off them; then he looked up into Theo's eyes, which were yellow cat eyes, golden and glowing.

Theo smiled kindly and said, "You've been heading here for a long time. But you know that now, don't you?"

Nathan took a shaky breath. "Yes," he said.

"And you know where we have to go?"

Nathan looked beyond Theo's shoulder to the place where the path led, unerringly, into the gaping maw of the woods, where the wolves prowled, and the spirits, and the witches who waited patiently for passing children; *I will wait for the children*, Nathan thought peacefully. He looked back into Theo's patient, inhuman face. *We will wait for them together.*

"Yes," Nathan said again.

Theo relaxed slightly. "Good." He held out his monster's hand. "Come on. We have to hurry."

It isn't too late. You can still go back. The choice is yours, Nathan.

He looked at this thing, shapeshifter, spirit of the forest, demon: a hundred names, a thousand, and none were exactly right. It was evil, a killer, a predator. It was a *thing*, just some *thing*. But he'd called for it. He'd made the devil appear.

I did that. Me.

The hand, clawed, held out before him, waiting, patient.

Evil, predatory.

But he loved it.

Loved *him.*

He loved it because it was horrible, it was loathsome, it was a killer, a murderer, a monster, and he loved him because he was beautiful, and he loved it because it thrilled him, evil things thrilled people, they always did. He loved it because it loved him; it echoed, he understood now, the same darkness he'd always known lived inside himself.

It was a place to belong. Nathan smiled. He'd finally found it; he'd found him at last. Evil, vile, beautiful.

Mine.

Nathan put his hand into Theo's. It was warm; it wasn't cold at all.

"It's your choice," Theo said softly.

Nathan smiled up into those golden eyes. "I'm ready."

Theo smiled back at him with adoration.

"Even though they tried to stop me," Nathan continued. "The Outsiders, the deaders, the lost boys—"

"I knew they would. They're jealous of me."

"But I didn't let them."

The wings that came somehow from Theo's back expanded then: a secret black, lined with myriad scarlet veins. They flexed and pulsed with each monster's breath he took. *They are beautiful and glorious,* Nathan thought, *just like we are.*

"You could see them," Theo whispered. "You were the only one."

"Yes," Nathan said.

"No one else could."

"Just me. I know."

"So I came to you. Because you wanted me more than the others. You called for me, you called for me *aloud,* you used your very own voice. You used your power. No one else ever did. I've never felt anything like that before. You." He drew a breath. "The lost boys, they wanted me, too. Even if they didn't call, I knew; I can always tell. They wanted to be taken away. It's what I am; it's what I'm built for."

"I understand," Nathan said.

"They're weak. Always so weak. But not you. You are strong."

"I don't feel strong."

"Yes, you do."

Surprised, Nathan realized, *I do.*

"I'm sorry they turned out so horrible. I didn't know that would happen. They've never come back before. There was never anyone to summon them back before." He sighed, smiled sadly. "They couldn't handle it. This life. This place. This *world.* I knew it. I *felt* it. So I came for them. But they screamed in the end. All of them did. In horror. In pain. In fear. Because of what I am."

Because of what you are, Nathan thought dreamily, *and what you did to them.*

"But not you," Theo said.

"No. Not me."

"You called for me."

"I did," Nathan said, squeezing the demon's hand. He leaned in and whispered into his ear: *"And I would do it again."*

He felt his eyes change; reflected in Theo's, he saw that they, too, glowed, hot and golden and split down the center like a cat's.

Theo closed his eyes; his wings vibrated with pleasure.

Nathan waited until he heard the soft purring as his shirt split, as wings of his own slid into the world and expanded. He knew they were as black as onyx, and lined with their own veins, crimson rivers of blood. They were grand, he knew; they were *magnificent.*

Then, almost shyly, Theo, marveling, said, "I love you, Nathan."

"I love you," Nathan said, "Theo," though that was just a name, and it didn't mean anything anyway, not really. None of the names ever did: not Logan, not Julian, not Seb. They were lost.

Let them go, let them be lost, he thought giddily. *Finally and forever.*

Theo was beaming. "Now we'll dance as I always promised you we would. We'll dance, me and you, and there will be drums, and songs, and fires, and the moon, and forever."

Holding his lover's hand, walking with his head held high and his back straight, each step deliberate and firmly, truly placed, Nathan followed Theo into the trees, then beyond, into the shadows which welcomed them both, until, at last, they merged and became one with the darkness.

September 2013–April 2022

ACKNOWLEDGMENTS

MY MOTHER PURCHASED for me a typewriter in the winter of 1987, when I was eight, and we lived on a microscopic farm near a microscopic town in windy, drought-ridden Eastern Montana, which inspired the horror stories I had long proclaimed I wanted to write; a typewriter, Mom knew, was just the thing a weird little budding author needed, and so she purchased it, mammoth, insanely heavy, and a beautiful metallic blue, from a sale at our school's library, and presented it to me for my birthday that year. I was fascinated, only a bit intimidated, and sat down immediately to compose.

My mother has always been my biggest supporter and is the first person who deserves thanks for the creation of this book. We'll put Shady Pines off for a few more years, whadda ya say, Ma? My father, too, deserves kudos for doing his best to understand the little queer kid he helped raise, and who has always been fiercely protective of me.

To my friend Amy Doty, proprietress of Frame of Mind, who inspired a similarly named character in *Black Forest* and who always acts as my champion, and for pushing this book across the finish line. Pillars of the community, unite!

To my friend Ashley Rhea, who read early drafts of *Black Forest* and offered considerate, honest critiques that helped shape the final draft.

To Sarah Nivala for that first editorial letter and for all our subsequent conversations about Nathan and his journey, and for your kindness and enthusiasm and belief in this book.

To Avalon Radys for helping me steer and for a million friendly emails.

To Pamela McElroy for helping me see the light, and whose editorial prowess during the final copyedits helped smooth away the remaining harsh edges.

To Adam Gomolin for believing in my writing ability and for offering writers such fantastic opportunities.

To Noah Broyles for his support and feedback and for helping me feel a sense of community.

To Davey Terry and Katya Mickelson for many a late night discussion of ghosts, the occult, and Gangly Mark / Scary Gary, and for reading a very early draft of this book.

To Fran Robert and Nancy Eron and Angie Loomis for twenty-five years of friendship, which has always included reading whatever nightmare I've dreamed up, and for all your love and faith and support.

To everyone who preordered *Black Forest* during that dangerous, sweltering summer of 2020: thank you so much for your patience and support!

And finally to my husband, Ryan, whom I love more than anything, and who believed that I could do this. Maybe he's right.

GRAND PATRONS

Amber Rose Mason
Amy Doty
Ashley Casseday
Beth Grove
Bjorn Sven Hanson
Brad M. Carlson
Brendan Shanahan
Cameron J. Brauer
Cathryn L. Watt
Colton Martini
Cynthia M. Randall
David J. Fox
David V. Terry
Deana Luetkenhaus
Elijah Miller
Frame Of Mind
Guy F. Haines Ii
Henry P. Maher
Izzy Milch
Jacob Carlsen
Jessica Brunsvold
Jennifer M. MacMurdo
John Powers Jr.

John W. Carraway Ii
Jordan B. Vakselis
Justin Finley
Leisa Greene
Matthew Woodcock
Melissa R. Trout
James Taft
Onya Winhofer
Owen Bauch
Rebekah A. Dodds
Rosie Ayers
Ruth A. Chananie
Samuel T. Steinmetz
Sara Hagen Hull
Seth Shaffer
S. Nigel Rogers
Tambre R. Massman
Terry Cyr
Thomas M. Campbell
Tia Gonzales

INKSHARES

INKSHARES is a reader-driven publisher and producer based in Oakland, California. Our books are selected not by a group of editors, but by readers worldwide.

While we've published books by established writers like *Big Fish* author Daniel Wallace and *Star Wars: Rogue One* scribe Gary Whitta, our aim remains surfacing and developing the new-author voices of tomorrow.

Previously unknown Inkshares authors have received starred reviews and been featured in the *New York Times*. Their books are on the front tables of Barnes & Noble and hundreds of independents nationwide, and many have been licensed by publishers in other major markets. They are also being adapted by Oscar-winning screenwriters at the biggest studios and networks.

Interested in making your own story a reality? Visit Inkshares.com to start your own project or find other great books.